I hope this true will be meaningful to, my best wishes,

Reed Mace

To: Janine + Family —

Learn from this what really matters in life!

Love
Dad + Mom

A birthday gift.
— 2005 A.D

The Potter and the Clay

Why Hast Thou Made Me Thus?

A Novel
Based on a True Story

Reed Moss

Library of Congress Control Number: 2004098593
ISBN: 0-9747376-9-0

First printing November 2004.

Printed at Falls Printing, Idaho Falls, Idaho, U.S.A.

Dedicated to John and Zelma, my parents, who never wavered from their dedication to family, despite extreme difficulties and tragedy.

Dickens, Hugo and Alcott would give this book two thumbs up. Heaven visits earth and a man's destiny is shaped by the event. He takes his young son and hitchhikes 300 miles to visit his daughter in a mental institution. His wife writes a textbook for motherhood by her every action and reaction. I loved the intense descriptions of rural life and the majesty of mountain refuges. I read it in the day and the night and every time I could get away. It became my feast; my great escape at the end of the day. I will be reading and rereading this book for the rest of my life and I hope my posterity will learn and savor its truths.

Luana Grigg, BA English, English teacher

I started reading this remarkable story last evening and most of today, unable to put it aside for very long. It's that kind of book. It should have a universal appeal. Every age group should have the opportunity to read this extraordinary story. *Bernice McCowin, BS, M.Ed.*

The Potter and the Clay has given me greater insight into loyalty for family and home. I was transported to a simpler time where I was entertained, uplifted, inspired and deeply moved. The images in the book have stayed with me, enriching my life, motivating me towards greater understanding for others, and giving me comfort and hope in the overriding message, which applies to us all.

Sheila Ann Olsen, National MS Mother of the year, 1987

I laughed, I cried, as I read the descriptions of rural life experienced by a remarkable family. This tender story touched my heart deeply. *Joan H. Robison, Idaho Falls, Idaho*

This book is a story of the struggles of a rural family in the difficult times of the Great Depression and World War II, and tragedies that befell their children. Yet a special happening guided and lifted this family through those deeply touching heartaches.

Lorraine Brown, teacher

The Potter and the Clay, is an appropriate title for this family's afflictions endured and seemingly impossible odds overcome. The land, trees, frost, animals, places, events and people came vividly to mind through this work of art in written form.

Shirley Larsen, home health administrator

The message that God does all things well is a great comfort. We appreciated this book's return to the grass roots values of years past. We believe that all who read the book will be better for the experience. *Edwin, M.D. and Jeanne Biddulph*

The author is a gifted writer. He uses simple, declarative sentences and active, well-chosen verbs. He uses anecdote and insight, rather than a dry recitation of events, to move along the story of growing up poor on an Idaho farm and his family's hardship, grief and happiness. I was involved and moved. *Dan Siegel, Salt Lake City, Utah*

ACKNOWLEDGEMENTS

To Elizabeth, my wife and best friend, I express appreciation for her willing support, her refreshing candor and helpful suggestions, and for the long hours she endured my sitting at the computer or doing research.

I also express my gratitude to Barry Reeder, who read a draft of the manuscript and energized me by his keen interest in the book and his encouragement to get it edited and into print. I also thank Paul Rawlins, my editor, for taking out the non-essentials, sharpening the focus of the book and helping to move the story smoothly along.

Launa Grigg, English major and teacher, read the original draft, expressed her excitement for the story, and volunteered countless hours going over every word with me to improve it.

My siblings and key players in this story, Joel Moss, Helen Shaner, Rhea Wray and Ruth Johnson, and their spouses, have been of inestimable help with research and in providing their own personal memories and insights about this drama as it unfolded over the years they were growing up.

Many others have provided generous support by reading the manuscript, making valuable suggestions, and expressing their interest in, and feelings about, the story. They include my seven children, Rebecca, Mike, Jeff, Carolyn, Angie, Annette and JJ and their spouses. They also include Sheila Olsen, my deceased law partner Dennis' wife and National MS Mother of the Year, 1987, Polly Mortell, my able legal secretary, Val Crapo, widow of State senator and a helpful mentor in the practice of law, Terry Crapo, Keith and Lorraine Brown, Bernice McCowin, Dr. Edwin and Jeanne Biddulph, Joan Robison, State senator Mel Richardson and his wife, Dixie, Dan Siegel, a client, Shirley Larsen, Lu Mecham and her deceased husband, an author and client, Lloyd, Maxine Wight and her deceased husband and my client, Monte, Darryl Harris, an author and client, Wayne and Marlene Peterson, Lee Baird, Betty Anthony, a Ririe native who knew Lael and the family well, and my niece, Gaylinn Thompson.

CONTENTS

AUTHOR'S PROLOGUE

This is a book about very ordinary, everyday people. "Common folk" some would call them. These were Idahoans from small villages and rural homesteads, farmers, ranchers, teachers, grocers, blacksmiths, etc. who coped with the twenties, the Great Depression and the Second World War. Yet some singular, even extraordinary, events happened in the lives of the principals, John and Zelma; things gratefully not reserved just to the elite and the sophisticated. It is those events and the lives and consequences involved in them that I have felt an urgent need to write about.

I have tried my best to report the facts of John's experience at the Grand Hotel exactly as they happened, based on his recorded statements; the countless times I personally discussed it with him and Zelma, and other evidence, including discussions among immediate family members and other intimates. Similarly, I have tried to be completely faithful to the truth of John's unique experience with Johnny, based on my own personal involvement. Those two experiences for John formed the "bookends" of mortal human life, and were sacred to him. Any inaccuracies or inconsistencies are my fault and should not be used to affect or distort the truth and reality of those events.

The members of our family and Grandma Fanny, Byron Mason, his parents, Cousin Johnny, his parents, our beloved Mary Jap, Cousin Cloyd, Dr. Walter West, Mr. Hemminger, Judge Larsen, Drs. Lowe and Allen, and a few others are true characters. I have tried to report their involvement in the book with reasonable accuracy, but have taken some small liberties as to some of the events in which they were involved, just to make the story flow from sequence to sequence. But no such liberties taken are intended to detract from their true character or disparage them in any way, or to deviate from the truth of John's extraordinary experiences.

Other characters, such as Dutch Caldwell, his wife, Darla, Sheriff Judkins and Lottie, his wife, Mrs. Snarr, Mr. Simmons, Kitty, Vilate Hatch, Miss Haltern, Mr. Hacking, Eddie Rogers, Danny Rosenthal, Karl Klinger, and a few others are fictional. However, they all bear a close resemblance to actual persons or a composite of actual persons or characters that made up the fabric of the Idaho rural society involved in the story; and the events described and involving such characters are actual events that happened, as nearly as I can remember them. However, certain time frames, the meshing of certain events with others, and the sequences of those events have been so utilized or altered as to better express the significance of those events in the lives of the principal characters, and to more succinctly depict life in this rural Idaho setting.

It is my hope that those who lose children, especially small ones to an early death, those families who have handicapped children, and those who are handicapped, may find considerable solace in Lael and Merlin's story, and come away with a certain and serene assurance that we need not "reply against God," for does not the "…potter have power over the clay?"

Antelope Flats,
Idaho *p. 25*

The South Fork of
the Snake River in
autumn. *p. 34*

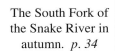

The one room "Hill
House" shack in
winter and summer.

Grandma Fanny

Lael's letter *p. 283*

Birdie's Bump *p. 51*

Mrs. Clifford's
house *p. 120*

Lightning lighting
them up like
massive indigestion.
p. 122

The majestic
Idanha Hotel
p. 231

Lael   Zelma   Merlin   Joel   John

**O Man, who art thou that repliest
against God? Shall the thing formed say
to him that formed it, why hast thou
made me thus? Hath not the potter
power over the clay...?
Romans 9:20-21**

Chapter 1

The Incident at the Grand Hotel

IT WASN'T *WHAT* JOHN had seen in room number seven of the Grand Hotel in Blackfoot, Idaho, the night before that bothered him. He knew what he had seen! The questions buzzing incessantly in his mind were: *Why* had he seen it? What caused it? Where did it come from? What did it mean? Why him? Why now?

Thus plagued, he left the Grand in the early morning of June 21, 1920, climbed into his battered Model T Ford, and headed north for home, Ririe, at thirty miles per hour. During the two-hour drive the beautiful spring landscape—green fields and budding blossoms—of southeastern Idaho escaped his attention. The sun rising brilliantly over the Tetons to the east posed no distraction. He was encased wholly within his mind. Wondering. Pondering. Reliving every detail of that incredible, surreal event.

Many years later I am sitting in my study staring out a big picture window across Antelope Flats, Idaho, similarly entranced by that event, having lived and experienced its aftermath and consequences. I am looking toward Burns Creek Canyon, which stands between the Grand Tetons and me. Brooding, melancholy Burns Canyon, even in bright morning sunshine. Its mood matches mine as my gaze shifts to an old photograph hanging next to the window.

Five faces stare back at me: There is a girl, about three; next to her, a little boy sitting on a sawed-off tree stump, about nine months; and another boy, about five, partly standing, partly sitting on the stump with his little brother. An oval photo of their mother hangs beneath the girl. A similar photo of their father hangs beneath the older boy. Each face reflects the delicate similarities and beauty of the others. The girl's name is Lael; her little brother's, Merlin; her big brother's, Joel; the mother's, Zelma; the father's, John.

"Funny how a photograph can take you back in time to places and embraces that you thought you left behind" some song says. I realize that intensely as my eyes focus on the girl. Her face is bright and beautiful, but her look is pensive. Is that the beginning of a tear in her left eye? Is it a scratch on the old photograph, a flaw in the paper? Is it my imagination wandering into the future she will face? That look transports me back over long years and brings a flood of bittersweet memories.

The look of the beautiful young mother, eyes slightly lowered and peering straight into the camera, is also somewhat mysterious. What is she thinking? Is it just a pose, or does she harbor some concern, some anxiety? Is it my fruitful imagination again? The father looks like an intelligent young man. *He was, in fact, an intelligent young man!*

I look again at the little boy on the stump. Now, even after these many years, his image still brings a twinge of pain. My brother's image. My sister's face. It is their story as it unfolds from the event at the Grand that needs to be told. It has worth. It has something to do with the universe, something to do with another significant dimension of human life, but I am not sure what. Perhaps telling it will bring that insight. Something restless inside me compels me to write it down, spell it all out, because I know it! I was there for most of it. It is true.

When I was twenty-five, in 1955, the event at the Grand was further authenticated by an unanticipated happenstance that left me deeply touched. I had just returned from serving in the military during the Korean War. My two sisters were staying in the bedroom upstairs opposite that of my parents, so Mother, Zelma, assigned me to the little six-by-ten fruit room downstairs with the mice! My mother and I built a little clothes closet under the stairs leading to the basement, painted the cement walls, hung a white sheet in front of the fruit jars and shelves, and hung a door on the entrance.

We pulled an old steel bed out of the barn and covered it with available cardboard, quilts, and sheets. It had only a crosshatch of horizontal springs and intertwining wire mesh that had to be covered with enough cardboard and quilts to eliminate stabs in the back. Mattresses cost too much. The room was cool in summer, bitter cold in winter, but quiet. It was home after an absence of five years.

We moved an old combination rolltop desk and chest into a space left over by the fruit jar shelves. The night I moved in I cleaned it out. Not much was in it except the accumulation of dust from the years it had stood unattended in the basement with the dirt floor. But on one shelf behind a little door some stationery lay neatly folded from top to bottom so all corners matched evenly, then folded once again in the center. The word *Save* was written in Mother's flowing script along the outside fold. It beckoned me to open it. As I did, the yellowed and crisp paper broke in several places along the centerfold. I used a Montgomery Ward catalog to smooth it out on the desk, then sat down on the edge of the bed and in the dim light from the single bulb above me began to read it.

It was a three-page handwritten manuscript dated December 5, 1927. It was a prologue to the lives of Joel, Lael, Merlin, my sister Helen, and me that I had heard so many times from the lips of my parents. This, however, had been written three years before I was born and some twenty-eight years before I found it and read it. It had details I had not known about the children who had been encountered before their births. It was a mother's view, outlining in rich detail the things that especially touched her, and it brought memories back to life.

It started on a beautiful summer evening, June 20, 1920. John and Zelma had been engaged four years earlier, but among other things, World War I had intervened, and while John was away they drifted apart and broke off the engagement. She had been nineteen, he twenty-three, both certainly of marriageable age under the custom of the times, but being apart and the war, as wars often do, took its toll, affecting their priorities, altering their perspectives. Carrying on a romance by slow mail also contributed to the status change from fiancés to friends.

In 1920 John lived in Ririe with his widowed mother. Zelma lived and worked in Blackfoot, fifty miles to the southwest. John sold aluminum pots and pans after his discharge from the military. He had driven his Model A to Arco, another fifty miles west of Blackfoot, to try to sell his wares and to visit a young woman he knew there. It had been a discouraging day, with no success with the wares or in meeting the lady friend. He started for Ririe in mid-afternoon. Passing through Blackfoot the thought struck him to visit Zelma at the laundry where she was working and at least say hello. He was tired anyway, and whether she was available or not, a good night's sleep at a hotel would help dispel the discouragements of the day.

He pulled up at the Grand Hotel on Main Street and walked into the nicely furnished reception area. The marquee had advertised "moderate rates." As John entered he was so impressed with the main floor dining room with its lavish furniture, china, silverware, and other trappings, he wondered just how moderate those rates would be. A chart on the desk satisfied him.

The proprietor came with the first ring of the desk bell; gave him a key, a washcloth and towel, and a partly used bar of soap; and sent him upstairs toward the back to room seven. In the room, John laid his small valise on the bed, poured some water from a pitcher into an adjacent washbasin, washed his face, straightened his tie, brushed off the dust from his trousers and shoes, and went downstairs and onto Main Street.

He stood looking up and down the street, then chose to go south where the greater number of businesses was located. He walked past unpainted buildings still open for business with signs fading, store windows dim with dust, wares still lying in their original crates used as shelves. He wondered if conditions here would ever improve to where Blackfoot might compare with the bright colors, lights, and general layout of the fancier stores he had seen in bigger cities in the east. Idaho, he mused, still lived in the Dark Ages.

He easily found the laundry. There was only one. He peered in through the large plate glass window and watched Zelma from behind as she wrapped a package of white shirts for a customer. She used brown wrapping paper, the same kind the butcher used for his meat and the baker for his bread. John noticed her crimson dress, her slim ankles and feet, how her figure flowed from top to bottom in a graceful cascade of balance and beauty. As she turned he saw that the front of the dress was open at the neck, sleeves rolled up; an apron, brightly colored and matching the dress, covered her front. She had a graceful walk, he noticed, as she delivered the package to a customer who smiled, took it, and exited the building. Her face looked a little flushed from working around the laundry, but somehow that made her all the more attractive, especially when she extended her lower lip and blew a little air upward to cool the blush on her cheeks.

John realized all over again that she was a beautiful woman, twenty-four years old, tan darkened, fine features, a full but trim body, a grace about her movements. He stared for some time till she, seeming to sense something, turned toward him. She recognized him instantly, despite the glare from the window, and she broke into a wide smile that lit up her face. She beckoned him to come in.

"Why hello, John. What a nice surprise. How did you happen here along?" Her voice was quiet, smooth, seeming to reach out and caress him. The "here-along" was one of her little trademarks. He remembered it from the past. Coming from her it sounded poetic, romantic, inviting.

"I was over Arco way, finished my business a little early, and thought I would stop by in Blackfoot and say hello."

"I'm happy you did." Her smile confirmed that fact.

"Seeing as how I am here and have a room at the Grand for the night, could we go out to eat and maybe take in a movie?"

Her face screwed itself into a "you're a typical man" stare. "It's too nice an evening to waste in a movie theater or a restaurant. If I put together a picnic basket, do you think we could spend some time together in Blackfoot City Park?"

"That would be even better. It's a nice warm evening," he replied, his hands toying with the keys to the Model A. She gave him an approving nod.

"I'm glad. I'll be closing up here in twenty minutes. So will you go to the grocery next door and pick out some nice carrots? They just got some from Utah, and also get a loaf of white bread. I have everything else at my place to make the picnic. Do you have money? If not, I have some."

"Yes, I have money for a few carrots and bread," he answered with a wide grin.

The groceries were easy to find, and by the time he returned she was locking the front door of the laundry. They strolled over to her apartment only a block and a half away. She asked what he had been doing in Arco. He told of his attempts to sell aluminum pots and pans from door to door but avoided the issue of the lady friend there. She didn't press him for details, just good-naturedly drew out of him what he wanted to tell. She was good at that, and he needed prodding to open up a bit anyway.

At the apartment he watched as she peeled and sliced the carrots, laid out the bread while directing him to spread mayo on every other piece, and had everything ready to go—plus her face washed, rouged slightly, and her dress changed into a mid-calf sack dress—all in less than twenty-five minutes. Impressed, he remembered how quick and efficient she was, with little fussing over her clothing or face because they fit her for all occasions, without primping.

Even though it was a warm summer evening, only a few people visited the park, so they were left to themselves. As a gentle breeze drifted through the trees and bushes, making little whispers here and there, they reminisced about prewar times as they ate. She asked him a question.

"John, you just turned twenty-eight yesterday (he noticed she remembered his birthday). Are you finding someone to marry and settle down with?" She said it not as any kind of invitation, only as a friend, because she felt no insecurity in her position. She was beautiful and popular and in no hurry.

His response was delayed, a trifle embarrassed. "I let myself get into a couple of business ventures, and I'm heavily in debt, almost hopelessly in debt. I'm not sure any sensible woman would want to tie up with me." He explained that he had invested in a sheep feeding venture and a grain warehouse, both of which had failed. This had left him burdened with some heavy debt and few assets, but he was determined not to take out bankruptcy because with his whole life ahead of him, a loss of creditworthiness would be even more fatal.

"What's debt got to do with life? I thought you always wanted a family with children, that your life would be a waste without them."

"But shouldn't both a wife and children have some security and a chance for a decent life? I can't assure any future child or wife any such thing. I might have to dig ditches or sell pots and pans my whole life, and I wonder if that would be fair to children or a wife." He let out a long sigh.

"You're mixing apples and oranges," she said with a teasing tug at his tie. They left it at that.

She had to work early the next morning, and he had to return to Ririe. He walked her back to her apartment and gave her a peck on the cheek, which she accepted with a smile. She unlocked the door and disappeared inside.

Deep in thought, he headed somberly back to the Grand. Even though it had been a long day, he knew he would not sleep for some time. Her comments had touched something deep inside. He was twenty-eight, a bachelor. His brothers, sisters, and most of his friends were married, settled down, having kids. Yes, he wanted a wife, a family of his own. The war had delayed all that, even contributed to the breaking of his engagement with her. Yes, the prospect of returning to the four walls of an empty room alone settled like a cloud of gloom over him. But what could he offer a woman? A lifelong struggle with debt! It would take forever to pay back what he owed, even at two percent interest, with wages low and an education that had been interrupted in the seventh grade because he had to work to help his widowed mother and family. Selling pots and pans would never do it.

Somewhere near eleven p.m. he entered his room, totally unsuspecting of what he was about to encounter. He turned on a light. His valise lay where he had left it on the bed. Besides the bed, pitcher, and washbasin, there were two chairs, a night pan under the bed, and to the right of the door as he entered, a dresser with an oval mirror above it.

He walked to the mirror. He needed a shave, but the whiskers did not show against the tan he had gotten while working on his brother's farm when he was not on the road selling. He took off his tie, rubbed his whiskers, scratched his full head of thick hair a couple of times, and noticed the furrow in his brow from the heavy thinking he had been doing about his fate and future.

He turned to cross over to the bed to retrieve his valise. But when he turned, the bed, the valise, the chairs, even the room were gone—completely vanished! The room had simply opened up! He was standing in nothingness. Yet it was light. He could see, but only vast empty space. No movement. No sound. Engulfing silence! He was stunned. His eyes searched through the emptiness. A chill crawled up his spine and tickled his scalp.

Suddenly his eyes caught movement coming from his far left where the corner of the room had once been. Emerging toward him out of the nothingness came five human forms, small, childlike ones. As they materialized he saw they were holding hands, smiling warmly and brightly, and were coming toward him with a happy skip and a hop. They came to the front of him, always smiling up at him, eyes aglow, grins wide. They stopped and stood in a line, still holding hands, saying nothing. The eerie silence prevailed. But, oh, how he felt; it was a euphoria and ecstasy he had never before experienced. He felt compelled, no propelled, to reach out and touch them, hold them, but was powerless to do so. He was not capable of speech or movement except to turn his head and inspect them and, gratefully, smile back at them. The fear had left him. He felt a perfect peace in their presence.

They were lined up five feet away, all smiling, still conveying a warmth and comfort he could feel but not describe. Who were they? Where did they come from? Why were they there? These and other questions flooded his mind and his feelings. Years later after he came to know them well, he would recall that had he looked at them carefully, he would have seen some of himself in them, certain facial and other characteristics. But the moment did not lend itself to such close inspection. He was too caught up in their joy and glee. They charmed him! They lifted his depressed spirits. Their love and warmth embraced him like a down-filled blanket. He felt a closeness, even a kinship with them—that they somehow belonged to him and he to them. The moment would pass, but its emotional ecstasy would last through all the years of his life.

The oldest boy came up to his shoulder. He was dressed in a dark suit and white shirt open at the neck. Next to him and to his right was a beautiful girl, a couple of years younger than the boy, but seemingly quite tall for her age. She wore a pink dress. She had dark hair with just a hint of auburn in it. Next to her and holding her hand was a small boy, not more than two feet tall, "a little bit of a thing," John later explained to Zelma. This boy was dressed in white clothing. He made for a dip in the otherwise gradually descending height of the children because the next child, a girl clutching his other hand, was two feet taller than he.

"He was kind of shriveled up. His face looked quite drawn—like he was…" John would wander off in midsentence describing him, wondering about him—and then continue. "He looked like a little old man. He was so much smaller than the other children and did not look healthy."

The girl to his right looked healthy and wore a white dress. A little boy stood next to her. *That little boy was me.* My father described me as a healthy looking boy with solid, sturdy legs, smaller than the sister next to me, but still taller than the little one in the middle. I was dressed in a white-and-blue-striped jacket, with knee pants and long stockings. John thought that we looked "tickled to death" to see him.

All at once we started to run, still holding hands. John said "they went around me four or five times fast, and then out they went" from whence they came, disappearing back into nothingness. The room closed back with John facing the bed to which he had originally turned. Everything was back to normal in the room. Yet, as he stood looking in the direction where we had disappeared, he began to feel as he had felt before, a good feeling, a happy feeling, as though we were back again, but now he could not see us.

The feeling stayed with him, replacing the gloom he had been feeling earlier. Later, he said, "I felt awfully good, and I felt like they had come back around me. Of course, I wondered about it for a long time. Then I undressed myself and went to bed." His wondering included the odd-appearing little boy in the middle. What was it about him? The rest were all normal, beautiful children, nicely dressed, and all, even the small one, were intensely happy, an infectious happiness that graced his sleep when it finally came.

Years later, even at his fiftieth wedding anniversary at age seventy-eight, he remembered the details vividly. Through those years the event and the feelings kept coming back. He had not dreamed it. It was real and somehow must be important, even sacred to him. He confided the event to his mother, Fanny, and his two brothers, Tom and Alma, upon his return to his home. They, though they believed every word of it, could not help him fathom its purpose. They told him that probably only time would tell, or not tell, which was small comfort to him.

Chapter 2

The Engagement

OVER THE YEARS I lived with my parents I heard "glimpses" of their ensuing romance and engagement following the event at the Grand Hotel.

The encounter in Blackfoot nourished and renewed John's interest in Zelma. She had a charming friendliness. She was beautiful. She was intelligent but not overbearing. She began to frequently intrude into his consciousness.

Other things intruded as well. John's debt depressed him. Salvage from the sheep and warehouse barely paid legal fees. The bankers were willing to extend but not forgive his debt. An ironic twist was that he had had more than half the amount he owed in savings in the same bank to which much of his debt was owed. But that bank took out bankruptcy, and, consistent with the law at that time, he could claim no offset against the bank or its creditors. He lost his savings, but his debt remained. Wages were low. He had no real education, which made finding a job with decent pay almost impossible. Discouragement clung to him like a soggy, wet shirt.

A few days after his visit with Zelma, during a restless night of little sleep, his loneliness and discouragement tortured him into a cold sweat. He was twenty-eight, heading toward twenty-nine. Would he still be alone at thirty-nine, forty-nine, fifty-nine? A fear only the lonely feel gripped his heart. With most of his friends married, he was beginning to feel on the outside of things. A lone man did not fit a couple-oriented society. Their interests and concerns were different from his. The endless "you ought to get married" quips were starting to play on raw nerves.

This scenario played itself out in his mind and imagination during this night, the darkness intensifying every ugly, foreboding thought. He was not typically a worrier. He loved life. He had a good sense of humor, which people liked about him. Yet the depressing impressions of that night would stab and sting at the oddest times, leave, then come back to disquiet him. His encounter with the children at the Grand also added to his puzzlement. How did that fit into his life?

He courted several young women during this time and several found him attractive, but nothing developed. None cured his yearning for something permanent, with substance and meaning. Zelma, too, had ample opportunities to be courted. Her beauty was legendary in the area. She had already turned down a couple of sincere proposals for marriage because she also found nothing secure in those men.

Zelma's family ran a little grocery and dry goods store on Antelope Flats, sixty miles from Blackfoot and ten miles from Ririe. Only rarely could she get a ride home. During one of those visits John had driven south of the store up Pine Creek Road to talk to his neighbors about helping with the pending harvest. He drove around the back of their house to park. While bending over to get a package out of the backseat, he heard a whoop and a holler followed by a loud peel of laughter. He stood up just in time to see a beautiful young woman—tanned, healthy, cheeks rosy from her ride—come racing by on a big black gelding followed by the neighbor's son on a handsome pinto. They were at full gallop, racing each other down the draw.

The woman was winning by two lengths. As she whipped by, John saw a plume of beautiful dark hair flying straight out like a flag from the back of her head. He saw only enough of the profile to notice the crinkles at the corner of her right eye, indicating a wide grin. She was urging her handsome steed on at top speed, apparently thrilling at the sport of leaving the young squire on the trailing pinto in her dust.

It was Zelma. He liked what he saw. Caught up in her competitive spirit, he smiled, even laughed, as she headed on down the draw and past the house, clearly the victor to be at whatever finish line had been chosen for the race. In those few moments John again felt pleasure at seeing her, sensing her exuberance and the challenges that she liked to tackle. He wondered if she might even take on the challenge of him and his debt.

After checking with the neighbor, John "chanced" to go by Zelma's father's store and saw her standing outside talking with one of her sisters. The black gelding was tied to the rail. He saw another of Zelma's father's horses also hitched to the rail and harnessed to a buggy. He was still nursing the feeling he had had as he watched her swoosh by on the gelding. A buggy ride with her beside him beckoned him on.

He stopped and talked for a while but was a little hesitant to ask the favor in front of the sister. Zelma, sensing that, sent her sister away on an errand, then waited patiently for him to speak his mind. After a few more pleasantries, he asked, "It's such a nice afternoon, do you think you could persuade your father to let me take you for a ride in that buggy over there?"

"I'll bet I can! I would like that! Wait here a moment, and I'll see if my father needs the buggy for a while." She went into the store and returned quickly to report that her father had given his consent.

As they were about to climb into the buggy John noticed the gelding still sweating and standing at the rail. "I think that poor horse of yours ought to be rubbed down and dried off before we go. You gave him a hard ride down Pine Creek Draw a few minutes ago."

"Where were you? I didn't see anybody watching me racing the pinto!"

"I was looking on from my car up at the Parks' place as you galloped by."

"Well, why didn't you say hello there?"

"I could never have caught up with you in my beat up old car."

"Then maybe cars won't replace horses after all, like they're trying to claim." She was warmed by John's sensitivity to the horse's welfare because she loved the big animal. They took the gelding into the barn where both rubbed him down with gunnysacks, John on one side and she on the other. When their hands happened to meet on the back of the horse they looked at each other and felt pleasure in the touch. They gave the horse a full pail of water and some oats and hay, then settled into the buggy to take a peaceful ride along the dirt roads dividing the fields of the Flats.

Some were in summer fallow, left without crop for a season to allow the moisture and nutrients from winter snow and summer rains to accumulate in the loamy soil. Other fields, fallow the year before, were planted in grain, mostly wheat for flour and barley for feed. It was early fall. Soon the straw stalks would be dry enough to pass through a thresher and yield the hardened kernels that could be stored without rotting.

Spring, however, was John's favorite time. He explained to Zelma that he liked to watch the rows of grain emerge out of the snow through the spring thaw, brownish leaves turning quickly to brilliant, almost transparent green with only three or four days of sunshine! The tiny green rows seemed almost to chase each other as they popped up around the fields; he could imagine them whooping and wahooing as they made their dash up and down the hills and along the contours of the slopes, jumping the little washes where topsoil and grain had been washed away with the spring runoff.

They ran side by side, those little green rows, turning, twisting, diving down, and then soaring up again over the slopes and hills in a harmony of symmetry, the brilliant green of the grain glistening against the dark brown of the rich soil. When they crossed each other at the corners of the fields, they looked like little armies fighting each other for turf. It was like watching a ballet of motion and order along the contours of the hills, each row obediently following the line where it had been sowed. Later, when the grain was up over a foot high and the rain was plentiful, the rows merged, intertwining their blades and heads, making their tops into more of a floor than rows, which ended their chase across the hills.

Then, almost sadly, John continued, "The hot summer sun takes its toll, turning the green to golden brown and later turning the heads to amber as the harvest approaches. By that time the heavy dark heads of the grain turn the fields into rows again, but without the brilliant green against the dark brown of the soil, they don't race or run or leap like before. They're still beautiful, but they never match the playfulness and exuberance of their youth. Now they are mature. They await the reaper's scythe."

Zelma knew most of what John had related to her from her own experiences around the Flats, but she had never heard it so poetically, even romantically described. She liked the mosaic of color and symmetry he painted. He seemed to see and feel much more in a field of grain than most men would.

Hardly noticing the passing time, they suddenly found themselves back at the store. John helped Zelma down from the buggy, taking a long time to release her hand. She didn't mind. There were several customers coming out of the store, so the situation did not lend itself to any intimacies. But he playfully bowed before her, thanking her for condescending to go with him. She smiled and said: "Such knightly demeanor certainly becomes you, sir John," and extended her hand for a final touch. He looked deeply into her eyes. She gazed intently back. He turned and walked to his car.

That fall the men were working from daylight till dark through October and into November to complete the harvest. Most were having a good yield, and grain prices were up considerably. Everyone was feeling good, even a little giddy, about their finances. Housewives, after months and sometimes years of struggling to make do, were buying more aluminum pots and pans. John's finances improved somewhat.

A few weeks after the buggy ride, John happened over to Zelma's father's store on a late fall Saturday afternoon, hoping she would be there for the weekend and was pleased that she was. Because of the distance from the Flats to Blackfoot, there were few chances for any kind of meaningful courtship except when Zelma was visiting at home.

They decided to take a stroll up the dirt road leading across Antelope Creek and south past the old schoolhouse. Painted light green like the fields in spring around it, the school was a large one-room affair, divided by curtains so first through fourth grades could be taught to the thirty or so kids attending. The bridge across the creek was made for buggies first, later for cars. Railroad ties lay in the direction of the stream atop a cement superstructure. Two two-by-ten planks had been laid crosswise of the ties in the direction of travel, thus completing the bridge.

Zelma started walking on one of the two-by-tens. A nail protruding from the board caught her shoe, jolted her suddenly sideways, and she slammed awkwardly into John's right shoulder, almost knocking him off his feet and off the bridge. He braced his left foot firmly against the other two-by-ten and recovered in time to balance himself and catch her as she fell, gathering her in and holding her fast.

She was chagrined by her clumsiness, and her face showed it as she looked up into his eyes. But as their gaze met, she saw a hint of turmoil mixed with pleasure in his eyes. Her instincts sensed that the turmoil was the loneliness his twenty-eight years were bringing upon him, and the pleasure was that he was perhaps finding in her an end to it. He saw in her face softness and an unmasked desire to be there in his arms. Without speaking he bent his head toward hers, softly kissed her tanned and glowing cheek, then moved easily into a full blending of their lips. She gave a little moan, relaxed into his arms, and kissed him back with equal vigor.

Nothing was said. Nothing needed to be said as they disengaged and he straightened her up. But from then on her hand found his as they walked along the dusty little road, both immersed in reverie, seemingly oblivious to all the beauty of their surroundings.

They came upon an abandoned iron-tired wagon half-buried over the years from wind-drifted dust. John playfully picked her up and sat her on the flat wooden bed of the wagon box. Then he sat closely next to her and gently put his arm around her back. She leaned her head onto his shoulder. They were staring past the old green schoolhouse across five hundred acres of waving amber grain into a brilliant sunset.

Zelma turned her head toward his and quietly whispered, "The time I like best here on the Flats is when the grain is about two feet high and just beginning to ripen into a bright orange, mixed with some lingering dark green. Then the wind starts up. It sweeps through the fields swaying the tall grain. I love the way it makes the heads and stalks bend in giant waves. It looks like a giant hand is gently brushing them, and all those brilliant colors intertwine with one another like a rolling wave on the sea! Or sometimes the millions of stalks and heads are like rows of dancing damsels, shimmering as if to shake out their robes, but still tied to their roots."

John turned his head to look down on her sunlit face. Her words stirred something in him. The good earth of the Flats was an integral part of his soul. He needed it just as he needed her. It pleased him that she saw more in a field of grain than just ripening straw.

"I like to watch the grain in motion, too, like the rolling waves of the Great Lakes I saw while I was stationed in the east. But wind can have an ugly downside. It can wreak havoc if the heads are heavy with grain. The stalks can buckle and lay the straw and heads on the ground flat as a pancake."

He didn't notice it, but Zelma was grinning brightly up at him. His response did not match the romance of her flight of fancy over the waving grain. Still she sensed and appreciated the practical side to his love of the land; the fate of many families was tied to these crops, and even a gentle wind could be a hazard to them, let alone drought, frost, hailstorms, and other disasters.

They returned to her father's store at dusk. At the doorstep, with only a lonesome frog croaking from Antelope Creek below and a few crickets chirping to break the silence, John reached for both her hands and drew her close to him. Looking straight into her eyes he said, "I think we have both matured a lot since the war. I want you to know that you mean a lot to me, more than ever before. I like being with you. How do you feel about me?"

The question caught her momentarily off guard. She looked into his face and could readily see how sincerely he meant the question. She liked that in him. He was an open book she could read and understand. There was no pretense, no playing games, almost an unnerving, even vulnerable honesty. She thought back over the war years, his absence, the breaking of their engagement. They had been young then, untested. Now they had both tasted loneliness, and he, his debt, and were finding that the carefree days of youth were shallow compared to real life, as they now knew it. She sensed he needed her, and yes, she needed him. She saw in him steadiness, loyalty, and trust. She might never be rich with him, but she would always be secure.

Her answer was soft, earnest. "I also like being with you. It pleases me. You have your concerns, your debts. I know they bother you, but they don't bother me. I'm young and healthy and ready to take on anything that comes along. But you are living in Ririe, and I'm in Blackfoot. They are miles apart. What can we do?"

Neither seemed quite ready to commit to the long term yet. But it was a start. He answered: "Let's work on it."

"Yes, let's do,"

He leaned to her, put his arms tightly around her, and held her close, his head next to hers. She nestled close. A feeling of relief, even fulfillment, swept through both of them, as though two halves were becoming one whole. They stood in that warm embrace for some moments, then kissed tenderly and parted. Each felt that this had been a gift, a gracious and beautiful Indian summer evening in Idaho.

Zelma's comment about the difficulties created by the distance between Blackfoot and Ririe proved prophetic. But they occasionally got together at social functions in Ririe or on the Flats when she would come to visit her family. The Ririe dances were a favorite pastime and attracted large crowds of young people. A fiddle, a cello, and a banjo would form a band at the combined school gym and community social hall, and the crowd would literally dance the night away. Some would come from as far as twenty miles away. They came early in the evening, while it was still relatively light. Nobody wanted to go home in the dark, even those with cars because they were so unreliable and had such poor headlights, if they had any. The horses would stand or lie down, tied to the hitching posts or rails outside. When the dancers tired, they would lie down on the dance floor and talk and tease and sleep until enough daylight filtered in to help them see their way home in the early hours of the morning.

The rekindling of their lost affections continued on these occasions. John's maturity over the years gave him a greater appreciation for Zelma's grit, her sensibility, her efficiency and charming friendliness. That affection also grew ever stronger out of little looks and smiles, little tosses of the head and peering out the side of the eyes at each other, even when dancing with someone else. It was honest, not flirtatious. It was like two magnets silently, vigorously pulling toward each other, a pull that intensified as they recognized each other's respective depths.

John remembered occasionally what he had felt as he had gazed at her through the window of the laundry, her natural grace and beauty, her cheery attitude, the quietude and peace he felt in her presence. Intertwined with those memories was his experience at the Grand, which seemed in some way to be connected to her. It would inevitably sneak back into his mind, bringing with it wonder and questions.

Through the fall of 1920 their love blossomed and deepened to the point where the distance between Blackfoot and Ririe became unbearable. Zelma made a sensible move. She quit her job in Blackfoot, gave up her apartment, and moved to Ririe where she found work as a clerk at the Golden Rod dry goods store. The proprietor and the people of the community welcomed her and her genuine friendliness.

In late January 1921, John's mother, Grandma Fanny, invited Zelma to come over to her house in the early evening for supper with John and her. Zelma eagerly accepted the invitation because she had grown fond of Fanny and enjoyed being around her. She finished work at the Golden Rod, took a few minutes to tidy herself up, and then walked the two blocks to Fanny's house on First West.

She was warmly greeted and was served some of Fanny's famous "dishrag soup"—a mixture of flour, milk, crushed pinto beans, and ofttimes a host of other ingredients Fanny "might have a-lyin around"—and some crackers. Fanny named the soup "dishrag" because it had a gray color similar to that of a well-used dishrag. The soup was complemented by an occasional swallow of

Fanny's famous dandelion beer, a nonalcoholic brew of dandelion brine mixed with water, sugar, and plenty of yeast. The meal was nothing elegant, but it was tasty and nourishing.

After supper Fanny graciously excused herself to go visit a sick neighbor. This surprised Zelma because it was she who had invited her to the supper. And when Fanny announced that she "would be gone a couple o' hours," Zelma sensed a bit of intrigue going on. She looked at John. He seemed oblivious to Fanny's disappearing, yet appeared to be a little on edge. Zelma's curiosity heightened, but she said nothing.

After Fanny left, Zelma and John sat down on the couch in the living room, Zelma's head resting on John's arm, both enjoying their ever-deepening companionship. Then John fidgeted for a moment and cleared his throat. Zelma sensed something important was going to happen, and she thought she knew what. But what she heard next surprised her.

"Do you remember when I stopped in Blackfoot to see you last summer?"

"Of course, it was a pleasant evening and picnic in the park."

"But for me it was a lot more than that."

"What do you mean?" She turned to look into his face.

He related to her in considerable detail his extraordinary experience at the Grand Hotel and then said, "I don't know what it means. I have had seven months to think about it, and I don't know any more now than I did then." Then he softly added, "But I do know I love you. I want to marry you. I want to be with you. I'm unhappy when you are not here with me. But before you choose to answer me, I thought you should know of that experience. After all, it happened just after I had taken you home."

Zelma quickly realized that this was something very important to him. The more she thought about it, while thrilling at and accepting his invitation to marry him, her instincts told her that it probably had as much to do with her as it did with him. She asked several questions about the clothing, the features, and color of hair of the children. She never doubted what he told her. He would never lie to her. She was particularly interested in the "shriveled one" and asked repeatedly for more details and what John thought about him.

"I don't know. I have no clue as to why he looked different. He was as happy as the others, but just didn't look healthy like they did. I wish I could tell you more, but I can't!"

Zelma sat deeply in thought for some time, nestling her head closer to his, her eyes closed. Then she started up, turned and looked into his face, and quietly exclaimed, "John, I think those are our babies. They have to be! I was with you just before it happened. There is no other explanation! I just can't wait to get my hands on them!"

Chapter 3

The Lean-to and the Flats

THEY MARRIED March 3l, 1921, and moved into a wood frame lean-to shack across the street from Grandma Fanny's house. A lean-to was half of a square or regular house. A half-roof sloped down from a bare wall with four-by-four studs forming one side. This wall awaited the other half of the house to be attached to it, but it was most often a long time in coming. The lean-to had a kitchen and a small bedroom. It had very little insulation. Water on the stove froze during the night in winter. The stove was wood burning, and the fire lasted only a couple of hours after John and Zelma went to bed. Then the piled-high blankets had to keep them warm. Nocturnal ventures to the out-house, forty yards away, were particularly trying. But the young couple was happy.

Across the street, Grandma Fanny's two-room house, badly in need of paint, stood on a large corner lot with a big garden plot, a barn with a cattle stanchion, a corral for a couple of cattle, a pigpen, and a chicken coop. Grandma Fanny, widowed twice, had lived there for many years. Now in her late sixties, she was a frequent visitor at the lean-to across the street. Just south of her house was another lean-to virtually identical to the newlyweds'. Karl Klinger, an old bachelor, lived there. The Donners, Artie and Will, lived in a two-room house south of Karl's place.

I look back at the picture in my study. Across the Flats, Burns Creek Canyon has a storm settling over it. Burns can have a hundred different attitudes in a single day. I look at the big brother in the photo. His white shirt is clean and nicely pressed. His hair is well groomed. All these attributes are a testament to his mother's touch and taste. "Joel" they named him when he was born on August 17, 1922. The doctor's fee was twenty-five dollars. There were no other costs since he was born at a relative's home in Rigby. Zelma stayed there for a week before the birth because John was busy working on Antelope Flats.

John was notified and arrived just before Zelma gave birth to this healthy baby boy. He leaned over to her as she cuddled the baby to her breast and whispered, "It's just as we thought it would be! That's the boy, the first of the litter. He'll have dark hair and a tan complexion, like yours. If the next one is a girl, then how can we doubt that I did, in fact, see our babies before they were born?"

Zelma lifted her gaze to his face, "When we got engaged, I told you I thought those tots were our babies to be. This is the boy. Then the girl will come, and then a boy that will have some kind of a problem, right?"

"I don't know. I can't interpret it. Life and time will have to do that for us; but I do think they are going to be a special little brood for us to raise."

Zelma gave him a little sigh of resignation and turned her attention to feeding the baby, gazing down on him with her dark brown eyes and long eyelashes, feeling nourishment and love flowing from her to him in a relentless stream. She would take them as they came, each to be tended and loved with all her heart and energy, each to have as much opportunity to grow and develop as she and her husband could provide.

Now that the ordeal of the pregnancy and birth was over, all was ecstasy, in which Zelma gloried. She had felt a deep and abiding love for John when she married him. This little baby not only enriched that but gave her a new level of joy and love she had never before experienced. This was her firstborn. She was a creator of a lovable human being with infinite potential.

But, she wondered to herself, am I really his creator, or has he been created elsewhere and I am only a temporary custodian of him? Was it him or just an apparition of him John saw at the Grand? His experience left her with more questions than answers. She only could assume that she was playing a part in a drama larger than herself, and the answers to her questions might be a long time in coming, if ever.

As Joel grew from tiny to toddler, he filled the little shack with squeals and laughter, was the focal point of their attention, and virtually their sole entertainment. They never tired of seeing what he would do next, how he would grow into one little capability after the other. His dexterity sharpened. His curiosity broadened. He ruled their little roost with his bright eyes, quick smile, and infectious giggle. He was healthy. He was cuddly. He was cute. He was more than they ever dreamed a baby could be. Their happiness grew with him. Their love for him strengthened and broadened them beyond themselves.

Next came Lael, on November 10, 1924, fully developed, healthy and beautiful. Her mat of dark hair added to a certain maturity that left her not seeming like a baby for very long. She came into John and Zelma's lives as Joel had come, bringing excitement and joy and more. She exuded a beauty and early charm that tantalized and beguiled them. She had a queenly quality that made them want to grant her every little wish. Their affection for her was akin to worship. Joel felt it, too. Everything about her was special, extraordinary and lovely.

As Lael grew older, Zelma was often touched by her dignified, almost regal mannerisms. When she started sitting, she sat erect, seldom slumped, and had a saucy little way of cocking her head to look at Zelma as she talked to her. Although she cooed, giggled, and fussed like a baby, she still maintained a self-assured dignity about her. After she learned to crawl, Zelma loved it when John got down on his hands and knees and chased her around the overstuffed chair or under the kitchen table. But when he caught her and held her close, she still bent her head at an aloof little angle that commanded a quiet respect.

John worked hard at selling his pots and pans but eventually gave it up to work full-time for his brother Tom on the Flats. He cleared Tom's homesteaded land of sagebrush, some as tall as ten feet, working from early spring till late fall. The wages were meager, but as a bonus at the end of several years, Tom gave him an eighty-acre tract of cleared land. Uncleared land was cheap. But land cleared of sagebrush, chokecherry bushes and aspen groves had good value. The eighty acres eventually became John's anchor to a bigger farming operation on the Flats.

"Antelope Flats"—not even the older natives can tell you where the name comes from. One early resident, long since dead, did leave behind a written report of sorts that stated that antelope once ranged over the area before the early settlers came. Today, one hundred miles east in the Pinedale and Lander, Wyoming, regions are large expanses of flat grassland where numerous antelope still roam. Perhaps their ancestors originally inhabited the Flats but migrated eastward as the homesteaders kept coming west.

The Flats offered some 30,000 acres of prime dry-farm land—nonirrigated, dependent solely on rain and snow. They are bordered on the west by Clark Hill; on the east by Conant Valley, a literal paradise of grassland meadows with the South Fork of the Snake meandering through it; on the south by a range of low-lying hills running east and west, with aspen coves and sparse but noticeable pines dotting the north slopes; and on the north by the South Fork of the Snake River and a row of mountains nestled along its north bank.

"Birdie's Bump" was the name given to a little prominence that sticks up out of those low-lying hills on the south. A lady named Birdie happened to live near there at one time. Since this little prominence was a natural landmark for wayfarers to chart their courses in early times, it was appropriate to name it so that all natives would have a common point of reference. The old timers claimed Birdie was a real "wild-eyed character" and that it was "fittin'" that this little prominence be named after her. Looking at the "bump," I don't think it was any singular honor to Birdie, but the name stuck!

The Flats have benefited from millions of tons of topsoil that have blown in from as far away as northern Nevada and settled between its little mountain and hilly borders. In some places the soil is twenty-five or more feet deep. Small wonder that it grew ten-foot sagebrush and would yield heavy stands of wheat, barley, and oats on only fourteen to twenty inches of annual rainfall.

John's eighty acres were nestled downwind only a mile north of Birdie's Bump. The "eighty" looked like a large loaf of bread lying in the direction the wind blows away from the Bump, with erosion drainages a quarter-mile apart lacing its sides. These scarred "loaves" are typical throughout the Flats. Viewed from Birdie's Bump on the south or the top of Burns Canyon on the north, they spread out in a grand panorama like a patchwork quilt of varying greens in summer, a soft blanket of white in winter. From Highway 26 the loaves on either side of the road, but especially the south side in early spring, resemble the bellies of a herd of zebras lying on their sides, with the snow cornices on the north slopes forming the white stripes, and the earth, dark and wet, forming the black. It was from this good earth, that John and Zelma would raise both crops and children.

John and Zelma resolved early on to be as frugal as possible and pay off John's debt as best they could, a process that would continue from 1921 to 1950. Zelma worked hard to help with groceries and other needs. She grew a garden with raspberries, strawberries, peas, beans, squash, potatoes, corn, radishes, and tomatoes. Much of this she traded at Brown's Grocery for store-bought goods.

Their thrift often led to a "thrifty" dialogue between them. Early one evening John returned from the farm dirty and tired. Zelma met him at the door. He stood below her at the foot of the little stoop leading into the lean-to, with her in the doorway looking down on him, all pretty and radiant.

"John, I'm out of potatoes and must have some to finish supper for you and the kids. Please run to Brown's Grocery and get me at least ten pounds so I'll have a few to spare. I need them right now!"

His reply was accompanied by a little smirk, "Well, if I have to go right now like this, all dusty and dirty, it'll cost you two dollars."

She stared down at him with a look of warm condescension. She knew the clerks at Brown's saw dirty and dusty farmers every day. She put her hands on her hips, gave him a "humpfh," took an about face, and sauntered back to the kitchen. John hurried to get the potatoes after dreamily watching her walk away.

Zelma knew how to please with her culinary skills. She cooked her meats with generous herbs and spices, fit for a gourmet. She baked potatoes, removed them from the peel, mashed them, then pressed them back into each half-peel, sprinkling each half with tasty grated cheese, which quickly melted. Zelma's meats and potatoes could bring any man worshipfully to his knees.

John always wanted to get to bed early and be up with the dawn. "There'll be no burnin' daylight," he was prone to say. In the kitchen after supper that night he dropped his longjohns, sponged himself off, then pulled on a clean pair "for sleepin'" and went into the bedroom. He thought Zelma would be reading by the dim light at her side of the bed, but was surprised to see her already in bed with the light out. She looked as though she were nestled in and fast asleep.

He sat down on his side of the bed to remove his slippers and socks, when he heard a rustle and then a muffled voice coming from off her pillow, saying, "Mister, if you set one foot in this bed it'll cost you five dollars!"

His shoulders hunched up playfully as though he had been stabbed in the back. He laughed, turned to put an arm tenderly around her, put his mouth close to her ear, and whispered huskily, "Only five dollars? How about a hundred and more? Really, sweetheart, to have you here beside me, you're priceless!"

In the mid- and later twenties, higher prices and good crops gave John and Zelma a bit of a nudge toward financial freedom. John's early venture into two failing enterprises made him a better manager of the money he earned. He calculated every penny, every source of revenue to pay the debt, live decently, and save and sacrifice for his children's education because of the special circumstances by which they had entered his life. It was a passion with him. He would give us, his children, every chance he could in life, and we, in turn, would be expected to make something of ourselves, something more than he had had the chance to be.

In addition to their garden, John and Zelma had chickens, pigs, two milk cows, and always a beef or hog for slaughter. With no money to spare for feed, John and Joel cleaned up any wheat, barley, or oats that spilled or leaked out around the Ririe grain elevators and used that as feed for their stock. They burned wood brought from the flourishing aspen groves on the Flats, wood they cut with axes and hauled on team-drawn wagons the ten-mile stretch to Ririe.

Ririe in the twenties did not yet have a movie theater, so often a group of citizens staged melodramas to help break the daily routine with some light entertainment. These attracted not only the locals but also people from neighboring cities, and homesteaders, farm laborers, and cowboys from Antelope Flats, all of whom were hungering for entertainment and a brief escape from their hard labor.

John was handsome, stood about 5'8" (which for those days was about average), and blended a nice sense of humor with intelligence that ofttimes landed him the leading male role. He played these parts opposite some of the area's nicest looking women. Mother told me that it bothered her a bit at the time, but she did not obsess over it.

When Joel was three, John was starring in a melodrama before a packed house and in his role as a bachelor was about to kiss the single leading lady. It was common to bring children, even a three-year-old. Joel was well behaved for the most part, especially during the scenes with the "villain." But when it got to the love scene he became bored, started fidgeting in his seat, and, without his mother's noticing him, finally slipped off it. He crawled forward under a couple of seats, then found his way to the aisle and started hurrying toward the steps leading up to the stage. The crowd paid him no attention because they were caught up in the love scene. Joel's timing could not have been more perfect. Seeing his father on the stage, Joel made his way up the dark side steps on his short little legs, still unnoticed. Then he burst onto the scene at full speed, and just as John planted his kiss on the leading lady, Joel grabbed his leg and hollered "Papa."

The crowd never forgot that scene. The cowboys and farmers slapped their legs and hooted and hollered and talked about it for days at the Ririe bars. The women howled and giggled about it at Relief Society meetings. It was embellished and exaggerated all over Jefferson and Bonneville Counties. And, of course, it came up in the Vilate Hatch show—which I will explain more about later. All the attendees claimed it was the greatest theatrical moment in the history of the town.

As the wild clamor of the crowd finally quieted down, John picked up Joel and carried him forward to the edge of the stage where he deposited him in the arms of his mother, who was blushing slightly but smiling coyly.

As he handed her the boy, she whispered, "That'll teach you to go around kissing other women."

"Well, why did you send a boy to spoil it all?"

She laughed quietly, "He did a better job than I could have ever done!"

For Joel it was probably his finest hour; an early entry into the saga of this family that was just beginning to play itself out amongst the hills, valleys, rivers, and communities of Ririe and Antelope Flats.

Chapter 4

Merlin

ZELMA WATCHED HAPPILY as John placed little Lael in the middle, taking her by one hand, Joel taking the other, as they started toward Brown's Grocery. Lael was eighteen months old, Joel almost four. Lael walked, but with short choppy steps, aided by her two "men." Joel anticipated getting a penny all-day sucker. Lael was pleased to be big enough to go on a date with her brother and father and was sure she would get a few good licks on a five-cent double-decker ice cream cone. John would also bring back a "remembrance" for Zelma, some nickel or dime thing that would not stretch the family budget. Zelma knew there would be a face and blouse, if not more, to clean up when they got home, but the thrill for the kids was ample compensation for all that. Life was good. She had a good husband and two healthy, wonderful children.

As she stood watching, suddenly she felt it! That first little "flutter." It caught her by surprise but was not unexpected. She had experienced it with Joel and Lael. In a short time that flutter would advance to a stirring and then a kicking. As for now it confirmed one salient fact: life was quickening within her womb. It would be a boy John had told her. The rest of the description was frightening, unnerving, especially now as reality hit. The boy had looked "shriveled" or "shrunken," had "a red pallor!" Was she growing a monster? No, the boy exhibited the same warmth and good cheer as the other children despite his odd appearance. Yes, he looked unhealthy, but he smiled and walked and ran with the rest of them, his little short legs bouncing up and down like pistons. No, he would not be a monster. But he would be different, probably not normal. Would he be a burden? Would he stretch their already burdensome debt with medical bills? Would he tax her emotions and her life beyond her energy and mental strength?

Such questions haunted Zelma over the months as she felt him growing inside her. Yet all that growing was so normal, so like the other two she had given birth to. Still, she could not help her anxiety. It sometimes sapped her strength, made her sit down and try to work it all out in her mind, but no answers came. The whole nine months were a tough pregnancy mentally, completely normal otherwise.

Merlin was born November 15, 1926. In the hours leading up to his birth, Zelma begged John to help her understand it. He had been exactly right about the first two, the boy and then the girl with features he had described to her on the evening of their engagement. Now the odd one was coming.

As the contractions started, she agonized over what was happening. It was unfair to be tortured with such depressing anticipation. John tried to comfort her as she lay in the bedroom of the lean-to, but no comfort came. The doctor came, but John did not feel he could tell him that this was going to be a boy and that he was going to be shriveled. The doctor would think he was crazy.

He reassured Zelma, "We'll love him and nurture him just like all the rest. I'll be there to help all I can. He is meant to be ours."

It was small comfort to Zelma. John had seen what he told her he had seen. The first two were proof of that. This one would be a boy, and he would be shrunken or shriveled or both. She was forced to reconcile herself to that. Nothing diminished her anxiety, her terrible struggle with the unknown! She was tied up in knots. This time the strain of labor and delivery was much greater than with the first two. Her concern gripped at her and tightened her muscles. She wanted the baby, yet she didn't want it!

When it was over she was all-in, reduced to a quivering, sobbing, per-spiring lump. Her sobs were deep, almost torturous, yet filled with intense relief, a hallowed, sacred purging of pent-up emotion and worry. She was cry-ing with delight. He was normal! He was healthy! He was not shriveled. He was not shrunken. He was a beautiful and completely normal baby boy. John bent over her and pressed his cheek against her flushed, wet face, blending his tears with hers.

He held her close as the doctor cared for the baby. He whispered, "I love you. I know what you've gone through." He loved her more in that moment than ever before. She was angelic, holy, pure, the symbol of all that woman and motherhood could be.

They named him Merlin. From the start he seemed to be on an acceler-ated schedule. He walked at nine months and began saying words about the same time. He had an infectious little giggle that made people want to pick him up and tickle him and play with him. He learned to say "Doel" for "Joel" quickly and had no trouble with "Lael" at all. He would run around the house calling "Dooeell" or "Laaeel" whenever he could not find his brother and sis-ter. He wanted to be with them all the time. When they slept he would exer-cise every little creative trick to find his way in between them, to cuddle and be warmed by their bodies. He loved being loved by them, being their center of attention, and they reciprocated with hugs and kisses, playing with his toes and fingers, and tickling him, just to hear that special giggle of his. It filled the house and made everyone just a little brighter and cheery.

From the moment of Merlin's birth John and Zelma worried and won-dered about the absence of his shriveled and reddish appearance. When they chose to talk about it, they could come up with nothing but speculation. Three of the five were here: boy, girl, boy. That was as far as their reasoning would reach. They would simply wait and see. In the meantime, they loved every moment of Merlin's life. He was a charmer!

Lael soon became Merlin's second little mother. She had a little brother, so she did not need dolls. She, with her regal airs, acted quite maturely by correcting him; keeping him out of danger, trouble, and mischief; looking after him; wanting to be with him. She adored him. She loved the little "Laaeeel" he would squeal at her. His mother was a necessity. Lael was his luxury.

John and Zelma often stood to the side and watched the little goings on and smiled. Lael and Merlin were a delightful pair, living in their little world of make believe or reality, whichever fit the occasion. Lael was always alert to Merlin's need for a change of diaper when her senses told her it was time. But, like a queen, she would condescend to tell her mother that a change was needed and then stand aloof while the deed took place. Joel reacted differently to his brother. His job was to make a little man out of Merlin, to tell him it was not manly to cry or act like a baby.

By now Joel was going with his father to the Flats and getting acquainted with machinery, horses, bridles, saddles, harnesses, brown furrows of freshly upturned earth, and endless rows of green growing wheat and barley, all of which fascinated him. He especially liked to run out in these crops when they were over his head and hide from his father, mother, and siblings if they were around. He wondered at how quickly they could find him, not yet realizing the telltale rustle he would make with the slightest movement in the tall grain. Lael would occasionally hide, too, but anything dirty or sticky was not for her.

The family moved to the farm on the Flats during the summer months, where they lived in various empty "shacks" located on the land John was renting. Eventually, with a hitch of six horses pulling it on logs placed under it, they dragged a shack of their own to the eighty donated by Tom. They dubbed it the "hill house" since it sat on a tiny knoll. It was one room—twelve by fifteen feet square—with a little lean-to made of boughs from willows growing along the nearby creek attached to its side. Joel and Lael slept there if the weather was right, dreamily watching the stars twinkle through the boughs while falling asleep. When it rained or the wind blew too strongly, they quickly jumped from their bed, bolted through the small back door, and climbed into their parents' bed. On the side of the room opposite the bed stood a small kitchen table and two two-seat benches. The adjacent corner held a wood box and a stand for washing face and hands. The wood-burning stove took up most of the remaining wall.

Once a week they returned to the "valley" to get groceries, wash clothes, care for the animals—except the chickens, which were brought to the Flats—tend what lawn there was at the little lean-to, go to church, then bundle up in the old car and head back to the farm. Grandma Fanny and neighbors were enlisted to feed the animals, milk the cows, and tend the garden while they were away.

After Merlin was born, the farm consisted of the eighty acres from Tom, another eighty they rented from Grandma Fanny, and another three hundred rented acres—the "Rowan and Forsyth" places—that included Birdie's Bump. The snowmelt and rain runoff had started to dig deep erosion channels across the Flats after the land was cleared for farming. The moldboard plow had a shear that cut down into the soil six inches or so. The "mold" part then turned the soil over—or upside down—as the plow moved through the earth. This left the topsoil loose, allowing the runoff to swiftly carry it away. A farmer could only hope there would still be enough fertility in each succeeding layer of the deep topsoil to yield yet another decent crop.

In summer after the plowing was finished, whenever a big rainstorm, and especially a cloudburst, swept across the Flats, the hills and slopes looked as though a giant tiger had raked the soil with its paws, tearing out mighty gashes that were then flushed down into ever-deepening erosion channels and thence to the Snake River, never to be retrieved.

John stood heartsick and helpless when he witnessed the mixture of the dark earth and rainwater, like rich milk chocolate, fill the gullies and go swishing and swirling in its headlong race to the river. Those gullies were cut deeper and deeper each year, leaving little canyon-like cuts across the face of the Flats, marring it, dividing it into a tangle of irregular pieces of land, each of which had to be worked separately from the others and made farming much more difficult.

John brought home an endless array of dirty clothes from the farm.

Zelma went at the washing with great energy, using a washboard in a big tub. It was a monstrous job, but it had to be done. After washing a batch and hanging it out to dry, she would sag into a chair, devoid of energy. Only the cry of a child could get her to her feet. So when they heard that the Donners across the street wanted to sell a used washing machine with a newfangled "wringer" for wringing out the moisture, they decided to look into it. The washer was stored at the lumberyard diagonally across the block from John and Zelma's lean-to.

A washing machine was an expensive luxury to John and Zelma, given their debt. Should Zelma continue with the old rubbing board? With three children already and most assuredly another two, they would have to get a washing machine sooner or later. Also, with Joel working on the farm with his father, there were additional dirty clothes each time they returned. Naturally, they wore the same clothes every day for a week and only bathed in the round galvanized tin bathtub when they returned on Saturdays. But the farm, the active children, and the dusty roads and playgrounds of the village created a large load of washing every few days.

On this day, October 25, 1927, having talked it over till there was nothing more to say, John and Zelma decided to go have one more look at the machine and then confirm the deal with the Donners. It was early morning, a bright sunny day. They had eaten a light breakfast while the children slept. It was a bit cold as they stepped outside, so Zelma turned back and put on a sweater. She peeked at the children in their beds. She thought they were still sleeping, so she quietly closed the door and left the lean-to. Unknown to her the children arose just after she and John left and wandered into the kitchen in their long nightgowns, with Merlin trailing his little wool comfort blanket behind him. The three tots stood in front of the stove, holding their hands up to enjoy its warmth.

Wood has little pockets of air and dried sap. When the wood gets hot, these little pockets explode, and sparks—sometimes inch-long cinders—spray out of the fire. The air-intake lid at the side of the firebox had been left slightly ajar to allow oxygen into the fire. A little cinder suddenly exploded through that open space and landed on Merlin's floor-length white nightgown. The gown only smoldered at first, giving off a pungent smell like burning hair. Joel and Lael, being so young, were unaware of what the scent meant and went on warming themselves.

Suddenly a puff of smoke and then fire engulfed the baby. The little boy's scream pierced the quiet as he fell backward onto his wool blanket and the floor. The blanket then burst into flames. Merlin's legs jerked and kicked against the fire, his little hands flailing at his face and eyes, trying to deflect the intense heat. Joel looked on in horror as the fire ravaged the head, shoulders, and torso of his little brother. Lael uttered a terrified cry as she rushed at him, but was quickly repelled by the searing heat.

Joel darted outside, flinging the door open and crying "Maaama, Paapa, come quick, come quick!" John, Zelma, and Mrs. Donner were just returning from the lumberyard. John did not hear the cry at first, but Zelma, always with an ear tuned toward the lean-to, heard. She saw Joel, with horror-stricken face, flying toward them. She could not see what was happening, but she knew tragedy was occurring in the lean-to. She could hear it in Joel's plaintive scream, could see it in his terrified look and the churning of his little legs racing toward her.

She flew to him, heard two utterly horrifying words—"fire" and "Merlin"—and with a shriek of dismay dashed toward the lean-to and through the open door. Her heart sank as she saw her little boy writhing in agony amidst the flames on the floor, heard his plaintive screaming, and smelled the burning nightgown, blanket, and seared flesh. She saw Lael trying to get at her little brother but unable to do so. The anguish on Lael's face was acute.

Wildly, Zelma picked her baby off the floor, dashed into the bedroom, grabbed a blanket, and pressed it around the little body to smother and extinguish the flames still eating at the remains of the nightgown and diaper. His intense pain was her intense pain—his anguish her anguish. His hair and eyebrows were burned off. His flesh was scorched. He lapsed into unconsciousness. Then he was back again, his little body jerking spasmodically. She tore at the remains of the smoldering diaper, throwing it from him onto the floor, where John, crashing into the room, furiously stamped out the last embers as the whole of the tragic scene enveloped him.

Zelma plucked wildly at the small shreds of nightgown, diaper, and blanket still clinging to Merlin's little body while caressing him, cuddling him, trying to bring him some relief. John rushed quickly to her side, urging her to hurry to the car so they could get him to the hospital. As they dashed through the kitchen, Zelma grabbed a little plate holding a pad of butter left over from breakfast, hoping it could somehow ease his shuddering agony. They would have to drive seventeen twisting, winding miles in their old car to get to the hospital in Idaho Falls.

"Oh, John," she cried "Did it have to be like this? Did he have to endure this torture, this brutal, ugly torture?" There was no time to respond. They rushed out, yelling to Mrs. Donner to take care of the two children and check for any burning ashes on the wood floor. Then they were in the car and gone.

En route Merlin threw up and kept jerking. He came in and out of consciousness, moaning, whimpering, and then was quiet but still jerking. Zelma tenderly spread the butter over the little body. In an act of desperation, she bared a breast and tried to get him to suck, to pull life out of her and into himself. It was hopeless. As they neared the hospital, the jerking stopped, the rapid breathing gave way to silence and stillness. He died in his mother's arms. He had lived only eleven months and ten days.

John looked over at Zelma, her head bowed, tears streaming down the smudges on her lovely face. He wanted to hold her, give and take comfort from her as the unbearable bore in on him. Through his own blinding anguish, he recklessly guided the car into the makeshift emergency entrance, slammed on the brakes, then rushed to the other side of the Model A and helped Zelma and the baby out and into the hospital through the newfangled twin glass doors.

Startled patients in the waiting room looked up and saw the two young parents and their baby. They smelled the burned flesh, looked at the large tear and butter stains on the mother's clothing and at her forlorn face. Two mothers standing by gasped at the scene. John and Zelma, noticing no one, rushed to the desk. They demanded to see a doctor. The doctor who came was Doctor West, Zelma's uncle, a big bear of a man. They went into a little room with a bed that had a white sheet on it. Doctor West gently took the baby from Zelma's reluctant arms and put him on the white sheet. He opened the little boy's eyelids to look in the eyes and then closed them with a gentle act of finality. He put a stethoscope to the baby's chest and then sorrowfully turned to John and Zelma. Embracing them both with a big bear hug, he solemnly pronounced their baby dead.

It was early afternoon, a bright sunny day, a little cold, but still bearing all the normal traces of a beautiful Indian summer day in Idaho. They stood there, the three of them, each immersed in his or her own thoughts of human life, fragile human life, bright and wholesome this moment, burned and extinguished the next. Zelma's grief turned to blame. Why had she ever left the children alone? But John, staring down at the charred little body of his delightful, happy little boy saw something through the ugly smudges of ash and butter and thought he recognized a familiar reddish pink pallor. But he was not shriveled, not yet. He thought he understood something, yet he did not understand.

Why this? He wondered. Why this torture for the little baby? Why this breaking of his and Zelma's hearts? Why did it have to be so ugly, so tragic, so agonizingly painful for all of them, but especially for the little fellow? What eternal purpose was to be accomplished in all this stupid agony?

He left the little huddle and made his way to the big window looking over the Snake River. "Slowly the rivers flow... We slowly follow after..." some song said. "They to the sea... We to the tomb..." Did his little boy come from some vast and mysterious sea of humanity, come to the earth to fill it with life and joy for only a moment and then return again to that unseen, silent sea to blend with those not yet come and those who had come and gone before? In his deep sorrow he could not comprehend it all. It would have to be sorted out later. He was too immersed in the present anguish.

Zelma left Doctor West's embrace and resolutely turned to a nurse who, through some silent signal, had come into the room. Zelma asked if she would please get a soft washcloth and some gentle soap and warm water. The nurse countered that she would take care of all that. But Zelma insisted. This was her duty, which she intended to execute faithfully.

When the nurse returned, Zelma took the washcloth, wet it, applied a little soap, and, sitting next to the bed bearing her little boy, gently started washing her little boy's eyes. The doctor had told her to start with the eyes, while the water and washcloth were clean. The little wisps of ashes, where the eyelashes and eyebrows had been, came away, leaving him looking waxen and unreal. She turned to the arms and hands, the little fists still clenched in pain. She dabbed gently, crying softly. But now skin came loose with the dabbing of the cloth. Blisters already were starting to pop up. She tried to continue, but she was hurting him, disfiguring him. With a gentle touch of kindness, the nurse pulled Zelma back from the bed, sat with her, hugged her and held her close as Zelma wept. Then the nurse stood, wiped her own tears from her eyes, tenderly wrapped the little boy in the white sheet, and took him from the room.

Doctor West sat down beside Zelma, put his arm around her, and pulled her close to him. He was a good uncle. He had taken care of all the sore throats and hurts and bruises and never sent a bill. Zelma took some solace from his embrace as she glanced at John still standing at the window. His teeth were clenching and releasing, his lower jaw expanding and contracting as a whirlwind of thoughts crashed through his mind. Now perhaps they knew what the reddish pink pallor had meant, or the shriveling. Or did they? A lifetime could not answer all their questions. The mystery of it was sealed up, closed, unfathomable.

"Would Merlin be or not be?" That was the question! John felt deeply that his children must have had some substance, some living essence, before they were born because he had seen them and had felt them. One did not feel "nothing." His prebirth encounter with his children provided him some measure of peace, despite all his unanswered questions. There had been presence there at the Grand, and there were feelings, emotions, intangible but real!

These were indelibly etched in his senses. On the other side of his little boy's life there should also be substance, presence, not oblivion. He found comfort in the thought.

Chapter 5

The Little Boy in White

ARTIE DONNER, LEFT BEHIND with the two children, surveyed the lean-to. On the floor near the stove lay the scorched remnants of a little night-gown and wool blanket surrounding a blackened spot on the floor the size of a small child. Breakfast dishes were askew on the table. One chair was over-turned from the parents' hasty exit. The bedroom floor was speckled with scorched pieces of diaper and nightgown. She carefully checked for sparks on the floor in both rooms.

Sadly she turned to the two children. Their frightened faces portrayed the trauma they had just witnessed. "Where did they take Merlin? Will he die?" Joel begged for an answer.

"Mama and Papa are taking him to the hospital in Idaho Falls so they can make it so Merlin won't hurt so much. We'll have to wait till your parents come home. Then we'll know how Merlin is." She had no idea as to what else to say.

She cleaned up the scorched debris and put it in a little sack on one of the kitchen chairs, cleaned up the dishes and the kitchen table, then bundled the children in their coats and started to lead them over to her house where she could watch them while she attended to her household chores. On the way she encountered two ladies and told them about the accident. They were aghast at the news but said they would spread the word and get some women rounded up to help at the lean-to.

Suddenly Artie realized that Grandma Fanny needed to be told. She turned in midstride, ran across the street and up onto the porch, and knocked on Fanny's front door. Fanny, not generally inclined to come to the door, yelled from her big upholstered rocking chair, "Come on in. It's open."

Artie shoved open the creaky door and ushered Joel and Lael in ahead of her. Lael rushed to her grandmother with a stricken face and with terror in her voice said, "Fire burn nightie and Merlin—Merlin cry."

Shocked, Fanny looked at Artie for an explanation, "Artie what in the world has happened to Merlin?" Artie told her of the accident and that John and Zelma were on the way to the hospital with the baby.

"I don't know how serious it is, but it looked just awful,"

"Oh my Lordy, what can we do?" Fanny exclaimed.

"All we can do right now is wait and see what happens. I didn't get to see the baby when they dashed out the door because they had him covered with a blanket. But it looked terribly bad! He was shrieking and jerking with pain! The floor by the stove was badly scorched. His wool blanket was burned to a crisp, and scorched bits and pieces of his little nightgown, undershirt, and diaper were all over the floor. I feel so sorry for that poor little thing. I've never seen such pain as he was suffering.

"I talked to a couple of ladies on the street, and I think they are getting women from the Relief Society to fix things up and prepare a meal for when John and Zelma return. But right now, all we can do is wait and pray. I'll take the children over to my house and take care of them."

Fanny started to cry. She grabbed Lael and Joel and held them close to her. "You kids behave now. Artie'll take good care of you. I'll slip over to the lean-to and help as much as this old carcass of mine will let me while we're waitin' for Mama and Papa to come back with Merlin." She tried to be optimistic.

Artie left with the two children in tow. Fanny dabbed at her eyes with a hankie, labored to her feet, got her coat and cane from the closest, then hobbled dejectedly across the street where she could already see ladies flocking to the lean-to.

Artie and the two ladies she had encountered in the street passed the news of the tragedy as best they could, hollering to neighbors across alleys and to passersby on the streets. The word spread like wildfire. Before evening the whole village of 465 people and those on Antelope Flats knew of the fire that consumed the little boy, Merlin. The little community would mobilize itself to support the family in their anguish.

Artie took off the kids' coats, sat them down on her big sofa, and tried to comfort them. She knew the children well. They came over often to play with her dog and cat. She loved them and enjoyed having them over. As yet she had no children of her own, even though she and Will had been married seven years. Her heart was heavy. She feared the worst after looking at the tragic scene in the lean-to.

Her immediate concern, however, was the two children. Lael kept looking up at her imploringly, saying, "Fire burn nightie and Merlin—Merlin cry. Fire burn nightie and Merlin—Merlin cry..." She repeated herself several times.

Lael had been traumatized by something like this before, during the summer when the family went to Jackson Hole, Wyoming, for an overnight trip. While they were in Jackson, the local Jaycees sponsored a mock stagecoach robbery at the city park, where hundreds of elk horns formed arches at all four corners. A stagecoach moved along Main Street adjacent to the south side of the park. Suddenly robbers came galloping along the street, and just as the stagecoach reached the intersection at the park's southwest corner, they started shooting their blank ammunition at the driver and the guard. The two fell off the coach. The robbers scooped up the cash box and made their getaway, with horseshoes clattering over the cobblestone street and sending sparks flying in every direction. Lael had looked on with wide-eyed horror.

For some time after the fake robbery, Lael, with great agitation, would shriek, "Man go bang bang, man fall down, horses run away. Man go bang bang, man fall down, horses run away!" Even as they lay in their bed among the cottonwoods where they had camped along the Snake River that night, Lael pulled her mother's face around to her, looked at her pleadingly, and whimpered, "Man go bang bang, man fall down, horses run away."

Finally Zelma pulled her close and whispered, "It was only play-like; the men were only playing, like you do with your toy dishes and Joel does with his little soldier men. No one was hurt." After several such assurances, Lael snuggled down into the covers close to her mother and Merlin, who had worked his way in between them, and went to sleep.

Now, however, Lael was a victim of stark reality. She had seen the fire. She had heard the baby scream in anguish. She had heard Joel screaming for his parents. She had smelled the burning nightgown and blanket and her little brother's burning hair and flesh. She had felt the heat and been repelled by it trying to get to Merlin. She knew he was hurting, burning, but had to stand helplessly by and see his blond mop of hair turn to ashes before her unbelieving eyes.

She looked intently at Mrs. Donner for comfort and answers: "Fire burn nightie and Merlin—Merlin cry... Fire burn nightie and Merlin—Merlin cry..."

Artie picked her up, sat down on the big sofa, and held her, pressing her little head to her breast, and soothingly said, "Mommy and Daddy are taking Merlin to the hospital where they will try to make him better." She also reached over and put a consoling arm around Joel, lending all the comfort her as yet untried motherly instincts could muster.

Finally, after the children had settled down somewhat, she went into the kitchen, made them a little breakfast, then brought them to the kitchen table and sat with them while they munched and drank. The intervals between Lael's repeated questions and Joel's more mature inquiries lengthened until they were ready for a nap, brought on by the food and their exhaustion.

The ladies from the Relief Society, aided by instructions from Grandma

Fanny, washed the dishes, scrubbed the floor, made the beds, and tidied up the lean-to as best they could. Several brought food that would stay fresh and laid it out pending the arrival of the young couple. They ordered their men to stock the indoor wood box and cut several days' supply of wood and stack it outside. This accomplished, they left two women and Grandma Fanny tending the house to wait for the children.

Artie brought Lael and Joel back home and, knowing they would be well cared for, turned to go fix her husband's supper. Will would be hungry after a long day's work. Just as she turned to go, she felt a tug at her dress, looked down, and saw Lael's sad and frightened little face looking up into hers. She had become Lael's island of security. Artie stayed. Will would have to fend for himself. He would understand.

Around eight in the evening John and Zelma returned. Joel recognized the clatter of the Model A engine and darted outside to see his parents and his little brother. Lael followed after. They saw their parents sadly climb out of the car and wearily make their way toward them. Lael ran to her mother, saying, "Mommy, fire burn nightie and Merlin—Merlin cry..." It was a question, not a statement of fact.

Joel asked his papa, "Where's Merlin?" Their questions had to be answered. But their parents would have to find a quiet moment to do so.

Zelma bent down and picked up Lael, oblivious to the stains and smudges that marred her dress and dirtied her face. She had washed her face at the hospital, but the inevitable tears came again and again, leaving their mark. She tried to hug Lael and take comfort from her. But Lael was too excited, too agitated. Zelma put Lael's head on her shoulder, patted her back, and carried her into the warm lean-to. It looked refreshingly lovely after the work of their neighbors that day. She felt a deep gratitude for their compassion.

John picked up Joel, carried him into the bedroom, and quietly told him, man to man, "Your little brother was burned so badly he could not stay in his body anymore. He has gone away to another place where we can't see him for a while." Joel grasped the dreadful truth immediately. He began to sob quietly as he realized that his little playmate and brother would live with them no more.

Zelma, with a subdued voice, thanked Mrs. Donner and the two ladies for their thoughtfulness and for caring for the children. She could see that they already knew the awful truth, so she did not try to explain. She turned toward the bedroom but stopped as she saw Grandma Fanny sitting at the kitchen table with a dejected, tear-stained face.

"Oh Mother, we've lost our little sunshine boy! I'm so sorry that you have lost a grandbaby too," she sobbed anew as she stood before her.

Death of dear ones was no stranger to Fanny. She had already discovered that a person could never adequately prepare for it, especially when it happened suddenly. Mrs. Snarr, twice Zelma's age and size, and a woman who had also lost a child and a husband, took Zelma and Fanny in her ample arms and whispered, "I know it's hard. I know it will hurt for a long time. But hold dear and treasure up in your hearts the memories of your little boy and grandbaby, and peace will come."

The neighbor women made sure all necessities were attended to. One, on discovering the hot water reservoir on the stove and the water bucket by the door were empty, went to the outdoor faucet twenty yards away and carried water to completely fill the reservoir. She left the bucket by the door full of fresh water. Then they bade the family goodnight and left. They knew this was a time for the little family to find itself.

———————————————

John told Grandma Fanny as much as was necessary to help her understand. Somehow talk of the incident now seemed so cheap. Fanny let it be. Satisfied that there was nothing more she could do, and worn out physically and emotionally, she asked John to escort her to her house and help her up the stairs.

It was dark and there were no streetlights. Neither spoke as they crossed the street. However, before Fanny went into her house, she turned to John. "Son, are you tying this to your experience at the Grand in Blackfoot?"

"I think I'm beginning to understand something, but I don't know what, or what sense it's all supposed to make." And with a tone of bitterness, he added, "I just can't make out why my little boy was shown to me shriveled and then had to go through this horrible tragedy to fulfill that destiny. He was such a bright little thing. He walked at nine months and started to talk about the same time. I feel such a terrible loss that I just can't get a grip on it all right now."

Fanny put a loving hand up to his face. "At least what you saw appears now, after what has happened today, to have been prophetic, so there must be some purpose and meaning to it." She hugged her son, then went inside to a fretful rest.

Zelma and John washed their faces, and Zelma changed from her dress into her nightgown. They ate lightly from the lovely meal prepared for them. Zelma then tended to the children, helping them into their nightgowns. She took Lael in her arms, sat quietly alone with her in the bedroom for a while, rocking her back and forth, and then responded to her repeated question, "Yes, I know. The fire burned the nightie and Merlin... and Merlin cried... But Merlin is okay now. He has nice white clothes on and is all clean and pretty. He doesn't hurt or cry now. The fire can't hurt him anymore."

Coming from her mother, Lael accepted the answer and let her innocent little mind rest. She and Joel were put to bed, but sleep came only slowly and with much fidgeting and fussing. When it finally did come, it carried them quietly away to a softer, gentler world and to peace.

The burning had been so intense that it left Merlin in no condition to have an open casket at his funeral service. Also, there was no way to quench the stench of the charred flesh. A picture of the little boy (the one on the stump) was to be placed on top of the casket to remind people of him and his short, cherubic life. John and Zelma were able to get through those four days from October 25 to 29, when the funeral took place, buoyed by the many kindnesses of their village folk.

On October 28 they made their way to the funeral home in Idaho Falls to complete the details necessary for the funeral service. They picked out the casket. It was so small! "How can such a small container hold him?" Zelma worried. "He was so much more than a body. He was a bundle of love, of joy. How could such a tiny space contain all that he was?" It reminded her again how he had been cheated of so much life. No growing up, no schooling, no career, no marriage, no children or grandchildren, no more brilliant sunsets and bright snowflakes and butterflies.

As they watched the undertaker put the finishing touches to the casket and then place the little body dressed in a white shirt and white knee pants in it, John and Zelma stood beside each other and with aching hearts looked down at their baby. They stood in silence for several moments, each lost in thought, holding each other, Zelma weeping for her son. Suddenly John's body stiffened. His face became pale and intense. He turned to Zelma, his eyes bright with tears brimming up. In a choking voice he whispered, "That's him. That's how he looked when I saw him at the hotel."

She looked into his face. Now she understood! All the questions and concerns about Merlin's condition, his reddish pallor and his shriveling, were resolved. Somehow it was as it was supposed to be. She did not know why. But she would not judge nor complain. She took comfort and strength from what they now knew. Their lives would go on. There would be more children. Somehow everything was in its proper order, despite her grief.

She said a silent prayer thanking God for the brief lifetime of her little boy and then nodded to the attendant to close and seal the little casket.

A few days after the funeral Zelma made a brief entry in her diary:

We know now what was meant by Merlin's odd-appearance when John saw him at the hotel in Blackfoot. Despite losing him I would not have wanted to miss even one small moment of his happy life. I see and live the world these children live in—perhaps all mothers do—as though I am living four lives, theirs and mine. I am grateful for this expansion of myself into them. Even though their pain is my pain, their joy is also my joy.

Chapter 6

The Monkey Trial vs. the Potter

THE THANKSGIVING AND CHRISTMAS seasons of the year Merlin died (1927) were hard on the little family. John and Zelma were still plagued with the question, "Why?" It hovered around them constantly. It wedged itself repeatedly into their thoughts, eager to jump into their consciousness at the slightest opening.

By mid-December there had not yet been much snow. John's eight horses were out on the Flats where they would roam until the snow covered their forage. Warm winds from the Baja Peninsula had streamed into Idaho on this unusually mild mid-December day. The winds brought a light cloud cover, which would maintain the warm temperature into the evening but did not threaten rain. John suggested that he and Zelma ride up to the Flats to check on the horses while Grandma Fanny looked after Joel and Lael.

The old car was not made for speed, so it gave the couple a chance to relax and enjoy the passing countryside. On half the land the fall wheat was now in the stooled-out stage giving the fields a "velvety lawn" look while the other half was in stubble. The pastel colored straw and lawn-green grain gave the countryside a "touch of taste," like a well-dressed woman wearing smooth and warm colors that beckon but do not shock the eye.

John stopped the car on top of the little hill that led a hundred yards downward to the dirt road leading to their summer shack. They leaned their backs against the car on the borrow-pit side of the road and let the soft breeze warm them as they gazed across their corner of the Flats toward Birdie's Bump. Occasional aspen groves dotted the landscape in little circular coves carved long ago by glacial ice. The aspen groves provided beautiful contrasts to the farmland, brilliant green in summer, with a soft, white bark, like birches, that made them look alive and stately, though leafless, in fall and winter. Near one of these groves stood the horses.

It was Zelma who said, "Don't we have a couple of halters or ropes in the car? I'd really like to take a ride up to the top of Birdie's if we can catch Old Jack and Tex."

"I think there are a couple of ropes in the back of the car, but there's no saddle."

"We don't need saddles! We can ride bareback. That's no problem!"

All the horses had names, and all the names had the word "Old" appended in front, whether the horse was old or young. As they approached they saw Old Tex was standing with Old Jack and Old Doll. The others were lying down. Tex was a true quarter-horse riding pony, not used for farm work except in emergencies. He was a dark bay with a white star in his forehead and white stocking feet in front but not in back.

Old Jack was a unique combination of saddle pony and workhorse. He was larger than Tex but not quite as large as the others. He had a stocky, athletic build and sported a shiny black pelt even with his winter coat on, except for a little streak of lightning-white on his forehead and white stocking feet. He was truly a handsome animal. John wished he had never been castrated. He could have been bred to John's mares and thrown some good-looking colts, which, John assumed, would have inherited not only Jack's good looks but also his intelligent and enthusiastic spirit. Tex and Jack were their favorites. They were like family to them.

"I think it would be well for you to ride Tex," John said. "Jack hasn't been ridden for a couple of months now, and he might be a little fidgety to start out."

Zelma shot him an indignant look at the thought that he was a better rider than she, but then pulled Old Tex around to a little mound of earth, deftly mounted him, and then pulled her long billowing dress up between her legs and the horse as a padding of sorts. True to form, Jack's high spirits kept him racing around in a circle while John held the rope taut. But eventually he calmed down, let John climb on, and they started off toward the pinnacle on Birdie's Bump. The other six horses decided to follow single file behind them.

Zelma used Tex's languid gait to turn her head this way and that and look wistfully out over the Flats and the Snake River Plain as they came into view, breathing in the still warm December air. She let herself drift into a melancholy trance as the splendor enveloped her. She needed nature's nurture. It had only been a little over a month now since Merlin's death.

John, too, was caught up in the unusual warmth and in watching his sweetheart sit erect and confident astride her horse. He knew she still thought often about her baby in the little cemetery on a little knoll one mile south of Ririe. He knew, because he would see an occasional tear steal down her cheek as she thought about him. Only a week before, they had purchased a marble marker, eighteen inches long and eight inches wide, with the simple inscription "Merlin Moss, November 1926–October 1927" and placed it at the head of his grave.

Anyone observing from Highway 26 would have seen two riding horses and their human cargo in the lead, followed by six other horses plodding along single file behind them, all working their way toward the top of Birdie's. Old Belle led the other six. She was a character. When hooked to a farm machine, she would lag back in the middle of the other horses, pulling as little as she needed to. This continued as long as the piece of land yet to be worked was still large, but as soon as she sensed that the unfinished piece of land was getting small, she would strike out eagerly, trying to hurry the other animals into getting the piece done so they could go home. For certain her IQ was greater than the other horses, except perhaps for Old Jack, but her character was flawed.

At the top of Birdie's Bump, Zelma slid easily off Tex's back, took the loop off his nose, and let him start feeding on the dry but plentiful grass. John was a few steps behind, so she wandered the short distance to the edge of the pinnacle, looked down, and then excitedly but silently beckoned John to come and look.

He looked down and saw what had excited her. Warming themselves on the face of the southerly cascade were two large bull moose, two cows, and two spring calves. One old bull looked up and saw the two humans peering down at them but sensed no danger and made no threatening gestures, nor did he attempt to move or induce the others to do so. All seemed half-asleep and bent on enjoying what might prove to be the last warm day for some time.

"I envy those mothers," whispered Zelma. "They still have their babies."

John took her hand, turned her from the tranquil scene, and led her to a large flat rock that was about knee high. They sat down facing the panorama of the Flats to their front and the valley below to their left. Gently putting his arm around her in an attempt to help her understand that he understood, he pointed to Old Belle who, instead of grazing, had drooped her head in a sleepy trance.

"Look at Old Belle's front knees and tell me what you see."

"They look like any horse's front knees."

"There's something a little more pronounced about hers than the others."

Zelma looked again.

"Do you mean those bones sticking out on the inside of her knees?"

"Exactly!"

"Don't all horses have them, except not quite so large or long as hers, especially that one on her left front leg?"

John looked at Zelma. "Yes, all horses seem to have them, but Old Belle's bone on her left front leg protrudes almost an inch out from the knee. The one on the other knee is probably half an inch long. I've always worried that someday when Belle is galloping along a side hill in the pasture, those bones are going to collide and give her a real jolt, maybe even cause her to break a foreleg."

"Well, why do they stick out of her knees like that?"

"The vet told me, and I have also read it somewhere in a book, that horses used to have a toe on each front foot. Those toes were attached to those bones sticking out at the knees. The vet said that time and evolution is supposed to have gradually left the toe to history, and only that bony remnant remains."

"Evolution?" queried Zelma. "Do you really believe in that?" Her voice had a slight edge to it.

"You remember the 'Monkey Trial' back in July of '25, when William Jennings Bryan and Clarence Darrow squared off against each other in Dayton, Tennessee?"

"Of course I do. It was the rage in all the newspapers and the news bulletins over the radio. The reporters claimed that Mr. Bryan made a complete fool of himself when he got on the witness stand and said we should be more interested in 'The Rock of Ages, than the age of rocks.' They said that Darrow cut Bryan to pieces. But what does that have to do with Old Belle?"

"You know I believe in God. I believe He gave me you. I believe He gave us our children, including Merlin. Now we know what was meant when I saw him at the Grand in his unnatural condition. What I saw was prophetic! It was a look into the future and what our future children would look like, all laid out for us to ponder, grapple with, but never to know what was meant by Merlin's condition until the fire took him. Evolution can't foretell the future. It can't prophecy! Only a higher intelligence could do that."

He paused and looked again at Old Belle. "Everybody followed the Scopes trial as closely as they could, especially Darrow's part in it, since he tried the case of the Miners' Union against the mine owners right here in Idaho in 1906. The prosecutors claimed that the union people planted a bomb on the house gate of ex-governor Steunenberg, and when he opened the gate he was blown to bits. Darrow got the three main conspirators, who were top union people, off with not guilty verdicts, even though the man who planted the bomb testified that they gave him the money to come to Idaho to kill the ex-governor."

John continued, "Darrow has been a devil of a competitor in the courtroom. I think his prowess in the Scopes trial turned many a person away from God even here in Ririe and on the Flats. After the fool Bryan made of himself, I wonder if Bryan's or anyone else's platitudes like 'Rock of Ages vs. age of rocks' should ever be relied upon to form one's faith in God."

"Well, what does all this have to do with Old Belle's knees?" Zelma asked.

"I am wondering what my experience at the Grand would mean to an intellectual like Darrow," John replied. "He would probably point to Belle's knees and say 'there lies your proof of evolution.' But then I would have to ask: Does evolution remove God, or some higher intelligence, totally from the scene? After hearing that trial discussed endlessly in Ririe and on the Flats, I think a lot of people believe in God only because they want to. It's a form of wishful thinking. Want Him to be and there He is!

"A lot of so-called atheists seem to act the same way. They simply make up their minds that there is no God, and poof, He's gone, just like that. By concluding that evolution is the ultimate answer for the development of man, the atheists and agnostics can claim that they have found their evidence for the absence of a creator.

"And, when I see Old Belle's protruding knee bones, a relic of her forebears' front toes, and when I consider Darwin's work on his evolution theory, to be honest, I feel compelled to accept evolution as one of creation's features. But when I ask myself, is evolution our sole creator, I have to concede that some higher intelligence showed me the future as to our children, and the only name I can place on that intelligence is 'God'!

"I suppose that Darrow, if he had me on the witness stand, would try to say that I fell asleep and dreamed it or that I was hallucinating, that I was having some kind of seizure, like an epileptic fit, or that I was simply a liar. He could claim that I didn't write it down, and this would be evidence that I had concocted it later after Merlin died.

"But I saw what I saw," John's voice rose. "I told my brothers and mother about it right after it happened. I told you about it the day we got engaged. I told you and them that I saw five children, and one of them was shriveled with a red pallor and smaller than it seemed he should be. When Merlin was born perfectly normal six years later that made me seriously wonder about what I had seen. Yet eleven months and ten days after his birth, you and I saw that shriveling and pallor, and it confirmed the prophetic certainty of my experience. As hard as it was on us to lose him, his death validated what I saw."

He stopped for a moment and then quietly said, "There's a verse in the Bible that says, 'O man, who art thou that repliest against God? Shall the thing formed say to him that formed it, Why hast thou made me thus? Hath not the potter power over the clay?' I feel that the intelligence that showed me those five children, including Merlin, has that power over all of us to serve purposes, probably meaningful ones, we know nothing about."

He continued, with marked intensity: "Now I'm going to say this. I told you there would be a boy, a girl, and the little shriveled boy, and then there will be another girl and then another boy. When those two come along, then the fact that I glanced into the future with the aid of the Potter will be absolutely undeniable!"

Zelma turned and looked intently at John. "It's probably too early to tell for sure, but I think the girl is on her way."

John bowed his head. A tear started down his dry cheek. He put his arms around her. She buried her head in his shoulder and he pressed her tightly to him. Old Belle still stood droopy and docile, oblivious to the dialogue she had started.

Almost without their noticing it, the sun had set and darkness was coming quickly. The earth was nearing its winter solstice. The horses stayed close by, seemingly glad to have their company. The children were secure with Grandma Fanny, and Zelma knew that Fanny knew that they might be a little late, depending on whether they found the horses and in what condition, so she would not be worried. The unseasonable warmth of the evening and the gradual changes in the beautiful panorama lying at their feet lifted their spirits. Everything was too lovely to leave.

Most of the residents of the Flats had moved to the valley for the winter, and those that stayed had only dim coal oil lamps for their homes. Electricity would not come to the Flats for another quarter-century. There was no moon piercing the light cloud cover, so darkness now prevailed over the Flats. As Zelma's gaze settled into this darkness, two miles to the northeast, apparently along Highway 26, a car's lights switched on. They illuminated a stretch fifty or sixty yards ahead of the car. The lights stayed on only briefly, then were switched off, and darkness reigned again.

This brief event triggered something in Zelma. She knew there was a car, substance, at one end of the lights and substance beyond where the lights shone. But she could see neither of these "bookends" to the light. She could only see the light shining across that short distance. It reminded her of her baby, Merlin. How he had burst into life with laughter, giggles, a budding intelligence, emotion, joy, pain, "brilliance" in a black universe, and then disappeared beyond that brilliance into what? Zelma was certain there was substance before his little life because John had seen him and felt of his presence. If such substance was there before his life, then why should it not be there afterwards, like the terrain lying in the dark beyond the headlights?

She pondered the thought as they left their cozy perch on Birdie's Bump, climbed onto their surefooted mounts, and gradually wound their way in the dark back to the car. The other horses again trailed after. John and Zelma petted and hugged Old Tex and Jack after they dismounted and to their surprise the other horses, led by Old Belle, came up to be petted as well.

As Zelma nestled into her seat in the car, serenity settled over her. The discussion there on Birdie's Bump and her thoughts about the car lights seemed to salve her soul into a luxurious solace. She would discuss that little episode with the lights with John, but not now. She sat in comfortable silence as the old car slowly brought them back to the lean-to in the valley.

Chapter 7

Lael – The Whirlywind

LAEL WAS LITHE AND ATHLETIC, graceful and lovely in her fourth, fifth, and sixth years. She stood erect, did not slump. She had a model's walk, unusual for a girl her age. The fire and Merlin remained bitter scars in her memory, but as the thirties approached she had her big brother, Joel, and her new little sister, Helen, as playmates. Helen was the girl standing to the right of Merlin at the Grand and was born on August 7, 1928. When her mother later announced that a little baby brother, me, would soon be born, Lael became very excited. In those years her games with little saucers and cups gradually gave way to other games: kick the can, anti-I-over, run sheepy run, softball, or swinging on swings.

It was summer, 1930. Warm winds wafted through the streets, whistled through the trees and around the buildings, blowing up little dust storms here and there. The louder gusts would whine as they shuddered through some natural or man-made device that acted like a pipe or flute. Southeast Idaho knows wind. The quiet days are refreshing, but "summer normal" is usually breezy. These mild and warm breezes brought out the best in people. They talked to each other over the backyard fences and hollered good-naturedly to passersby on the streets while the summer sun hung long in the western sky.

Joel was coming on eight, Lael on six. The grade school playground was not far from the lean-to, so when Joel was not working on the farm, he and Lael became frequent visitors. They made a beeline for the "slickery slide" and the swings, which Lael especially liked. Rising above earth in sweeping curves, holding her head erect, and surveying her domain fit her regal bearing. Joel obligingly helped push to get her swing moving, and he taught her how to "pump" the swing so it would keep up its motion when he left to go to the slickery slide.

On this day they arrived later than usual. Afternoon winds, stirred by the sharply rising temperature, started acting up. Miniature funnel-shaped tornadoes not more than fifteen feet high were seen occasionally. "Whirlywinds" they called them. They were little playthings compared to their monstrous cousins in the Midwest that carved wide paths of destruction, debris, and desolation.

Movietone News at the theater showed Ririe's residents pictures of those "killer tornadoes." Every kid was horrified at what they saw and fretted that they might strike their little town. Their parents assured them that Idaho's mountainous terrain would only allow the whirlywinds, not the killers. Kids, even young adults, liked to run after a whirlywind and try to get directly into its path so they could be twisted and tousled by the rotating wind and feel the terrifying, though only momentary, incapacity to suck in air. The little funnel clouds helped create a little excitement on the long summer days.

Lael had settled into her swinging routine, enjoying the thrill as she reached the apex of each arc. On one swoop she swung forward to her high point and took a big breath. She then exhaled as she swooped backwards. Just as she was about to take another breath, a whirlywind crossing the playground collided with her from her left as the swing swept nearest to the ground. Her mouth was wide open to suck in a fresh breath, but suddenly it was filled with bitter, choking dust. Instinctively she swung a hand over her mouth, letting go her hold on the swing chain. This twisted her so violently to the side that her other hand lost its grip. She fell backwards out of the swing onto the hard ground, striking the back of her head a vicious blow.

She had not screamed. It was too sudden, and the dust that filled her mouth and throat made it impossible to make a sound. Now she lay unconscious and motionless. Joel was unaware of what had happened until he finally glanced over to watch her and saw her seemingly lifeless form crumpled up on the ground, the swing making its final undulations above her.

He ran to her, gently picked up her head, and looked into her ashen face. By this time other children were gathering around whispering, "Is she dead?" Joel screamed for someone to find an adult to come and help. Soon Mrs. Snarr arrived, huffing and puffing as fast as her big frame would allow. She bent over Lael's face and listened. She detected breathing and whispered a quiet "Thank you, Lord." She could not bear the thought of another tragedy befalling this young family. She pulled a hankie from her purse and told one of the bystanders to wet it at the water faucet and bring it back.

She brushed the dust from Lael's face, dress, and stockings and held her head as her breathing returned to normal. Lael began to moan. Mrs. Snarr looked for broken bones, scrapes, and cuts, but found nothing serious except a small cut on the back of her head. She used the dampened hankie to wipe the blood from the cut and then remove the remaining dirt and dust from Lael's face and eyes. Then she folded it and put it on Lael's forehead to soothe her.

Slowly, painfully, Lael opened her eyes as muddy tears oozed out the corners. Mrs. Snarr could see that her eyes were rolled back in her head. Slowly they returned to normal, and Lael, though dazed, eased back into full consciousness.

"My little dearie, you scared the daylights out of us for a few moments there. Are you okay now?"

With a bewildered look, Lael responded, "The back of my head hurts, and I have a heady-ache over my eyes."

"Well, lie still for a little while until it gets to feeling better." She told one of the boys who had a light sweater over his T-shirt to remove it so she could wrap Lael in it to keep her warm. Mrs. Snarr draped the sweater over Lael and put her big brown purse under her head. Then she turned to Joel.

"Joel, are your parents home?"

"Yes, Mama is."

"You run fast and fetch her while I stay here with Lael."

Joel darted as fast as his legs would carry him, churning up the dust and the distance to the lean-to, reminiscent of another time he had quickly run to fetch his parents.

Even before reaching the lean-to, he was hollering loudly, "Lael's hurt—she fell out of the swing. Hurry, come!" Zelma heard the cry, ran to the door, and opened it just as Joel raced around the corner and skidded to a halt. He looked wild—his hair all tousled and a worried look on his face, a look Zelma remembered. Joel excitedly told her, while gasping for breath, that Mrs. Snarr was at the playground and had sent him to fetch her because Lael had fallen off the swing and looked like she was "hurt real bad."

Zelma, six months pregnant, checked on Helen, who was taking a nap in her crib, then walked and ran as fast as her condition would permit, fretting all the way about Lael. Medical bills were another big worry. They had little money even for groceries.

Zelma rushed up to Mrs. Snarr, who was still sitting on the dusty ground calming Lael with kind words. She heard the children asking each other how badly Lael was hurt; some speculated wildly about what caused her to fall. One sat in a vacant swing looking over at Lael, awestruck by the drama.

Zelma breathed a sigh of relief to learn that Lael seemed to be back to full consciousness, even though the back of her head was very sore and she was complaining of severe pain over her eyes. Zelma knelt down beside her and soothingly asked her where it hurt, assuring her that Mommy would take care of her now. Lael tried to smile, but it was too painful.

As Zelma looked at her, she noticed, but only for a very brief moment, that Lael's eyes crossed and then straightened again. It was so fleeting that Zelma wondered if she had really seen it. But, she thought, if I didn't see it, why am I even thinking about it?

She and Mrs. Snarr again checked Lael carefully for broken bones. There were none, but the cut on the back of her head was still oozing drops of blood. Mrs. Snarr wiped it away with her handkerchief, which she had washed again at the fountain. They gently lifted Lael to her feet. She tipped to her right as if she would fall. They straightened her up and the dizziness seemed to pass. She walked, but very slowly, each footstep jarring the ache in her head. There was no way to get her home except by walking. Zelma, after thanking Mrs. Snarr for her kindness, put Joel on one side of Lael and told him to hold her hand. She took the other, and the threesome began a slow walk toward the lean-to.

On the way, Zelma asked Joel for more details about what happened, but he honestly told her he did not know, except that she had fallen out of the swing. Lael was confused and found it hard to talk or explain, but she did mumble something about a whirlywind taking her breath. About halfway to the lean-to Lael suddenly bent over and gagged, spewing the contents of her stomach into the dusty street. She gagged a couple more times and then straightened herself up. With a few kicks in the dirt Zelma quickly obliterated the mess, and the trio continued toward home. Lael's steps firmed up more and more, and eventually she resumed her regal bearing, walking the last fifty yards by herself. Zelma sensed that Lael must be all right after she resumed that cute little walk of hers.

Zelma bathed Lael, washed her hair, and treated the cut on the back of her head with the only antibacterial of the time, Mercurochrome, which gave Lael another few moments of stinging pain. Her mother gently persuaded her to lie down and take a nap, telling her that it would help to take away the ache above her eyes. Lael went willingly to the bed. As Zelma bent over to give her a kiss on the cheek, there came that fleeting look again, the eyes momentarily crossing. Zelma knew that it was real once it happened the second time. She tried to dismiss it as a normal result of the fall, but somehow it unnerved her.

John returned from the Flats later that evening. Lael had slept soundly and long, awakening just in time for supper. She was still drowsy and complained of the back of her head hurting, but she said the heady-ache over her eyes was gone. John asked what had happened. Zelma, with Joel's excited help, told him of the accident with the swing. John cradled Lael on his lap and asked to see the back of her head. The red Mercurochrome had spread out over her scalp, making it look matted and nasty, but the wound, though swollen, looked like it was healing. He kissed her tenderly on the cheek and told her it would soon be better, that she had a strong body that would heal the wound by itself.

The family had a quiet meal. John and Zelma read to the children and then tucked them in bed. Lael's condition and the intensely crowded lean-to hung in Zelma's mind as she and John climbed into their narrow but comfortable double bed. Zelma turned over toward John and told him of the two fleeting incidents when she saw Lael's eyes cross.

"The first time didn't bother me so much, but when the second happened quite a while after the swing accident, then I began to worry. Do you think we should have a doctor look at her? I'm sure Uncle Walter will be examining the children at school before it starts. Perhaps I could ask him to look at Lael."

"What frightens you about the eye-crossing? Don't you think it's temporary; just a result of the fall from the swing?"

"I don't know. I wish I did know! I don't know what there could be in a person's brain or head that would make the eyes cross. But I don't like it. It must mean some kind of damage in there."

"If you're that concerned, then I'm concerned. Get your uncle to look at her as soon as he comes to the school. I don't like the eye-crossing either."

"I think we'll both feel better if we check it out. My other concern is that I don't know how he can look into her head to see what's going on."

"There might be something in his book-learning that would give him a clue as to what is happening, if anything."

"I worry about medical bills, but if my uncle is true to his usual form, he will waive off any charges."

"That'll help a lot, but I hate to impose on him."

Zelma decided that since money problems were already in the discussion, she might as well get to her other lingering concern.

"There is another concern I have. We haven't talked about it, and maybe it isn't even worth talking about. But this little lean-to is getting awfully crowded with three children, and now with that 'sturdy built boy' coming, we're going to explode out of this place."

"Yes, I know. Believe me, I've been thinking about it, too, but I don't know where to turn. Wheat prices have dropped considerably and my eighty and the rented places are too small an acreage to get ahead on, but I can't quit farming and go find another job at a dollar a day either. I don't see how we can pay any more rent and still meet our other obligations."

Zelma had an idea, but she wanted it to come from John. They lay in silence for a few moments. Then she snuggled up close, put her left arm across his chest, and quietly said, "Karl Klinger says he's going back to Austria to die. He'll be leaving soon."

Karl, the bachelor who owned the lean-to across the street next to Grandma Fanny's house, was almost sixty-five years old. As a young man he had migrated to Idaho from Austria. He had never married and lived alone for well over forty years, the last ten in his lean-to. He had homesteaded 160 acres and bought another 160, both of them lying side-by-side up on the Flats. He rented the 320 out for a third of the crop, while he did menial jobs around town. He was a good handyman and could fix anything. He wasn't very sociable and spoke with a thick Austrian accent, but people liked having him around because he was so "doggoned handy."

When he announced that he was going back to his homeland to die, the townsfolk became quite emotional. They didn't want him to die or to leave. But Karl, in the last few years, had become quite sentimental about his homeland and the places he knew and loved as a child growing up. More importantly, he had long ago left a beautiful and beloved young bride-to-be there with the intention that he would come first and earn enough so she could soon follow to their dreamland in America.

Soon after he arrived in Idaho he got a sad letter telling him that she had been killed when a horse bucked her off and she fell, striking her head against a rock. With barely enough to live on, he had never been able to return to his homeland. And although he did not want to tell the townsfolk this, he felt a strong urge to go back home and be buried beside her, thus, in some way, fulfilling their dream of being together.

Grandma Fanny's house just north of Karl's lean-to was a "regular house" in that it had a two-sided roof, sloping on both sides, with a porch in front and a little landing for a porch in back, both of which the two lean-tos lacked. In fact, they didn't even have a back door. But like the lean-to, Fanny's house only had two rooms, a kitchen in the back and a bedroom in the front. "Front" meant the bedroom was located on the street side of the house just off the front entrance porch. It served as both a bedroom at night and a living room for Fanny and any guests during the day.

Unlike many of the houses in town, especially the simple lean-tos, Fanny's house had once been painted, giving it a fairly elegant look, though now the paint had peeled off in large patches. Most important of all, and again unlike the lean-tos, Fanny's house had a basement, albeit a dirt-floor basement. That basement conjured up in Zelma's mind many possibilities for her growing family. Fanny's house also had one other enormous luxury. It had "piped-in water" to the kitchen. The lot, with its huge garden spot, the old barn with a cow's stanchion, a corral, pigpen, and chicken coop would all lend themselves well to a growing family, Zelma reasoned.

With Karl leaving, Zelma wondered if it might be possible to get his lean-to for Fanny to live in and move her family into Fanny's house. It would probably require going into debt again, but the prospect of getting that basement to go with the two upstairs rooms motivated Zelma to apply pressure where pressure might accomplish something.

Fanny was stubborn as a mule in a good-natured way. If she said "No," that was that, period! She spoke her mind, without apology. In fact, her speech could get colorful at times. A few days earlier, she had gone to pick some dandelion leaves to make dandelion beer. She asked little eight-year-old Joel to help her. As they were gathering the plentiful leaves along the ditch bank, Fanny had to kneel down. When she tried to get up she got a painful kink in her back. In desperation she hollered at Joel.

"Come over here by me and stand tall and fast while I grab a hold of your shoulder and lift myself up!"

After succeeding, she remarked, "Ain't that plain miserable that an old buzzard like me has to have an eight-year-old kid help her to git up? These old bones a mine ain't worth shootin' no more. Maybe I oughta jist lay me down 'n die."

Joel, being a well-bred boy with tender concern for his Grandma Fanny, replied, "Grandma, you shouldn't talk like that!"

"Waall, dadburn it, sometimes I jist can't find no other way to describe the way old age is a catchin' up with me. So you'll jist hafta get used ta it."

Joel reported the episode about Grandma wanting to die to his mother. He was told that Grandma had had a hard life, which had shaped her language and her disposition. "You shouldn't get too upset about it," Zelma assured him with a big smile. "She's such a tough old bird, you can just bet your boots that when the grim reaper comes to take her away, he'll think he's finally met his match."

Fanny liked Karl and was pretty upset about his leaving to go back to Austria to die. They shared a common beginning in America: she had emigrated from England, he from Austria. They often sat on her front porch and reminisced about growing up in their native lands. He always helped her with repairs around the house, even helped her plant and care for her big garden for a while, until it got to be too much for her even with his help. She finally gave it up and let it go to weeds.

She would miss him. But Karl had made up his mind. He had sold the 320 on the Flats for enough money to get him back to Austria and give him a little time to live off it. After that he figured he could do handyman work so he could live and have shelter. In mid-August during one of their chats, he told Fanny he would be leaving the first of October and asked if she knew anyone who might be interested in buying his lean-to. Fanny replied she didn't rightly know but would talk to him about it after she did some "thinkin' on it." As a matter of fact, when she learned he was leaving, she had already begun thinking about it.

The long and short of all this was that two worlds were coming together, Zelma's and Fanny's, although they did not yet realize it. Zelma left her remark about Karl dangling in John's mind as they fell asleep that evening. As John went through the routine of repairing equipment and getting granaries cleaned out for the new harvest, Zelma's "thought" cropped up repeatedly, and by a slow process of reasoning over the next few weeks, he saw a solution to their housing problem.

They could hopefully arrange a mortgage to buy his mother's house to assure her some money to live on, and suggest she consider using a part of the money to buy Karl Klinger's lean-to. An added benefit was that their two lots would connect, and his family could help care for Fanny. They would have the dirt-floored basement for a sleeping room for at least two of the kids. The other two could sleep on cots in the kitchen at night, like at the lean-to, and he and Zelma could sleep in the bedroom-living room.

He was so exhilarated by these possibilities, and the sensibility and simplicity of it all, he was finally prepared to tackle trying to get a mortgage on Fanny's house and then tackle Grandma Fanny. He knew Fanny rebelled at "changin' things," but with gentle persuasion and a little time it just might work out. John decided to discuss it with Zelma one evening over supper and was pleasantly surprised to realize just how smart a man she thought he was to come up with such a fine suggestion for a solution to their growing family's housing needs.

Meanwhile, the weeks following Lael's swing accident were hectic. The kids had to be ready for school. Joel would go into the third grade on account of being "skipped" by his teacher and the principal who determined he was too bright to stay behind in second grade. Lael would be entering first grade before turning six, which was approved by the principal because she would probably have Joel's intellect. To get ready, clothes were mended, washed, and ironed. Holes in stockings were sewn up. Used textbooks were handed down among family members or among neighbors. Seldom were any bought. Used pencils were rounded up and sharpened. Old spiral paper tablets were scoured from desks and drawers with last year's notes being ripped out and the unused pages reclaimed for the new school year.

Zelma also worked at the "psychological preparation" for Lael to take on this new adventure. Zelma explained that Joel would be at the same school and would go and come back with her every day. Her cousin, Johnny, would be there too. Miss Haltern—twenty-six, tall, good-natured, still looking for a man—would be her teacher, and Lael would like her a lot. She would learn how to write and read and do arithmetic. She would have tasty "school lunches" prepared by some of Ririe's best cooks. There would be hot dogs and hamburgers, spaghetti, fun desserts, and all kinds of other good foods. It paid off. Lael was ready and eager to go.

The injury from the swing accident had healed itself quickly, with one exception: the crossing of the eyes. There were a couple more instances where Zelma noticed it happen. She wondered how many there had been that she had not seen. Zelma's sister, Lila, or "Aunt Tiny," as all her nieces and nephews called her, was the school district nurse. She managed the health care for the schools in Jefferson County, including the one-room schoolhouses scattered about the county. Through her, Zelma learned that Uncle Walter was coming to Ririe to do routine examinations before the kids started school. He would check throats, teeth and gums, put a stethoscope to the lungs and hearts, and under certain conditions give shots and vaccinations.

Zelma arranged to take Joel and Lael to see him, and to Zelma's delight, Aunt Tiny was also there. Zelma was ushered into the little school library where the medical exams were being conducted. Lila greeted her warmly, and Uncle Walter gave her a big hug, with, "How's my niece with the fat little belly? What's it like to be absolutely gorgeous and pregnant? I never had that privilege!"

Zelma shyly shushed him up and did not respond to the question. Lila, the baby sister of Zelma's family, beautiful like Zelma and single, smiled at the little interchange and was very happy that her sister was expecting another baby.

Dr. West first checked the two children according to his normal routine and cleared them as healthy. Joel was sent out then and Zelma proceeded to tell her uncle and Lila about the swing accident and the eye crossing. Dr. West asked how many instances she had noticed. There had been several. Had she ever seen it before the accident? She had not. Were they increasing in frequency or in duration? Not to Zelma's recollection. Were they decreasing in frequency or in duration? Zelma could not say. Did Lael exhibit any nausea, any unusual behavior? Not that Zelma had noticed. She maintained her regal little mannerisms, talked pleasantly, walked gracefully, and played with an athlete's poise and skill.

Dr. West had Zelma put Lael on her lap, drew his chair up close, and shined a flashlight into each of her eyes, looking into them as deeply as he could. He covered one eye, shined the light into the other, and then moved the light quickly away to check for dilation, then did the same with the other eye. He touched her temples on each side and asked Lael if they hurt.

" No."

"Do you have a headache over your eyes or anywhere else on the sides or back of your head?"

"No."

"Do you hurt anywhere?"

"No."

"Have you felt dizzy since the accident?"

"No, except right after it happened I had a heady-ache and the back of my head hurt."

He felt the back of her head where the cut had been.

"Does that hurt?"

"No."

Nothing seemed to be swollen. He gently rubbed the sides of her neck, kneaded her shoulders on both sides, asking if that hurt.

"No."

He asked Zelma, "Has she complained of any headaches since the accident?"

"No, not that I have noticed anyway."

Reasonably satisfied, he told Zelma he could not detect anything wrong and that he knew of no other way to check her because he couldn't see into her head other than through her eyes. He told her she should watch carefully to see if the eye crossing continued, and if it increased in frequency or duration or both, he would want to know. He simply had no answer for it right now.

Somewhat relieved, Zelma thanked him, gave him a hug, and said, "We need to pay you for these things you do for us. We have no money, but I have a whole crate of fresh raspberries from my garden, and there are plenty more to be picked. You and your family would enjoy them if you will just stop by and pick them up."

"Now Zelma, you know that our family blood is thicker than medical bills, so don't you worry about them. But if I get time I'll certainly stop by and take a few of those raspberries with me."

Dr. West and Aunt Tiny had many other students to attend to, so they parted. After finishing at the school, Aunt Tiny stopped in to visit. She liked to visit with the little family and was always a welcome guest. She usually brought chewing gum, all-day suckers, or other treats that the kids enjoyed, and they eagerly awaited her visits. Dr. West didn't stop by.

Lila expressed her concern about Lael's condition and wanted to know more herself about the swing accident. She suggested that Zelma not let the eye crossing worry her, but to watch Lael carefully and also ask Lael's teacher to let her know if anything unusual occurred with Lael, such as nausea, headaches, and the like.

Zelma took Lael to school on her first day and told Miss Haltern about the accident. She assured Zelma she would watch Lael carefully.

Chapter 8

The New House

IT WAS THE END OF AUGUST, 1930. A huge rainstorm halted the harvest for almost ten days. John decided to use the time to approach his banker with his proposition for housing the family. He and Zelma drove to Idaho Falls the morning it started to rain. The seventeen miles seemed to Zelma, in her anxious state of mind, to take forever, going thirty-five on the straight stretches and fifteen to twenty around the corners. And corners there were! Half of the road had been laid out along the square section lines, so they drove right a mile, then left a mile, and so on for half the distance to Idaho Falls.

The bank manager was a woman, short, plump, but always immaculately dressed. John borrowed "operating money" from time to time to buy seed and plant his crops, so he had had previous engagements with Millie, the banker. If he had a short crop, he would dutifully come to Millie to get an extension. Millie would take liens on John's cows, hogs, chickens, horses, and any equipment not already mortgaged, and then release the lien on the crop so he could sell it to meet other obligations and to live on. John always came through as agreed. Millie had developed a great trust in him.

John and Zelma parked the car in one of the parking places located on the street in front of the bank. There was no parking lot. These street-side parking places were ample for the limited number of cars in the city. John and Zelma patted their clothing, checked their hair, and went into the plush offices of the bank. They asked for Millie. People didn't have to make appointments; in fact they could not with no telephones. They just stopped in. Millie had a customer, so John and Zelma sat down on the inviting upholstered couch in the bank's waiting room.

Zelma sighed as she felt its lovely material caress her body as she sank into it. What would it be like to have such an elegant piece of furniture in her living room? she wondered. She could have lavish parties with some of the "fine" people like the school principal, teachers, businessmen, farmers, ranchers, the sheriff, the mayor and their spouses and let them enjoy her lovely furniture and house. The dream quickly evaporated as she saw Millie, finely dressed and businesslike, coming toward them.

Millie was fifteen years their senior in age but had a youthful face and a perpetual smile. She liked her job. She liked herself. She was the daughter of a prominent banker. This, of course, helped her get a position at the bank. But she had also done her part. She was married and had raised two children, but she had simultaneously completed a bachelor's degree in finance and banking and entered into the banking business. This was quite unusual for the times. She was a woman in a man's world. Early on it took a little adjusting for John to get used to dealing with a woman banker, but over the years they had become good friends and developed a mutual respect.

Zelma had heard John talk about Millie. Zelma was curious to meet her. The first step toward her great dream rested with this woman. If John could get his plan to acquire Grandma Fanny's house approved, then he could go face Fanny with the deck stacked in his favor.

Millie sized the couple up as she invited them into her office. They were a handsome pair, both tanned and healthy looking. Zelma was pregnant and pretty. Millie could see from the way Zelma's arm intertwined in John's that they were in love. She knew of the tragedy involving their burned little boy and had been impressed with John's serene acceptance of it. She knew their financial affairs probably better than they. They were struggling with three living children and a fourth on the way.

Millie liked what she saw in this young woman grasping her husband's arm and exuding an appealing self-assurance. She sensed that John got a lot of his determination and confidence from her. She said a friendly "hello" to John but grasped Zelma's hand in a warm handshake of equals. The reciprocated pressure on her hand and the way Zelma's eyes met hers were just right, friendly but not fawning.

After a few pleasantries, Millie asked, "What can I do for you?" John cleared his throat, leaned intently toward her, and told of their desire to persuade his mother to sell them her house for his growing family and then have her use some of the money to buy Karl Klinger's lean-to.

"Is that the house right across from the Ririe High School, the small one with the large garden area?"

"Yes."

"But isn't it only a two-room house like the one you are living in now?"

"Yes," John responded.

"How will that help you other than to go from a lean-to to a regular two-sided home? You already have two rooms in your lean-to."

"Mother's house has a half-basement, a room as big as the kitchen, and that will provide another sleeping room for our two boys. The two girls will sleep upstairs in the kitchen. We'll sleep in the front room, which will double as a living room in the daytime."

Millie looked perplexed. "I thought you lost your other boy and only have one boy and two girls now. Did I hear you say your two boys?"

John hesitated, taken aback by his inadvertent reference to "two boys." Zelma quickly intervened. "The one I am carrying is a boy."

"How do you know that?"

"We know," was Zelma's firm and frank answer. Millie gazed at her for some time, looking her straight in the eye. Zelma's reciprocated gaze held fast. Millie sensed the truth of the assertion although she knew of no way they could know. She looked at John. His gaze was also firm. Something in their manner made her a believer that the coming child would be a boy. She stored the thought in the back of her mind and went on to discuss the amount of the loan (the full purchase price since they had no money for a down payment), security for the loan (the house and John's eighty acres), the payback provisions, the interest rate, and the other necessary details.

Millie liked dealing with them. Their candor was refreshing. There was no hidden agenda. Nothing about their affairs was concealed, nor would they ever attempt to do so. John was frank to tell her they had no money for a down payment and that both "the deal" and the purchase price still had to be negotiated.

"But before I tackle my mother I want to be able to tell her we can get the loan. I can't even imagine, much less guarantee, what she will say. But I have to start somewhere, and getting the money for her so she can buy Klinger's place is the first step. If I can tell Fanny that you will back us on the loan, it should help greatly to get the thing done."

Millie knew Fanny and understood what John was saying. She also knew the approximate value of the eighty, around ten to fifteen dollars per acre, and the approximate worth of Fanny's house, around one thousand dollars. The security and payback terms were adequate. She had the authority to grant the request on the spot. She looked at them again. Their confidence was refreshing to her. When she asked about furnishings for the new house and was told that they would "make do with what they had until their fortunes improved," she quickly understood that they would sacrifice personal gratification for honest debt retirement. That made the cornerstone of the loan.

She stood, reached for John's hand, and shook it. "The loan is approved, go tackle Grandma Fanny, and good luck with her. You may need it!"

She walked around the corner of her desk and reached for Zelma's hand. With her other hand she softly patted Zelma's protruding tummy and with conviction said, "I have enjoyed getting to know you. Now I think I know what makes John tick. Take good care of that boy!"

Zelma smiled a knowing smile. They understood and liked each other.

Nothing more needed to be said, except to thank Millie for approving the loan, which she did.

That evening John went alone to speak to his mother. The ensuing dialogue was colorful and interesting.

"Mother, we're cramped up like sardines over in the lean-to. There's so little room I have to go outside to change my mind. When the cat comes in we get fur in our teeth 'cause everything is so close there with me, the wife, and three kids, soon to be four!"

"Waall now, that is a mite close all right, but what can you do about it?"

"Well, Karl is going back to Austria, so his lean-to will be vacant. How would it be for you to sell us your house and you buy Karl's lean-to and move over to it?"

"Waall now, you and Zelma are poorer than them church mouses they talk about. How would you be gettin' the money to buy my house? And besides that, how will my house help? It's only two rooms which ain't much bigger 'n what you already got!"

John explained about the basement and told her of Millie granting a loan on her house with the eighty acres as added security.

Fanny had been thinking along those lines herself, but she had been working on a list of things she wanted if she agreed to move. She had not got them all sorted out in her head yet, so she postponed further negotiations to another time.

"I'll have to do some tall thinkin' about that afore I could make such a major change. But you can go talk to Karl if you want. I already told Karl that I might be interested in his lean-to since it ain't got no stairs to climb. The price oughta be no more 'n $300 to $400 for the house and lot, what with it havin' no basement and no piped-in water." John said he would check with Karl.

Then Fanny asked, "When is that next baby due, by the way?" This will be the other boy, right?"

"He should be born about the same time as Merlin was, in November."

Fanny wanted one more answer. "Was this one you seen healthy? Any blemishes or any problems with him?"

"No, he looked as healthy as all the other healthy ones."

John went back to the lean-to and reported the conversation to Zelma. She encouraged John to speak with Karl while he was still waiting for the grain to dry. He did, getting Karl to agree on a price of $350 cash.

Things moved quickly. Six days after the first encounter with Fanny, John wandered over to his mother's house and told her of the price Karl was asking for his lean-to and lot. Then he asked, "What do you think about your moving to his lean-to?"

"I been thinkin' we might as well do it, 'cause there are a couple advantages for me over there. Karl's place only has one small step up into it in front, while this one has three, both front and back. With me gettin' feebler all the time, I've decided I'd rather take the lean-to, and I don't care about the basement here 'cause I can't go down the stairs or at least could never get back up them. For all I know there could be a whole bunch o' animals livin' down there, 'cause I ain't been down there for a month o' Sundays. So you younger folk can handle it better 'n I can."

Then Fanny emphatically added, "I got some conditions I want to be clearly understood and carried out to the letter if we do it."

"What are those?"

Fanny pulled out a piece of yellow, lined paper on which she had made a list of notes. "You know Karl's place don't have runnin' water like here. The faucet is out at the front of the lawn next to the street. I'll take care of the water for the house durin' the spring, summer, 'n fall, but with the first snow, then Joel or Lael or somebody has got to haul my water in for me, keep the bucket and the reservoir on the stove full, and haul extra when I take a bath in the old tin tub. I'll do that every Saturday. Agreed?"

"Yep."

"Second, durin' those same seasons I'll probably be able to git to the outhouse in back all right. But when the first snow hits, I'm a gonna be usin' the night pot right regular, so one of you or the kids is goin' to have to come over every mornin' and evenin' during the winter and take that out. Agreed?"

"Yep, I guess we'll have to handle it."

"Third," Fanny continued, "you and Joel will have to keep my wood box full of chopped wood and kindlin'. When you're a cuttin' yours, you can cut mine, too, and haul it over. Karl has been doin' some of this stuff for me, and with him leavin', I gotta turn it to you and the kids."

"We'll assign Joel to do that and hauling your water as part of his chores."

"Fourth," she looked at her notes and back up at him, "I'm startin' to get some little dizzy spells, and when I have to get up in the middle of the night I'm afraid I'll fall and break a hip. So when I feel I'm in a dizzy spell mood, I want somebody big and strong enough to come over and sleep durin' the night so they can help me do the things I sometimes gotta do at night."

"How often do you get those?"

"Well, just off and on, maybe once ever two or three months, but with me a growin' older, it could be more than less."

"Well, with the kids having school and everything, and with me working on the farm, we may have to parcel that job out among Tom and Alma's kids, too."

"Well, talk to them about it and get something worked out, 'cause we gotta care for one another as we grow older!"

"OK, I'll get it worked out," John replied with a bit of a furrow building in his forehead.

"Fifth, I always wanted you and Zelma to have this house anyway, so I don't mind sellin' it to you. The price is $800. That's low, but fair. You'll have to get your banker lady to work out terms you can meet. But I know you're gonna have chickens and a cow or two and a few hogs, and for that gracious price, I want the privilege of goin' in the coop and gettin' me an egg or two anytime I want, and I would expect you to give me some milk, a little slab o' bacon, and a little beef and perhaps a half a chicken from time to time."

"Yep, no problem there." John looked at the paper notes and wondered if they were getting near the bottom.

"Sixth," she said with a very serious tone of voice, "I have told the Ririe

School Board that if and when this place with its big garden and lot is ever sold from outa my family, that they would have first right to buy it. I'll rest easier when I die knowin' you and Zelma have a secure roof over your heads but also knowin' that my agreement with the school district will be honored. They want it for expansion, they said."

"But what price did you quote them?"

"Fair value to be determined at the time by that Rasmussen boy who sells real estate over in Rigby. He's honest and will give it a fair price."

"Is that in writing anywhere?"

"Nope, our word is our bond, and that's that!" was her emphatic reply.

"Well, I guess I can live with that as long as I know we can keep it in our family as long as we want."

"It's the right thing ta do," she said, dismissing the subject with a wave of the hand.

"Is that everything on your list?" John asked with a little hesitation.

"Yep, those are the terms. Go talk it over with Zelma, and if you two agree, give notice to your landlord on the lean-to, get your paperwork done with your banker lady, and then we'll pay Karl his money, get his deed, and start the movin' process."

Zelma quickly agreed that most of those "conditions" were things they would be doing for Fanny anyway, and more, so the deal was struck with a handshake and a hug.

Karl Klinger cleaned up the lean-to beautifully, trimmed what was left of the growing lawn at that time in the fall, and prepared to leave. For a week before his departure, people dropped in and left a little trinket or a quarter, a fifty-cent piece, even a silver dollar, or some other little token of affection as thanks for the good service he had rendered them and their community. There were many tears and a lot of hugs, especially from Grandma Fanny. Karl had trouble handling it all, being quite shy. When the day arrived, he dressed up in his best suit and tie, put on a bowler hat, and looked "mighty princely" said Grandma Fanny. She could not walk the three blocks to the railway depot, so she stood out on her front porch and waved him good-bye.

She said with a choking voice, "Karl, you belong to America! But I understand, I do understand, so go with God my dear friend and may He be with you and comfort you to the end."

Several saw Karl off at the train station. No one heard from Karl again.

Chapter 9

Dutch Caldwell

EVERYONE EXCITEDLY PITCHED in to help with the move across the street the week after Karl's departure. Mother cleaned out the basement and set a few mousetraps at strategic locations. (When I eventually slept there, instead of counting sheep, I counted the "clicks" of the trap and the screeches of the mice). Papa laid boards across the dirt for a floor. They hauled down a bed large enough for two with a straw-filled mattress, plenty of blankets, and two heavy flannel sheets. This is where Joel would sleep until I (the soon to be newborn son) would be old enough to go down there with him. Papa fixed the small window in the basement, which looked out at ground level, so it would let a little fresh air into the dank interior, which smelled like a potato cellar.

Meanwhile, Lael was loving her first year of grade school. She learned to read and write. She especially enjoyed the "Dick and Jane" books, and she loved her teacher, Miss Haltern. Miss Haltern noticed early on that Lael was developing beautiful handwriting, especially for a first grader.

During the school year Miss Haltern was courted by an old beau from her college days. He took Miss Haltern away as his bride at the end of Lael's first grade year. When school was over for the year the other teachers had a bridal reception for Miss Haltern. Lael, with Mother's help, embroidered a little doily on which were imprinted the words, "I love my teacher, Miss Haltern, Lael." She wrapped it in brightly colored paper and personally delivered it to Miss Haltern at the reception.

Miss Haltern opened the package, bent her head downward as tears welled up in her eyes. She pulled a hankie from her purse, wiped away the tears, and polished her nose. She asked Lael to come to her. She took her on her lap and whispered, "I want you to keep a big secret, okay? You are very special. You are one of my favorites. I will never forget you. Thank you for this lovely doily. I hope my husband and I have a bunch of kids just like you."

Lael was very pleased but cried as she threw her arms around her teacher and they embraced for a long moment. Then Miss Haltern set her down, and Lael walked gracefully away, unashamedly wiping her wet eyes with the sleeve of her blouse.

Lael's school adventure was enhanced by her fondness for her cousin, Johnny, who was two grades ahead of her. He was not only Lael's cousin but also her good friend. With Johnny and her brother going to school with her, Lael felt secure and happy in her first few years of grade school. Joel was a bright student. He soon captured the respect and admiration of his teachers who predicted "he would become somebody."

In the midst of these goings on, I finally came on November 21, 1930, rounding out the five. Then, to the folks' pleasant surprise, Mama gave birth to two additional girls. The first "extra," Rhea, was born on May 8, 1933. The other "extra," Ruth, was born January 31, 1938.

"Why weren't we seen?" This was a question they raised anytime Papa's experience at the Grand came into a conversation.

"You were given to us for good measure—running up and heaping over!"

Papa had no better answer, at least until sometime later in the family saga. Papa saw only five but seven were born. The "extras" rounded out the family.

It was a hot summer Sunday in the mid-1930s. Papa was already at church with Joel at a special meeting for the men. Mama was bringing Lael, Helen, Rhea, and me to the main church service, which started at ten a.m. Lael was ten. Helen was coming on seven. I was nearing five. Rhea had turned two just a few weeks before. Lael was sometimes carrying and sometimes dragging Rhea, who became distracted by every bug and flower. We were dressed up neatly in freshly washed and pressed clothes. We were a little late, and Mama was trying to hurry us along to be on time.

Our path took us to the intersection where we could see Mary Jap's hotel a half a block to the east. Mary Awoki owned the Ririe Hotel. It was located only a block from our home at the corner of Center Street and Main. It was a wood frame building with a restaurant downstairs in the front, living quarters and a kitchen in back. It had six single rooms on the second floor, accessed by an arching set of stairs, the front of which led up to the rooms, the back to the outdoor toilet behind the hotel.

Mary could only speak Pidgin English. Ofttimes you didn't know what she was saying, but you almost always knew what she meant. In the community, she was known simply as "Mary Jap." Like "Birdie's Bump," no one meant to give offense, and nobody, not even Mary, got upset or cranky about it. After all she was full-blooded Japanese but also a naturalized U.S. citizen.

The hotel was run down and sold cheaply when Mary bought it. She had been twice widowed, and without a husband to help support her, she needed some way to make a living. She had two sons, native-born Americans by her first marriage, but they were long since gone from home. They seldom came to visit because of inadequate transportation and the cost. When they did come, Mary was all a-flutter because her boys were her link to earlier, happier days.

Mother knew that Mary endured a sad and penetrating loneliness. She lived alone, and she was different from the Caucasian community. At least, some in the village figured she was different, with her slanting eyes, her shuffling walk, and her funny way of speaking. Also, she was a Buddhist, the only one in town. Yet she made and kept friends in her own special way, paved by her big-hearted tolerance and her compassion for the down and out, to whom she gave free meals and rooms. Her good-natured attitude, her charitable ways, and her compassion endeared Mary to the community.

The morning after Merlin's funeral, Mary appeared on Mother and Father's doorstep with a warm breakfast of rolls, freshly made, and bacon, eggs, and hash browns. In her broken English and with tears streaming down her cheeks, she told them how sorry she was that they had lost their little boy. She didn't say much because she could not adequately express her feelings in this foreign tongue. But from her face and demeanor they could tell that she felt deep pain for their little family. She was invited in but, true to her normal behavior, she graciously declined and went back to her hotel. Every day for a week she came with breakfast, demonstrating her sympathy in a humble, helpful way.

On our way to church that mid-summer day, Mama looked toward the hotel and saw Mary sitting on the back stairs, weeping bitterly with her head buried in her hands. Mama rushed over. She put an arm around Mary, drawing her face out of her hands and wiping the tears away with a fresh diaper she had in her hand. Mama begged Mary to tell her what was the matter. Between sobs, Mary blurted out the name Dutch Caldwell and in her broken English explained that about midnight Dutch had come banging on her door and demanded he be given a room for the night. He had been drinking at both Ririe bars just down the street, and after they closed, he could not find his car, let alone drive it, so he had stumbled down the street to Mary's hotel.

Dutch had a reputation. He was the forty-three-year-old, spoiled son of a father who had put together a fine farm and cattle operation on about 2,000 acres. His parents had built a beautiful home for the times and had state-of-the-art cattle corrals and chutes, silos, and storage facilities. Dutch's mother had died of cancer when Dutch was eighteen. His father never remarried, never thinking he could find anyone to replace his bride of twenty years.

Dutch's father died of a heart attack at age sixty-three, just a few weeks before the stock market crash of 1929. Dutch was his parents' only child. In school he did only enough to get by, but liked to play the school's brand of six-man football and was good at it when he did not let his ego interfere. When it did, he would throw tantrums when he was not given the ball as halfback as often as he wanted it.

Dutch had become an alcoholic, although he would never admit his addiction. He also chased women despite being married to Darla, a decent girl from Idaho Falls, who brought some bit of dignity to his life. Even she was unable to keep him home to herself and was powerless to stop him from strutting like a stud horse whenever a good-looking woman was around.

Upon his father's death Dutch inherited his family's estate, which was without debt. But his lifestyle soon required that he sell seven hundred acres to pay off gambling and other debts. His hired men, first engaged by Dutch's father and loyal to him, his wife, and the spread, were dismayed by their new boss's behavior, but tried to keep things going for Darla and the family's sake. Dutch's frequenting of the Ririe bars was typical, and the night before this Sunday was no exception, other than his stay at Mary's hotel.

Mary said she had let him in and helped him up the stairs to a room. She said he had been foul mouthed and cussed her all the while she was trying to help him. They finally made it to the top of the stairs, where he staggered and stumbled into the room, slamming the door in Mary's face with a bang. For more than an hour he had stomped, yelled, cussed, stumbled over furniture, and slammed repeatedly against the walls. Finally, he fell onto the bed and went to sleep. About an hour ago, she said, Dutch quietly tiptoed down the stairs and went away, without saying anything to Mary and without paying for the room.

Sobbing bitterly, she added, "He broke up room. Furniture's broke up and big mess all over everyting."

Mama answered, "Let me see it."

"You no wanna see, make you sick." But Mama insisted. She put her arm around Mary, and together they went in the door and down the hall to the room. Mama called back to us to stay where we were and for Lael to mind the baby.

Five minutes later Mama, looking pale and distraught, but with fire in her eyes, came out the back door and down the stairs with Mary. She told Lael to take her baby sister into Mary's café and keep a close watch on her. She told Helen and me to come with her and Mary. We went into the kitchen, where she and Mary assembled a collection of buckets, mops, brooms, dustpans, cleaning rags, and hot water.

Mama also put big dishtowels on Helen and me and tied them securely so they covered up the front and most of the back of our nice Sunday clothes, then said with a frown, "I probably shouldn't make you two endure this, but we need your help, and you might as well get used to some of the seamier things of life. Lael has to stay down here and tend Rhea."

She and Mary put on aprons, and our quartet climbed the stairs, lugging the cleaning paraphernalia. As we approached the door of Dutch's room we encountered an overwhelming stench. Instinctively, Helen and I covered our noses and mouths, almost overcome by those fetid fumes. I wondered how I could possibly enter such a foul den.

Mama's stern voice cut through all that hesitancy, "Now get a grip on yourselves, and let's get to work."

Timidly, Helen and I looked into the room. We could not believe what we saw. The grimy floor was splattered with puddles of partially digested, regurgitated food and liquids, with footsteps that had slipped and sloshed through them. The lone chair was lying on its back with its two front legs suspended from a pair of wires that had been used before to repair and steady them. (This was the normal condition of half the chairs in Ririe.)

The mirror, still hanging on the wall, was cracked downward through the middle, and the bottom part had broken out and fallen onto the dresser above which it had previously hung. The dresser was tipped over onto its front, and two of the three drawers were broken and lying around like pieces of kindling wood. In the wall next to the mirror was a big tattered hole through which it looked like a fist or a boot had been thrust. The bed was worst of all! Unmentionable grime was splattered here and there on quilts and sheets. Even the pillow had not escaped. Lying in the middle of that sordid mess, but partially hidden by a fold in the quilt, was a pair of yellowed and filthy false teeth.

Under Mama's stern prodding, and aided by handkerchiefs she tied around our mouths and noses, we went to work to clean up the mess. Her resolute demeanor literally dragged all squeamishness out of us. First thing, Mama took a washrag and picked up the false teeth with it, dropping them into a glass jar she had brought with her. She set the jar down just inside the door, probably as a grim reminder of the formidable task that lay before us.

The mirror was taken down, the chest of drawers righted, and the broken drawers laid outside the door for eventual repair along with the broken chair and mirror. The quilts, sheets, and pillow were ripped off the bed and shaken out onto the floor to the extent their contents would "shake out," then thrown out into the hall to be taken to the washing machine. Helen and I were given a broom and dustpan and assigned to the floor to scoop the grime into a bucket and haul it to the weathered two-hole toilet out back. Then we had to get down on our hands and knees and mop the floor sparkling clean, the only way Mama would tolerate it.

Midway through the process, Joel, Lael, and the baby, Rhea, appeared on the scene. Joel said Papa had sent him to find us because we had not shown up at church. Mama at first wanted to keep Joel there and give him part of the job, but rather than dirty him up she told him to go tell his father what had happened and to come as soon as he could to Mary's hotel. Joel left, but Lael stayed, her face turning white from the stench and the grimy scene before her.

Without warning, Lael let out a gasp and a gurgling sound, vomited onto the partially cleaned floor, and then fainted in a heap just inside the door. Mama rushed to her, took a clean cloth and some clean water, and started to wipe her face. Simultaneously, she dragged Lael into the hallway by the window, opened it, and let the breeze waft over Lael's ashen face. The breeze and cool water soon brought Lael around, but as she opened her eyes, they crossed again, except this time they stayed crossed for several seconds. Mama told her to play with Rhea there by the window where the air was fresh while we finished cleaning the room.

Eventually we completed the difficult and disgusting task. The quilts, sheets, and pillow covers had been taken to the washer and were making progress toward coming clean. Mama insisted that Mary wash them twice, just to be sure that every last vestige of Dutch Caldwell's filth was cleaned away. Mama told Mary to leave the chair, chest of drawers, and the mirror be, and she would have John pick them up and get them repaired. Finally, a strong detergent was spread across the floor and wiped onto the remaining furniture to try to sanitize it and eliminate any of the stench of Dutch Caldwell that was left in the room. But the false teeth were left in the jar just as they had been found. Mama had a plan for them.

———————————

Papa returned with Joel just as we were descending the stairs with our pots and cleaning tools.

We took the cleaning supplies back to the kitchen. Papa told Mary he would come over on Monday morning and fix what he could of the furniture and then have a carpenter do the rest. It had been an exciting morning, one that I would remember far more intensely than most of the Sunday mornings I had spent in church.

Before leaving Mary's place, Mama asked Papa to take the baby and the other kids and start for home. She told him there was a roast cooking on the stove, and he was to check it and set it off the hot part of the stove and let it simmer on the side if it was done; otherwise, he should put more coal (we now used coal when we could get it) on the fire and let it continue cooking.

After the others had gone, Mama took Lael into Mary's kitchen and sat her near the open window. She bent down and looked deeply into her eyes but saw nothing unusual, no crossing. She got some warm water and a clean washcloth, soaked it, wrung it out, and then began to wipe Lael's face.

"Do you know what happened upstairs?"

Lael's look was a blank at first, but then she said, "I got sick and threw up in that awful room. I don't remember what happened then, Mama, cause the next thing I remember I was out in the hall on my back in front of the window. What happened to me, Mama?"

"You passed out, and I brought you out into the hall and let the fresh air from the window help revive you. When you woke up did you feel anything different or funny?"

"Yes, Mama, everything was black when I began to feel the air from the window. Then things looked real fuzzy. Then everything got okay. But I also felt like somebody was pushing on both sides of my head real hard, like they were trying to squeeze an orange."

"Do you feel that way now?"

"No, I don't feel the squeezing, but I can hear my heart pounding in my head. It sounds like there's a drum beating in there."

"Does your head hurt now?"

"No, I just hear this funny thumping in my head is all."

"Is that getting any better or softer or louder?"

"No, it has stayed the same from the time I woke up by the window, but the squeezing I can't feel anymore."

"That's good. I think you are going to be okay. But I have one more important question. You said everything was black, then fuzzy, then cleared up as you were coming to. Has that ever happened before?"

Lael's response was guarded. "No, I can't remember any time like that. Why? Is that something bad?"

Mama's answer was also cautious. "I don't think so. I think you were just overwhelmed by the awful stench and those awful things you saw in that room. We should be careful about suddenly exposing you to something like that. But now let's make sure your dress is clean and you look as pretty as before. Then we will hurry home."

Lael had one more urgent question. "Why was that room so awful, and why did it stink so bad?"

"Well, you know that a man stayed there last night. He was drunk and he made a mess of the room. Mary has been a good friend of ours and helped us in some of our bad times, so we just wanted to help her clean up that horrible mess."

"But why did he do it, Mama?" Lael insisted.

"When a man gets drunk sometimes it makes an animal out of him, like the one that stayed there last night in Mary's room."

With that, Lael was satisfied, at least for the moment, and after being carefully inspected by her mother and a few flecks and a stain on her dress were cleaned off, the two bade Mary good-bye, accepting her profuse thanks. The two walked on home, hand in hand. Mama brought the jar containing the false teeth, but kept it covered with the cloth she borrowed from Mary.

The Sunday dinner was delicious as usual. It was topped off by a piece of Mother's special "$100 Cake." Its name had a story to go with it. A very wealthy man ate a delicious dinner at a fabulous restaurant in New York City one evening. He finished his main course and said he was full and wanted nothing more. But the waiter told him he should try this very special cake and that he would not be disappointed.

With the waiter persisting, the man ordered a piece. After he ate it, he was so excited about it he told the waiter he wanted the recipe. The waiter said the cook would not give it to him. The man asked the waiter to take him to the cook. The reluctance of the cook to part with the recipe was soon assuaged by the tender of one hundred dollars. Once he owned the recipe, the man published it in a recipe book, giving it that name. I was really aware of only three things about that cake, and that was enough. First, its name; second, that it was somehow made "with a base of mayonnaise instead of eggs," whatever that meant; and third, it tasted delicious! I ate all that Mama would allow me at any one sitting.

During and after the meal, I could hear my parents talking about the events at Mary's hotel. It was then I found out that Mama had brought the jar with Dutch's false teeth home, covered with the cloth. Those teeth, still in the grimy condition they were discovered, led to a heated confrontation with Dutch in front of his wife. Mama exchanged them for one hundred dollars from Dutch to repair the damage done to Mary's room. Call it blackmail if you will, but Dutch decided to pay it in lieu of Mama reporting the incident to the sheriff. All this was a stellar blow to Dutch's inflated ego, something he had trouble forgetting.

Chapter 10

The Great Depression and the Vilate Hatch Show

WHILE OUR FAMILY was busy growing, around us the Great Depression had descended upon America and the world. The tight finances that were always part of those days induced interesting thought processes. In fact, while waiting for me to be born, Papa and the doctor and his wife, who helped him, had an animated conversation.

"John, I've got a string of girls going. I think yours'll be a girl too. It must be in the water."

"No, this one will be a boy!"

The doctor and his wife laughed good-naturedly, "Now, John, this baby isn't going to break my string of girls. You just watch and see!"

He said it with such conviction that a thought sneaked into Papa's mind. Why not bet him double or nothing for his fee if this baby turned out to be a boy? The temptation was quickly repulsed. He couldn't exploit what he knew for material gain. But I did break the doctor's string of girls.

I knew money was scarce in the thirties, and we raised our own fruits, vegetables, beef, pork, eggs, milk, and butter and traded garden produce and eggs for store bought goods. I knew wages were low because my father paid a worker one dollar for a full day's work on the farm, sunup to sundown, and the worker paid seven dollars a month to rent a two-room lean-to. He was glad to have the work. But in my early years I remember nothing of "depression." This was the atmosphere in which we and the other children of Ririe were born and raised. One of those others was Danny Rosenthal. He had Saint Vitus' dance. He was also retarded. There were no development workshops or other "shelters" for such kids around Ririe. They either roamed the streets or went to school, where the teachers simply did what they could with them. Danny couldn't sit still in school, so he wandered the town, his daytime campus.

The whole village helped out with Danny. At lunchtime some mother would spot him, make him a sandwich and give him a glass of milk, check him for bruises and scrapes, and then send him on his merry way. Later, toward evening, someone would either walk Danny home or give him a ride in a wagon pulled by a team, or, if he was really lucky, he might get to ride in a car.

One time, and one time only, some boys got Danny drunk to see how alcohol and Saint Vitus' dance mixed. They didn't. When the boys' mothers found out about it, and they always found out, those boys got the "lickin'" of their lives. Those village mothers had a network of communication that upstaged modern technology. They knew which boy kissed which girl and when and where, and they knew it almost as soon as the event happened, or sometimes even while it was happening!

I know that wheat prices dropped sharply, from five dollars per hundred-pound sack to one dollar in those Depression years. Everybody struggled to get by. Bank loans were extended. Many took out bankruptcy. In the meantime, people simply made do with what they had. Many lived off what they could grow or feed. Still, while the Great Depression may have been a fact, we were not depressed. If nothing else, Vilate Hatch saw to that.

Out from behind the long, black curtain on the stage of the community center stepped a middle aged, pleasingly plump woman with a voice like a foghorn. She wore well-worn, loose-fitting bib overalls and had a large, round alarm clock tied to her waist by a piece of electric cord—her "timepiece" she called it. The floppy hat atop her disheveled hair gave her an irreverent look, which matched her monologue. Vilate Hatch, Depression-era talk show host, looked out at the audience as though all were dressed in red longjohns, walking up and down along the curtain smiling broadly until she spotted Jed, the barber. She pointed to him.

"Now we all know that Jed over there cuts our school athletes' hair at a fine little discount, a-tryin' to have them lookin' pretty for their ball games. Well, I have it on good authority, uncompromisin' rock solid authority, that Sid, our star basketball player, was a gettin' his hair cut last Tuesday afternoon for a big game on Friday night. Why, Old Jed worked right diligent on the left side of Sid's head but kept takin' little sips out of a cup handily placed on his back bar. As the haircut progressed, so did Jed's glow!

"Old Jed got a purty good job done on the left side. Then with great flair he swooshed the barber's sheet off Sid (she ceremoniously mimicked the act), shook it out, and thanked Sid for comin' in.

"Sid, all perplexed, looked in the mirror and said kinda pleadin' like, 'But Jed, you only did one side.' To which Jed briskly replied, 'Son, you tryin' to tell me how to cut hair?' 'No,' whined Sid, 'I just wanna get the other side cut.' At this Old Jed was highly offended, held out his hand for his fifteen-cent fee, and told Sid he should hurry on home.

"Poor Sid saw it was useless to argue, so he gave Jed the fee and went home to his ma. She looked at him all puzzled like, seein' as how he was shaved all whitewall on one side and still had a full crop on t'other. She promptly put on her coat and escorted Sid back to Jed's shop, but when they arrived the door was locked tight. Peekin' through the window they could see Jed stretched out on the couch, oblivious to the goins on o' this world. They returned home, where she took her sewin' scissors and a comb and made the best of it she could. When Sid played on Friday night the crowd was a whole lot more entranced by Sid's haircut than they were with his ball playin'!"

Jed enjoyed Vilate's report as much as everybody else.

The times gave rise to "Vilate" because she kept people laughing despite their woes. She loosened people up by telling outrageous, but mostly true, stories on anybody in the area she chose to, young or old, saint or sinner. It didn't matter.

Vilate just had to play up the rumor, which was fact, about Junior Weinberg and his episode with his tractor and truck.

"Junior was a-plantin' wheat over on the Wilkins eighty. He had a yaller D-6 tractor, his pride and joy, which he treated better 'n his wife," Vilate huffily reported.

"Junior went round and round that eighty, leavin' the four corners unplanted till he could do 'em out after he had the main eighty planted.

"To plant wheat," Vilate continued, "you need a truck to haul the wheat seed to the field. Junior, bein' the intelligent farmer that he is, drove his finely painted red truck in on one o' them unplanted corners. Each time he would fill her up (meanin', o' course, the drill and not his belly), then he would drive the truck farther into the field along those corner strips. This meant that when the corner is done out by the drill, then not only are those strips planted, but the truck tracks are also obliterated (now that big word means 'covered up' for most of you out there in the audience)!

"Now," as Vilate carefully pointed out, "when the drillin' was about finished, Junior had that thar shiny red truck a-sittin' out there somewhere purty near the middle o' the eighty on one o' those corner strips. Junior came up with a brilliant way to kill them so-called 'two birds with one stone.' He put that D-6 in low gear and let it go forward along those strips a-plantin' all by itself at one slow little mile per hour. In that gear it would hold a true course. So Junior climbed off that thar Cat, ran ahead to the truck, climbed in so he could back it outa the field, while that Cat, true-blue, came crawlin' along plantin those strips. He was in a hurry so he could back the truck out to the end of those strips, park the truck and run back and climb onto the D-6, finish that strip of corners, and be done with the eighty."

Vilate now had her audience on the edge of their seats: "Junior turned on the ignition and shoved down on the foot-starter button. But the bright red truck didn't start! He shoved down again. Same result. A third time, the same! Then Junior started gettin' mad, and the madder he got the more he forgot," exclaimed Vilate. "Because all of a sudden Junior looked up with a scream to see his dutiful D-6 climbin' right up over the nose of that beautiful truck, bringin' drill and all with!"

It was a true story. But Junior lived it down. People understood. They were all human. Everybody made a mistake now and then, and the more people could guffaw them away, the better it was. All were grateful that Junior's dutiful D-6, which was built like a tank anyway, came away unscathed, as did Junior.

For our community, Vilate was better than Leno or Letterman as life went on in Ririe in those years. Times were tough, and the Depression was on, but we were not depressed. Vilate Hatch took care of that.

Chapter 11

The Frost

I WILL NEVER FORGET a day in late June 1936, even though I was only five-and-a-half years old. Papa woke up early, and his stirrings around the kitchen, a slam of the rear screen door by his going out and another by his coming in a moment or two later, and the quickened pace of footsteps back and forth between the bedroom-living room and the kitchen woke me up. I was sleeping alone in the basement below. Joel was away on some outing. I heard some muffled conversation between Papa and Mama but could not make out the words, only the tone of their voices. It seemed agitated, worried. It disquieted me, chasing sleep away. I climbed out of bed and made my way up the stairs, still rubbing the remnants of sleep from my eyes and wondering what I was going to encounter upstairs.

As I opened the door into the kitchen, I saw Papa and Mama looking out the window and talking to each other. Papa said, "If this frost has hit the Flats, we're in big trouble. The grain is in the boot, and the frost will kill the emerging grain kernels because they are so tender at that stage. I have seen the temperature get below freezing this late in the year down in the low spots occasionally, but this frost has put ice on the cows' water trough outside here in the valley. This could be bad enough up on the Flats to hit our whole crop."

I didn't know what "boot" and some of the other big words meant, but from the worried tone in Papa's voice, I could tell something was troubling him badly. Even at my young age, I had started to take a keen interest in the farm, rode with Papa on the equipment, and begged each time to go to the Flats with him, which Mama occasionally allowed. What I was hearing sounded like tragedy.

Papa said, "I'm going to have to go up there and see what has happened. We have our whole future tied to that crop."

"Papa, can I go with?" This was the first they noticed me. They were surprised that I was awake so early. Papa made an inquiring look at Mama and got an approving nod.

"Yes, I think I'm going to need some company, and it might as well be my little farmer pal. Go get your farm clothes on and come and have a bite of breakfast as soon as Mama can get it together. We'll take off right after that."

I was excited and ran quickly to climb into the set of clothes Mama insisted I wear to the farm. The pants were hand-me-downs from Joel and had some tears in the knees and frayed edges along the bottom. The shirt was not much better, but they covered me adequately. Since I knew it was cold, I got out another hand-me-down, an old jacket. Then I pulled on my proudest possession.

Grandma Fanny had bought, right out of the Golden Rod Store, a pair of high-topped farm shoes just for me. She had brought them unannounced in the back door of the house and thrown the brown box onto the kitchen table, saying, "That boy deserves to have some good shoes to do his chores around here and to work on the farm. I got 'em a little big, so he can grow into them over a couple years, but they oughta last."

I was just tall enough to peek my head across the table and see the box, and a smile a yard wide crossed my face. I ran to Grandma Fanny and gave her a big hug, almost knocking her over in the process.

She recovered quickly, saying, "You're becomin' a good little worker, a-cuttin' my wood, gatherin' me an egg, and pickin' me a bowl o' raspberries now and then, so you wear them farm shoes right proud, and keep a-workin' and studyin' real hard, and you'll grow up to be a real good man."

Mama looked on the little scene and heard the dialogue. "But Grandma, those are expensive shoes. You should save your money for yourself and not give it away like that."

"Waal, you know I am gittin' that little Social Security check each month nowadays, since the Congress and President Roosevelt have set up a little retirement program for us old cusses. I feel jest a little generous now and want to help this boy have the work shoes that are gonna help him become a real farmer like his pa."

With that she left and went back to her lean-to, "looking mighty proud of herself and rightly so," Mama said.

Back upstairs we ate a quiet breakfast of good crisp bacon, fried eggs, and fried potatoes, all flushed down with a generous helping of milk from our two cows in the back corral. The milk was cooled in our ice chest. Papa hauled the ice in the late winter from the Flats and buried it in a hole in the backyard covered with straw so it could be pulled out from time to time and put in the ice chest to keep things cool.

We also had toast lathered with rich yellow butter Mama had made a day or two before in our old wooden churn. I usually had to take my turn at cranking the handle but didn't mind because I could occasionally peek in and see the yellow butter separate itself from the milk, turning what was left of the milk to gray whey, which our sow and her eight piglets loved to drink.

Mama bade us farewell with a worried look on her face. Underway, Papa told me some things about the debt he was carrying and other financial things that I couldn't understand or appreciate. But when he talked about the crop and wheat being in the boot I was all ears. The farm had become an unalienable part of me. Everything about it fascinated me: the crops, the fertile little vales and the not-so-fertile ridges, the horses, the machinery, the spring work of plowing, the summer work of weeding the acreage to keep the weeds from stealing nutrients for the next crop, the fall work of harvesting the old crop and planting the new crop on the summer-fallowed fields.

I liked to play in the "Antelope loam." It was soft and ran through my fingers like silk. When rain came it would clod up a little, but a touch of the hand would quickly break it down into that fine silt that had such a magic fertility. Mama liked it so much she made us shake our farm clothes out onto her flowerbeds when we came home all dusty and dirty.

I listened intently to Papa tell me about the frost and what it might do to the crop. The wheat had been planted last fall. It would come up only a couple of inches, then stool out, as a round circle of green leaves formed from the planted kernel. Then the plant would go into a hibernation stage as the cold weather hit, stopping its growth and staying dormant during the winter under the snow. Somehow it shielded itself from the freezing temperatures, and the snow acted like a blanket. When the snow melted in the spring, the warm sun brought the plant to life, and the stooled-out leaves would start growing straight up. When they got about a foot above the ground, the head of the wheat would begin to form in the bottom of the long stem about two inches above the ground. The bottom of the leaf stem looked pregnant, because the head, the beards, and little nibs that eventually make the kernels were all taking shape down there. You could see and feel the bulge where this was happening. If frost killed the little nibs, the head would emerge out of the leaf stem intact but barren of any kernels. The plant would be useless straw.

The "crop" was beginning to be to me like the beat of my heart or the breathing of my lungs, an appendage that was a part of my being. When something happened to the "crop," it happened to me. When it suffered, I suffered. So did Papa and Joel. I knew it meant more than a loss of money. It was a loss of hope, dreams shattered, a loss of accomplishment, of reward. Losing a crop was like losing a loved one, so intense were our feelings for the "crop."

Still, I did not fully grasp, at my young age, how devastating losing a crop was to future plans. Debt payments would have to be postponed—if a charitable creditor would understand. No new clothing would be bought. Old books and pens and pencils and notebooks would be re-tooled for the oncoming school year. We would cut out going to movies because we couldn't afford the six cents for a ticket. We would buy less gasoline for the car and drive less to visit relatives or go to town (Idaho Falls) to do any shopping.

We would have to postpone Mama's long-suffering dream of adding two bedrooms and a bathroom onto the north side of the house. There were other things too numerous to mention that would require adjustment. Although I didn't understand it all, I could tell that Papa was mulling all these thoughts over in his mind, trying to get a handle on what he would have to do if his initial fears became reality. Sensing all this, I held my chatter as we proceeded along the ten-mile stretch up to the Flats.

After leaving the main highway, we drove along the dirt road leading to the eighty acres called the Home Place, but just before arriving, Papa saw Dave Billings, our neighbor who lived half a mile below our summer shack on the Home Place. He was walking the three-fourths of a mile to Highway 26 to get his mail out of the mailbox. He looked concerned, had a real frown on his face.

Papa stopped and rolled down his window. "What do you make of this arctic cold, Dave?"

"It's a bad un," was his grim reply. "The temperature up here dropped to twenty-two durin' the night, so any fall wheat in the boot will have little chance of makin' grain. Most of mine, and I'm afraid most of yours, will be hit hard because we were plantin' about the same time last fall. Most of mine is in the boot, so I am sure yours will be, too. Just a few minutes ago I went and checked mine in the field there near the house. It's probably too early to tell, but I could feel a cracklin' as I touched the bulge of the boot, so the frost had probably penetrated it. The only possible salvation for me is that 160 I planted after that heavy rainstorm last fall that kept me off the grain drill for about a week. That 160 is not yet in the boot and should survive."

Papa's response was quiet and depressed. "I had mine all planted before that storm, so it's in the same stage as that fall wheat by your house. I'm afraid I've lost it all. Do you think the frost hit the ridges, too? I know it would hit the valleys, but sometimes the ridges survive."

"At twenty-two degrees I think the frost blanketed the Flats, ridges and all, and there was not even a whisper of wind to move the grain and keep it from freezing. I imagine it caught the potato crop in the valley, too, so there are gonna be a lot of farmers and bankers who'll be hurtin' after harvest this fall."

"Sometimes I wonder if we shouldn't get rid of our land and machinery and go put the money on a roulette wheel somewhere. It wouldn't be any worse of a gamble," Papa said. He bid Dave good-bye and drove on up to the summer shack. Dave continued his dejected stroll to the mailbox.

We got out and walked behind the shack, past the old log shed where the horses' harnesses and saddles hung, and out into the field where the hill we liked to run down on warmer summer days faced us. Papa looked at the green wheat stalks and saw the melting frosty dew glistening on them.

"You're probably gonna get those nice farm boots a little wet from the dew, and your pants might get a little soggy if you come with me. You will either have to stay in the car or walk by yourself up into the field. I can't carry a big fella like you up that hill. We have to see what the frost did down in this swale next to the house and up on top of the ridge."

I told him I wanted to go, so we went together. He sometimes took my hand when I got winded. He stopped several times, pulled out a stalk of wheat and rolled the little bulge down at the bottom between two fingers, then peeled the protective sheath away from the little bulge, looked at it soberly, shook his head each time, and trudged farther up the hill. He did the same on the plateau at the top of the ridge.

Finally, with a look of sadness and worry, he said, "It looks bad, son. We better check the other fields." We did, with the same results.

We kept some chickens at the Home Place. They ran uncooped around the farmstead, eating grasshoppers, bugs, grass, and anything else lying around, and laid eggs loaded with heavy yellow-brown yolks. We gathered the eggs and counted the chickens. They were all there. They had evaded any weasels so far. We spent a good part of the day there, cleaning the shack, stocking the wood box, and checking the pasture to make sure the horses were okay.

Papa made one more tour of the field on the Home Place in the afternoon, checking the boots of various stalks, and came away ever more certain that tragedy had befallen the Flats. We drove home in silence. I could see the muscles on the side of Papa's face flexing and relaxing, flexing and relaxing, as he drove deep in thought toward Ririe.

We arrived home just before supper. We hadn't eaten all day, which was not uncommon on the farm. Papa reported to Mama what we had found out about the crop.

Her terse response was, "We'll just have to make do," and she busied herself getting supper on the table and getting us all around it.

Papa asked Helen to say grace on the food with, "I'm just not up to praying tonight." Mama looked up at him somewhat perplexed, but with understanding. We were a religious family. But this evening was one of frustration and concern.

The food was tasty to me as always, but Lael began fidgeting with her food and after only a couple of bites set her fork down and with a disgusted tone, said, "I don't want this stuff!"

"Eat it anyway," said Papa with emphasis.

"No, I don't want to!" was her quick and defiant response.

Something exploded in Papa. He jumped up, tipping his chair over backwards as he lunged for Lael across the table. She jumped back to avoid his grasp. His arms fell down into the bowl of stew we were eating. He went berserk, jumped around the table, grabbed her, and dragged her into the living room where he could find a chair. He sat down, yanked her onto his knees, and started to pound her backside with a fury I had never seen in him before.

Lael was screaming, "Don't, Papa! Please don't, Papa!"

Papa responded with even more rage, "You naughty little brat, you're gonna behave and do what you're told!" He continued hammering with loud slaps at Lael's backside, while pieces of stew and juice flew off his shirtsleeves.

It was a horrible scene. We were terrified, not believing what we were witnessing. Finally, Mama could stand it no longer. She seized Lael from his flailing arms, placed herself between Lael and Papa, and screamed into his face, "If you're going to keep this up, you beast, you'll have to do it to me!"

Papa's face turned from rage to stupor in the twinkling of an eye. He sat dumbfounded, as if he had been somewhere else and then suddenly found himself sitting in front of his wife screaming at him in her fury. Dazed, he stood without saying a word, walked into the kitchen, took off his shirt, threw it into the dirty clothes basket, and walked out the back door toward the cow barn against the setting sun.

Lael was hurting and sobbing. Mama told the rest of us to go finish our meal. She stayed with Lael, shutting the door to the bedroom-living room. She pulled up Lael's dress and pulled down her bloomers to inspect her backside. It was red and obviously hurting badly. She told Lael to lie on her stomach on the couch while she got some ointment to put on it. She came into the kitchen without a word, went to the cabinet where medicines and first aid supplies were and pulled out a tube of ointment, then went back into the other room. As she opened the door, we could still hear Lael's sobbing. Mama was trying to soothe her, telling her that Papa just wasn't himself tonight and something about the crop on the Flats.

We picked at our food. Helen tried to feed Rhea in her high chair, but we all lacked the energy and desire to eat. We loved our parents and always felt secure with them. They had disciplined us but had never beaten any of us before. We had never seen such rage in either of them. It left us cold and helpless. Lael's sobbing ebbed somewhat but was replaced with periodic deep shuddering gasps of air as Mama soothed and consoled her.

When she was finally quieted, Mama came in and told us to clean up the dishes and wash them as always, with Helen to do Lael's job as well as her own tonight. As soon as we were finished we were to get our teeth brushed, get into our pajamas, say our prayers—there would be no family prayer tonight—and go to bed. She hurriedly made Helen and Lael's bed in the kitchen area, cleaned up Rhea and put her in her crib in the living room-bedroom with a bottle of warm milk, then just before I left to go down to my basement bed, Mama brought Lael into the kitchen and helped her into her pajamas.

She sat us down on the edge of the bed and said, "Papa has had a bad thing happen to him, to our family, today. He is terribly upset. We must be patient and try to help him and each other. We lost our crop on the Flats. It got froze out, and it's going to be hard to pay our bills and buy our food. But we will just have to get by, and we will! We can do it!"

After we were in bed and quieted down, Mama pulled on a sweater and walked out the back door. When she got outside, she realized the evening was warm, and she didn't need the sweater, so she put it over her arm and headed toward the cow barn.

How could it have been so cold as to freeze last night and now we are having a warm June evening? How could one little thrust of arctic air swoop in leaving such broad spread devastation in its path, and then disappear just like that? she wondered.

She found Papa in the cow barn sitting on the three-legged milking stool, his head buried in his hands. As she opened the door, he raised a tormented face and looked at her.

She said softly, "You turned into an animal in there, John! I have never seen you like that before. I realize we have our troubles now with our frosted crop, but that doesn't mean you can take it out on the children like you did with Lael just now."

"I know, I know," he muttered, with tears welling up in his eyes. "I'm terribly ashamed of myself. You know I love my children more than my own life. How could I let myself go like that?"

She didn't answer.

He asked, "Is Lael okay?"

"She will be in a few days, but her backside is all red and hurting her pretty badly right now. She went almost hysterical in there." She paused. "And that is the thing that is worrying me the most!"

"What do you mean?"

"Something is not right with Lael! Some little things are showing up in her that puzzle me. I watched her put on her shoes the other morning. One of the laces had come out of its hole. She fidgeted with it for some time, then finally was able to get it in the hole. But then she was awfully slow getting her shoes tied, like she was trying to remember how to do it. And," she continued, "I didn't tell you this because I didn't want to worry you, but the day we cleaned up at Mary Jap's, Lael fainted when she came into that filthy room. I pulled her out into the hallway by the window and put a wet cloth on her face. But when she came to, her eyes crossed and stayed crossed for several moments. It was not one of those fleeting instances like before. I'm so worried about her, but I don't know what we should do. With the crop frosted, that means no money for medical bills, and I don't know what a doctor can do about it anyway. These little happenstances with her are not like an attack of appendicitis or a disease. They just creep in for an eerie moment, then flit away again."

Papa stood up, wiped his face with both hands, and looking at her intently, said, "Will you forgive me? When you stood in front of me and called me a beast, I realized how deep into a pit I had let self-pity thrust me. You and those kids are more important than anything else to me. My life would be utterly meaningless without you and them. I realize that now as never before. And with these strange things happening to Lael, I feel even more shame."

Mama could feel the intensity of his sincerity. She loved him. She was committed to him. The events of this day would be overcome because they as a family would simply overcome them. They both had the strength and courage to manage it.

"Of course, John, I forgive you. What I saw tonight was a departure from everything I've known about you. I hope we have killed that beast that flared up tonight so that he will never reappear."

They embraced and returned to the house.

Upon entering the kitchen Papa went straight to Lael and Helen's bed, where he knelt down on Lael's side. She was lying on her stomach. Her head was turned toward him. She was awake; her eyes wet and wide open.

Papa whispered, "Sweetheart, that spanking I gave you was awfully mean of me. I am ashamed. When we have problems we should talk them over, and I should not get mean. You need to be obedient, and if you don't like your food or something else, you need to tell me why or I need to ask you why, but I should never be mean. You mean too much to Mama and me to ever treat you like that again. Can we be friends again?"

She didn't answer. Instead she reached out her arms and put them around her papa and buried her face in his shoulder. That was answer enough. He held her tight, nuzzling his face into her shoulder as well. After a few moments, he whispered, "Thank you, sweetheart," and laid her back onto her pillow. She looked up at him in the fading daylight with a look of reconciliation as only a child can do. Then it happened! For the first time he, too, saw the eyes cross and stay that way for a long moment. Then they returned to normal. She closed them and drifted off to sleep. Helen heard the dialogue between them. It brought comfort to her, and enabled her to settle into sleep.

Papa came downstairs to my bed. He sat on the edge, put his hand on my head, and tousled my hair. I was still very much awake, rethinking all that I had witnessed that evening. He sat there for several moments, seemingly lost in thought.

"Do you remember that day this spring when we went up to the Flats and saw that bull, cow, and calf moose, kind of a moose family?" he said after a time.

"You bet!" I answered.

We had driven to our shack on the Home Place early one morning. As we got out of the car, Papa suddenly said, "Look!" and pointed to a patch of willows adjacent to the little stream that ran seventy-five yards from the shack. A big black bull moose was standing fifteen feet on our side of the willows. He was at least nine feet tall. He had a magnificent rack, two huge spoon-shaped antlers with jagged edges jutting out around the outer fringe. He had a massive necktie of hair hanging beneath his jaw. He was snorting, pawing the earth, shaking his rack, and looking directly at us as though he were going to attack.

Papa said, "If I had a rifle, I could drop him right there. He knows it and I know it. Normally he would take off up the creek and be gone before I could shoot. I wonder why he's acting like that?"

The question was answered almost immediately when a cow and calf emerged from behind the willow. The cow's right front leg was broken at the knee, and as she tried to move on her other three legs, the bottom portion of the bad leg swung uselessly in the air. We could see that she was in pain, maybe had just broken it in a fall, as she hobbled toward the bull. The calf stayed right with her on the far side from us. She moved behind and past the bull up a little slope toward a patch of aspen trees lying another sixty yards away from us threatening humans. The bull placed himself between her and us as she slowly, painfully crossed the open slope to the small grove. The bull kept his eyes on us as he moved with the cow and calf. At intervals of fifteen or twenty feet, he would turn and face us directly, making the same threatening gestures with his antlers and front feet. The calf stayed with the cow the full distance and on the opposite side of the cow from us.

The cow and calf disappeared into the little grove. The bull placed himself at the edge of the grove and stood facing us with intermittent threatening gestures. We watched silently for about five minutes.

Papa broke the silence. "The cow must be lying down and trying to rest, and the bull is guarding her and the calf. Let's go on up the road to the machine shed and pay them no attention; then the bull will understand that we mean them no harm, and he will quiet down."

Upon returning an hour or so later, we could see no more of the moose and decided to cautiously inspect the little grove. There we saw a little bedlike mold in the grass where it was obvious the cow had lain. There were bloodstains where the right front leg would have been. They had moved on out of the grove and disappeared. Papa reported the incident to the Idaho Fish and Game Department when we got home so they could try to find the little family and see if they could anesthetize the cow and help her.

Papa continued, "That bull put his life on the line to protect the cow and calf. To me that is the ultimate devotion one can give. Also, the little calf, even though it was probably terrified of us, was obedient and stayed close to and on the far side of the cow so it was shielded from us by her and the bull. As a family, we can learn a lot from those moose. I want you to know that I feel as responsible and as caring for our family as that bull felt for his family. He loved the cow and his calf so much that he put himself in danger, even faced the threat of death, for them. That is how I feel about your mother and your mother and I feel about you kids. We would do everything we could to protect you from danger, even if we faced the threat of dying for you.

"You saw me make a terrible fool of myself tonight. I let our frosted crop make me lose control. That was evil of me. It will not happen again. I am responsible to help our family love each other and be good to each other. So please forgive what you saw me do tonight. I told Lael, and I want to tell you, that you children do have to be obedient, like the little moose calf, but when we don't like something, the food, our clothing, our chores, or whatever, or even when we are in a foul mood, we should talk things over and then go and do the right thing in a loving way. Will you help our family do that?"

"Sure, Papa."

That sufficed. He tenderly touched my forehead with his hand and then went back upstairs.

In bed that night with Mama, he turned to her and said, "Honey, I marvel at many things in life, and I give God credit for his design in all of life's wonders, but most especially the manner in which He brings two young people together to get along with each other, to build a home and a family, to work, to pray, to struggle, to enjoy, to love, to plan, to see the children grow, to accomplish everything side by side. A good wife is heaven's best gift to a man. I am grateful that I found such a woman. You make the cares of the world seem easy."

"You must have done a lot of thinking sitting out there on that old three-legged stool." Then with a sigh, she said, "Life is not easy. I am especially worried about Lael. I think we knew there would be hardships when you saw Merlin's condition before he was born. But that helps me to also believe that we will somehow be equal to the task of raising these kids, frosted crop or come what may."

Papa muttered something more or less under his breath. "What did you just say?"

"I read somewhere in a little story about Adam and Eve written by Mark Twain where he told about Eve dying first, and on her tombstone Adam put the words, 'wherever she was, there was Eden.' You're my Eve." Then with a soft peck on her cheek, he turned over and let the worry and weariness of the day slip away into dreamland.

Mama lay quietly beside him for some time, pondering his last comment and feeling a soothing peace slowly settle over her, a peace that seemed to reinforce and intensify her commitment to him and her family.

A footnote to that unforgettable day: That fall the wheat stood tall and straight, the bearded heads standing erect on the stalk. There were no kernels to make them bend over. Papa wanted to cut the straw to help it break down and blend into the soil and provide much needed nutrients for the next crop. It was too difficult to get the straw to slide into the combine, however, because there was no weight in the heads to force it through. So, on a windy day, the whole family went out along the sides of the fields and set fire to the crop. We watched with disheartened faces as the tall, thick straw crackled and popped and melted away into a deep blanket of black ashes across the fields. It would have been a bumper crop, providing much needed financial help to the family, but it was not to be. The fire carried our dashed dreams with it through the burning fields.

Chapter 12

Lael, the Middle Years

TWO WEEKS INTO the school year that fall, Lael's teacher, Mrs. LaBelle, stopped by to see Mama in the afternoon of a brilliant and warm late autumn day. Papa was at the farm. Grandma Fanny was in the kitchen with Mama when Mrs. LaBelle's knock came on the door. Mrs. LaBelle was a tall, stringy (Grandma Fanny's descriptive word for her) woman with sharp features and a sharper nose that came almost to a knife-edge point just above her upper lip. She had four children, was a kindly soul, and took great interest in every student in her care.

Mama had not expected the visit but appreciated her stopping by and asked if she could get her something to drink.

"A cool glass of water would suit me just fine."

Mama suggested she come into the kitchen and say hello to Grandma Fanny while she obliged with the water. Grandma Fanny and the teacher exchanged greetings. They liked each other, and Fanny respected Mrs. LaBelle "for havin' the gumption to git an education and do somethin' with it durin' these hard times."

Of Grandma Fanny's six children, not one had been able to finish high school because they had to work to support themselves, their siblings, and parents. Fanny always told us she thought "gettin' an education was like turnin' on a light inside a person's head and made him or her a cut above the ordinary." Fanny appreciated Mrs. LaBelle and invited her to sit at the kitchen table on one of the better chairs.

When Mama returned, with a look of tenderness Mrs. LaBelle said, "I need to talk to you about Lael."

To Mama it was not unexpected. She had become aware that Lael had developed a learning problem. She was also troubled by other things she had been noticing: the shoe tying, the eyes crossing, and occasional lapses of memory when Lael would forget to finish a job she was given. Mama had talked to Dr. West again, and he had checked her over, especially her eyes. He had recommended corrective glasses, since Lael was becoming nearsighted. The glasses were also supposed to help keep her eyes straight. He could find nothing further. She was otherwise healthy and athletic.

Mama asked, "Is there a problem?"

Mrs. LaBelle looked inquiringly at Grandma Fanny.

"If there is a problem about Lael, both Fanny and I should know so we can both help her. She is very special to both of us."

"I am concerned," Mrs. LaBelle admitted. "Something is not right with her. She is having more difficulty grasping the lessons, and many times I will find her absentmindedly looking out the window instead of paying attention in class. There is one other thing I have noticed and wondered if you had."

"What's that?" Mama asked.

"I've noticed a time or two that she grinds her teeth when she gets that absentminded look on her face. It's like she's chewing gum only in slow motion. She doesn't do it all the time, but it has happened at least a couple of times since school has been in session."

Mama looked at Grandma Fanny. Both shook their heads.

Mrs. LaBelle continued. "I talked with her teacher from last year. She said that Lael seemed to start out fine at first, but for a good part of the last year, especially toward spring, she noticed Lael getting slower in her school-work. She said Lael still wrote with a nice flowing hand and could read quite well, but she was having considerable difficulty with arithmetic and grammar."

Mama told Mrs. LaBelle about her visits with Dr. West, that they had ordered glasses for Lael and they should be ready soon. "John and I and Fanny are all concerned, but the doctors can't find anything wrong with Lael. In fact they tell us she is a real specimen of health and vitality."

Mrs. LaBelle quickly agreed, "Yes, she is a healthy young lady, and during recess and at lunchtime she goes out and plays hard on the swings and in the games the kids play."

"So what can we do?" Mama responded.

"I talked to the principal about it before I came. He encouraged me to tell you what I observed because he wants to be sure you knew what's going on." She paused, looked down for a moment, cleared her throat, and then plunged ahead. "He's going to require that Lael repeat last year's grade. This is not uncommon. You know that some students are skipped ahead, like Joel was. Others are held back because they are not quite as ready to go forward as others."

Mama interjected, "But what if it gets worse? Will she be held back again and again?"

"The principal told me to assure you that as long as Lael can learn, even though at a slower pace, she is entitled, even required by law, to continue in school. So we will just have to work together to help her. I am glad to hear about the glasses. That might help considerably."

Mama looked out the kitchen window into the bright afternoon sun and gave a sorrowful sigh. "We really have no choice. I'll tell John, and if he has any questions, we'll get back to you or the principal. We want to do what's best for Lael."

With a doleful look on her face, Mama thanked Mrs. LaBelle for her interest and concern.

"Zelma, don't get me wrong. Lael is a delight. She is such a graceful and loving young lady. I have loved having her in my class just like her other teachers have. I hope this is only a temporary thing that will resolve itself."

She stood and bade the two ladies good-bye, thanking Mama for the refreshing water.

Fanny sat staring off into space for a few moments, then looked at Mama. "What could possibly be goin' on inside that beautiful girl's head? She acts so dignified and she treats me so kindly, like I was somethin' special. On the outside she is the picture of health and beauty, probably, like John always says, 'the fairest of them all,' but somethin' jest ain't right. I've noticed it. You've noticed it, and now the teacher and principal have noticed it."

"We simply don't know," Mama said. "We have to be patient and loving and help her all we can to do her homework so she can finish school. She's not like Danny Rosenthal who can't even go to school. She has come along reasonably well till now."

Fanny, looking rather wistful, made the chilling comment, "Lael's mind is slipping, and the worst of it all is that I think she knows that, too."

Mama's response was quick and terse. "John said she looked completely normal when he saw her at the Grand, and she looked about the age she is right now. That means something to me, something hopeful and comforting. I believe with all my heart that Lael's going to be all right. Otherwise there should have been something to give us a warning, like there was with Merlin."

Fanny's response was subdued, almost a whisper. "I hope and pray you're right. But I've been a wonderin', why wasn't your baby, Rhea, shown him? What's it supposed to mean that she was left out? There wuz only the five shown. Was Rhea a replacement for Merlin? And do you expect to have any more children?"

"I don't know. I wish I did know what it all means. But Lael was tall and lovely and NORMAL!" They left it at that.

The eyeglasses and the love and attention focused on her at home and at school all helped but did not solve the problem. Lael continued in school and was passed from grade to grade, but her ability to learn continued to diminish.

When I started in the first grade at school, no sooner had I discovered "Dick and Jane" stories and learning to read and write, than I began to hear little taunts from some of the other students.

"Your sister is a nut."

"Your sister is dumber than a post."

"Your sister is a screwball."

"Your sister is weird."

Even though Lael was still beautiful and had traces of her former regal mannerisms about her, mental retardation takes a light out of a person's face and eyes, leaving them looking somewhat odd or empty. Schoolmates were beginning to notice. Kids started shying away. She was not invited to play in the recess games like before, and mean kids would shove her away from the swings and other outdoor playthings, taking advantage of her as some children will do at that age. There was one notable exception: her cousin, Johnny, continued to be her friend and to look out for her. That would never change.

I think we were considered "poor" people because we were still living bunched up in our little two-room house (with basement, of course). We did not have the prettiest of clothing. They were obviously hand-me-downs, and it was not uncommon to have patched-up little holes or tears in our pants or dresses, but Mama always kept our clothing clean. Papa cut our hair to save money, so it looked accordingly. Yet, aside from Lael's burgeoning problems, the rest of us were doing well in school. Joel, Helen, and I were each skipped past the second grade and were treated with great deference by our teachers.

As the principal had promised, after Lael was held back one year, thereafter she simply continued into each succeeding grade until she finished the eighth grade. After graduation, she would probably be able to handle household chores or do menial tasks not requiring great concentration, but not much more. The high hopes and expectations with which this charming girl started school with Miss Hollern were dashed.

Then came mid-November, shortly after Lael's thirteenth birthday. My classroom had a large glass window facing out onto the playground area. It was noon recess. We had just had an early four-inch snowfall. The temperature was cool enough that the snow had not melted, but it was wet enough to make good snowballs. I had a cold. The teacher had let me go eat my school lunch but would not let me go outside for recess. I stood at the big window enviously looking out at the students on the playground.

As I glanced to my left, I saw Lael descending the steps to get onto the playground. She was bundled up in one of our family's hand-me-down coats. As she alighted from the lowest step, a hail of snowballs caught her in mid-stride and forced her to double over and back up toward the brick wall. Another volley hit her, two snowballs striking her in the head. Another caught her in the neck, sending cold snow down into the front of her dress. There were five eighth grade boys laughing heartily and keeping up the volleys of snowballs. Lael, backed up against the wall by the onslaught, curled up and tried to pull her inadequate coat around her to defend herself.

Lael began to cry and was begging them to stop, but the volleys continued, with snowballs hitting in her hair, on her legs, and all over her body that was shielded only by that tattered coat. I had never felt such anguish before. The incident pops into my mind even now with an intensity that I still cannot adequately describe. I was furious. I looked about for a teacher to help my sister.

As I turned to run out into the hall to find someone, my eye caught movement out on the playground next to the wall. Cousin Johnny had apparently come from the high school during his noon recess. He was small for his age and not much bigger than the boys throwing the snowballs, but he jumped to Lael's side, where he started picking up the snowballs lying around her and furiously throwing them back at the perpetrators. Lael had sunk to her knees, wet, bedraggled, and shaking and crying.

The volleys of snowballs intensified now that the perpetrators had two victims. Finally, another group of students standing nearby rushed over to

Lael and Johnny and started throwing the hard, wet snowballs back at the attackers. This finally brought the onslaught to an end. The attackers dispersed, still laughing.

I watched as Johnny tenderly wiped the snow from Lael's coat, dress, and hair and tried to console her. I could see from the stricken look on her face that she could not comprehend why she had been so viciously attacked. Worst of all, I could see that she was well aware that she was not normal. Her graceful and dignified bearing was giving way to her developing retardation. And she knew it was happening! That was the cruelest blow of all.

Finally, a teacher was made aware of the attack, and I watched as she helped Johnny pick Lael up and bring her into the school. The lady teacher took Lael to the bathroom and, with the help of a lot of towels, dried her off and tried to comfort her. However, the brutal attack and the jolting awareness of her retardation would not give way to consolation. So the principal, Mr. Hacking, put Lael in his car and took her home.

Mr. Hacking was a kind man with four children of his own. He had known Lael from birth and had been a witness to her gradual mental deterioration. When he helped Lael out of the car once he got her home, her beautiful, tear-stained face and her lovely hair, all matted and wet, brought a catch in his throat. He wondered how God in heaven could ever allow this graceful young lady to slip off into some never-never land in such a degrading and demeaning way—and that she had to be aware of each step. He vowed that he would protect her, and an idea as to how to do it was already forming in his mind as he helped Lael up the three steps onto the porch.

Mama answered the door and was shaken as she looked at her daughter's stricken face and the condition of her hair and clothing.

"What's happened?"

The principal asked if he could come in, and he would explain it to her and John. He had never been in their home before but had heard that though it was crowded with only two rooms and two adults and four children living there, Mama always kept it neat, clean, and attractive. Little handmade doilies were displayed on the end tables next to the couch. A tasteful painting of a still life hung on the wall, and everything was dusted and clean. He also noticed a black upright piano tucked into one end of the small room and sensed that these children were being given an element of refinement, despite poor finances, beyond that which his grade school could provide.

Papa greeted the principal respectfully. It was an honor to have him in their home. Teachers and school principals in those times were treated with great respect, like bankers, doctors, and lawyers. They were educated and held the future of the village children in their hands. Papa thanked him for bringing Lael home. Her wet clothing and matted hair, the evidence of a fierce snowball attack, outraged him.

While Mr. Hacking agreed to wait, Mama took Lael into the kitchen and cleaned her up some more, sat her down at the table, and gave her a large cup of hot chocolate and peanut butter and honey on a piece of bread. She wanted to hear from her what had happened, but felt it impolite to keep the school principal waiting. She asked Lael to stay there and eat while she and Papa spoke with the principal.

Mr. Hacking told them about the attack and said that he would try to find the perpetrators and get their parents involved to see that they were properly disciplined and firmly admonished to treat Lael with respect.

He added, "Knowing the nature of some children, I wanted to tell you that I'm going to undertake a special program to help Lael. I will enlist the aid of three or four of the more mature students, who command the respect of their peers, to help Lael. I'll give each the assignment to watch out and stand up for Lael. If they see she is being picked on or being taunted or teased, they should immediately intervene and protect her and then report the incident directly to me. I will also instruct the teachers to be on the alert so that an incident such as happened today will never happen again.

"I know that you realize that Lael is not progressing in school and has developed an obvious mental handicap, almost like an older person slips into senility. I am sure you want her to complete her schooling, and I feel that by law we are required to see that she does. But I think we need to provide these special arrangements to make life as peaceful and happy for Lael as we can. I can already tell that she now realizes that something is not right, and that is the most troubling thing of all for me."

Papa replied. "It's heartbreaking for Zelma and me to see our beautiful girl slip away. We never dreamed it could happen. She was always so bright and pleasant to be around, blessed with a special dignity right from birth." His voice caught and he could not continue.

Mama spoke in his stead. "We are grateful for your help and concern. It's comforting to know that others are willing to help with our dilemma."

Papa, having regained his composure, continued, "Yes, we are grateful and appreciate your suggestions. We hope you can find some good young people who will carry out your plan."

Mr. Hacking replied, "I know I can. It will work."

Papa and Mama thanked him again and bade him good-bye. As he departed, he was handed a sack of cookies Mama had baked that morning. She told him to have some and take the rest to his wife and family. He smiled his thanks and departed.

They turned their attention to Lael to console her and prepare her for the next day of school. They assured her that Mr. Hacking would see to it that those mean boys would never do anything to her like that again.

But Lael had one nagging question: "Why do they treat me like that?"

Papa could find no answer.

Mama simply said, "Some kids can just be mean for dumb reasons, especially when they are in a pack like a bunch of wolves, and that makes them just as dumb as their reasons. You continue to be nice and treat everybody with respect. Mr. Hacking will see that this doesn't happen again."

A few weeks after the snowball incident I was walking along the main school corridor when suddenly I noticed a large boy had Lael backed up against the wall, talking to her in hushed tones, but with a menacing look. He was holding out his hand, and I heard him gruffly hiss through his teeth.

"Give me your lunch money, dummy."

Lael looked terrified, like a trapped animal. Small as I was I started toward the bully from behind, but before I could reach him, suddenly from my left came a furious blur of a human being. He grabbed his schoolmate and shoved him up against the wall.

"You leave Lael alone. If you ever even look crossways at her again, or threaten her in any way, I'm going to beat you to a pulp, and then I'm going to take you to the principal, even if I have to drag you there kicking and screaming!"

The furious blur was Josh, the captain of our six-man football team. He was a good student and a straight arrow. Everybody respected Josh. After the tongue lashing, he dragged the perpetrator fifteen feet down the hallway away from Lael and told him to get lost. Then he came back to Lael and looked at her like an equal.

"Lael, you are a very nice girl. You deserve to be treated just like anybody else. If somebody ever threatens you again or teases you or treats you mean, just tell me about it. I want to be your friend and help you any way I can."

Lael struggled to regain her composure, then looked at him shyly and said, "Thanks, Josh, for being nice to me."

Mr. Hacking's plan was beginning to work. Those students with mischief on their minds soon learned that Lael had friends, respectable friends, who immediately came to her aid whenever anyone tried to abuse or demean her. Gradually the taunts and teasing subsided, and Lael was able to continue with her schooling.

Later a cruel twist of fate would eradicate virtually all she had learned. Yet to the degree that her retarded status would allow, she retained bits and pieces of her prior self. She eventually graduated from the eighth grade. But this proved later to be part curse or part blessing, depending on what certain people made of it.

Chapter 13

The Plow That Broke the Plains

IN MY TEEN YEARS I happened upon a musical composition that for me captured the human spirit of the Great Depression and the war years. It was Andre Kostelanetz's inspiring album *The Plow That Broke the Plains.* It was a good title for its soothing music with a semi classical western lilt. It portrayed the motivation, the dedication, the inspiration that men and women from the "country" needed to open the Great Plains and western America to farming and ranching. The music recalled within me the struggle, but also the ecstasy that came from occasional triumphs, associated with farming and ranching, which I had experienced firsthand growing up on Antelope Flats in Idaho.

In some of its more somber tones, the music told of the serious injuries and even deaths that were an inevitable part of farm and country life. Ours was not the only family that suffered losses. A few years before he lost Merlin, Papa had been plowing on one of Tom's fields just across the country road from the Clifford log house. He had six horses hitched to a two-bottom plow. He was sitting on the old iron seat that stuck out above the plow and was attached by a flat piece of steel to the main frame. This steel was a half-inch thick, four inches wide, and about two feet long. Its flexibility allowed the seat to bounce up and down in soft little rises and falls that made the ride quite pleasant. In fact it had about lulled Papa to sleep when suddenly his eyes caught a frantic movement across the road. Mrs. Clifford was flailing her arms and running about excitedly, a stricken look on her face.

He stopped, tied the reins to his seat, and made a dash for Mrs. Clifford, clearing the three-strand barbed wire fence on both sides of the road by several inches.

"I've lost my baby girl. I can't find her!" screamed Mrs. Clifford. "I've looked all over. There are no trees and no hiding places, and there's only pastureland around the house, so there's no place she can hide. But I have called and called and she doesn't answer."

By now Mrs. Clifford was beside herself with worry and fear. Papa was sure that it could not be a kidnapping or a wild animal. The little girl had to be somewhere nearby. He started turning in a circle, surveying a one-hundred-yard-diameter distance as he did. Two-thirds of the way around his gaze lighted on the little four-by-four wooden well sticking up out of the ground in a slight hollow sixty yards down the slope from the house.

Without a word, he raced to the well and peered down into it. There, floating face down on the surface of three feet of water, not more than five feet below the surface of the ground, was the little girl, her blue cotton dress floating in a wide arc about her still, quiet body. Not knowing what else to do, he hollered back to Mrs. Clifford, "She's down here!"

Mrs. Clifford let out a shriek and started running toward the well, while Papa climbed into the water beside the little girl. He plucked her out of the water, held her head with his left hand, and pushed on her back with his right, trying to get any water out of her lungs. But none came, only a bit of clabber. She had not drowned. She had suffocated. The look of horror on the mother's face burned indelibly into his mind as he handed the little girl up to her. He could see not only the loss she was suffering but also the horrible guilt bearing in upon her for letting her daughter wander away in an inattentive moment.

A neighbor on the Flats, Eddie Rogers and his wife, lost a girl at birth, then a boy in the influenza epidemic that swept the region in the late teens and early twenties. Another boy, only four, was riding with his father on a horse-drawn rig that cut wheat so it could be pitched on wagons and hauled to a stationary threshing machine. Eddie had turned his head for a moment, and when he turned back, he suffered the sickening sight of his little boy tumbling off the platform directly into the path of the machine's "bull wheel." This wheel had large steel triangle cleats. One of the cleats caught the boy's shoe and pulled him down and under the wheel before the machine could be stopped. The boy suffered a brutal death before his father's horrified eyes.

In other sections, Kostelanetz's music reminded me of nature at its best and worst, of lightning storms, some with horizontal and others with vertical bolts flashing out. The horizontal lightning played along the underbellies of the clouds, lighting them up like massive indigestion, but never shot a bolt toward the ground. These were especially beautiful in the evening and at nighttime. On the Flats at 6,000 feet above sea level, this lightning and accompanying thunder were giants in proportion to their valley cousins below because we seemed to be standing right in the middle of them. In the vertical lightning storms, giant bolts literally parted the sky while blazing down onto some lightning rod on the earth. The music even helped me to smell again the special scent of "electricity in the air" when lightning hit, which most never experience because they don't work out in it like a farmer or cowboy.

The aurora borealis, the famous northern lights, also found their way onto the Flats and into Kostelanetz's music. They splashed broad ribbons of pastel colors up and down against the backdrop of the black northern sky because there were no city lights to distort or diminish the brilliance of their dazzling dance. The music also reminded me of how the stars blazed like diamonds in the clear dark nights on the Flats, the deep black of the night enhancing their brilliance, and how the Milky Way indeed looked like a bright splash of milk against that black vastness when the moon was absent.

It told of the harvest moon rising bright, huge, and majestic out of the eastern horizon, enlarged and reddened by the mist of dust and chaff that floated up off the fields as dusk gave way to night. Its subdued and mystical rays covered the landscape like a blanket of silk, giving just enough illumination to take away the edge of the darkness. At times, even, it was bright enough that we could work by its light, and by its soft glow everything seemed to run smoother, softer, faster, better, quieter.

The music told of the pungent smell of moist earth when turned by a plow or disk, a scent of freshness, newness, an awakening of nature's awesome power to produce food and fiber. And it seemed to bring out the honorable scent of strong men, boys and horses bathed in sweat while straining to accomplish the hard work of tilling the earth and making it productive. It told of women and girls working alongside their men and boys, to grow babies and nurse and tend them, to do all the unending chores around the farmstead, gathering eggs from under the chickens, slopping the hogs, milking the cows, feeding the calves, shucking the corn, planting, tending and harvesting the gardens, and feeding their tired men folk when they trudged wearily home from the fields.

In a way, even as she descended into the dark world of her retardation, Lael also captured for us some elements of that time and place like Kostelanetz's music did. Ofttimes she would not sleep well and would rise from her bed in the middle of the night and wander through the house or sit by a window and look out into the darkness if there was no moon, or into the soft moonlight if there was one. I cannot fathom what she was thinking during those nocturnal ventures. What does a person think who gradually deteriorates mentally? Does she think of what might have been? Or does she have the faculties to philosophize over her plight? Probably not. I would guess that her thought process was more one of confusion and frustration, like wandering into a strange and uninviting land without familiar landmarks to guide her path.

One thing remained constant with Lael, however. She loved animals and she loved nature. She delighted in letting the wind blow through her hair, to savor an ice cold drink of water, to run in the breeze, to smell the sweet scent of a blooming wildflower, to watch the fuzz of a dandelion drift aimlessly away with the wind as she held the stem firmly in her hand. She loved the feel of water on her feet, to catch a snowflake and enjoy its symmetry and beauty before it turned into a tiny drop of clean, pure water in her outstretched palm. She loved spring. She loved to watch the aspen groves on the Flats materialize out of their stark, silent, sticklike forms into a slight blush of pastel green as though an artist, with the most delicate touch of his brush, had created only a hint and not the real essence of the color, and then to watch the hint turn to a brilliant burst of ever-darkening green as the leaves matured. The pines bursting out new growth in spring fascinated her. The delicate beauty of a butterfly entranced her as it flitted here and there, and when it would land she watched in awe as its symmetrical wings silently maintained it atop its precarious perch.

One weekend in the late fall we had driven to the Flats to sleep overnight. It was cold, so we all slept inside, parents in the bed and kids on the floor. In the wee hours of the morning Lael began one of her nocturnal wanderings. The shack was so small there was little place to wander, so she sat by the window to watch the night pass toward day. To her surprise, everything was white. It had snowed a couple of inches, but there was more than glistening snow in this bright moonlit panorama. Before her wondering eyes she beheld billions of glittering little lights, like billions of fireflies frozen in place with their lights softly aglow. She was staring at the hill that rose behind the shack as moonlight peering out of the clouds of the weakening storm glistened off those fascinating objects in the snow. She could not tell what they were but was spellbound by their brilliant spectacle.

She rushed to her mother, still sleeping, and urged her to "come look!" Mama started up, concerned about Lael's apparent agitation, but soon realized that it arose not from worry or problem, but from excitement and thrill. She followed Lael to the window and was awestruck by the incredible spectacle. She had never ever seen anything like it before. She woke the whole family, and we all took turns gazing upon this majestic phenomenon. Quickly we dressed warmly and rushed out into the moonlit night toward the glittering hillside.

By some blessed magic, the combination of snow, temperature, and humidity had created countless little ice crystals, each and all looking exactly alike. They were a quarter-inch wide and a half-inch tall. They were standing vertical in the snow and ran in long lines up the hill, like crystal dominoes, shimmering and glistening in the soft moonlight.

Lael plucked some from the ground and looked at them wonderingly, as though she were holding a handful of diamonds. We asked Papa and Mama how it had happened. They didn't know. They had never seen anything like it before. It was another of nature's magical moments. We spent more than half an hour amidst the crystals and then returned to our beds in the shack where sleep again overtook us. Early in the morning as the sun brought its warm rays to bear on our little hillside, our field of crystals disappeared, never to return.

It seemed that Lael, even as one world was closing, became more and more in tune with nature's magic and music, and despite her muddled mind, she involved our family in some of nature's most memorable displays. I realized that beauty is truly in the eye of the beholder, and that beholder need not be a genius or even of normal mental acuity to appreciate and cherish it. Lael had her place in life, in our family. We learned from her to appreciate nature and each precious moment of the great adventure of life. We also got an intimate insight into the changes that took place in her and the struggles that came with watching it happen. None of us pass a handicapped person without feeling a deep empathy.

One mighty change that took place on the Great Plains, and one that changed our lives in the thirties as I was growing up, Kostelanetz's music did not capture. It was the music of the "tractor that broke the plains." What great works could have been written about the incredible "crawler tractor." It was geared down to a top speed, fifth gear, of five miles per hour and a powerful slowest speed, first gear, of one mile per hour. With only limited horsepower it could pull many times its weight, the motor transferring through giant sprockets all that geared-down power to its sixteen-inch-wide steel cleats. The driver and his crawler became one powerful force moving in harmony through the fields, hour after hour, day after day, pulling incredible loads, overcoming gravity and inertia, tilling the firm, dark soil of the earth.

In the thirties, the crawler brought not only a revolution in farming but also in family life. Farm work could be accomplished in much less time than it could with horses. The crawler pulled more, never got tired, never got sick, never had to take time off to eat and sleep. It never got out of its pasture, never got sores from the harness or bridle, never got cranky or mean, never had a "crupper" around its tail to aggravate it, and it never died (unless it broke down). Instead of working from mid-April through mid-November every day, all day, sunup to sundown, except rainy days and Sundays, the crawler freed men so they could have periods of "slow time" to spend with their wives and children. Its advent on the farms of the Snake River Valley and Antelope Flats revolutionized farming and family life like nothing before.

A couple of decent crops, better prices, and farm subsidies provided by Franklin D. Roosevelt's "New Deal", after the frosted crop, provided Papa with the necessary money and credit to buy a small International crawler in the late thirties. These circumstances also enabled him to expand his acreage to a size that provided a decent living. He added the "Adamson and Clifford places," bringing the total to 640 acres. These purchases were on credit. Under the conditions brought on by the Depression, Papa was granted a "crop-failure" clause in each contract, allowing him to pay only the annual interest (two percent) when the crop yielded less than fifteen bushels per acre and postpone the principal payment to one year following the original contract term. Fortunately, he needed to invoke the clause only once.

The "Plow That Broke the Plains", immortalized by Kostelanetz, broke them like never before once it had a tractor to pull it, and the crawler, perhaps much as the plow had done centuries before, changed farming and ranching, and with it, family life on the Great Plains and Antelope Flats forever.

Chapter 14

The New Addition

IN THE SPRING OF 1939 the snow was gradually melting on the Flats, leaving crystal white snow cornices amidst the shiny dark soil. These formed broad bands of black and white across the fields—the "herd of zebras" look. Papa and Mama brought the family to the Flats after school on a Friday evening to spend the night and clean up the old shack to ready it for summer use. This early spring ritual let us experience again the enticing scent of moist earth mingled with thawing snow as it was carried abroad on the cool, crisp breezes of spring.

The grain of the previous fall yielded a good crop. War, one of the dreaded four horsemen of the Apocalypse, was threatening to again engulf the world, and this only twenty years since the last world war. Ironically, the imminence of the pending conflict produced one beneficial result for the family. Grain prices began to improve significantly.

With everybody pitching in, the accumulated dirt and dust on the floor, windowsills, tops of the furniture, and bed quilts was quickly shaken out, swept up, dusted off, or mopped away. When I took the bed covers outside and shook them out, dust billowed up into my face. Lael washed the dishes clean in warm, soapy water heated by a roaring fire in the stove. A couple of mice surprised by the commotion scooted out from under the stove and were quickly stomped on by Papa and Joel's heavy boots.

Mama and Helen, helped or hindered, as the case might be, by five-year-old Rhea, prepared an early supper of fried chicken, beans, baked potatoes, and delicious gravy. It was quickly eaten because everybody wanted to get outside in the sixty-degree fresh air. Papa asked us kids to hurry and do the dishes and then to stay and play around the shack while he and Mama climbed the hill behind the shack to "look at the sunset," he said.

I noticed that Papa took Mama's hand as they trudged up the hill, and they seemed to be having an animated discussion. A couple of times Mama leaned in toward Papa, and before they got to the top of the hill their arms slipped around each other's backs. The scene held my attention. It looked as if something very interesting, even exciting, was happening.

When they got to the top of the hill, where the setting sun silhouetted them against the skyline, I saw Mama suddenly leap into Papa's arms. He twirled her around and around and then put her back on her feet. Both buried their heads in the shoulder of the other in a long and seemingly emotional embrace. Then they turned toward the sunset, Mama nestling her head on Papa's arm and shoulder, both looking into the brilliant sun-inspired colors etched on the undersides of the few clouds standing against the wide western sky.

They watched until the sun finally set and the colors faded. Then they began a giddy descent to the shack. They occasionally stumbled and teasingly collided with each other, both laughing as gravity accelerated their descent. Upon arrival they called us to come inside quickly because they had something exciting to tell.

Papa added some wood to the stove and lit the old coal-oil lamp, which cast a little light and a lot of shadows about the room, along with its warm glow. We sat on the bed, on the floor, and on the couple of available stools, all looking with eager anticipation to our parents for some clue as to what they were so excited about!

Mama, with a look of sheer ecstasy on her face, said, "Guess what you kids."

"Aw, come on, Mama, how can we guess what?" I asked. "All we know is it sure looked like you were having a good time up there in the sunset."

"Well, we were having a good time, one of the best times I've ever had!"

"What do you mean?" insisted Joel, speaking for all of us.

"Well, your Papa has just told me that, with the good harvest we had last fall and better prices for our crop, we are going to add two bedrooms onto the north side of our house, build a nice little porch on the front, and add a washroom on the back this very summer!" She was almost shouting.

We all let out a collective "Yea" and "Yippee."

"But, that's not all!" Mama quickly injected. We all hushed immediately.

"We are going to add a bathroom between the two bedrooms!"

The thought of an indoor toilet and a built-in bathtub was almost too much for us to grasp. But our ardor was cooled a bit as she went on.

"We can't afford to complete the bathroom this year, but we'll have it all plumbed in and ready to install the toilet and tub as soon as we can get the money to do it. But we will build in a washbasin where we can wash our hands and faces and not have to use the kitchen sink anymore!" Her voice was rising again. "And, as soon as we can we'll buy a water heater to heat the water for the washbasin, tub, and kitchen sink so we'll have hot water right at the tap!"

Everybody was excited that beds would not have to be put up and taken down every morning and night. The folks would sleep in the new bedroom facing the street. Our little baby sister, Ruth, would sleep in the crib in their bedroom. Helen would sleep in a rollaway bed, and Lael and Rhea would sleep in a double bed in the other new bedroom. I would still sleep downstairs. Joel would be off to college. Once the bathroom was completed, then no longer would we have to endure the bitter cold of the outdoor outhouse or the tight fit of the old galvanized tub for our baths on Saturdays.

It turned into a festive evening. The little one-room shack literally rang with laughter. Mama started preparing the beds for the night, but at frequent intervals I saw a happy smile sweep across her face. It was a monumental blessing for her and her family, the realization of a luxury she could only dream about before. Finding shelf and closet space for eight people was impossible, putting up and taking down beds was always so tiring, and living in such cramped quarters tended to put everyone on edge. Now all that would be ending. Mama's smile was beckoning us into a whole new style of living.

The work on the new addition started immediately so the bedrooms and bathroom could be completed before school started in August. Millie at the bank approved the money for the construction. Papa had already told Grandma Fanny about the new addition but had begged her to keep the matter secret until he could arrange the right time and place to break the news to the family. Fanny could hardly handle it. In the end she was glad she did because she oohed and aahed with wide-eyed excitement as we told her the good news.

We watched with great anticipation as the south part of the roof was extended upward to a higher peak by two-by-four trusses. Then the new roof arched downward on the north side to cover the added bedrooms, closet spaces, and the narrow little bathroom. Joel and I helped Papa dig the hole and trenches for the septic tank and cesspool into which the wastewater would flow. We unhooked the old rusty drainpipe from the kitchen sink that led to the underground gravel drain field and connected the new pipe to the new septic tank and cesspool.

We never forgot that summer as we saw one of our fondest dreams become reality. Lael was especially caught up in watching the new addition. That this was a major improvement for the family she could still understand, and she could still fully appreciate the sheer joy it generated.

The bedrooms were small, with the built-in closets consuming some of the space, but they were adequate. They freed up the living room for raucous and fun-filled family evenings. The kitchen could now be used exclusively for cooking and eating, except that until the bathtub was installed, it continued to serve as the location of hilarious Saturday baths in the old round tub.

The outside of the whole house was stuccoed over to cover up the peeling and fading paint on the old part and match up with the new part. It took some time for the stucco to dry out, and when it did, for some reason the new part didn't exactly match the color on the older version. But we were not into "fashion," nor were the townsfolk, so differing shades of stucco were acceptable.

All went as planned, and the move-in was completed before school started in August. Lael went again into the next higher grade with the rest of us. Her sleepless nights and nocturnal wanderings continued, however. But now, from her new bedroom she could sit on her bed and look out the window toward the backyard with its cattle corral, pigpen, chicken coop, and large garden space.

She could also see the two milk cows sometimes doing their own nocturnal wandering around the corral, feeding from leftover hay in the crib or leaning and scratching themselves on the old wood barn that formed one side of the corral. The cows were Lael's particular friends, or at least one of them was.

One night about two o'clock in the morning, Lael woke to a strange and unnerving sound. She listened intently. A woeful, haunting wail was coming from the backyard. She got up and peered out the back window toward the corral from which the sound was coming. After a few moments of intense listening, she rushed through the hall into our parents' bedroom and shook Papa vigorously.

"Papa, Bessie's crying!"

Papa, coming slowly out of a deep slumber brought on by a heavy day of harvesting, shook his head and said, "What?"

"Bessie's crying!" Lael urgently repeated.

"A cow doesn't cry."

Insistent and quite agitated, Lael said, "Quick, come and listen!"

Papa got up and went with her through the kitchen to the back door, opened it, and both listened intently with ears cocked toward the corral. To Papa's amazement it did sound like the cow was crying. By this time Mama was at his side also listening.

"She must be having her baby and is having trouble, big trouble the way she sounds!"

Papa dashed out to the corral in his bare feet and white long johns. He took a quick look into the corral and hurried back to the house.

"Zelma, please go wake up Reed, and all of you get your dirtiest clothes and coats on and some rubber gloves if we have them, or at least leather gloves, and let's get out there. Bessie's in real trouble!"

Within minutes all four of us were climbing over the pine-pole corral fence and running to the cow. Bessie was lying on her left side with her hindquarters close to the barn. A large Holstein bull calf was halfway out of her body. The calf's head had turned under its body into the muck, which, along with Bessie's hindquarters' proximity to the barn wall, made it impossible to come farther out of the cow. Both Bessie and the calf were suffering.

Lael knelt down by the cow's head and began consoling Bessie. Mama started rubbing her belly, trying to stimulate the muscles to action, while Papa and I took up positions between the back of the cow and the barn.

Papa had me lift on the partially born calf, which was slick with slime, while he began maneuvering the head out from under its body. It wasn't easy. Lifting the calf was akin to lifting half the cow because he was still halfway inside her. Papa finally got the calf's head straightened out and its body angled along the barn wall so it could slide out of the cow. We then each grabbed a front leg of the calf, holding onto the slimy forelegs as best we could.

Papa looked at Mama. "Tell us when to pull!"

"She's so exhausted I doubt she can push anymore, so you might as well start pulling!"

We did, and to our pleasant surprise one pull brought the calf completely out of the cow. I watched as a sickening, slimy and bloody mess of afterbirth oozed out of the stricken cow right after the calf. Papa immediately busied himself with the calf, cleaning out his mouth and nose and making sure he had not swallowed his tongue. He was alive, but listless. With continued swabbing of his air passages, and after a few helpful lifts of his slick and slimy body, we finally got him on his feet. Meanwhile, after resting only a moment and realizing the birth was complete, unbelievably, the exhausted cow staggered to her feet, turned immediately to the calf, and started licking it.

I looked over at Lael and Mama. Mama was hugging her and telling her how her concern for Bessie had saved Bessie and her calf and how grateful we were. Now we would have rich, tasty milk and butter for a long time.

Animals, I am convinced, perceive things we often don't give them credit for. After that evening, Bessie had a special affection for Lael. When she would come to the corral, Bessie would walk to her and expect to be petted on the head and, if Lael allowed, she would stick out her big, long rasp of a tongue and give Lael a loving swipe on the cheek.

From the back window of the new addition where Lael sat, the cows' movements were traceable when there was moonlight. Without the moon she could only see shadows cast by a recently installed, dim streetlight at the intersection just north of the house. Out by the back alley, the old outhouse still stood like a weary sentinel.

All this was a nightscape Lael could still understand and enjoy.

Chapter 15

Hitchhiking

IT WAS LUNCH RECESS, early spring, 1940. We had already eaten our lunch. Mr. Simmons, my likable and very interesting fourth grade teacher, was holding a group of us in the cafeteria spellbound with a story about riding the rails during the Great Depression.

"I was sixteen back in '32 when I began ridin' the rails all around the country with a friend my same age. We got odd jobs here and there in places called Los Angeles, Biloxi, and Omaha. We went through Omaha a lot since it was a major railroad crossroads—and the same with Chicago. Other cities I remember were San Diego, Ogden, Spokane, and there were so many others."

These were names as foreign and far away to us as the moon or Mars.

"I calculated it on a map one time and figured that we traveled close to 20,000 miles in the three years we rode the rails. But it came to an end when we were riding into Phoenix one day. It was July and hot, close to 120 degrees. There were five men in the boxcar, my friend, three strangers, and myself. We had thrown the doors on both sides wide open to tempt any little breeze into blowing through while the train was slowly pulling into the outskirts of Phoenix.

"My friend and I were sitting in one of the open doorways with our feet dangling over the side. One of the strangers stood in the same doorway leaning his right shoulder up against the open door frame. He looked to be about twenty-five, tall and thin. He had on a loose-fitting brown shirt and a pair of faded blue pants that looked like they once belonged to a good looking suit. But now they had a four-inch tear on the outside of the right leg and were soiled and dirty. He held them up with a piece of electric cord that he tied around his belly with a figure-eight knot in front.

"He had on a pair of ragged looking boots with only parts of laces that came up about three inches on the eight-inch high shoes. The tops of the shoes, where no laces were, flapped out like big wings.

"The stranger was fixing himself a cigarette, holding his little Bull Durham sack in his right hand and shaking the tobacco onto the cigarette paper he was holding with the other. The other two strangers, who were just as raggedy looking, were sitting in the doorway opposite us also with feet dangling over the side of the boxcar."

Mr. Simmons paused with a vacant look on his face, like he was lost in memory. Then he resumed with some animation.

"Suddenly, even though we were only moving about fifteen miles an hour, the car lurched so hard that it almost threw me and my friend out headfirst, but sitting down held us just fast enough to stay put. The tall stranger didn't fare so well. He was still fixing his cigarette, with both hands being occupied, when that big lurch came. The cigarette and Bull Durham bag went flying. He was not quick enough to grab hold of something with his hands before he went flying headfirst out the doorway, too.

"He arced out as though he was going to do a swan dive onto the neighboring tracks. Instead, the tear in the right leg of his trousers or one of the wings on his right shoe, or both, caught firm on the bottom latch of the open door frame, and that swung him down under the car onto the rails where he was cut in two by the large steel wheels."

Mr. Simmons didn't want to talk about the incident more than that. But we did come to understand that neither he nor his friend, nor the other strangers, who apparently didn't know the victim either, wanted to get involved with any of the "authorities" over the incident. So they just left the stranger lie as the train moved on, and as soon as they could they all evacuated the boxcar. Mr. Simmons said that it sickened him and his friend so, they never rode the rails again.

I never rode the rails, but it was common in those years and during the war for people to do a lot of hitchhiking by automobile. Drivers expected to see people on the highways, sometimes more than one, and even now and then a family of three or four. I did a lot of automobile hitchhiking from the time I was seven until I was ten—and almost joined Mr. Simmons' unlucky stranger.

In the summer, we took our chickens to the farmstead on the Flats, and when we had slack times from work and no one was going to the farm, I was assigned to hitch a ride the ten miles to the Flats every three days, walk the mile plus to our summer shack, make sure the chickens were okay, and gather all the eggs. I carried a little burlap bag that folded neatly into a little flat packet I could carry in my pants pocket until I needed it. It held the eggs nicely and left enough room at the top so I could get a good grip on it to carry it back to Highway 26, hitch a ride, and bring the eggs home.

No one thought anything about a kid hitchhiking. It was normal for the times, and usually the first car would stop. Many were neighbors from Ririe or the Flats, but often strangers gave me a lift. Most were courteous, and some on the return route even drove me right to my house in Ririe. One time a nice stranger gave me a dollar bill. It was an incredibly generous gift! I guess he thought I was poor or something.

My hitchhiking came to an abrupt halt in early August 1940. I had walked the three blocks from our house to Highway 26 and easily caught a ride. The driver dropped me off at the T intersection on the Flats where the dirt road led up to our summer shack. I trudged up the dirt road and checked to make sure everything was okay in the little shack. We never locked the door. In fact, the door didn't have a lock on it.

I counted the chickens, found them all there, and otherwise tended to things as Papa had directed me. Then I pulled the burlap bag out of my pocket and went about gathering the eggs. Most of the chickens liked to lay their eggs in the nice nests we prepared for them in the coop, but a couple of hens, who wanted baby chicks, built nests in the willows or other hard-to-find places. I had to scour the area within a hundred yards of the coop to make sure I found all the eggs.

I carefully put them in the burlap bag, got a nice handhold, and walked back to the highway. It was an overcast day and a typical Idaho breeze was blowing, probably twenty miles per hour. The wind coming from the southwest was warm. I had to walk against the wind up to the shack, but it carried me along on the way back, which was nice.

Mama insisted I wear a straw hat to keep the sun off my scalp and face. The breeze gave me trouble keeping it on, so I took the ends of the two laces it came with and tied them under my chin to cinch the hat down tight. The dirt road joined Highway 26 on the true flat part of the Flats, but only a few yards directly to the west was a little hill that vehicles had to chug up as they left the level terrain. I always found hitching a ride easier at the top of the hill because the cars, and especially the trucks, had to slow down to fight the gravity of the hill anyway.

With eggs in hand and hat secured, I walked to the top of the hill and parked myself in the borrow pit on the right side of the road to wait for westbound vehicles. Traffic was slow, so I lay down in the borrow pit to wait till a car came. After twenty minutes I heard a car coming quite fast along that smooth part of the highway leading to the hill. I quickly jumped up and made a bad mistake that I didn't realize till later. Instead of holding up my right hand and thumb in the typical hitchhiking signal, I held it up high, with fingers together and thumb extended, with the palm facing the onrushing car.

I held the little burlap bag of eggs in my left hand.

At first it looked as if the car would rush on by, ignoring me. Suddenly the brakes screeched, and the car came to an abrupt halt about forty feet beyond me. I was glad for the ride and rushed toward the car. The driver meanwhile jumped out, sort of staggered, and with an unsteady gait, walked toward me.

"What's wrong, kid?" I recognized him immediately. It was Dutch Caldwell, Mary Jap's nemesis. The one who had the heated confrontation about his grimy false teeth that cost him $100.

"I just need a ride to Ririe."

He countered with an agitated voice, "What in blazes are you holding your hand up like that for? You know dad gummed well that's not a hitch-hiking signal. That's a distress signal! We thought you were sick or injured or somethin' when you were lyin' down in the borrow pit and then jumped up signalin' like that just as we came along. What's your name, anyways?"

I noticed the slur in his voice, but I told him.

He looked at me for a moment or two, then with a peculiar look on his face asked, "You Zelma's kid?"

I said, "Uh huh," rather warily.

He thought for a moment, when suddenly a sort of funny woman's voice hollered from the car, "Hurry up, Dutch, we gotta git goin'."

I could smell alcohol on his breath and assumed from the sound of her voice that the woman was in the same condition as Dutch. I looked at the car and could see another couple in the backseat. The car was a little MG roadster, able to hold only four, so I assumed I would have to get another ride.

Dutch, after putting his hand to his chin and rubbing it sort of softly, said, "OK, come on, we're headin' for Ririe, and you can ride on the right front fender. It has a place for sittin'."

Being young and trusting, I climbed on the right front fender and took hold of the ornament in the middle of the hood. It was firm and solid and provided a good handhold. I didn't realize how desperately I would soon need it. I held the burlap bag in the middle of my chest with my right hand. My left hand gripped tight around the ornament.

I looked back over my shoulder into the car and saw the woman in the passenger's seat. It was not Darla. It was a woman called Kitty who lived a quarter-mile or so outside Ririe. I had only seen her once or twice. She was ten or fifteen years younger than Dutch. The other couple I didn't know, but they appeared to be about Dutch's age. I assumed they were coming back from an all-night party in Jackson Hole, Wyoming.

Dutch climbed into the driver's seat with considerable difficulty and a bunch of swearing. He slammed the car into gear and started off with a big lurch that jerked me backwards and just about sent me, with the eggs, sprawling off the fender. With each shift of gears the car lurched again, but I was able to hold on. Then things got frightening. As we went around the first curve at the bottom of Clark Hill, the car came up on its two left wheels it was going so fast. I glanced back with a frightened look at Dutch and the woman, but they were laughing at me trying to hold on. The speed limit before the war was fifty miles per hour. I'm sure Dutch was going eighty, careening around corners, revving that roadster up to its top speed.

By the Byington Store in Poplar, five miles east of Ririe, going around a curve, the car swung way over onto the shoulder. I thought we were headed straight for the borrow pit. I was holding the ornament so tightly with my left hand that my knuckles were white, probably like my face. As the car started to dip into the borrow pit, out of sheer desperation I let the eggs and burlap bag go flying out of my right hand and used it to quickly grab onto the underside of the fender just over the tire where I was sitting. I held on for dear life with both hands. This brought another raucous laugh from the occupants of the MG.

I was sure I was going to die, either in an accident where I would be the first object to hit any tree or fence or whatever was in the path of the roadster, or I would fly off the fender and roll endlessly in a bloody heap on the asphalt roadway. The knot tying the laces on my hat came loose, and the hat went flying into a neighboring field, aided by the crosswind and the reckless speed of the car. Riding on the front fender was like riding on the wing of an airplane.

There was no opportunity to get off. I could only hold on and hope.

I survived the last five miles, but almost did not survive the stop at the Ririe intersection. Dutch hit the brakes so hard that the tires screeched and I smelled burning rubber. I almost went flying ahead of the vehicle, but thanks to my double handhold, I was able to maintain my perch until I jumped off even before the car had stopped. I guess a scared and bewildered kid can look awfully funny because as they drove off, all four occupants were laughing and pointing at me.

I quickly ran the distance to our house, totally shaken but glad to be alive. When I arrived bareheaded and with no eggs, Mama was furious until I told her of my wild ride and how I lost the eggs and hat. I thought she was ready to go find Dutch and kill him. But she calmed down and worked hard at soothing my jangled nerves. At suppertime I was asked to again relate the whole incident. The family had an animated discussion about it and about hitching. Mama and Papa quickly decided there would be no more hitchhiking without an adult going along. They were both relieved that I was safe. Papa looked at me intently and gave me counsel.

"You are never to ride with a drunk in or outside the car. And remember that even as a child, especially as a child, you always have a special right, the right to say 'NO!' You can always walk away and say 'No thanks' to any situation. Just be sure to never get into such a predicament again."

Those instructions helped Lael and me a little later. It was one evening at dusk when Lael and I had bought a Pepsi at Mary Jap's restaurant and were on our way home. A stranger drove up and stopped beside us. He looked about fifty. He rolled down his window and asked us how to get to Rigby. We told him.

Then looking rather intently at Lael, he asked, "Can I show you something interesting? Climb in and take a peek." He opened the door for us to get in. I climbed in the passenger's seat but kept the door open while Lael leaned in and looked on. We thought the man was probably some kind of a salesman who wanted to show us his goods.

To our amazement he pulled out two photographs showing him and some woman, both naked, with the woman sitting on his lap. Both were looking directly into the camera. Lael quickly covered her eyes and exclaimed, "Those people don't have any clothes on. Shame on them." And I quickly said, "No, thank you!" I jumped out, almost knocking Lael over, slammed the door shut, and we both ran for home. As soon as we got to the house, we told Mama, who promptly got hold of Sheriff Judkins and gave him as much of a description of the man and his car as Lael and I could remember. But we heard nothing more about him.

On the night of my wild ride, my parents sat down in the living room after supper to talk about the incident and how they should deal with Dutch Caldwell. They decided not to talk to Sheriff Judkins about it because they figured it would be the word of a nine-year-old boy against Dutch, Kitty, and the other occupants of the car. They thought of talking to his wife, Darla, but decided she had been through enough anyway, and it was not her problem. Besides, rumor had it that she was seeking a divorce.

A short while later, on a late afternoon when Dutch and Kitty took off in his pickup heading for Jackson Hole, they traveled through the Flats and were heading down into Conant Valley. The descent from the Flats was along a narrow and steep two-lane dugway, which had an abrupt, hairpin turn near the bottom. The police report stated that the pickup was "traveling at a high rate of speed and missed the sharp turn about 400 feet up from the bottom of the valley. The tire marks indicate that it went straight ahead onto a little plateau adjacent to the curve, then sailed out a hundred feet or so and crashed in a piece of pastureland not far from the bank of the Snake River. The pickup caught fire. Neither occupant survived."

Chapter 16

Danny Rosenthal –
a Child of the Village

RUMORS ABOUT DANNY ROSENTHAL, the boy with St. Vitus' dance, hummed through Ririe. He was getting to be a man, becoming big and strong. Whiskers were growing on his face. Some mothers wondered just where all this might lead. The event with the man with the dirty pictures quickly spread throughout the town. Many worried what might happen if Danny got caught in the clutches of that "dirty old man" and got all "heated up" from some dirty pictures.

Idaho had two mental institutions. For want of a better term, one was called the "insane asylum." It was located in Blackfoot. The severely and criminally insane were housed there. The other was called "The Nampa State School and Colony." It was for the less handicapped and was located in Nampa, on the west side of Idaho near Boise, the state capital. A debate raged in the village about these two institutions and Danny, with a sort of "us against them" attitude developing. Some were of the opinion Danny should stay in Ririe and let the town folk take care of him like always. Others thought he should go to the Nampa school, where he could be supervised and trained to do something useful within his limitations. The less compassion-ate were quite vocal that he "belonged in the insane asylum."

One Sunday afternoon when Grandma Fanny was over for dinner, she started to ask Papa and Mama what should be done about Danny.

"That's none of our business!" Papa promptly and emphatically respond-ed. He had friends on all three sides of the debate and did not want to com-mit himself. More importantly, he was well aware that any opinion he might express could come back to haunt him.

As soon as the topic came up, Mama quickly told us to go outside and play. It was clear that the Danny Rosenthal issue was not for children.

Grandma Fanny pursued her course, "It's gettin' time for somethin' to be done afore a disaster strikes. Danny is gettin' big and strong, and I'm sure he's got the same urges that other young men have, but he probably don't have the brains to bank and cool 'em. Some of the mothers who have girls in their teens are gettin' mighty worried about him wanderin' the town like he does."

Papa loooked down and frowned.

Mama responded. "We have a girl in her teens, and she has urges, too. I worry constantly that someone might take advantage of her. It's hard, it's dev-ilish to even think about, but I worry that one day we may face with Lael what the Rosenthals are facing with Danny."

They sat in silence. No one knew what to say. But each realized that a bitter moment of truth was coming. The discussion ended as quickly as it began.

Out on the front porch, I sat with Lael on the steps. The weather was warm, the afternoon lazy, when a car full of teenage boys came driving slow-ly along our street. They looked like decent guys. The car, a late model Buick, probably belonged to one of their dads. Two of the boys looked our way. The one in the rear passenger seat on our side suddenly hollered for the driver to stop and back up. Both the driver's and the rear passenger's windows were rolled down.

The one at the rear poked his head out and very politely addressed Lael. "Hi. I haven't seen you here in Ririe before. I'm Tom Clayton from Rigby.

Can I talk to you a minute?" He motioned for Lael to come to the car.

She walked from the front step to the car with that graceful gait of hers. She presented a figure much like that in Mama's pictures in her early twenties. She had shapely legs, slender curves, and was tall, tanned, and beautiful. The sun glancing off her auburn hair created a halo-like effect about her head.

I couldn't hear the conversation at the car. It didn't last long. The driver bent his head forward, coughed, and turned with a funny look on his face toward the passenger beside him. The boy who had called her over was trying to make conversation but quickly realized Lael was retarded. I could tell he was trying to be polite but also to extricate himself from the encounter.

The car started forward, leaving Lael looking after it. She watched until it was a block away, then turned and walked back toward me, her face down and dejected, her shoulders sagging. I saw a look of ugly pain, bitter disappointment, and demeaning embarrassment. She wanted to be normal, but she was not.

Big tears splashed down her cheeks as she sat down beside me on the porch step, buried her head in her arms and knees, and cried, shaking uncontrollably. I tried to console her, but couldn't. I couldn't find the words. I put my arm around her shoulders feeling in some small measure the agony she was enduring and asking myself, "Why this ugly misery for my sister?"

Not long after that incident Danny disappeared. One day he was there, roaming the village. The next day he was gone. There were no public displays of affection, gift giving, or "seeing him off" like there were with Karl Klinger, though he had been every bit a part of the village scene as was Karl. We later learned that he had been sent to Nampa to the State School and Colony. At the time, however, few of the villagers knew what was going on behind the scenes. Danny simply was gone.

A few weeks after Danny disappeared, Eddie Rogers invited our family to his place on the Flats to have a picnic with his family and spend an afternoon. We were delighted. Just forty yards southwest of Eddie's shack was a rocky outcropping out of which flowed a beautiful stream of cool, crystal clear water that made the lips tingle. A bed of watercress plants had seeded themselves just a few yards downstream from the mouth of the spring. Fenced from animals, the cress flourished. Those natural delights were one reason we were always happy to visit at Eddie's shack. Eddie also had a tire swing on a long rope that Lael especially enjoyed.

Eddie also saddled up two tame ponies and let us take turns riding them. It made us feel so superior to be on their strong backs and feel the quiver of their powerful muscles beneath us, muscles we could deftly control with a little bridle and twin reins. Lael, Papa, Eddie, two of Eddie's daughters, and I were standing around the ponies waiting to ride them.

Nearby were Eddie's twenty head of cows and calves, moved from their upper pasture down to the pasture below his summer shack because the little creek that watered them up there had gone dry. He told us his family had formed a human chain, each person about twenty feet apart, and drove the cattle before them to the end of the upper pasture, then out the gate and down to the lower pasture a hundred yards away.

As Eddie was explaining this, Lael, always interested in animals, asked, "Why is that little cow up there in the corner bellering? She looks real sad."

We all turned and looked. A small heifer with a bally (white) face and black and white markings was standing on a little hill in the corner of the lower pasture, facing toward the upper pasture. She had her head held high and made a loud and constant mooing noise that had a plaintive edge to it.

Lael said, "She's not happy."

Eddie responded, "I dunno about her. She's been a real strange one. She belongs to a neighbor in Ririe. He asked if I could put her with my cows for the summer so she could get bigger and then get bred next spring and have a calf. Ever since we moved them down here from the upper pasture she has hardly eaten and keeps goin' to that corner and bellerin'. I wonder if she thinks there's a coyote or wolf up there that has her all anxious."

The mother cows at that moment seemed to be totally content. They were lying together and chewing their cud. Their calves were scattered around, some lying, some grazing. While we were watching, the whole herd of mothers suddenly jumped up and ran toward the bally heifer. They looked as though they were going to stampede right over her and on through the pasture fence. Yet they all stopped within only a few feet of the little heifer. Then all started mooing loudly, while the heifer started acting more peculiar. She dropped her head low to the ground and began running back and forth along the fence, mooing softly.

Suddenly, from the brush a hundred yards beyond the lower pasture fence burst a very small newborn calf, bally faced, with black and white markings. Its hair was still matted from its birth, and it was trailing at least four feet of umbilical cord, pierced through with numerous twigs and thistles. As the calf emerged from the brush it appeared confused and weary, but when it saw the cows it became excited and raced the distance to the pasture fence, the umbilical cord whipping wildly to and fro. It charged underneath the wire into the lower pasture but then seemed uncertain as to whom it belonged.

It was obvious it had not eaten since its birth two or more days ago. It was now certain to all of us that it had just barely been born when the cattle were moved out and had been left behind. During the summer the thought of the bally heifer being with calf had never crossed Eddie's mind.

The calf raced straight past the little heifer to the group of mothers. What happened next was completely unexpected. The cows formed a circle around the calf, as though to fence it in, each of them mooing like mother cows trying to comfort their own calves, except that all their attention was riveted on the newborn.

Then something unprecedented in our collective experience occurred. The newborn, prodded by a desperate hunger, picked out a mother cow in the circle, ran to it, and began to suck. And she let it! The calf stopped only briefly to suck from the first cow, then went from one to another in its bewilderment and excitement. All of them let it suck as long as it wanted, all of them mooing softly. Not one engaged in any of the usual kicking and turning away when a strange calf would try to suck.

The bally heifer watched from outside the circle for several minutes, perhaps as long as five. Then she moved toward the circle, which by some silent signal opened to let her in. She gently nudged the calf back out the gap by which she had entered and moved it thirty feet away. Then she guided the little newborn to her udder.

"Good Lord," whispered Eddie, "I never noticed her udder before. Look how large and swollen it is. It must be aching badly. How could I not have noticed?"

As the calf sucked, the mother licked its backside, and when brief interruptions from sucking came, she attended to the face, ears, neck, and front flanks of the little animal. The calf kept stepping on its umbilical cord, almost pulling itself over at times. Eventually it would drop off, but in those moments it was a nuisance.

Eddie, looking on in wide-eyed admiration, said, "In all the years I've dealt with cattle I've never seen anything like that! Normally those mother cows would be kickin' that little calf to pieces if it tried to suck from them. To see those cows form that circle to corral the little fella and let it orient itself to the herd and suck at will has gotta be one of the grandest displays of compassion, and from so-called dumb animals, that I've ever seen."

Lael observed, "Now they're all happy."

Papa had been very quiet during the incident. He seemed deep in thought, then spoke: "I've never seen nor heard of anything like that either in my experience with animals. Do you know what it reminds me of?"

No one answered, but the question hung with its own intensity in the air.

"It reminds me of how the village mothers took care of Danny Rosenthal, fed him, tended to him, bandaged up his cuts and bruises, looked out for him, saw he got home. He was the child of all of them, just like that little calf and those mothers."

Even at my young age, the tone of Papa's voice and the look on his face betrayed a deeper concern about the future of his own family—and Lael.

Chapter 17

Byron Mason and Other Heroes

A SINGLE LIGHT SHONE straight down from above, illuminating only the boxing ring. Everything else in the packed hall was pitch black. All eyes were riveted on the ring. Byron Mason—native son, short-cropped dark hair, clean-shaven, tanned muscles gleaming—was in the fight of his life. His opponent was two inches taller, five pounds heavier, two years older, and blond and muscular. In the fifth round he had bloodied Byron's nose, and just before the bell rang ending the round, a strong left jab split Byron's right eyebrow open. Byron was literally saved by the bell.

The referee separated them and sent them to their corners. Byron's mother, horrified by all the blood, screamed for the fight to be stopped. Byron quickly looked her way and mouthed the words, "Mom, I'm OK." The referee came to Byron's corner.

"You sure you want to go on, son? Those are pretty bad cuts."

"I'm OK." His voice was calm but had an edge to it, his eyes a determined gleam.

The bell rang. Byron's opponent, anxious to capitalize quickly on his gains in the previous round, rushed toward him. Byron painfully stood up.

He had a bewildered, even dazed, look, an open invitation for the kill. The blond made a wide arching swing with his right hand, a blow that could have taken Byron's head off. Suddenly Byron was wide-awake. He ducked. The blow sailed over his head. Then he brought his right glove from off the floor with a force that caught under the chin of his opponent and literally lifted him off the canvas. The blond didn't stagger. He didn't lurch. He simply collapsed in a heap on the floor, out cold.

Byron waited for the count to ten, then knelt down and helped the handlers pick the blond off the canvas and take him to his corner. The fight was over, another in a long string of victories for Byron.

Joe and Nell Mason lived down the street two blocks and left a half block from us in a "basement house." This meant a home that was only a basement for now. A hole for the house had been dug six feet deep. Eight feet of concrete was poured around the perimeter into molds to form the basement walls that stuck up two feet above ground level. Floor joists and rough flooring for the upstairs level of the house were laid over the basement hole. Black tarpaper—America had not yet entered the plastic age—was laid over the flooring and tarred down to keep it from blowing away. The tarpaper was intended to prevent leaks of rain and snow into the home below, but the flatness of the future floor made this nigh impossible. The covered stairwell, which provided entrance to the basement house, looked like a large inverted V sticking up out of one corner.

The basement house was a cousin to the lean-to. They were both meant to provide temporary housing until the next stage could be completed, which might take as long as twenty years. Oftentimes they were never completed. It was not uncommon for children to be raised in the basement portion and be gone before the upstairs could be built. That's how it was with the Masons. Most of their children, Byron too, were gone before the house over the basement was completed.

Nell was one of those special mothers who saw that children like Danny Rosenthal and Lael were looked out for. Lael was in her Sunday School class and developed a close bond with her, especially as Nell began to notice Lael's developing retardation. Nell made sure that Lael was treated with dignity and understanding by her children.

Joe and Nell were a little taller than the average. Consequently, their children were generally taller than most kids, and they were uniformly considered to be very good looking. Byron was especially handsome and had such a charismatic personality that Lael always felt comfortable around him. He greeted her kindly and spoke pleasantly to her whenever she encountered him. Lael was an adoring fan of Byron, who was several years her senior. Byron had plenty of fans in Ririe, as boxing became the sport of the day, maybe even the decade.

———————————

There were the two great heavyweight bouts between Jack Dempsey and Gene Tunney in 1926 and 1927. (The latter involved the "long count," when Dempsey did not immediately go to a neutral corner, so the referee delayed the count. Tunney rose at the count of nine, which was probably fourteen, and went on to win.) These took place before I was even born but were rehashed so often in conversation for many years thereafter, and also were made into a movie, that I knew all about them. These were bouts that people never tired hearing about, and they served as a prelude to, and whetted appetites for, yet another boxing classic.

In 1930, Max Schmelling from Germany became the World Boxing Association champion. Soon thereafter Adolph Hitler began to fashion his national socialist culture in that country. Schmelling only retained the title for two years, 1930 to 1932. But he loomed large on the world boxing stage again when he knocked out Joe Louis, America's up and coming "Brown Bomber," in June 1936. This was a major triumph for Germany, a staggering defeat for America! Germany and Schmelling were touting the Nazi line that Negroes, Jews, and others were inferior races to the Aryans, a worldview promoted by Goebbels, Hitler's propaganda meister. They continued their farce even after Jesse Owens, a black American, embarrassed Hitler and the Nazis at the 1936 Berlin Olympics, feats we watched on the Movietone newsreels in the theater.

In 1937 Joe Louis knocked out James L. Braddock, the WBA champion, in the eighth round of their title fight, bringing Louis the WBA title. In the nine months following the Braddock fight, Louis defended his title three times: once against Tommy Fair, then against Nathan Mann, and finally against Harry Thomas. This led to a groundswell of enthusiasm for a rematch between Louis and Schmelling. It would be held in Yankee Stadium on June 22, 1938, and it became a battle of America versus Germany, American Negro against Hitler's Aryan, good against evil. In Ririe it was the major topic of conversation.

The newspaper reported an incident between President Roosevelt and Louis before the fight. The president, with his polio-afflicted limbs, remained sitting but asked Louis to come close so he could whisper something in his ear. Roosevelt made a point of feeling Joe's well-trained and powerful muscles, and then, as at least one journalist reported, Roosevelt whispered to Louis: "We need muscles like yours to defeat Germany." In the mainstream press it came out: "Joe, go beat Schmelling to prove we can beat the Germans." When this was reported in the American and German press it stoked excitement over the bout to a fever pitch.

Shortly before the fight, eighteen Americans were indicted as being spies for Germany. This heightened the already tense relationship between the two countries, and those tensions found a focal point in this rematch. Scalped tickets to Yankee Stadium sold for two hundred dollars and were rescalped for as much as five hundred dollars. The newspapers, radios, and Movietone News were filled with the international intrigue that seemed to be focused in this particular fight. It would be broadcast worldwide by radio.

The big day came. The whole world tuned in to listen, including Germany, where, because of the time differential, the fight did not start until three in the morning. Louis weighed in at 198.75 pounds, Schmelling at 193. Both fighters were in excellent condition, having trained vigorously for months.

Our family gathered in Grandma Fanny's lean-to to hear the broadcast because her radio picked up the signal much better than ours, though even her fine radio would frequently go into a long, piercing whine, cutting out the broadcaster's voice. Her radio was a beautiful thing, three-and-a-half feet high and two-and-a-half feet wide, with elegant woodcarvings adorning the front and sides. Radios were such an important household item, they were made into beautiful pieces of furniture to fit with the most lavish décor. Grandma Fanny's was no exception. It occupied a very prominent place in her living room, around which chairs could be arranged so all could hear.

On the night of the fight, the whole family—six kids, two parents, and Grandma Fanny—hovered around her radio, hanging on every word. Grandma kept the volume as high as she could so as not to miss anything. We practically memorized the sequence of the fight.

In the opening moments of the first round, Louis connected with a vicious blow to Schmelling's head, which sent him reeling against the ropes where he hung, turned three-quarters away from Louis. The referee started the count. Schmelling turned around. Louis staggered him with another punch, and the German went down for a three count. He got up only to face another solid blow and went down again, but only to where his gloves touched the canvas. He dizzily arose once more. Louis connected again with a grinding blow that this time sent him flat onto the canvas.

Referee Donovan counted to five and then realized that Schmelling was finished and stopped the fight. Louis had knocked out Schmelling two minutes and four seconds into the first round. The black man had triumphed over the Aryan. America, the melting pot of all races, had triumphed over Hitler's "super race." All of us, parents and Grandma included, were screaming as the referee ticked off each second of the count. Joe's triumph brought praise and respect to his race and to America, a home for all races. Joe, as did Jessie Owens with his Olympic victories, represented freedom and victory, American style.

Before the advent of television, boxing was one of our premier forms of entertainment. The other was dancing.

Ririe's two bars (usually called "pool halls") were side by side on Main Street, except for a small vacant lot full of weeds, beer and whiskey bottles (they didn't have beer cans then), and other debris that separated the two. Adjoining the southernmost bar was the Ririe Pavilion, built just for dancing. We had a movie theater but could never count on how long it might take to see a movie. The film frequently broke and had to be mended, the projector lamp often blew out, and the projector itself was unreliable. The dances usually followed the boxing matches. People came from all over southeastern Idaho to those dances. Papa's brother Alma, Johnny's father, owned and operated the dance hall.

When microphones and speaker boxes came along, Alma decided to put a big outdoor speaker, or "boom box," on the roof of the pavilion. This blared out country dance tunes over the whole village. I often went to sleep to the loud but mellow voice of some country western singer who, with deep baritone richness, sang, "Have I told you lately how I love you? Could I tell you once again somehow?" or the woeful lament of a female, "You can't be true dear. There's nothing more to say. I trusted you dear hoping we'd find the way. Your kisses tell me that you and I are through, but I'll keep loving you although you can't be true." Gene Autry sang one of the most popular western songs of all time: "I'm back in the saddle again, out where a friend is a friend, where the longhorn cattle feed on the lowly gypsum weed, back in the saddle again. I'm ridin' the range once more, totin' my old forty-four..."

The villagers loved the music. The foxtrot beat from the boom box caressed the town like a velvety blanket. Old-timers and kids were lulled to sleep by its soothing melodies while the teens and young adults danced. No one protested the booming speaker, which played on until midnight each night a dance was held. Nobody thought it was "noise pollution." Only a few people in town had radios, and those that did could never get the richness of the melodies that played from that big boom box on top of the Ririe Pavilion. Uncle Alma and Aunt Lizzie were roundly praised for installing it.

The pool halls kept busy with people traipsing from the dance pavilion to one or the other and back, and there would inevitably be a bare-knuckle fistfight or two during each evening a dance was held. These occurred in the vacant lot between the two pool halls. Since there was no building between that lot and our house, we were close enough to hear the dialogue that took place with the fights (accompanied, of course, by that lilting music from the boom box). If there was enough moonlight, we could even get a good view of the fights. The voices of the fighters were always raised and shrill, agitated or passionate, depending on what the men were fighting over. Sheriff Judkins had the attitude that a fight between two young "roosters" would settle things faster than a night in jail and a bunch of legal process that cost the taxpayers money. As long as the fights didn't get out of hand or turn into a riot, he let them be.

One night I was lying in my bed listening to an ardent love song drifting across the way from the boom box. Suddenly I heard the makings of a very loveless fight going on. It seemed so ironic that two men could ferociously beat each other, even draw blood, to the tune of some touching melody of love and romance. The fight, from what I heard of it, had to do with some non-native coming into one of the pool halls, slapping down a silver dollar on the bar, and yelling to the bartender, "Give me a shot o' whiskey for this damned, teetotallin' Mormon dollar I got here." Jake, a non-Mormon was sitting at the bar next to the out-of-towner.

After a brief outburst of profanities, Jake invited the out-of-towner out to the vacant lot. Jake made it clear that the "furriner" shouldn't act and talk that way. The two combatants had loud voices, so I was eagerly leaning on their every word.

Jake yelled, with considerable "amens" and "you bets" from those who accompanied him, "You cain't come in this here town o' ours and talk demeanin' about our Mormon friends and their dollars like you did jist now, so I demand you apologize right here, right now!"

The response was instant and loud, also supported by voices from friends of the other combatant, "Your Mormon dollars and a apology be damned. I kin speak as I choose."

The talking ceased, and the sound of bare fist against bare flesh took over. I could hear the clash and the loud voices from across the street and through the block through my partially opened basement window.

Suddenly a man's shrill voice shouted, "LOOK OUT JAKE! HE'S GOT A KNIFE!"

Then I heard a woman screaming, "HE'S CUT HIS BELLY WIDE OPEN. HIS GUTS ARE SPILLIN' OUT!" Then everybody started screeching and hollering. I jumped out of bed, ran upstairs, and dashed out onto the front porch to see what was going on.

Lael, the light sleeper, was already there, peering through the dusky shadows with a look of terror in her eyes. I could tell that the screaming voices, the general pandemonium, and probably the very ugly images blazing into her mind were upsetting her terribly.

She started to cry and began screaming, "They shouldn't fight! They shouldn't fight! Go tell them they shouldn't fight and kill each other!"

No way would that wild bunch ever listen to ten-year-old me! Besides, Papa and Mama would never tolerate my going over there. I stood there dumb, torn between Lael's torturous sobbing and the bloody scene across the way. Completely bewildered, I wondered how a little silver dollar could cause such a heated and near-fatal fight.

Mama barged out onto the porch trying to tie the loose waistband on her nightie and get to Lael, who was becoming increasingly hysterical. Mama put both arms around her and drew her head onto her shoulder. She looked up at me and asked what was going on. I told her as much as I knew.

Just then the sheriff's car arrived at the scene with his light flashing. He jumped out, and the screaming and pandemonium quieted.

In the warmth of the evening air, Mama sat Lael down on the love seat and continued to hold her close, speaking quietly to her. It took some time for the sobbing to cease and for peace to settle over Lael.

She asked, "Why do they fight, why do they try to kill each other?"

Mama didn't try to answer the question. She held Lael close and told her that it was not our concern and not to worry about it.

I sat on the edge of the porch looking at them, wondering where all this was leading to with Lael. This event piled yet another layer of worry on top of all that had previously accumulated within her. She was becoming extremely sensitive to violence in any form. Every argument, and especially a fight, upset her terribly. We tried to avoid even talking about such things in her presence. As closely bonded as the two of them were, Mama's consoling hugs and comforting words were having less and less of a soothing effect on Lael. Her mind was conjuring up ugly images that left her terrified and insecure. An irresistible force was pulling her down, down, in a relentless slide into a foreboding purgatory from which none of us could retrieve her.

I later learned that this time the out-of-towner spent several months in jail. Jake was given first aid while lying there on his back amidst the weeds and other debris. Then he was whisked off to the hospital in Idaho Falls. He lived and was hailed as a hero by the whole village.

That was probably the most colorful of the fistfights I witnessed, other than the boxing matches involving Byron Mason. But his fights were never brawls. They had finesse. Had Byron been there, I thought, the out-of-towner would have been flat on his back within seconds, knife or no knife.

Like Joe Louis, Byron Mason became a household name throughout southeast Idaho because boxing had become so popular and he was our local champion. To box like Byron became the dream of every red-blooded Ririe boy. I even boxed in a couple of preliminary bouts to Byron's main bout, but soon learned I did not have Byron's skill.

Because of her close association with Nell and the way Byron treated her like a cute little sister, Lael was also caught up in the Byron wave that swept the area. Byron was one of Ririe's special native sons and a legend in his own time throughout the region.

Byron's name came up in our home for a different reason one evening when Grandma Fanny came for supper. She brought disturbing news. "I jest got word that Byron Mason has decided to enlist in the Navy. A couple of the ladies over at the Golden Rod Store told me they heard it straight from Nell's mouth. She told them that Byron jest plain knew he was gonna be drafted anyways with the things a goin' on in Europe and all that Hitler nonsense, so he wanted to choose which branch of the armed forces he would be a servin' in."

Mama countered, "I wish he wouldn't. He's jumping the gun! They're only fussing around over there in Europe. It doesn't involve us. Hitler is only trying to get some of the land back that Germany gave up in the big war. Surely America will not be drawn into that neighborhood squabble."

Her voice betrayed considerable concern, however. We knew where that came from. Joel was approaching draft age. He was only a few years younger than Byron. She was obviously worried about his life if America got itself entangled in another war.

Papa sat toying with his fork in his food, his face a solemn mask. "If Germany attacks England, I think Roosevelt and Congress will insist that we get involved. To lose a vital ally like England will leave America vulnerable to Hitler's further aggression. Everything I hear and read says to me that we are going to be sucked into this fight one way or the other."

It was all pretty big for me to understand, but the tone of Papa's voice, Mama's agitation, and the sigh of resignation from Grandma Fanny left us children a little shaken, especially at the possibility that Joel, Byron, Cousin Johnny, and other young men would have to fight in a war.

Suddenly Lael began an earnest chant: "Joel can't leave our family! Joel can't go to the army! Joel can't go to war! Byron shouldn't go! He should stay here in Ririe!"

Mama could tell that frightful images were developing in her mind. She grabbed Lael's hand and looked into her eyes. "Lael, Joel doesn't have to go yet. No one has made him do it. We hope no one will. Byron had the choice to go or not. No one made him do it. He liked the Navy and chose to go. Right now there's no problem, so put these thoughts out of your mind, and we'll only worry about them if and when we have to."

Lael quieted down. But we went to bed that night feeling our little Idaho village might not be so remote from the rest of the world after all.

As Joel and I lay in bed that night, being enamored with the idea of traveling the world or even flying a fighter plane, I asked him how he felt about the things we had talked about at supper. He responded in his usual balanced and thoughtful way.

"I guess it would be interesting to see all those faraway places like Germany or England or Italy, but to be there as a soldier and to see those places as battlegrounds doesn't sound very fun to me. All the old soldiers from the last war say it was a horrible thing, and you should never get caught up in any notion that war is fun or romantic. I am not excited about going to any kind of war!"

"Well, what do you think of Byron joining the Navy?"

"Byron is a boxer and a fighter. Maybe he can see some excitement and romance in it all, especially the Navy where he can sail around the world on big battleships and not be a foot soldier slogging through mud and wind and rain. But being on a battleship surrounded by miles and miles of water and having the chance of getting torpedoed by a submarine, bombed by an airplane, or shot at by big guns from an enemy ship doesn't sound all that exciting to me."

I went to sleep troubled by a dream of being adrift in a vast ocean wearing only a Mae West life preserver with thousands of miles of water between land and me. The allure of distant lands and cultures was still immensely appealing to a young boy from a small village, but not when coupled with the menacing scourge of war.

Lael fared no better that night than I. She woke the next morning after a troubled sleep with renewed anxiety over the prospect that Byron, Joel, Johnny, and others would be going to war. It was not easy to console her.

Chapter 18

That Unforgettable Sunday

IT WAS SUNDAY. For a December day it was unbelievably warm, another of those rare but precious Indian summer days that occasionally came in late fall. The villagers came out of doors, soaking in the sunshine and warmth. Most were off work and could relax and enjoy the incredible gift of such weather. I still wonder how such a beautiful day could end in triple tragedies.

The whole family went to church in the morning and then quickly changed to comfortable clothing to fit the weather. We hurriedly ate an early dinner and unanimously elected to climb into our new Chevrolet car and drive into the hills. The car still had that new car smell that was a constant reminder that things were looking better financially for our family. In fact, we had finally installed the flushing toilet and bath to go with the sink in the new bathroom.

Equally pleasant was our first refrigerator, which replaced the messy ice chest. My sisters made endless ice cubes and put them in everything we drank. They even tried them in milk! They found a recipe in the refrigerator's instruction book to make ice cream in the ice cube trays, so we had ice cube tray ice cream daily for a week or so. We soon realized, however, that it had scores of little bland ice crystals in it, tasted flat, and came nowhere near the homemade ice cream from the hand-cranked churn. We went back to the churn. To have cold milk, ice cubed water, and to keep lettuce, vegetables, meat, jams, jellies, eggs, and fruits crisp or cool or fresh, or all of the above, however, was a luxurious delight. But we still had to trudge to Brown's to get our frozen meat and other frozen food from the freezer-locker. A residential freezer had not yet been invented.

There was more! Papa had bought and installed a water heater in the basement to supply warm water at the tap and to the bath. Perhaps even more importantly, he had bought Mama a brand new electric stove! The old wood-burning stove had been carted out to the barn, where it was carefully covered with a canvas tarp instead of being hauled to the junkyard. Papa was sure bad times would come again when we could not depend on electricity and would have to haul the old stove back into the house. Papa carefully sealed the round stovepipe hole in the chimney with the bottom of a tin can and painted over it to match the rest of the chimney. He placed the blackened stovepipe atop the wood stove so that when the inevitable need arose they could be reinstalled on a moment's notice.

The new Chevrolet was black and sleek looking. It even had those wide white-sidewall tires that gave it a jazzy look. It also had an electric starter. You just had to turn on the key, press your foot down on the little round knob to the right of the accelerator pedal, and bingo, it would start to purr.

Joel had been sent on a church service mission to the Japanese people in Hawaii and was supposed to have arrived there at the end of September. We had not received any mail from him, so we did not yet know where he was assigned on the islands. We all envied his opportunity to go to such a paradise.

That left five kids at home: Lael, just turned seventeen; Helen, thirteen; me, Reed, eleven; Rhea, eight; and baby Ruth, three, plus Mama and Papa. We all fit nicely into the four-door sedan, with Papa, Mama, and Ruth in front and the rest of us in the backseat.

Papa drove the posted fifty-mile-per-hour speed limit with care because it seemed not only plenty fast for him but almost more than the narrow asphalt roadway leading out of Ririe would allow. It led five miles to the bridge across the Snake River. Then we traveled east at a slower pace along the narrow dirt roadway that led up to Heise Hot Springs.

Heise had artesian hot springs. These were among a long string of hot springs that begin in Alaska, pop up down along the Rockies through Canada and into Montana, and are especially prominent in Yellowstone Park. From there they wind into Idaho where they supply warm water for the swimming pools at Green Canyon north of Rexburg, Heise, and Downata south by Downey. They emerge again at Wasatch Hot Springs in north Salt Lake City, then farther south at Saratoga Hot Springs south of Salt Lake.

A German immigrant who had fought in the Civil War, a widower, came with his pretty daughters to southeastern Idaho. He suffered from rheumatism. He was told about some warm springs east of Ririe on the north side of the Snake River, which the Indians emphatically touted for their healing effect. Old timers even told him they saw deer warming their feet in the water of the springs. The immigrant, Richard Clamor Heise (whose last name means "hot' in the German language), filed a claim on the springs. He envisioned a resort there patterned after European spas. He built a hand-hewn log lodge for guests, constructed a shelter for the springs, and with the help of his daughters, made Heise Hot Springs into a favorite fishing, camping, and swimming resort.

We did not swim or intend to on this beautiful day. Instead, we continued past Heise on up the winding dirt road about four miles, where we veered southeastward and descended down a slight dugway to the north bank of the Snake. On the opposite side, the footstool to the Flats began, that portion lying just west of Clark Hill. Its dominant feature was the "Hogsback." As you approached from the west, you saw a narrow ridge two hundred yards long suddenly rise up before you. It truly did resemble the back of a hog, with the north end of the ridge dipping down to form the neck. When anyone was near the Hogsback, he was sure to be either entering or leaving the westerly footstool to the Flats.

At the bottom of the little dugway we entered a world of stately cotton-wood trees. The bottomland on which they flourished was located at the western edge of the lower Snake River Canyon (the lesser known one downstream from where the Jackson to Alpine, Wyoming, whitewater canyon runs). Across the river Highway 26 ascended on up Clark Hill and thence onto the Flats, leaving the river six hundred feet below. There the walls of the canyon are laced with multiple layers of lava-flow outcroppings on both sides. The once mightier Snake coming out of the Ice Age must have cut through that lava like a hot knife through butter, leaving those resplendent walls as a backdrop for the lush cottonwood groves and fertile meadows adjoining the river's meandering courses, at their base.

On this December day the cottonwoods, bare of leaves, allowed the afternoon sun to slant through their high branches, creating a busy patchwork of light and shadow as we drove through them. The shadows played across our faces and torsos with a strobe-light effect. Papa slowed the car so we could roll down the windows and smell the water from the Snake and the moistened leaves lying abundantly at the foot of the trees.

We rounded a curve and suddenly came to a dozer cut in the riverbank where small boats could be launched. Papa turned the car into the cut and stopped the motor. He stared across the river, seemingly lost in thought, remembering. It was a tranquil scene. The river flowed smoothly by, the southern sun glancing off its surface. Some evergreens and naked cottonwoods on the opposite shore laced the bottom of the sheer lava wall like the flaring hem of a beautiful dress.

Papa spoke quietly, almost reverently, "A year ago last September I was here at this very spot on the morning of a beautiful sunny day like today. Your mother knows about it, but I haven't told you kids. A good friend of mine, Art Barrow, had died after a long bout with colon cancer.

"Art asked a special favor of me. Art loved to fish the Snake throughout this lower canyon. He spent many happy hours here. He told me he wanted his body cremated and his ashes sprinkled in the Snake right along here. He also wanted his fishing pole thrown into the river after the ashes. He asked me if I would do that for him. At first I worried about cremation because I was not sure that was the way to treat his body. But Art assured me he and his family felt just right about it. So I agreed. Art's daughter and son-in-law went with me to the mortician's to pick up the container with the ashes, and we drove to this spot pulling Art's boat.

"The son-in-law backed the boat into the river. He started the motor and drove us directly out into the middle. He pointed the bow upstream and set the throttle so the speed of the boat matched the pace of the river going by so we could stay stationary right out there where I'm pointing."

Papa's voice became quieter, more subdued. We had to strain to catch every word. We were now as completely absorbed in the event as he.

"I remember hearing birds on both sides of the river above the gurgling of the water and the purr of the motor. The sun was etched in fiery yellow in the south against the deep blue of the harvest sky. The cottonwoods were just beginning to turn yellow, and the berry bushes and laurel were a fluorescent red. It was a scene and a moment I will never forget." His voice caught. He hesitated.

He cleared his throat, somewhat embarrassed, and then continued. "The metal urn had a lid with a hinge. When I opened the lid, the urn was almost full to the brim. The ashes were a gray-white color, and there were little hard gray pieces here and there about the size of a pea.

"I stood up, braced myself against the side of the boat, and leaned carefully out over the edge. Then I let the ashes slide out in a long thin stream of gray-white against the dark blue of the passing water. They hung momentarily on top of the water like a mist, then dissipated and were no more to be seen." Papa became silent.

Being curious about other things, I asked, "What about the fishing pole?"

Papa seemed to shake himself out of his reverie. "Art's son-in-law gently lowered the pole into the water with the reel and bottom of the pole downstream, the tip upstream. The reel end plummeted to the bottom first. It seemed the pole was buried and forever lost. But the reel must have caught on something, because suddenly the tip began to rise silently out of the water. It made a slow, majestic arc upward past our staring faces and then gently nestled back into the water. It seemed to memorialize Art's birth as the tip came up out of the water, his life as it slowly made its arc, and then his passing as it laid back into the water and vanished. It was also a fitting final wave of good-bye from Art."

Even at my young age, I felt something special as I looked out across the river after my father's story and watched the water drifting by just as life drifts by.

Lael broke the silence. "What does cremated mean, Papa?" She had not connected "cremation" with burning and ashes.

Papa looked at Mama for help! She turned to Lael with a pleasant smile.

"We'll talk about that later. Right now we have this gorgeous day to enjoy, so let's hurry on up the road and get out and run and play in this warm sunshine before it gets cold."

Grateful for her thoughtful response, which avoided any discussion with Lael of a body burning, Papa started the motor, backed out of the cut, and drove on up the river canyon. We came to a sun-drenched meadow where Papa let us out of the car so we could suck in the clean smelling air and run and play to our hearts' content. This warm and cozy December day was truly a gift to be appreciated by our family, because from that day on our lives would never be the same.

Soon the sun began sinking low in the southwestern sky. It was time to leave this happy family outing and return home. The new car did not have a radio, so we were totally unprepared for what was to happen as we drove into the driveway between our house and Grandma Fanny's lean-to. Upon hearing the car turn in, Fanny burst through her front door and came shuffling painfully toward us, a look of horror on her face and tears pouring down her cheeks. Papa quickly rolled down his window.

"My word, Mother, what's the matter? What's happened?"

"The Japs attacked Pearl Harbor in Hawaii this morning! The American fleet has been almost totally wiped out. Thousands of soldiers and sailors are dead. It was a sneak attack. Nobody had any idea it was a comin'. The last report said the battleship Arizona wuz sunk. Byron wuz stationed on that ship! And Joel is there somewhere in Hawaii and may be dead or injured. How can we find out what's happened to him? Oh Lordy, it's just awful. Now we are for sure goin' to be in a war with the Japs and probably the Germans, too!" Her voice closed off in a shuddering sob.

We were in total shock. Lael became almost hysterical and started to chant, "Joel can't be dead. Byron can't be dead." Her agitation over this news was so intense she started to grind her teeth and an occasional fleck of saliva spewed from a corner of her mouth. For a few moments she sat on her seat in the car, placed her hands in the middle of her lap, and started to rock back and forth, groaning. Then she jumped out and ran to Grandma Fanny, looking pleadingly at her, as if to beg that she take the awful news away.

Mama ran after her, locking Lael and Grandma Fanny in a consoling embrace and saying, "Lael, we don't know what's happened to Joel and Byron. We have to wait until we find out. We have to hope for the best. Joel arrived in Hawaii at least a couple of months ago, so maybe he was not there where the attack happened. And we don't know if Byron was on the Arizona when it sank!"

She took Lael's face in her hands and pulled it toward her, looked deeply into her eyes, and said, "Please let your mind rest. We are all worried, but we just don't know what's happened to Byron and Joel, and it will be better to wait and not let ourselves get all upset until we do know."

Papa asked Fanny, "Are they still broadcasting the news of the attack over the radio?"

"Yes. It's been on all afternoon."

"Then let me come over to your house and hear everything that's going on with your radio. Ours doesn't work that well. In the meantime, Mama can get the kids quieted down and Reed can feed the animals and do his other chores. I'll be back to the house as soon as I've heard all the news, and we can talk this over some more at suppertime. If I'm not back by six, Reed, then you start milking the cows. Be sure to put some bag balm on the Guernsey's udder and tits. She's been lying in the mud and got them all caked up." He took Fanny by the elbow and returned with her to her lean-to while Mama, with an arm around Lael and with Helen, Rhea, and baby Ruth in tow, returned to our house.

I changed my clothes and went about my chores, my mind buzzing at this ugly yet oddly exciting news. Papa did not return by six, so I milked the two cows. First I massaged the Guernsey's udder and tits with bag balm and then let the balm do its soothing work while I milked Bessie, the other cow. Whenever I came into the house to carry eggs or milk, there was always much animated discussion going on, with Mama trying to answer every conceivable question my sisters' young minds could think up.

There was no relief from this news. The anxiety over Joel and Byron's fate was unbearable. We had to wait for news from Papa. Mama busied herself putting together a light supper. Papa returned a little before seven. Mama had us wash our hands and faces and sit down in our places while she served our supper. We looked inquiringly at Papa.

But Lael spoke first, her mind trying to grapple with what was deeply, and perhaps sorrowfully, affecting our village and our family. She asked, "Is Joel dead? Is Byron dead? Is there going to be a big war? Is everybody going to get killed?"

Papa looked at her with tenderness. Here was a little-girl mind in a seventeen-year-old body trying desperately to grasp the significance of a horrible event.

"Sweetheart, we just don't know. We have to be patient and wait. It will be tough, but in a few days we'll know."

He told us that a huge armada of Japanese aircraft carriers, battleships, and other vessels had bypassed all the traditional shipping lanes and somehow escaped detection as they steamed toward Hawaii. They positioned themselves northwest of the islands, and early on this Sunday morning had sent squadron after squadron of airplanes to attack Pearl Harbor where most of our battleships were anchored. They also attacked and destroyed our planes on air bases on the island. It happened totally without warning. He said there had been a blip on a radar screen indicating planes coming in from the northwest, but personnel at the radar site thought it was a group of bombers they were expecting from California and gave no warning to anybody.

Most of our battleships were either badly damaged or destroyed, and, yes, the Arizona had been sunk in the harbor where she was at anchor. There was no news about who or how many were on the ship and might have gone down with her. He said the early reports indicated that mostly military targets were hit, and if Joel was on Oahu, he would have been somewhere in a city and might have escaped injury. That news was small comfort, considering how devastating and destructive the attack had been and how certain it was now that young men from the village and the Flats would soon be caught up in a war that would span the globe.

The only bright spot in the news was that no aircraft carriers had been tied up at Pearl Harbor, so America would have at least a start toward arming itself. Papa also reported that President Roosevelt was going to ask Congress to declare war against Japan, and it was anticipated that war would soon be declared against Germany and Italy. That was as much as we heard that night.

We went to bed troubled and anxious about Byron and Joel. None of us slept well, Lael least of all. She got up and padded around the kitchen and living room in her slippers. Then she sat down by the window overlooking the street. Around midnight she suddenly began to cry, sobbing uncontrollably. Mama and Papa rushed to her. Helen, Rhea, and I also woke at the sound of her loud sobbing and went to see what was the matter.

Mama and Papa were alternately holding her, soothing her, trying to bring her comfort, but it fell on deaf ears. She was inconsolable. I could almost envision the demons that were going back and forth through her mind, bedeviling her, taunting her with all sorts of ugly and violent images. She said hardly anything. She couldn't—the unstoppable sobbing overpowered everything else.

Mama, seeing the three of us out of the corner of her eye, gave a stern motion of the head that said we were to return to our beds and not come back. We did as directed. But Lael's hysteria rang throughout the house, echoing, it seemed, in every corner. It lasted the whole night. Papa, Mama, and Lael got no sleep. The rest of us only got sporadic naps.

Toward morning, Lael became exhausted and faded into a fitful sleep in Mama and Papa's bed. Papa stayed with her while Mama made preparations for breakfast and getting us off to school. Our questions about Lael went unanswered.

"You'll have to go to school and do the best you can; then hurry home as soon as school is out and try to get a nap."

Mama, looking haggard, had no strength to say anything more.

Chapter 19

Lost in the Abyss

WHEN I RETURNED from school that afternoon of December 8, 1941, I looked up from outside into the window of our little living room, which faced the street. Lael was sitting there, staring out the window. I waved, but no recognition dawned in her face. I could tell her eyes were crossed. She looked hollow-eyed, vacant of the light of intelligence. I opened the front door and said hello to her. There was no response, just that vacant stare as she turned toward me, and then back to the window.

During that terrible night we lost the Lael we knew. She sat now for endless hours at the living room window where the crying commenced that night and looked out into we didn't know where. She would take a pencil and spiral notepad and write her name, "Lael," over and over and over, page after page after page. Often she would lay the pencil down and start crying again, bedeviled by we knew not what.

A telegram came a few days later stating that Joel was alive and well. He had been stationed on the island of Kauai where no attack had occurred. Greatly relieved, my parents tried to communicate this to Lael, but she was unable to grasp it. I am not sure she even knew now who Joel was.

A telegram from the War Department brought the Mason family the tragic news that Byron had been on board the Arizona and was presumed dead, one of 1,177 sailors who were on the ship and perished when the attack came. Whatever station he was at on the Arizona became Byron's final resting place. It proved fruitless to tell Lael of Byron's death. In her transformed condition she could not understand, perhaps did not even remember him, and if she had grasped it and did remember him, the news would have undoubtedly triggered an even deeper descent into her abyss.

My parents promptly made a visit to the Masons. With Grandma Fanny at home to care for the kids and Lael, they started out on foot. By now the weather had returned to normal winter weather, with the temperature in the low twenties on this mid-December afternoon. There had been a couple of inches of snow since the seventh, so they wore galoshes and coats.

When they reached the first intersection, Mama stopped, looked to her right where Mary's hotel stood, then looked at Papa and said, "Let's ask Mary to go with us."

Papa looked at her in shock, thinking what an affront that would be to Joe and Nell. Then he made a prompt attitude adjustment, looking admiringly at his wife. "You're absolutely right. We have to hold the door open to Mary in all our hearts, and this is exactly the time and the way to start."

Mary's restaurant had no customers. She was alone, sitting in her kitchen, as Papa and Mama came through the front door and made their way to find her. Mama was suddenly beside herself that she had failed to think of Mary in all that time since the attack on Pearl Harbor. Yes, she allowed herself to reason, she had had her problems with Lael and the awful waiting for word about Joel, but how could she have forgotten Mary for all that time?

She ran to her, put her arms around her and her cheek next to hers, and whispered, "Oh Mary, can you forgive me for not coming sooner? You should have been the first thing on my mind. But I let other troubles get in the way. Please forgive me," she pleaded.

Shy Mary was at a loss for words. She simply buried her head in Mama's shoulder and whispered back, "You done come, you done come, you done come! You help me! You help me! I sorry for Byron. I have love him very much. I love Joe an' Nell, but dey hate me now. Dey hate me now!" She began to sob.

Mama grabbed both her shoulders and shook her. "Mary, Joe and Nell don't hate you. You must realize that. You had nothing to do with this. You are an American, like everybody else in our village."

"But I no look lak American, I no talk lak American. I different, and dey all hate me now."

"No, no, you must not even think that! You must always remember that you are an American and no one has the right to claim otherwise. You are a blessing to our village. People know of your goodness. You are one of us."

Mary calmed down somewhat and asked them to sit down at her kitchen table.

"But I don' have no customers no more. Dey don' come no more."

Papa spoke. "Give them a little time. We all need time to accept what has happened and to get our thinking straightened out. Byron's death has made it harder for our little village, but it changes nothing. Now, that said, we thought it would be nice if you would go with us to visit Joe and Nell and express our regrets at their losing Byron."

"Oh no, no," moaned Mary. "I canna do dat. Dey no want me around. Dey mus' hate me and all Japanese."

Papa replied, "You know the Kramers, don't you?"

"Yes."

"Should you and Zelma and I hate them because they come from Germany?"

"But dey look American. Dey speak English. I no can do."

"What has that got to do with anything? Their circumstances are no different than yours. They are naturalized citizens of America just like you, and they speak with an accent. Now please put on your coat and come with us to visit Joe and Nell. They need us, all of us!"

Mary stared at both of them a long time, her doubts and worries about the venture showing on her face.

Mama spoke again, "Mary, we need to hold the door wide open for you to continue to be a blessed part of our village. I can't think of a better way to do it than for you to come with us to see Joe and Nell. It's the right thing to do, and it's the right time to do it!"

Mary had always trusted my mother. She relented and retrieved her coat and galoshes from the closet. She locked the doors and went with them.

That three block walk sent a signal throughout the town. Villagers peering from their windows and passersby on the street took notice of that little trio making their way to Joe and Nell's basement house. They were going to pay their respects. To most of the inhabitants it was a reality check akin to the one Papa experienced at Mama's request that they take Mary with them. Mary was one with them and, if they thought about it long enough, a beloved one. Her Oriental features made no difference. Although it would take time to blossom and bear fruit, that idea took firm root in the village on that mid-December afternoon.

When they arrived, Papa climbed the two steps leading up to the inverted V that formed the stairwell. He knocked loudly. There was a small moment of silence, and then Joe's deep bass voice rumbled up the stairwell, "Whoever it is, come on in." There was no sense in climbing the stairs to let someone in when his voice would do just as good a job.

Papa opened the door and let Mama and Mary precede him into the stairwell. Joe was standing below looking up. Mama could see the anguish written all over his craggy face. She also thought she saw a look of surprise as he detected Mary following her down the stairwell, but it vanished quickly.

Nell hollered from the kitchen, "Who is it, Joe?"

"We got company, Nell. Come on in the living room." He invited the trio in as Nell came out of the kitchen.

Nell, the lady, ever the lady, on seeing Mary rushed past Zelma to her and embraced her, saying, "Mary, oh Mary, thank you for coming! Thank you for coming! I have been so worried about you. Are you all right?"

Mary answered, "I so sorry you lose Byron. I have love him vera much, an' he was so nice to me an' done come often with his friends or girlfriend to my restaurant. I feel bad. It hurt deep inside me," she said, pointing to her heart.

Nell responded, "I know how it must hurt you. I hope people have been nice to you. You are such a noble lady and have done so much good. I hope they never forget that. Joe and I never will. I am so pleased that you came to visit us. Please take off your coat and sit down."

Then Nell turned her attention to my parents, both she and Joe receiving warm embraces from them. They thanked them for their kindness to come visit.

Mama spoke: "We should have been here sooner. Please forgive us. We let our concern over Joel and some problems with Lael hold us back. But Joel is all right and we are grateful for that. Now what can we do to help you?"

Nell responded, "What's wrong with Lael?"

"We don't know. After we first heard of the attack on Pearl Harbor, we were worried about Joel because we didn't know where he was in Hawaii. Lael had a terrible night. She cried the whole night. I'm sure it was because of her worry over Joel and Byron. Since that night she has left us and gone off into a world where we cannot reach her. But we'll take care of that. We just want to tell you how the whole town and everyone on the Flats is mourning with you. Byron was special. He was a part of all of us. Everyone knew him and loved him. How are your children doing with this news?"

Joe answered, "They are coming to terms with it, but it's hard. We're worried that Byron will only be the first of many our town will lose. We fear it's going to be an ugly thing, for our town, our country."

He paused, took a deep breath, exhaled, then said, "We wish we could bring him home and have him with us out in the Ririe-Shelton cemetery, but indications are they are going to leave the Arizona where she is."

Joe choked up, and it was obvious that this additional element of the tragedy had also deeply impacted Nell. Not only had she lost her son, but also his body would remain submerged in a watery grave thousands of miles from home. There was an awkward silence as each reflected on that burdensome fact.

Papa broke the silence, "Nell, Joe, even though we also lost a son, our little Merlin, I doubt that I could ever fathom your agony in losing Byron, a grown son, especially to a war. But after we lost our boy, I found great comfort in a little scene described in a biography of Abraham Lincoln. He was losing his little son, Willie. He was dying from a lingering illness. Lincoln could not sleep through Willie's last days, so he spent the nights at Willie's bedside with a nurse who was tending him.

"She told him she was a widow and that her husband and two children were in heaven. She added that she saw the hand of God in it all and that she had never loved Him before as she had since her losses. 'How was that brought about?' Lincoln asked. 'Simply by trusting in God and feeling that He does all things well,' she replied."

Papa continued, "Lincoln thanked her gently and said, 'I will try to go to God with my sorrow. I think I can trust Him, and I will try.' After the funeral service, a pastor from New York approached Lincoln and took him aside. He firmly said to President Lincoln, 'Your son is alive.' 'Alive!' exclaimed Lincoln. 'Sir, you mock me!' 'No,' said the pastor, 'Do not seek your son among the dead. He is not there! He lives today with God! This is God's most precious truth! Doubt it not!'

"I feel that way myself," Papa continued. "I feel that immortality is God's most precious truth and that God really does do all things well, despite all the heartache we sometimes have to endure."

Joe and Nell, especially Nell, found a measure of peace in the thought even when later her youngest child, a son, was also taken into the armed services and his life was put in the same jeopardy as Byron's.

———————————————

Where before she could, Lael was no longer able to go to the movies with us. The images on the screen could not penetrate into her new world. She could no longer go to church because she would get up and wander aimlessly about, oblivious to what was going on. Occasionally, when someone was not carefully watching her, she would slip out of the house and wander the town. Though mainly she sat for long hours at the window and wrote her name, over and over. Someone old enough to control her had to stay home with her at all times.

Some of us did go to the movies and were treated to the reality of the vicious attack on Pearl Harbor as we watched the Movietone News play over and over the carnage some brave cameramen had captured on film. Worst of all, we saw the heartbreaking sinking of the Arizona, and each of us re-lived Byron's torturous end. We saw the ammunition magazine ignite from a bomb and explode, heaving the ship upward several feet where, at the apex of its ascent, its hull cracked like an egg. Then we watched in slow motion as the hull closed back together and the ship settled down under the water. We hoped that Joe and Nell never did see that ugly scene.

A touching memorial service was held for Byron. The church was filled to overflowing, a fine tribute to Joe and Nell and their family, as Ririe's first victim of World War II was laid to rest vicariously.

Author's note: While writing this book I visited the Arizona Memorial at Pearl Harbor. I gazed solemnly down at the outline of the great ship lying several feet beneath the water, thinking of Byron. I went into the inner sanctum and read the scroll of the dead. Byron is listed as "B. Mason". I wondered, why couldn't they have listed his full name? B. Mason could be anybody. Byron Mason was a special native son of our town and its first victim of World War II.

The United States Congress declared war against Japan on December 8, 1941, (Congresswoman Jeannette Rankin from neighboring Montana being the only one voting against the declaration). Germany and Italy declared war against the U.S. and vice versa on December 11. Christmas and New Year's came and went. The celebrations were subdued. America was preparing for war. Some people in Ririe still had some adjustments to make!

School was in recess in the summer of 1942. I was playing marbles on the earthen walkway by Mary's hotel. Suddenly my friends and I smelled smoke. We looked up to see it billowing out of an upstairs window of the hotel. Within minutes several men were racing up the stairs with buckets and a hose attached to an outdoor faucet to battle the blaze.

Mama came up beside me. She had her big shopping bag with some quart milk jars to be returned to Brown's Grocery. She asked one of the men standing around how it happened. He didn't know. She asked if Mary was okay. He said she was in the café getting dishes and things ready to haul out if the fire was not controlled.

Mama started for the café. Behind her a drifter who stood gawking at the fire let out a bellowing, "Let the damned Jap place burn!"

Mama turned in fury and swung her shopping bag right into his face. I heard bottles breaking. He staggered backwards, cupping both hands over his nose and screaming that it was broken. It was bleeding profusely. That was inconsequential compared to the rebuke issuing from Mama's mouth.

"You mean and miserable, lousy slob. Mary is more American than you! How dare you speak such garbage! If you weren't so stupid you oughta be up there risking your life to save her hotel. Now get out of here before I hit you again!" He ducked his head, pressed a dirty hankie to his nose, and hastily departed.

I was impressed. Mama was usually quite reserved and pleasant. Only once before had I seen such fury, and that was the time with Papa over Lael. Her anger quickly turned to concern for Mary, and she rushed into the café to help her. In only a matter of minutes the volunteers had subdued the fire. They reported it had only burned a long drape hanging by the window and scorched the wall a little. A replacement drape and a little scrubbing and paint on the wall would remove all traces of the fire, just as Mama's shopping bag had removed all traces of the drifter.

Chapter 20

War – and the Sheriff's Visit

THE SNEAK ATTACK on Pearl Harbor galvanized America into one common state of mind—"Victory at all costs." The Depression was over. People had gone back to work. Factories all over the country began to churn out the destructive tools of war. Gasoline, rubber, sugar, meats, butter, fats, oils, shoes, canned foods, farm machinery, and other items were rationed. To stave off inflation Congress gave President Roosevelt the power to freeze prices, salaries, and wages at their levels on September 15, 1942, and not too much later rents were frozen. War slogans such as "A slip of the lip may sink a ship" sprang up. "Uncle Sam Wants You!" signs with a picture of Uncle Sam pointing a finger directly at passersby appeared all over Idaho.

The cost of the war would soar. The United States would sell E-Bonds and other instruments of debt in excess of 150 billion dollars to finance it. The U.S. government spent less than nine billion dollars in 1939. It would spend over 100 billion in 1945, more than a tenfold increase! In southeast Idaho, and probably throughout the country, speed limits were drastically reduced. In our area the maximum speed was reduced to thirty-five miles per hour. The restrictions were implemented to save on gasoline and tires.

The radio and Movietone News began spouting strange sounding names: Bougainville, Tarawa, Corregidor, Okinawa, Guam, the Marshall Islands, Kwajalein, Guadalcanal, and Iwo Jima from the Pacific. From the east came names like North Africa, Stalingrad, Warsaw, Luxembourg, Sicily, Tabruk, Normandy, and many more. These places were mere dots on the world map, but they became household names as each day we listened intently to the news.

A bright spot occurred when, just over four months after the Pearl Harbor attack, on April 18, 1942, the United States gave Japan a surprising jolt. A squadron of sixteen B-25 bombers led by one of the early heroes of the war, Lt. Colonel James E. Doolittle, took off from the carrier Hornet about 650 miles east of Honshu, Japan. The bombers dropped payloads on Tokyo and other cities and then headed toward friendly territory in China and even Siberia. Most of the planes had to ditch because they ran out of fuel, but the underground fighters for China helped save Doolittle and sixty-three of his men. Two pilots were captured by the Japanese and executed, but the unmistakable message had been sent. The sleeping giant (America) had awakened.

News of this raid created great excitement in Ririe. It was announced over the radio, in the schools, and made headlines in all the local newspapers. In my class at school when the raid was announced, a monstrous cheer went up. You would have thought we had just won the war. It was a psychological lift to America and must have had a depressing effect upon Japan when it realized its cities and citizens were not immune from attack.

The decade of the forties also produced a significantly different weather pattern for southeastern Idaho. Many claimed it resulted from all the explosions going on around the globe. Whatever it was, that decade was one of the wettest on record for Antelope Flats. In the thirties the Flats fared little better than the dust bowls of Oklahoma and Nebraska. The increased rains in the forties produced bumper crops on the Flats. With prices reasonably high, the local farmers' financial conditions improved considerably. Their one frustration was that despite their mounting savings, they could not buy farm equipment and other necessities due to short supply caused by war production.

Papa's acreage now handily provided a decent living and some savings for the eventual purchase of equipment when it became available. Most importantly, however, these good times assured the means to see that every one of his children, except Lael, obtained a bachelor's degree at a university. The two sons went on to doctorates in sociology and law.

Less than ten percent of my class went on to college. Papa, however, was literally obsessed with the challenge of sending his children to college. He started little savings accounts for us at the bank. He added to them when he could. He insisted that we deposit our earnings from baby-sitting, picking potatoes, other farm work for neighbors, and from selling garden produce, in those accounts. They yielded less than two percent interest, but built up to respectable amounts over the years. Those accounts were top priority, ahead, even, of buying a refrigerator, installing a bath and toilet, and other luxuries. Papa was rigid in his determination. If his children's college educations could be secured by his and Mama's labor or sacrifice, they would be given every chance to achieve the potential he had sensed lay within them since he first met them in that hotel room.

Lael, however, became the family's great concern of the forties. Her fateful transformation made prophetic Papa's observation about Danny Rosenthal and the lost newborn calf at the Eddie Rogers' ranch. It was becoming impossible to keep track of Lael all the time. She would sometimes slip out of the house when no one was watching. The village mothers took care of her like they did Danny, but a beautiful but retarded girl going on eighteen wandering the streets caused intense concern among the villagers and, of course, the family.

One evening when Helen was coming from the dance hall with two of her friends, she spotted Lael alone on Main Street. A car with three men in it had just pulled up beside her. They were trying to talk Lael into getting into the car when Helen and her friends intervened and quickly brought Lael home.

It was a summer afternoon in 1942. Mama, working in the kitchen, heard steps cross the front porch and then a loud knock on the front door. From the sound of the boots on the wood flooring of the porch, she knew who it was. Anxiety gripped her. Although the visitor would be kind and friendly, she feared his visit would be like a call from the grim reaper. Sheriff Judkins was a large, imposing man with a deep bass voice that could shake the rafters when he wanted to speak to the wayward with the full authority of his office. But it could be soft, low, and consoling when other duties of his office required it.

There was a lull in the farm work, so Papa was also at home. Lael was sitting at her window writing her name and occasionally staring outside. Mama answered the door.

"Good afternoon, Sheriff, what brings you here along?"

His voice low, he asked, "Is John home? I wondered if I could speak with the two of you for a moment?"

The tightening in Mama's stomach intensified.

"Yes, he's right here in the living room. Please come in."

Papa was sitting in an easy chair opposite Lael. He was staring at his daughter's silhouette in the frame of the window with a worried frown on his face. When he heard the sheriff's voice asking to come in, he, too, felt a sickening dread come over him. The moment of truth he had feared was creeping in on him like a sickly vapor. He got up, shook hands with the sheriff, and asked him to take a seat on the living room couch. The sheriff, seeing Lael, asked if they could meet in the kitchen. They obliged, leaving Lael at her post, seemingly oblivious to the visit.

The water in Ririe always tasted cool and fresh. Mama offered the sheriff a large glass. She set a glass in front of Papa and poured one for herself. A cool glass of water, anything to put her hands on, to hold onto, she desperately needed. They sat at the kitchen table, the sheriff on one of the two-seat stools, which fit him quite well, with Papa and Mama occupying a similar stool on the other side. Sheriff Judkins laid his hat on an adjacent stool and cleared his throat.

"Things are starting to stir here in the village like they did before Danny went to Nampa. People are concerned about Lael. She has changed drastically in the last little while. Occasionally she gets out and about and doesn't know how to get home. She's hard to communicate with, and she can even be difficult to persuade to come home. The whole village knows about that car with the three strangers who were trying to get Lael to get in with them.

"I feel it's my duty to bring these things to your attention. I'm sure you know this and probably a lot more." He hesitated, took a sip of water, and then continued.

"As hard as it is for me to say this, it's getting to a point where something should be done for Lael's protection and welfare. You have lived with her all her life and been absolutely exemplary in your care for her, I know, but since she has worsened in the last few months, I have to suggest that you consider placing her in an institution like Danny."

The blow had landed. Mama's heart sank. Her mind wandered back over the years, Lael's very normal birth, her dignified and queenly grace, her start at school with Miss Haltern and how bright her future looked then. She remembered the fall from the swing, the eyecrossing, the episode at Mary's hotel. She remembered Mrs. LaBelle's visit, confirming their fears that Lael was slipping behind. She remembered the snowball incident and many more. In many respects, as a mother, she had suffered Lael's developing retardation as keenly as had Lael.

Somewhere, way off in a corner of her mind, she knew this day would come, especially after that bitter night last December. The fact had been suppressed, repressed, hidden, seldom allowed to penetrate her thoughts. But now it was here in all its bitter truth.

"I know you have our best interests at heart, and Lael's. But it's so dreadful, so awful, I don't know how to even answer you. To think of my lovely, sweet Lael being ripped out of our family, away from those she loves and who love her—it's heartbreaking. It's terrifying!"

Papa was desperately trying to control his emotions but with limited success. His voice was almost a whisper. "Do you think she could go to Nampa, like Danny? She can't go to Blackfoot. It would destroy her! You have known her all her life. You don't think she belongs in the insane asylum, do you?"

"I know she went through the eighth grade and learned to read and write, which is much more than Danny did. So she could very well be a candidate for the Nampa School, which is more for the handicapped than the insane. They might even be able to bring her out of her lost world and teach her some basic skills so she could do limited work and keep herself occupied. I suggest you try Nampa first."

"We'll have to talk it over. It will be the toughest decision we've ever faced. If we do decide to do something, how do we go about it? Do we just write to them and ask them to take her? How did the Rosenthals do it with Danny?"

The sheriff looked at Zelma across the table. He could see agony, a deep forlorn agony, spreading across her beautiful face. She was middle aged but slim and youthful looking. His duty hung heavily upon him as he looked at her. He noticed how her shoulders slumped in resignation and despair. Could this be a mother's worst nightmare, worse even than the death of a child? He looked back at John. There was a pained hollowness behind the eyes, the very depths of sorrow.

He swallowed, then took another sip of water, pausing momentarily to regain his composure. "Do you know the prosecuting attorney for Jefferson County, Bill Hemminger?" Papa nodded.

"One of his duties is to handle cases like Danny's. First, he'll have to see if he can get the Nampa School and Colony to accept Lael. They have certain requirements for admission that are mandated by state law. When you talk to him about Lael, he will ask you for a whole bunch of information about her, her history, her schooling, and her mental condition. He will provide this to the superintendent at Nampa.

"Once he gets word from Nampa that they will accept her, he will have to file a petition with the probate court asking that the court declare Lael so mentally handicapped that she needs to be placed in an institution. There will have to be a hearing before the court and enough evidence produced to satisfy the judge that Lael should be institutionalized."

"Who will have to be there? Will this be a public hearing?" Papa inquired.

"No, no, it doesn't have to be a public hearing, but I am sure a doctor will have to testify or provide an affidavit to the effect that Lael and the family are no longer capable of caring for her needs. One of you will also have to confirm to the judge that you feel it is in Lael's best interests to be sent to Nampa."

The sheriff could see that the reality and the complexity of this were beginning to wear on John. He decided to leave the matter there, saying, "Think it over and talk it over."

He looked at Mama. "I know it's hard. The whole village wishes it could ease your pain. They went through it with Danny and know how it is affecting you and your family. But you have to consider your other children and your own personal welfare. Lael is getting to be too much to handle. Your energy will be sapped. Your nerves will be worn thin. In fact, I think that process is already underway."

Although his words seemed to be falling on deaf ears, they sank deeply into Papa and Mama's souls. They had been losing a daughter by inches over the years, but since December, it had been by yards, by leaps and bounds. The whole seventeen-and-a-half-year process of raising Lael was closing in on them, beating up on them, literally eating away at their sanity, their faith, their hopes, their aspirations for their children.

The sheriff determined it was time to leave. The heavy burden of his duty had not been lifted by his visit. He bid John and Zelma good-bye, took his hat from off the adjacent stool, and walked back through the living room and out the front door.

Lael still sat unmoving, staring out the window, with her pencil and spiral notebook lying in her lap.

Chapter 21

The Preliminaries

I WAS ELEVEN at the time of the sheriff's visit. I was too young to appreciate all that was going on, but I did notice the concerned faces of my parents. I saw gray starting to appear in Papa's sideburns and little streaks forming in Mama's hair. I saw furrows develop in Mama's forehead and crow's feet at the sides of her eyes. Under those eyes, dark circles were now common.

There were many hushed conversations. There were many more telephone calls than usual, though with a five-party line it was a tedious procedure to get the line free. With the harvest underway on the Flats it was not until late in September that Papa could get away to do the one thing pressing on his mind.

———————————————

Bill Hemminger's office in Rigby, the county seat, was piled high with books and files. John could hardly see his desk for the clutter. It was obvious that he was an extremely busy man. As John looked at all the files and books, his apprehensions about the task before him heightened immeasurably. Would this busy man have adequate time and energy to handle what for John was the most sensitive and delicate issue that could ever come before the law—the institutionalization of a human being, his daughter?

Those fears were quickly allayed. Mr. Hemminger greeted him warmly and asked John to sit down in one of the comfortable client chairs. The attorney made the setting more comfortable by coming out from behind his desk and taking the client chair opposite John. They sat knee-to-knee and face-to-face.

"John, I suppose you know that Sheriff Judkins has already told me that you might be coming in to talk about your daughter."

"This is the hardest thing I've ever had to do!" John said. "It's devastating to my wife and family. I'm beginning to understand now what the Rosenthals went through with Danny."

"Yes, I see these cases quite regularly. It's the toughest part of my duties. We have retarded children all over the county. Some are hopeless cases. Yet some are salvageable."

"What do you mean by salvageable?"

"I mean that in some cases there is good that comes from it. It brings relief to the family knowing that their child will be under constant supervision and care by professionals. It might help you and Zelma to know that Danny Rosenthal is now taking a medication that has controlled his illness. He's learned to cut hair and is a barber at the Nampa School and Colony."

John was amazed. "I'll report that to my wife. That could give her the grit she needs to let Lael go. Perhaps with the right care and medication, they can bring Lael back from wherever she's gone and give her some semblance of a happy and productive life."

"Let's hope so," was Bill's positive response.

"The most important part of all of this is that it would be absolutely unbearable for the family, especially Zelma, if Lael had to go to Blackfoot. Is there any way you can be sure she goes to Nampa, or if not, that we can stop the proceedings and take care of her ourselves?"

"You can always stop the proceedings, with one exception. That would be if someone else, for example the sheriff or a member of the community, were to seek her institutionalization. In that case, it would have to proceed, and you would have to fight it. But I can't imagine anyone would do that against your and Zelma's wishes."

"We have exhausted ourselves talking and worrying about it. We have decided to proceed with the understanding that you will do everything possible to get Lael into Nampa. She went to school, learned to read and write, progressed reasonably well for the first grade or two, but then slowly deteriorated. She did graduate from the eighth grade at age sixteen."

John further explained the sudden change in Lael, but told him that even though she seemed farther out of reach than ever before, she could still read and write and even do some decent coloring with crayons.

"Those are facts that should help get Lael into Nampa," Bill assured him.

John felt considerable relief as the conversation proceeded. He asked what the next step would be. Bill produced two printed forms and told John these should be carefully and truthfully filled out, signed by the proper persons, notarized, and then brought back to him.

"When I get these forms back from you I'll send them to the superintendent at the Nampa School and Colony. He will evaluate the information and advise me whether Lael meets the requirements to be placed in Nampa. If so we'll start the formal proceedings before the probate court."

John asked about those proceedings and was reassured that they would be closed to the public and proceed basically as they had been outlined by the sheriff.

John asked about costs for the proceedings.

"The family will have to pay the costs of the physician, but the county will stand all other costs, including Lael's transportation by the sheriff to Nampa. But," he cautioned, "you'll have to file an affidavit about your finances. Under certain circumstances the judge might order that the family pay a certain portion of Lael's care. That is a determination he must make during the commitment proceedings."

"We'll do what we're required to do," John responded, but then asked, "You said the sheriff will transport her to Nampa? Why is that? Can't we take her?"

"No. Once she is committed, she becomes a ward of the state and falls under the sheriff's jurisdiction to deliver her to where she is committed."

"That will be one more nail in the coffin to see her hauled off like that. But with gasoline shortages, we might not be able to take her to Nampa anyway. That's almost three hundred miles away," John said.

Bill was silent. He saw in John's solemn face what he had seen in many cases before: the hesitancy, the wish to escape, the concern and the worry for his own flesh and blood, the further demeaning of his daughter. John stood, thanking Bill for his time and kind help.

With heavy hearts, leaden minds and limbs, my parents reviewed the documents.

Mama muttered, "It looks like most of these will have to be filled out by Uncle Walter since he has all the information about Lael's medical and mental history. The only part we can answer is the page about our family history."

With a sigh, she added, "I'll have to make an appointment with him."

"Yes, go ahead, but don't talk about why we need the appointment or someone on the line will hear it and spread it all over. I want to keep all our options about Lael wide open."

Mama called. The receptionist put her right through to Dr. West. The usual pleasantries were avoided as Zelma quickly but quietly said, "I need to talk to you about Lael." That brief comment and the tone of her voice told him all he needed to know.

"I've got to come to Ririe tomorrow. I'll be there at your house at ten in the morning, and I'll bring plenty of time."

Mama was sure he was not scheduled to come to Ririe, but wild horses could not keep him from coming.

Her voice broke as she whispered into the phone, "Thank you, Uncle Walter. I need you more than you will ever know," and she hung up.

With a worried frown and deep in thought, Dr. West slowly set the phone in its cradle.

He called out to his receptionist, "Cancel everything tomorrow until at least three o'clock in the afternoon. If there are any emergencies, make arrangements for them to go to the Marsh Clinic. I'm sure they'll help out. Tell them I've had an emergency come up."

When Dr. West arrived the next morning, Mama met him on the front porch and embraced him warmly. "What could I ever do without you?" She looked him straight in the eye. "I know you are not scheduled for Ririe today, but I knew you would come at the drop of a hat. I can't tell you how comforting that is to us."

"Lael needs special care, doesn't she? I figured that out the minute I heard your voice yesterday. But let's face up to it and try to work out something that will help Lael find some happiness and your family some comfort, if that's possible."

Mama led him into the living room. Lael was sitting at the window writing furiously in her spiral notebook. She looked up at Dr. West without recognition. She turned back to her notebook. Dr. West glanced over at it and saw a page full of the word "Lael." She went to the next page and continued her furious writing. He went with Mama into the kitchen.

Papa had been outside tending to the cattle, but on seeing Dr. West's Cadillac drive up, he quickly came into the house, went to the bathroom to wash his hands and face, then came into the kitchen. He shook Dr. West's hand and thanked him for coming. They sat down at the kitchen table on the customary stools. Papa told him of the visit from the sheriff, his visit with Mr. Hemminger, and the need for a doctor's affidavit. He produced the documents Mr. Hemminger had given him.

Dr. West looked at John and Zelma as they sat across from him. He could tell they had been through much agony and soul-searching since the sheriff's visit. But he also detected a certain resolve. They had been through the depths of indecision, frustration, and despair but had emerged ready to see this through. That was good, he mused. It would take all the resolve they could muster.

Dr. West filled in the forms in his own handwriting. The "Personal History of Applicant" section asked, among other things, for Lael's weight, 110 lbs.; her height, although hard to read, appears to be 5'6"; color of eyes, blue; color of hair, dark brown; does she destroy articles or clothing? no; her attitude toward parents, affectionate; physical deformities or imperfections? no; normal use of limbs? yes.

Under the "Measurement of Intelligence" section, does applicant talk? yes; is memory good or poor? fair; feed self? yes; dress and undress? yes; sleep well? fair; attentive to call of nature? yes; started school, age six; what progress? read and write simple things; stop going to school? age sixteen; in what grade? eight; can applicant read? yes; write? yes; count? yes; add? no; multiply? no; divide? no; understand form (square, round, short, long)? yes; recognize and name colors? yes; realize the difference between right and wrong? yes; play musical instrument or sing? sings.

Other interesting or significant questions on the application were ages of parents at applicant's birth, father, 30, mother, 27; has applicant other siblings and are they normal mentally and physically? yes; were parents or grandparents related by blood? no; was either parent subject to overtax of mind or body before conception of applicant? no; was the mother, during this pregnancy, subjected to continuous anxiety, hardship, or exposed to any shock, accident, or especially painful emotion? no; was applicant's condition congenital or result of accident or acute sickness? influenza at two years, very sick at this time (but no mention of the fall from the swing); was the child born full term? yes; was labor ordinary or difficult? ordinary; were instruments used? no; was there deficient animation at birth? no; was the child nourished by mother or artificially fed? nourished by mother; any peculiarities in early nutrition? no; was applicant sickly or strong as a baby? strong; at what age was feeble-mindedness first manifested in applicant? at six years, unable to learn at school (but she did learn in those first few grades to read, write, etc.); is applicant's condition improving or growing worse? growing worse; is applicant epileptic? no; is there imperfection of speech? no; of movement? no; general health of applicant, good; classification as to type of mental deficiency, moron, imbecile, idiot, answer: moron, 10-12 year mentality; in event of death, what disposition of remains? parents notified and body sent home for burial.

Dr. West signed both documents, verifying that he had known Lael all her life and was well enough informed to provide the answers indicated. They arranged for a notary public to acknowledge Dr. West's signature on the forms, but she was not informed what the documents contained. The acknowledgment is dated September 23, 1942.

With that process completed, Mama exclaimed, "Uncle Walter, you're not going to get away this time without having a nice dinner (meaning lunch in those days). So why don't you men go in the living room and talk while I prepare it. You might also try to engage Lael in some conversation." She busied herself with the lunch while Papa and Dr. West went into the living room.

Dr. West pulled up the piano seat and sat by Lael. He took her hand and patted it, looked into her face, and smiled. This beautiful girl whom he had treated for the usual childhood diseases and watched grow into a lovely young lady had become a vacant shell with eyes that crossed.

"Lael, do you remember me?" No answer, only a blank stare with those eyes that seemed to look everywhere but nowhere.

He tried again, "Lael, would you like a Pepsi Cola from Mary Jap's restaurant?" There appeared a slight indication of interest, but it evaporated quickly.

"Lael, are you happy?" No answer.

"Lael, do you love little baby Ruth?" She muttered a soft "yes" under her breath. He was getting somewhere.

"Do you like the milk cows?"

A subdued, "Yes".

"Do you like to drink their milk?"

"Yes."

"Do you like to gather the eggs from the chicken coop?"

A more animated, "Yes."

"What are you writing in your notepad?" She lifted it to show him— "Lael, Lael, Lael" in childlike but very readable script.

He asked, "Who is Lael?" She looked a bit puzzled, then answered by pointing to herself. With gentle prodding this went on for some time, but though she raised somewhat to his baiting questions, she soon lapsed back into her vacuum.

Dr. West looked at Papa. He was staring at Lael and then muttered more to himself than to Dr. West, "She was the fairest of them all."

"Yes, she's been a beautiful girl and still is. I know we ordered a couple of electric shock treatments back a few months ago. The report did not indicate any favorable result. Have you noticed any difference since then?"

"No, not really, and I would never put her through that again. She was absolutely terrified, and for a while she was totally inconsolable. But we got through it." Then with a certain firmness, he continued, "We see no alternative but to try to get her to Nampa where they might be able to bring her back to her former self with medication and therapy. Bill Hemminger told me that Danny Rosenthal has been taking medication and has learned to cut hair in the school's barbershop."

Dr. West was amazed. He knew Danny's condition before he went to Nampa. "That should give you some hope, John. I know it's tough, but in the end some good might come of it." Mama came to the door and said that dinner was ready.

They ate a light, refreshing meal of split pea and ham soup, with crackers and cold whole milk from the refrigerator. Lael ate with them silently. She took small bites, absentmindedly chewing them for some time before she swallowed. Little touches of saliva and chewed food would spill occasionally from one corner of her mouth. She usually took care of it with a napkin as the need arose. When she forgot or did not notice, Mama gently reached over and touched up the spot.

Dr. West thanked Mama for the lunch, saying that split pea and ham soup was one of his favorites. He was trying to bring a touch of pleasantness to the situation, but gloom brooded over them all. It was hard to say or do anything that even momentarily lifted the spirits of his beloved niece and her husband, let alone lift Lael.

Mama went to the back porch and brought a bag of freshly picked corn from her garden and ordered Dr. West to take it. He protested but knew it would make her feel better if he did. He laid the bag down on the kitchen table and drew her into his arms and gave her a long, tender embrace.

She looked up into his face and with an emotion-checked voice whispered, "Are we doing the right thing? Is there no other way? Nampa is so far away! We won't even be able to get enough gasoline to visit her and remind her that she has family."

He looked down into his niece's tormented face, wishing that he could somehow make that face happy again. But that would take time and healing.

"Yes, dear Zelma. It's the right thing to do. You must let your mind find peace. You have to consider how it will tax you and John and your children to keep Lael here at home. As Lael gets older it will become increasingly difficult for all of you. She will require constant care and supervision. She could even become easy prey for hoodlums. Those are hard things to say, but they are realities.

"Most importantly, you have to consider Lael. What is best for her? Can Nampa, with medication and modern psychology, help her more than your family? Think of Danny Rosenthal. He is living a productive life. This must be a blessing for him. You should hope that the same might be done with Lael. That would be a great blessing to her."

His words were soft and wise. They helped my parents take that ugly fork in the road they were now facing. They strengthened the resolve to go forward with the application.

Papa picked up the bag of corn to carry it to the car for Dr. West. Dr. West strode over to Lael and took her in his big arms in a tender embrace. He put his lips to her forehead and gave her a soft, lingering kiss. He felt for her.

Surely she had suffered the most of all. Tears welled up in his eyes.

She put her arms around him and gave him a light but meaningful squeeze; then, detecting a slight shudder go through his body as emotion overwhelmed him, she looked up into his face with a puzzled look and gave him a soft smile. Then she turned, picked up her notebook and pencil from off the couch where she had laid them, and went back to her chair at the window.

Watching this little drama overwhelmed Papa. Tears crept into his eyes and dripped down his face as he and Mama followed Dr. West to his car. It was a very nice car, he noticed, but somehow that didn't matter. It was a thing, only a thing! It was of such little significance compared to a world of tender emotions and deep feelings. He carefully put the corn on the backseat, straightened up, wiped his eyes with the sleeves of his shirt, and took Dr. West's hand.

"Thank you for all you've done for us. You have been an anchor in a turbulent sea of distress."

Dr. West thanked him, nodded tenderly to Zelma, looked back through the window where Lael sat with a vacant stare, then climbed into his car and drove away.

Chapter 22

The State School and Colony Responds

THE CAR SHUDDERED as it crossed the tracks on the eastern outskirts of Rigby. Papa was startled back to reality. He had been so deep in thought during the trip he didn't realize that he had arrived at the city. The admission papers for Lael lay on the car seat beside him in a large brown paper grocery sack. It was October 16, 1942.

He was ushered immediately into Mr. Hemminger's office.

"I've been thinking a lot about you and Zelma, John. These things are never easy. I want to lend any support I can to ease your concerns."

Papa thanked him and reluctantly handed him the paper bag.

"The wife and I have hardly slept; we've lost our appetites and have worried ourselves sick over this thing. But it's become clear that we don't have any real alternative but to try to get Lael into Nampa. Zelma will never let her go to Blackfoot. Please see if we've filled the papers out properly. Then tell me what else we should do."

Mr. Hemminger studied the papers for some time, carefully scrutinized the notary acknowledgment and seal, looked up over his bifocals, and said,

"They appear to be in order. I'll send them off to Nampa today along with a cover letter asking for a prompt decision on whether Lael will qualify to go there."

"Is there anything more we can do to help see that she makes it into Nampa?"

"No, I can't think of anything else. We'll have to be patient and see what they decide. The actual decision may be more subjective than objective, so it may come down to the superintendent's personal choice. But Lael, having completed the eighth grade and being able to read and write, makes me seriously doubt that he would ever recommend that she go to Blackfoot instead of Nampa. I hope waiting it out won't be too burdensome for you and Zelma."

To help shore up Mr. Hemminger's own convictions, Papa repeated much of the history of Lael's early childhood, the swing accident, her seeming normalcy in the first couple of grades in school. He told of the snowball incident and the school principal's help to enlist a group of "friends" for Lael who helped her through the last grades. Mr. Hemminger was impressed.

"We've had several incidents of bullying going on in some of the schools around the county. I wonder if that approach might help the underdogs in those situations. I think I'll suggest that to some of the school principals."

He paused momentarily, looked out the window and then back at Papa with a positive smile. "Lael sounds like a perfect fit for Nampa. I really think we'll succeed."

Papa thanked him for his kind help, stood up, looked apprehensively one last time at the application papers, then turned and with leaden tread left Hemminger's office.

Hemminger immediately invited his secretary to bring her pencil and notepad so he could dictate a letter to the superintendent at the Nampa School and Colony.

October 16, 1942
Dr. Chas. R. Lowe, Medical Superintendent
State School and Colony
Nampa, Idaho

Dear Sir:

I am enclosing application and medical statement in connection with the admission of Lael B. Moss to the State School and Colony, Nampa, Idaho. Advise whether you will make further investigation and if so about how long it will take, as these people would like to have this girl committed as soon as possible. Let me know whether the patient properly classifies and when you will have room to accommodate her so that I can have the commitment made.

Wm. P. Hemminger

The response to Mr. Hemminger's letter was not long in coming.

October 19, 1942

Wm. P. Hemminger
Prosecuting Attorney
Rigby, Idaho

Dear Sir:

We have your application for admission of Lael B. Moss, seventeen-year-old girl, to this institution. Same will be placed on file. It appears from the information contained in this application, if it is correct, that she doesn't belong here. She is said to have begun school at the age of six years and, at 16 years, had reached the eighth grade. That is almost a grade a year. It is my contention that anyone that is capable of doing eighth grade work should not be classed as feeble-minded, according to the gradings used.

No reason is given why they wish to send her here. We have considerable trouble, at this institution, at this time, preventing people of very much lower mentality than she appears to have, from being taken out of here. We think for no other reason than that someone thinks they can get valuable service from them at this time when laborers seem to be at a premium.

Only a few days ago a sheriff of one of the counties threatened to begin court proceedings to get three or four members of the same family out of the institution, including a mother and two sons, and according to the records here, there isn't any of them that have a mental age of over six years and the mother cannot read or write. I realize this has no real connection with your prospective patient; however, I mention it to show you the sort of demands that are made upon us.

I cannot tell you, at this time, just when we will be able to accept this girl even if she did properly classify here. We have accepted a number from other counties, which have not yet been delivered and should they change their mind and fail to deliver them, it might give us an opportunity to accept some others in another locality.

Dr. Chas. R. Lowe

As soon as he received the letter, Mr. Hemminger dutifully called Papa. Realizing it was a party line, he was brief and circumspect: "John, I need to see you the next time you are in Rigby. Please call and let me know when you can make it so I'll be here."

"I'll be coming for parts for a machine in the next couple of days and will drop by then," Papa responded.

Both of them recognized that with gasoline shortages and rationing, combining the trip with other purposes was the only thing to do.

Pressing work on the farm made for a nerve-wracking three days before Papa could get away. He kissed Mama lightly on the cheek, as he got ready to leave and told her he would find out what was going on.

"John, if they say she has to go to Blackfoot, tell them we'll keep her and make do. Her tender heart could never survive there!"

He mumbled a troubled "OK" and went to the car.

He picked up the machine parts he needed but was so nervous the parts manager asked if he was feeling all right. Papa had been buying parts there for years and was usually upbeat and had a few humorous stories to tell. Today was markedly different.

"Yes, I'm OK," Papa said, but his eyes and demeanor belied the fact. He had no other response and without any form of good-bye, walked out carrying the parts, which seemed to weigh him down.

He put the parts in the car and left it unlocked. He knew no one would disturb it. He hurried to Hemminger's office a half block away. Hemminger produced Dr. Lowe's letter and let Papa read it line by line. Papa was surprised. He lifted his eyes from the page.

"Dr. Lowe apparently doesn't realize what happened to Lael in December last year, nor does he likely know that the principal at the school just kept her moving through those last few classes despite her inability to learn."

"Probably not. He only has the application and medical statement to go by. Lael's going through the eighth grade probably threw him a bit of a curve."

"What do we need to do to straighten things out? Here we were worried about her going to Blackfoot. Now maybe we can't even get her into Nampa!"

Hemminger rubbed his forehead with his right hand, looking out his window for some time, deep in thought.

"I think we need to have Dr. West explain the situation in more detail so the superintendent will understand her complete history. Given that, he should be able to accept her under the 'gradings' as he calls them. Do you think you could get Dr. West to write a letter clarifying things for Dr. Lowe?"

"We'll see what we can do. How soon do we have to respond to Dr. Lowe's letter?"

"He says he's not certain that he could take her even at this time, so I doubt that it's a matter of great urgency. I think you are the ones to decide how fast to move this along."

Papa looked down and seemed to be counting as he placed the tips of his fingers against each other. "With Thanksgiving and Christmas right around the corner, we might save a lot of heartache if we wait till after the first of the year. Do you think Dr. Lowe will be offended or take it out on us if we put it off till then?"

"I doubt he would care one way or the other. He seems to have so much going on that a little respite from this decision might be doing him a favor."

Papa sat for some time staring down at his hands and then quietly said, "I'll talk it over with Zelma and get her to talk to Dr. West, then let you know."

Enroute to his car, two thoughts dominated Papa's mind: The timing of the reply to Dr. Lowe and when to confront the family and Fanny about committing (a hard word) Lael to an institution. Procrastination can be a blessing at times. With Thanksgiving and Christmas coming, a delay would give them a little respite; an interlude to help prepare them all for this hard step.

Mama met him at the door with an anxious look. He quickly reported the contents of Dr. Lowe's letter and Mr. Hemminger's willingness to delay the response until after the first of the year. Mama welcomed the news. She, too, had been worried about taking Lael out of the home before these particular family holidays and had a hidden hope that begged for time while they came and went.

They decided to wait to tell the children until the commitment to Nampa was secured. They knew, however, that they would have to bring Grandma Fanny into their confidence long before that and the sooner the better. She was "ailing" as she called it. Her sleeplessness was becoming worse, and she needed more help during the nights. She had turned eighty-seven years old in April of that year. Her limbs had been giving her a rough time for many years, but her mind was keen and sharp. She would be a "fierce force" to tangle with if they did not tell her what was happening.

While the kids, except Ruth and Lael, were in school, they decided to talk it over with her one afternoon in early November. They took Ruth and Lael with them. Neither would be able to understand what they were discussing anyway.

Fanny was mildly surprised. Most visits were one on one these days, and Lael was seldom brought over anymore. She was glad to see them. She loved her son, and she loved her daughter-in-law. Baby Ruth was always welcome with her bright cheery smile and intensely curious nature. And Fanny had always harbored a special love for Lael.

Fanny was briefed on what had transpired in the last few weeks, starting with Sheriff Judkins' visit up through the last letter from Dr. Lowe. She listened intently.

"John, I've thought about this so many times and have probably asked you about it a bunch, too. When you first saw Lael before she was born, did you see anythin' at all in her that would have given you some clue to what was gonna happen to this beautiful child, like you saw with Merlin?"

"Not a thing. She stood there looking wholesome and healthy. Naturally, I couldn't look into her head, but her eyes and smile were bright."

"It appears best that you do what Mr. Hemminger suggests and get Dr. West to write an honest opinion that will help persuade that persnickety Dr. Lowe to take her. He should be told everythin' so he can make the right decision."

They told Fanny about delaying until after Christmas and not telling the children until a commitment to Nampa was firmed up. She agreed.

She looked over at Lael. She had seated herself by Fanny's small front window and was looking out beyond the grass now turning brown in the front yard, beyond the stump where in 1927 she, Merlin, and Joel were photographed, out beyond the street and across the vacant lot between the pool halls. She seemed oblivious to it all.

Fanny wondered, Is her mind vacant? Are no thoughts going through it? If there are, what are they? Are they total confusion? Are they ugly or happy images? She could come to no answer. She stared at Lael's beautiful hair, the light from the window highlighting its slightly auburn cast. She was a young, tall being weighing a slender 110 pounds, seemingly absent the light of intelligence that normally graces the body and personality.

Tears started down Fanny's cheeks. She wanted to let her emotions burst out of her in an agonizing gush, but in deference to Lael she held them back lest she upset her and her parents.

As they left, they all gave Fanny a hug, including Lael, who muttered a quiet, "Bye bye, Grandma Fanny." Mama took Ruth's hand. She clutched it tightly, wanting to find in her youngest daughter some security in the gloom swirling about her.

Chapter 23

The Proceedings

MAMA CALLED UNCLE WATER and made an appointment to see him in mid-December. They met at his office and discussed the letter from Dr. Lowe. She explained that the family wanted to wait until after Christmas, but asked if he could please help them to get Lael into Nampa by giving Dr. Lowe a better understanding of her condition.

"It sounds like Dr. Lowe has the impression that Lael is only subnormal and not truly mentally defective. The graduation from the eighth grade seems to stick in his craw. Yes, I'll write a letter after the first of the year and try to help him understand the situation a little better. To whom am I supposed to address the letter, Mr. Hemminger or Dr. Lowe?"

Papa replied, "Mr. Hemminger thought it best that you address it to him, and he'll send it to Dr. Lowe."

For Christmas the family got a nice surprise, a gift from Santa of a medium-sized suitcase. It was dark blue, made out of a "canvasy" type of cloth, and had a shiny black leather handle on it.

Helen asked, "Why would Santa give us a suitcase?"

Mama replied, "Well, as you kids get bigger and older, you'll be going off to college, and you'll need a suitcase to take your clothing and other things. I think Santa just wants to get us prepared for the time to come."

Lael got new panties, socks, a new pair of shoes, a new dress, a new hair-brush, and other sundries. She even got a new toothbrush. Equally intriguing, she got a couple of packages of gum, which were becoming scarce with the shortage of sugar. She also got a new spiral notebook and two pencils. The other children, caught up in their own gifts, didn't seem to notice. Grandma Fanny did.

Dr. West sent his letter to Mr. Hemminger, who called Papa to tell him he thought it should do the job.

January 5, 1943
Mr. William P. Hemminger
Rigby, Idaho

The letter of Superintendent Charles R Lowe of Nampa, Idaho, concerning the condition of Lael B. Moss of Ririe, Idaho, has been called to my attention.

In this letter Superintendent Lowe mentions as a fact that this girl had received and passed the eighth grade examinations. This is entirely a misunderstanding on his part and should be called to his attention. This girl was allowed to pass from grade to grade but not because she finished the work or was capable of doing the work. The teachers early in her schooling found she was mentally unable to grasp and comprehend her studies and therefore only because of her physical growth she was allowed to progress in school.

I am positive this girl does not approach beyond a second grade education and mentality. I think she is definitely feeble-minded and should be committed to the institution.

Dr. Walter West

Mr. Hemminger sent Dr. West's letter to Superintendent Lowe on January 6, 1943, with a cover letter:

Dr. Charles R. Lowe, Medical Superintendent
State School and Colony
Nampa, Idaho

Dear Sir:

I am enclosing a letter from Dr. Walter R. West who made the medical statement in connection with the admission of Lael B. Moss to the State School and Colony at Nampa, Idaho. His letter seems to explain some of the questions raised in your letter to me under date of October 19, 1942 and after you consider the matter further I would like to be advised as to whether this girl can be admitted to the institution so that I can have a commitment made.

Wm. P. Hemminger

Superintendent Lowe was surprisingly prompt in his response to Mr. Hemminger's and Dr. West's letters.

January 8, 1943
Mr. Wm. P. Hemminger
Prosecuting Attorney
Rigby, Idaho

Dear Sir:

In reply to yours of January 6th in which you write, again, concerning Lael B. Moss will say we now have two statements concerning this girl's progress in school. Just which one is right we are unable to state. It always seems to me to be a rather sad commentary on our school system to state that they will do such things as is stated in this case; namely, that a student is promoted from grade to grade when they know very well they cannot do the work and haven't done it. However, that is a very common statement made to us and it may be a true one.

We have not had very good luck with the patients we have gotten from Ririe. Most of them seem to belong in an insane hospital rather than here; however, things have change [sic] a bit since we last wrote you and we think we have room to take this girl at the present time, so, will take another chance and see what we get.

If you will have this girl taken before your Probate Judge and committed to the institution, then send her, together with an Order of Commitment, to the institution, we will accept her.

Dr. Chas. P. Lowe

Hemminger arranged with the probate judge for a hearing of commitment on January 28, 1943. Despite the inconvenience of the telephone party line he was able, without leaking any notice to the community, to have Dr. West, Lael, and my parents at the hearing. Lael was required to attend since she was the one whose liberties would be restricted.

It was a cold, ugly morning. The temperature would hover around zero for most of the day and had sunk lower the night before. Starting the car was a chore. The starter growled as Papa shoved it down. He worried that he was going to run the battery down, but at long last it coughed and sputtered, belching a bunch of half-burned fuel out of the exhaust before it finally began to purr. Mama and Lael huddled beside Papa in the front seat, trying to keep warm till the car's heater warmed up. I stood looking at them leaving, wondering what was happening. They told me later.

Mama reflected on that bitter October day in 1927 when they had rushed Merlin to the hospital in Idaho Falls. That had been a typical Indian summer day in Idaho, and even though it lent no cheer to the tragedy with Merlin, at least it did not add insult like this cold and ugly day was doing to Lael's leaving the family.

George M. Larsen, the probate judge, had a commanding presence. When all were seated in the stately courtroom, he made a solemn entrance in his flowing robes as all rose in respect as ordered by the clerk. He sat down in his large upholstered chair on the elevated podium, gently placed a file folder in front of him, opened it with some flair, and began reading the contents. As he read he occasionally looked at the group in the courtroom. He knew them all except Lael, so he narrowed his vision to her. She was modestly dressed in what appeared to be a brand new garment. She was an attractive young lady in her late teens, but there was a distraction about her eyes. They were obviously not focused, which gave her a furtive or mysterious look. In fact, as she raised her head once to peer at him, he got the odd impression that she was looking past his right ear at something behind him. The stare was hauntingly vacant, hollow; no recognition of any object behind him seemed to dawn in her face. He looked at Mama. Her suffering face told all.

He ordered the clerk to shut and lock the door. He wanted no intrusions. He solemnly stated, "For the record, this hearing is in the matter of Lael B. Moss, a resident of Jefferson County, Idaho, for commitment to the Idaho State School and Colony at Nampa, Idaho. Mr. Hemminger, are you ready to proceed?"

"I am, your honor."

"Since this is a matter involving a restriction of liberties of a resident of the county, should there be a special guardian appointed to represent this young lady?"

"I see no need and can find nothing in the law to require the same where the parents, who are the natural guardians, are here to represent her interests."

Judge Larsen asked, "John, do you accept the responsibility to act in the best interests of this girl as her parent and natural guardian?"

"Yes, I will," was his subdued answer.

"Very well," declared the judge. "We will proceed."

Papa was put on the witness stand, sworn to tell the truth, and in answer to Mr. Hemminger's questions, he testified about Lael's history, including the "transformation" of December 7, 1941. The judge had no questions.

Dr. West then took the witness chair and clarified the record pertaining to Lael's "graduating" from the eighth grade. He also clarified the seeming discrepancy between the application and his letter of January 5. The judge asked a few questions to be sure that Dr. West, in his medical opinion, felt that the best interests of Lael would be served by confinement to the Idaho State School and Colony at Nampa. Dr. West emphatically endorsed the proposal. In his opinion Lael needed twenty-four-hour-a-day supervision and care, but hopefully, with psychological counseling and medication, she might be brought back at least to her pre-December 7 status, where her life and her self-esteem might improve. The judge was satisfied.

He asked Mr. Hemminger if he had prepared a draft order of commitment. Hemminger nodded and asked the judge if he could approach the bench to deliver the proposed order to him. Hemminger laid the draft on the judge's desk and returned to his seat. The judge studied the document for several minutes. He raised his head to look at Dr. West.

"Everything appears to be in order, but I will have to have you sign the Physicians' Certificate, which confirms what you have testified to and what you have observed here today." He handed the document to the clerk and motioned for him to take it to Dr. West. "Please read it over carefully, Dr. West, to be sure you agree with its contents."

PHYSICIANS' CERTIFICATE

W. H. West and _____, *being duly sworn, each for himself, deposes and says that he is a legally qualified physician; that at the request and in the presence of Hon. George M. Larsen, Judge of the Probate Court of Jefferson County, he has heard the testimony of the witnesses and personally examined the said Lael B. Moss in reference to the charges of being feeble-minded, and finds that said person is feeble-minded. This is not a case of INSANITY, SENILE DEMENTIA, ACUTE OR CHRONIC MANIA OR MANIA A*

POTU, and is not a proper subject for a county poor farm or hospital. The further facts appertaining to said case, as nearly as can be ascertained, are set forth in the questions and answers in form now on file in the office of the Medical Superintendent of the Idaho State School and Colony under the titles "Application for Admission," "Measure of Intelligence," "Personal," "Family, and "Etiological History."

Walter R. West, M.D.

The judge questioned Papa about his finances and filled in the Financial Statement pertaining to his assets. It showed eight thousand dollars in assets and four thousand dollars in debts. Upon reviewing it, the judge firmly stated, "I find no basis for burdening the family with any of this girl's care. They have other children's needs to attend to. The State of Idaho will assume that charge."

The judge signed the statement verifying its content and solemnly affixed the seal of the court over his signature. Then, looking again into Mama's troubled face and Papa's dejected one, he said, "I am ready to sign the order of commitment. Does anyone have anything to say before I do so?"

Mama started up, as if coming up out of a deep stupor. Papa tenderly put his hand on her arm. She settled back with a look of tormented resignation. She felt in that moment as she had felt as Merlin died in her arms that long ago day. With the stroke of a pen the judge was now severing Lael from the family, relegating her to an unknown, perhaps unfriendly, realm.

ORDER OF COMMITMENT

Lael B. Moss being brought before me, George M. Larsen, Judge of the Probate Court, Jefferson County, State of Idaho for examination on the charge of being feeble-minded, and I, having heard the testimony of John W. Moss and _____, witnesses best acquainted with the accused during the time of the alleged feeble-mindedness, and doctors _____, W. R. West_____ and _____, graduates of medicine, after having heard the testimony of witnesses, and after personal examination of the accused in open court, having made the certificate by law required, and being myself satisfied that the said Lael B. Moss is feeble-minded and not insane and is one whose mental defects render her a menace to society, prevents her from receiving proper training in the public schools and taking proper care of herself, and after satisfactory proof as to the truth of all set forth in the certificate of said physicians, I do hereby make the order that the said Lael B. Moss be confined in the Idaho State School and Colony, at Nampa, Idaho, and the Sheriff of Jefferson County is hereby ordered to deliver the said Lael B. Moss to an attendant of said Idaho State School and Colony, and take proper receipt for said feeble-minded person.

Dated January 28, 1943.   George M. Larsen, Probate Judge

The judge handed the order to his clerk and told him to make the requisite copies and certify them so that the sheriff and the superintendent would have certified true copies upon which to act. He then stood and came down from the bench, shook hands with Dr. West, and thanked him for appearing before him. Next he went to my parents and Lael.

"I can see that this is very tough on you. I wish I could ease your pain. She's a lovely girl and is just entering the prime of her life. I doubt I could even anticipate what you're going through and what she has had to go through. I wish you well and God's comfort."

He turned to Mr. Hemminger and softly said, "While the family is here, you might stop by the sheriff's office and arrange with him when to take Lael to Nampa." Mr. Hemminger nodded in agreement.

The judge then turned and looked at Lael. She had no comprehension of what was happening to her. Yet she was modest and reasonably dignified, he thought. He patted her tenderly on her right shoulder and then with head bowed and a troubled frown, he walked back through the door to his office.

———————————————

Sheriff Judkins was in his office at the courthouse. He stood and shook hands, smiling a wan smile in greeting. He knew what had been going on. He looked at Lael. She was there only in body. The rest of her was elsewhere.

Mr. Hemminger said, "I wanted to be sure you were in so I could go get two certified copies of the order of commitment from the clerk to give you so you will have one and can give one to the superintendent in Nampa. Please excuse me while I do that. In the meantime perhaps you could make arrangements with John and Zelma as to when you will be able to take Lael to Nampa."

The sheriff sat on the edge of his desk and studied his calendar. He looked up. "With my schedule, the only time I really have right now is tomorrow. The day is clear enough that I could leave early in the morning. Would that be too soon?"

Papa looked inquiringly at Mama because she would have to make most of the urgent preparations for Lael to leave. She sat in a puzzled stupor for a moment.

"If not tomorrow, when could you?"

The sheriff looked again at his calendar. "Probably not for at least a week."

"It's probably best for the other children and Fanny that it happens sooner than later. What time would you like to leave, sheriff?"

It's a long way, about 300 miles. It would be good to leave early. I could pick her up at eight in the morning if you will have her ready."

Zelma looked at Lael, then back at John, then at the sheriff, and in a soft, almost inaudible voice said, "We'll have Lael and her belongings ready by eight. It'll be a miserable night, but doing it this quickly may save us many more miserable ones."

She took Lael's hand and began to stroke it, bowing her head as she fought back the tears that began to brim in her eyes.

The sheriff looked at her sympathetically. "OK, I'll call the superintendent right now and ask him if the school will be prepared to receive Lael when we arrive late tomorrow afternoon."

He placed the call himself through the long distance operator who, after about a five-minute wait, confirmed that she had the superintendent on the line. The arrangement was approved. The sheriff hung up the phone and confirmed that they could go forward with the plans for tomorrow, January 29, 1943.

Mama asked, "How will you take her, by car or train or what?"

"I'll take her by car."

"Should one or both of us go with you?" The sheriff saw a troubled look come over Zelma's face.

He responded in a quiet, soothing voice, "I would recommend against either one of you going with me. You would only be prolonging the misery you've already suffered. I strongly suggest that you all make your farewell to Lael at home where the whole family and Fanny can be there."

Turning to Mama, he said, "I'll take my wife with me so she can be a companion for Lael and help her at the stops we'll have to make during the drive." Mama nodded in relieved acquiescence and resignation.

Chapter 24

The Departure

MAMA SAT DOWN HEAVILY on Lael's bed. She pulled out a sheet that had accompanied the Application for Admission. It was hard to concentrate on the document. So many things were pressing in on her—the depressing hearing before Judge Larsen she had attended that morning, the children, the community, Fanny—all had to be told. But she also had to pack. Her eyes scanned a paragraph of the document.

The patient should have in his (her) possession when received the following articles of clothing:
FEMALES: 1 good dress, 3 work or wash dresses, 1 white dress, 3 sleeve aprons, 3 underskirts, 3 underwaists, 3 suits underwear, 3 pairs drawers, 3 nightgowns, 4 pairs hose, 4 handkerchiefs, 1 pair heavy shoes, 1 pair light shoes, 1 pair leather slippers, 1 comb, 1 hairbrush, 1 toothbrush, 1 hat, 1 coat or sweater, hairpins or ribbon.
Patients of untidy habits should be provided with a larger quantity of washable clothing.

The last sentence did not apply to Lael. Despite her handicap she was tidy.

Mama reached under Lael's bed and pulled out the new suitcase. She opened it and looked into its depths. She was staring into a black hole, not a suitcase. Her daughter and her meagerly earthly belongings would be climbing into it, and then the lid would be slammed shut and locked!

Papa finished his chores outside and came into Lael's bedroom. He laid his arm around his wife's shoulders as she was bending over the bed carefully placing items into the suitcase. He hesitated, wondering if he should disturb her with an added concern.

"I've been thinking a lot about Dr. Lowe's comments in his letters. He sounds quite annoyed that Lael is coming to Nampa. I worry that when he actually sees Lael he might try to force her into Blackfoot. It has just dawned on me that he would now have the authority to do that because Lael is his ward. We might have nothing to say about it."

This comment landed like a heavy thud in Mama's heart. "Do you really think he might do such a thing?" she pleaded.

"I don't know. I just worry that he might. I thought that I might send him a letter explaining the situation a little more for him. None of the papers and letters really tell about that terrible Sunday and how much less handicapped she was before."

Mama's shoulders sagged: another worry, another potential dilemma to face. She hadn't thought of that possibility. With a face haggard from sleeplessness, worry, and emotion, she looked up at her husband. His concern was real, intense! This new possibility robbed her of her energy.

"Blackfoot houses the criminally insane, the psychopaths, and others with the most severe insanities. Lael could never survive there! Yes, write a letter! Tell him about that horrible night and also about her gradual decline before then, about how delightful she has been over the years, despite her handicap. Before her change, she could do housework, write, read, paint, sing, help with the animals and chores. She could have been reasonably productive and self-reliant if that awful night had never happened!"

"Yes, by golly, Dr. Lowe needs to know that! We'll make him understand that Lael needs help and that help should come from his school!" He left to finish his chores.

Fanny brought little Ruthie home, knowing that she would want to be there to greet her brother and sisters returning from school. She opened the back door without knocking and wandered through the house until she found Mama. Mama took Ruthie in her arms and laid her head carefully on her shoulder. She looked up at Fanny with red and swollen eyes. She would have preferred to wait to tell Fanny about Lael leaving until the next morning and had firmly resolved not to tell the children so they could get some rest that night. But Fanny had to know, despite the fact that she would toss and turn and fidget the night away.

Mama sent Ruth from the room, telling her to stand on the porch and watch for the kids. Lael was at her post at the living room window. Mama then told Fanny about the order of commitment and that the sheriff and his wife would come at eight in the morning to pick up Lael.

"So durned soon?" Fanny gasped.

"It's the only time the sheriff can go unless he waits and goes a week later. He suggested the sooner the better, and we agreed rather than put you, us, and the children through another week of misery!" The words came spilling out in a burst of agony and emotion.

Fanny replied, "Yup, it's the right thing. We'll just havta get on with it. Can I help you with anythin' so you can be ready?"

"No, I have it all packed. I'll close the suitcase and put it under the bed so the kids won't notice. Please don't say anything to them. Otherwise we'll have a night of crying and howling. We'll get them up early in the morning, have our prayers, eat a nice breakfast, then about 7:30 sit down and explain it to them. Would you like to be there?"

"You're doggone rights. It's tearin' my heart out, but I gotta be there to tell Lael good-bye. Maybe I can help a little with the kids, too."

"Yes, that would be good. They'll need all the consolation we can give them."

Papa, Mama, and Grandma Fanny hardly slept that night. As it usually does, the dark intensified the dread and gloom. The haunting question, "Are we doing the right thing for Lael, for the children, for us?" hung over them like an evil vapor, mocking them. If Lael were ever to be brought back to where she was before, would she have a better chance in the family atmosphere, where those she knew and loved would be there to support her and cheer every slight improvement? Yet how could the family, without training, without medication, without any knowledge of what had happened inside Lael's head, ever be able to help her? And perhaps staying here might drive her deeper into the ugly pit she was already in. These, and others, were the stinging, torturous thoughts that heightened their anxieties and kept them from sleep.

Mama woke us at 6:30. She said she was getting everyone up a little earlier today because the family had something important to discuss. We were instructed to wash our faces, comb our hair, get dressed for school, and be in the kitchen for breakfast at seven.

Promptly at seven Papa came in from doing chores, and, to my surprise, Grandma Fanny came through the door with him. Her eighty-seven years seemed to weigh heavily in her face. Dark circles and big bags hung below her eyes. She looked uneasy, solemn. Then Lael appeared from her bedroom. She was dressed differently from other days. She had on a new dress, clean anklets, and nice clean shoes. Her dark hair was brushed out and looked neat and pretty. Her face was scrubbed clean, but traces of toothpaste where she had brushed her teeth were evident. We began to sense that something was different, eerily so.

Papa instructed us to kneel down around the kitchen table, except for Grandma Fanny, in deference to her "old bones," who sat quietly in one of the chairs. Papa led the prayer. It included phrases like "please protect Lael," "please give her comfort and peace of mind," "please bless us to help Lael in any way we can." Then there was a pause, followed by, "Please help us to understand these things." The pleading in his voice as well as the words filled me with anxiety. What was menacing our family? The prayer concluded, and we took our customary places at the table. There was a marked quietude. Even the clatter of the spoons against the oatmeal bowls was subdued.

The dishes were promptly cleaned up and stacked in the sink. Then Papa asked us to go into the living room and sit down. Lael took her seat over by the window, looking out into the beyond. With anxious faces we turned to Papa, then to Mama, and then back to Papa. He cleared his throat, coughed, started to speak, and then stopped because nothing would escape his lips. He swallowed twice and started over.

"Lael will be leaving our family today. She'll be going to a special school in Nampa, which is way over on the other side of the state by Boise. It's the school where Danny Rosenthal went. She can't learn in the schools you are going to now. She has to have special help. Mrs. Judkins and the sheriff will be here at eight o'clock to pick up Lael and take her there. She won't be able to come back and visit us. We might be able to visit her there from time to time, especially after the war when gasoline shortages ease up."

"How come the sheriff and his wife are taking her, Papa?" Helen asked.

"When a child goes to that special school at Nampa she becomes a 'ward,' or 'patient,' of the state and has to be taken to the school by someone authorized to act for the state. In this case, that's the sheriff."

"If we can't go see her, can we write and send her things?" asked Rhea.

"Yes, I'm sure we'll be able to do that."

"Well, I'm glad," responded Rhea, "because I know she'll want some candy and apples and gum and stuff."

Mama responded, "Yes, she will, and we should all do that for her. She will love receiving those things and know that she is still a special part of our family."

Grandma Fanny put her arms around Rhea and Ruth, realizing that they did not fully comprehend all that was going on. She could find no words to help them understand, but her loving arms conveyed a message more consoling than words.

My head was swimming. Lael, a special part of our family all my life, would be gone. She would leave an emptiness that could not be filled. We heard the sheriff's car pull up in the crunchy snow out front.

Mama grabbed Lael's coat and hurriedly put it on her and then pulled her own sweater tightly around herself. The rest of us grabbed our coats or sweaters and walked out onto the porch in the bitter cold January air. I felt a chill beyond the chill in the air. I worried about Lael. She knew us. She didn't know "them," whoever they were, where she was going. Would she suffer more than ever before?

From the porch I looked to the east. It was not yet light. The sun was still below the horizon. My gaze was attracted to a long, white, even luminous blanket of fog that was gently lifting off the twists and turns of the Snake River from the east of town up past Heise, past the Hogsback, and farther east along the north side of the Flats. The river was yielding a bit of its warmer water to the bitter, cold air above it.

The sheriff and Mrs. Lottie Judkins simultaneously climbed from the car. Mrs. Judkins was a tall, gracious lady with slightly graying hair. She came directly to Mama and took both her hands in hers.

"Zelma, I'll take good care of her and see that she is assigned a room and given something to eat and feels comfortable before we leave to come back." Mama thanked her.

The sheriff took the suitcase from Papa and put it on the passenger seat. Lael and Lottie would be sitting in the backseat together.

The sheriff said, "I might as well bring this nice suitcase back for you to use because Lael won't need it there."

Papa nodded. They shook hands, the sheriff indicating by his businesslike manner that it would be best to get underway. We each took a turn giving Lael a farewell hug, quietly, quickly. We were all crying. Grandma Fanny was trying unsuccessfully to staunch the flow of tears and drizzle that escaped her eyes and nose with a special hankie she had remembered to bring just for that purpose.

Lottie climbed into the backseat and moved to the other side. Mama hugged Lael warmly, tightly. Then, as Lottie reached for Lael's hand, Mama helped Lael inside the car to the backseat behind the front passenger seat. The sheriff shut the door. Then he quietly reached with his key and turned the lock in the door, a gesture none of us missed. That act also triggered something in Lael.

As the sheriff disappeared around the back of the car to go to his driver's seat, Lael peered out through the window and with a bewildered, even desperate, look at Mama, and with a voice we could not hear, mouthed the word "Maaamaaa" as tears began to splash down her cheeks. Lottie quickly put both arms tightly around Lael, pulled her head down onto her chest, and the car drove off.

Lael was eighteen years and eighty days old. We all stood there empty. We waved but no one saw it.

It was so cold Grandma Fanny ushered us kids inside, but Papa and Mama stayed looking after the departing car. I went to Lael's window and looked out at them. Mama had put her left arm around Papa's back. He had his right arm over her shoulder and had drawn her close to him. I saw sparkles coming from Mama's cheeks. The bitter cold was freezing her tears into ice crystals! She tried to brush the crystals aside with her free hand. Papa was looking toward the car; the muscles of his jaws were flexing and relaxing, flexing and relaxing. His lips screwed themselves up into a narrow white line across the lower part of his face. They watched until the sheriff's car turned right onto the main highway three blocks away. They both waved a silent good-bye and turned toward the house, their faces haggard and downcast.

I looked toward the east where the long, white bank of fog along the Snake continued to grow and lift into the brightening morning sky.

Chapter 25

The Torturous Torment Continues

THE DAY AFTER LAEL ARRIVED at the school the records show that Dr. Lowe personally conducted a thorough physical examination. Some of his observations: "Hair is abundant, color dark brown; teeth are fairly clean, one decayed, a number filled; on auscultation (listening with a stethoscope) the breathing sounds are increased but no rales are heard; on auscultation the sounds are heard; there are no murmurs but they have a peculiar sound. The first sound appears to be about the same intensity as the second. Hearing is good, she states. At times there is a suggestion that she might be hearing voices by her actions; entertains herself a great deal of the time by looking in the mirror; she doesn't cooperate very well."

Meanwhile, Papa had worked on the letter to Dr. Lowe. He had hoped he could send it with the sheriff, but he needed time to think it through and draft after draft just would not come right. Lowe's words, "We'll see what we get," pounded like hammer blows in his brain. Lowe would get Lael in her post December 7 state, not the lovely but retarded teenage girl she was before. That's what he would *get*! Papa finally mailed the letter on February 1, 1943.

That letter has disappeared from the records, but Dr. Lowe's response was caustic and unnerving.

February 3, 1943

John W. Moss

Ririe, Idaho

Dear Mr. Moss:

In reply to yours of February 1st, in which you write concerning Lael B. Moss, will say, I wonder why you didn't place this information on the application that you filled out when you made an attempt to have her admitted to this institution. It was my opinion, from the information you did give, that the girl should not be sent here.

I am not prepared, at this time to say whether she has always been feeble-minded, but I feel quite certain that, at the present time, she is mentally sick and is suffering from a psychosis which is in addition to whatever feeble-mindedness she may have had. She doesn't cooperate very well and I'm sure she hears voices. She talks and laughs to herself, spends a great deal of time scribbling on a piece of paper although she doesn't write anything intelligible. She will frequently scream for no apparent reason. She doesn't eat very well; however, she is reported to be doing a little better in that respect. Even the other patients can understand that she is different from what they are.

I feel that it was a mistake that she should be sent to this institution as we are not prepared to take care of the insane. Whether she improves or not I still feel that she could have been cared for much better in a hospital that is supposed to be equipped to care for such patients and, in addition to that she would not disturb the whole ward as she does here. I don't know what the future may show but it is very possible that she may develop, with the frank mental reactions that she has, so we would be unable to care for her at all here. She certainly can do nothing in school, at this time. In fact, she doesn't cooperate in any way, so far as doing any work is concerned.

Very truly yours,

Medical Superintendent

Mama and papa were visibly upset after reading Lowe's letter. His tone was antagonistic. How could he, with such an attitude, help Lael? Having barley weathered the agony of her departure, now they faced yet another dilemma.

The hope that the Nampa School could bring Lael back from insanity to feeble-mindedness was fading. It was agony for my parents and Grandma Fanny. Papa felt that Dr. Lowe did not really understand Lael or her history. He resolved to meet personally with Dr. Lowe and encourage him, even challenge him, to help Lael come back from wherever she had gone.

Papa's resolve was fortified by a constant return in his thoughts to the Grand Hotel in 1920. Lael not only looked normal, with no crossing of the eyes or anything else unnatural about her, but was the personification of beauty and dignity in that premortal glance. Didn't he have a duty to be sure that EVERYTHING was done to try to restore this lovely young girl's sanity? And if such a miracle were to be wrought, then wasn't the state school the place to start? The thought was a constant nag. In the nighttime and during quiet moments, it would spring into his consciousness to plague him.

Mama had sensed his uneasiness from early February through the spring work, but in early June 1943, as the spring work on the farm was coming to an end, Papa came to a decision. One evening he asked Mama to go with him to see Grandma Fanny.

Fanny did not look good. The bitter cold winter, Lael's departure, and Fanny's many years had been pressing in upon her. But her mind was still bright and alert. She welcomed the visit. She welcomed all visits because she was not able to get out and about much anymore.

"Wa'al what's on your chest, son?"

"I've been thinking about Lael. I can't get her out of my mind. Am I," he caught himself, "Are we doing everything for that girl that we should be doing? You both know about Dr. Lowe's letters and the hopelessness they convey. I'm worried that Lael is being stuck off in some closet somewhere and isn't being given any kind of help."

Mama looked fondly at her husband. To him, family was a solemn, God-given duty, something from which he could never escape, no matter how heavy the burden. She felt blessed to have such a husband.

Mama asked, "What more can we do? I want to do everything humanly possible, too, but I'm at my wits' end."

Fanny sensed that her son already had something in mind. "I know you bin doin' a lotta thinkin' durin' the last four or so months, and what has all that thinkin' produced?"

"Dr. Lowe has never seen any of us. He probably thinks we are white trash from a little podunk place called Ririe who have tried to foist their insane daughter off on him. Maybe he needs to get acquainted with us so he will better understand our concerns and our hopes for Lael."

"How d' ya aim to do that?"

"I think I should go to Nampa and have a talk with Dr. Lowe. Besides, it would give me a chance to see Lael again and let her know that we love her and miss her."

"How d' ya aim to do that? With rationin', you couldn't get enough gas ta take you the seventy mile or so down ta Pocatello, let alone clear over ta Nampa. My lands that's 250 to 300 mile if it's one!"

"I'll hitchhike and take Reed with me. Having a twelve-year-old boy along would help us get rides, and with gas rationing, those that can get gas are a little more inclined to give a man a lift nowadays. That would save the cost of taking the train or a bus."

"Waal, I'll be durned. You mean you would hitchhike with Reed clear across southern Idaho? That trip could take you three or four days. Where would you stay?"

"I figure if we leave early in the morning, we could probably get to Boise the first day and stay in a cheap hotel; then the next day we would hitch a ride on over to Nampa and see Dr. Lowe and Lael. Then we would hitchhike back toward Ririe as far as we could on that same day, and maybe even make it all the way."

Mama saw the wisdom in having a young boy along on the hitchhike. It ought to ease the minds of those thinking about giving them a ride.

Grandma Fanny looked into her son's face. He meant what he was saying. He had to do this. Perhaps it would give him a sense of relief, of duty done, no matter how things turned out. She looked at her daughter-in-law. Dawning in her eyes was a certainty that this was the right thing to do. It would help to bring peace to John's mind, and this visit, within five months of Lael's departure, would help maintain a connection between the family and Lael.

Fanny said simply, "It's the right thing. Do it, and give that girl all the hugs and kisses you can muster from all of us back here at home."

"OK. Reed will finish school this week, so we'll get up early next Tuesday morning and get outta here!" He said it with a semblance of a smile. "If I have to I'll literally beg Dr. Lowe to keep Lael at that school and give her all the help he can!"

Papa hated the telephone. He didn't like talking to someone he couldn't see, and especially someone he didn't know. But he timidly picked up the receiver on Friday morning of the week the decision to go to Nampa was made. It was not a dial phone. They didn't have those then. He waited at least sixty seconds before the operator came on line, but it seemed like an hour. The fact that he would be calling clear across the state to Nampa, the attendant cost, and the need to make an appointment with the testy Dr. Lowe made the long wait agonizing.

Finally the operator clicked on. "May I help you?"

It startled Papa at first, but he quickly cleared his throat and in the most masculine bass voice he could muster, said, "Yes, I would like to speak to Dr. Lowe or his secretary at the Nampa State School and Colony in Nampa."

"Do you have the number?"

"No, I don't even know how to get the number. Can you get it for me?"

She laughed, "Why of course. But it will take me a minute or two to get it and then connect you. Do you mind waiting?"

Papa was so impressed with her kindly attitude, he began to think that perhaps the telephone was not such a bad gadget after all. He responded, "Yes, I'll wait, and thank you for helping me out."

She answered with a friendly, "You're welcome," and left the line for another minute or so while she dialed information and got the number, then connected with Dr. Lowe's secretary. She came back on the line. "I have the superintendent's secretary on the line. Please go ahead."

Papa said, "Hello?"

A lady answered with a voice that seemed as close as the next room, "This is Dr. Allen's secretary. How may I help you?"

The name "Dr. Allen" threw Papa off guard. He asked, "Isn't Dr. Lowe there anymore?"

"No," was the friendly response. "He was replaced by Dr. C. Sanford Allen on March 22 of this year."

Papa was perplexed. He asked if she would wait just a moment. She said she would. He put his hand over the mouthpiece and turned to Mama, who was straining to hear as much as she could.

"Dr. Lowe isn't there anymore. A Dr. Allen has taken his place. Should we still go?"

Mama's response was instantaneous, "More than ever now! Dr. Allen will surely know less about Lael than Dr. Lowe. This will give you an opportunity to explain everything, get acquainted, and have contact with him while Lael is there."

Papa agreed. He spoke into the receiver, "Yes, this is John Moss from Ririe. I was wondering if Dr. Allen would be in next Wednesday. I'd like to visit with him there in Nampa at the school if possible."

"Oh, you must be Lael's father. She is the only Moss we have here."

"Yes, that's me."

"Wait just a moment and I'll ask Dr. Allen. Do you know about what time you'll be here?"

"I can't gauge it for sure, but I hope I could be there by ten in the morning. I'm not sure we can be there right on time, so could you ask Dr. Allen if he could allow me a leeway of about an hour, say sometime between ten and eleven?"

"Yes, I'll do that. Please stay on the line and I'll be right back."

Papa waited another interminable sixty seconds or so until her pleasant voice came back on the line. "Yes, Mr. Moss, Dr. Allen will expect you sometime between ten and eleven next Wednesday morning."

"Thank you," Papa said with a grateful voice, then added, "Would we be able to see Lael while we're there?"

"I'm sure that will be no problem. I'll alert the supervisor of her ward so she can have her ready for your visit. How long do you anticipate talking to Dr. Allen?"

"I think for at least a half hour or even a bit longer if that'll be all right with him."

"With your coming this long way, I'll see to it that Dr. Allen reserves plenty of time for you, and we'll make arrangements for you to see Lael also."

"Come to think of it, I'm bringing my twelve-year-old son with me. Perhaps he could visit with Lael while I talk to Dr. Allen. Would it be possible to arrange that?"

Her response was most pleasant. "I'll see that those arrangements are made."

"You've been very kind to me. Thank you so much."

"You're very welcome, Mr. Moss. We'll see you and your son next Wednesday then, and I'll have those arrangements made to see Lael."

Papa hung up the telephone with a big sigh, almost a shudder of relief. Things were working out all right, thanks in great part to the kindness of the operator and Dr. Allen's secretary.

Chapter 26

The Big Hitchhike
Across Southern Idaho

THAT TUESDAY MORNING Papa came downstairs to my bedroom with a loud clatter on the stairs, sort of a pre-awakening stomp. As he leaned over to wake me, I opened my eyes and asked him what time it was. He said it was 5:30, and we had to hurry so we could get out onto the highway. He had already discussed the hitchhiking trip with me. To think that I would be seeing most of southern Idaho, fifty times more of the state than I had previously seen, made me eager for the trip and quickly dispelled all sleepiness.

I dressed in what I thought was some good looking casual and comfortable attire. When I came upstairs Mama took one look at me and took me back downstairs to find a nicer looking pair of tan slacks and a nicely cleaned and pressed light green, short-sleeve shirt that matched. She wanted me to look good for the hitchhiking and the visit with Dr. Allen and Lael. I looked in the mirror, realized that I looked pretty sharp, and appreciated her good taste. Papa had dressed up in a suit and tie and had his "go to meeting" hat lying on the chair by the door. He intended to make a good impression as well.

After a hasty breakfast Mama ushered us out the door. On the front porch she kissed Papa tenderly on the cheek and told him, "I know you're doing the right thing. I'll be praying for you when you visit Dr. Allen. He has just got to understand that Lael can't go to Blackfoot. Tell Lael that we miss her and love her. Tell her that we are taking good care of the cows and chickens and the dog. She'll want to know that if she can still understand."

She turned to me. "There is some gum, a coloring book, and some peanuts in a little bag in Papa's valise. Be sure to give those to Lael."

Papa looked at her with fondness. "I know how you have suffered through all this. We'll do the best we can to help Dr. Allen understand about Lael."

She turned again to me. "You're a good hitchhiker. Make sure you teach your Papa how to do it so you two can get over to Boise by tonight. And have a nice visit with Lael. Give her a big hug from all of us, and tell her about home, about her family, about the animals, about Ririe. Help her to know that she still has family."

Proud to be a part of the goings on, I answered, "I sure will, Mama. I'm glad I get to see Lael again. I'm excited."

It was just a minute or two after 6:30, but the sun was already rising over Antelope Flats to the east. The weather was warm, the wind calm. No sooner had we entered the highway going to Idaho Falls than a truck from the Ririe Kraft cheese factory stopped for us. We knew the driver, Kim Carlson. He was delivering a load of cheese to the main Kraft factory in Idaho Falls and was glad to give us a lift. For me it could not have gotten any better! He had a medium sized paper sack about half full of brand new, white cheese curds, still warm from the night crew batch. I sat next to him. Papa sat by the window.

Kim put the sack on my lap with a big smile. "Reed, when your Pop and I ain't reaching for a curd, you can take a turn. I know you like fresh curds, 'cause I see you all the time comin' into the cheese factory after school and askin' for curds to 'take to Grandma Fanny!' But I betcha there ain't half those curds gets to her after you carryin' them the two and a half blocks to her lean-to." He laughed.

I laughed, too. "That's hard to have those fresh curds right under your nose and keep out of them."

He chuckled again. "We all know what's goin' on at the cheese factory. Grandma Fanny is one of the better excuses we hear from you kids a wantin' curds. Some of them excuses get so outlandish we can't help but burst out laughin', 'cause we know whose belly they's a gonna wind up in."

Kraft fed free curds to about every kid in Ririe, and there were a lot of grown-ups that got in on them, too. Papa was an avid curd eater, so he enjoyed the half-hour drive to Idaho Falls as much as I did.

The Kraft factory was located on the south side of Idaho Falls, another fortunate beginning to our big hitchhike. All we had to do was get out of Kim's truck and walk 100 yards down to the main highway toward Pocatello. We hadn't walked ten minutes before a big shiny red Cadillac stopped for us.

Papa pointed to the license plate. "This could be our lucky day. That license plate says IA on it, and that means Ada County, where Boise is. He might take us all the way to Boise!"

The driver said hello, shook hands with Papa, motioned me to the back-seat of that spacious automobile, and asked us where we were going. Papa told him we were headed for Boise.

"That's where I live and that's where I'm headed, so welcome aboard. It'll be nice to have some company to keep me awake."

I sat on that plush backseat and felt the soft float of the marvelous springs and shocks of that great automobile. It was like riding on a cloud in that seventh heaven people talk about. My tummy was full of fresh cheese curds. I was riding like a king to Boise. It had taken only two hitchhikes. Providence was smiling down on us. It was only a little after seven in the morning, but with two-way narrow roads and reduced speed limits imposed by the war, the ride would still take most of the day. Still, we were doing much better than we had ever hoped.

The driver, Wally Barnes, asked Papa why we were hitchhiking to Boise. Papa told him that he had a daughter in the Nampa School and Colony and we were going to see her and talk to the superintendent about her care.

"That's tough," Wally replied. "I admire your wanting to stay connect-ed to your daughter and your concern about her welfare." Wally seemed kind-ly respectful of Papa and me and deeply sympathetic.

Papa and Wally also had an animated discussion about the war and pol-itics. Most of it went over my head, but during the times I was awake I learned a lot. The Allies, primarily America, England, and Russia, Wally said, had taken Tunis and Bizerte, wherever they were, and had essentially brought German and Italian resistance in Africa to an end.

In fact, Wally said he had read a report that the Allies were preparing to invade Sicily and Italy. I got the impression those places were somewhere across some sea from North Africa. Apparently the fierce fighting in Russia was also slowing down the German advance.

"When the Russian winter comes along," Wally said, "that could be a major turning point."

Wally also told us that some big German field marshal named Von Paulus had surrendered to the Russians. Signs were beginning to indicate that, like Napoleon in 1812, Wally said, Hitler's army was meeting its match in the valor of Russian resistance, Russia's unending vastness, and Russia's bitter win-ter weather. Papa agreed that things were beginning to look up on the European front.

I got even more of a history lesson about the war involving Japan. I had always been more interested in that war because the Pearl Harbor attack had cost us the life of Byron Mason, plus Lael's ugly transformation, and it had created difficulties for our family's friend, Mary Jap. The war with the Japanese was more personal because of them.

I learned that shortly after Pearl Harbor the Japanese military captured most of the islands spreading southward from Japan, through the Philippines, Singapore, Borneo, and also eastward through New Guinea north of Australia, and the Gilbert, Solomon, Mariana, Marshall, and other islands. But Japan's expansion across the Pacific had come to an end in a mighty battle over the little island of Midway about one thousand miles from Hawaii. Wally said it was one of the most decisive battles in history. In that two-day battle the

Japanese had lost four aircraft carriers and a large part of its airplanes, which ended the threat of Japanese attacks on either Hawaii or the mainland.

The Japanese had recently either been driven from or deserted some of the Aleutian Islands southwest of Alaska, which they had occupied right after Pearl Harbor. From the discussion I listened to for a large part of the trip to Boise, it sounded as though things were turning around in the Pacific as well as in Europe, with the Allies going on the offensive on both fronts.

To a twelve-year-old the talk about a turnabout in the war raised the hope that one day I would be able to buy a decent candy bar, some good chewing gum, and even some good tasting pop once real sugar became available again. It also held out the hope that Papa would be able to upgrade his farm machinery. I might even be able to drive a brand new tractor pulling a brand new plow or disk.

In a much deeper sense it meant the end of killing and losing men like Byron. We were regularly reading obituaries of young soldiers or articles about young men being injured or maimed for the rest of their lives. These were young men who were only six or so years older than I! It would be wonderful to see those obituaries and injury reports come to an end, for I knew that my brother Joel and my cousin Johnny would be put in harm's way in just a few months when they would be drafted into military service. The sooner the war could turn around, and better yet, the sooner it could end, the happier and less afraid all of us would be.

Chapter 27

The Idanha Hotel

WALLY RECOMMENDED a hotel called the Idanha in Boise and was kind enough to not only take us right to its front doorstep but also go in—taking Papa with him—and talk to the manager, a friend of his. Wally arranged for a room and negotiated a special businessman's rate for us. This meant that even though it was probably the best hotel in Boise, that rate would about equal what we would pay at what Wally called a "fleabag" hotel. It seemed that Wally liked us and had enjoyed his long visit with Papa. I think he felt a kindly compassion after hearing Lael's story.

I told him, "I sure liked that nice ride in your beautiful car," and thanked him with a twelve-year-old's handshake.

Wally smiled and patted me on the head. "It was nice to have you along. I wish you both well in your visit with Dr. Allen." He turned to his shiny red Cadillac, climbed in, and drove off. I was glad to know there were such nice people around outside of Ririe.

We started looking around the lobby of the hotel. There were elegant sofas, chairs, and other beautiful furniture, marble on the floor and on the walls, beautifully carved wood around some of the perimeter walls, and many other beautiful things I had never seen before. I thought I was in a fairyland. All around us were men and women who were elegantly dressed in suits, ties, and long, flowing dresses. It looked as if they were going to have a lavish party in one of the big rooms just off the lobby. I was glad Mama had "re-dressed me up" before leaving. Even with Mama's help I didn't feel I fit in with those elegant people. Papa's best and only suit seemed shabby and out of place among all that finery.

Papa took me into the men's room just off the lobby, where I was fascinated by the urinals, a whole row of them, all made out of the purest white ivory looking stuff, with beautiful tile coming up from the floor along the back wall about four feet high, and above that, expensive-looking wallpaper that went clear to the high ceiling. Then came a real surprise. All the toilets were enclosed in little cabinets. On the door of each was a handle that could only be activated by putting a nickel in a slot just above the handle. Papa put in a nickel, and both of us occupied the same cabin. For Papa, coming out of the Depression years, doubling up on the nickel was a matter of sound economics.

Papa had already registered us at the front desk under Wally's watchful eye, so we took our key and went up to our room. To our chagrin we found that our room had its own private toilet, bathtub, and a funny looking thing sticking out about five feet above the bathtub.

"We coulda saved the nickel," I said.

"Well, when you've never been in such elegant surroundings before, you have to experience it first before you know what you've got. I just assumed that all the hotel guests would be using that big restroom just off the lobby."

"What's that funny thing sticking out above the tub on the wall there?"

"That's a shower. Instead of filling the tub, you can stand in it and let the water sprinkle over you like warm rain. We used to have those in the army, but there were usually five or ten in a big room where that many men could shower at the same time."

I replied, "I gotta try that warm rain!" I have never bathed in a tub since, so long as a shower was available.

An alarm clock on the dresser told us it was 7:30. It had been a long day. We had eaten Mama's sack lunch, even shared it with Wally so he could keep driving. But now we were hungry again. We hustled down to the lobby and started for the hotel restaurant. On the side of the main door hung a menu. Papa looked carefully at the prices, pointed his finger at a couple of items for me to see, shook his head, and then took me outside.

"We'll find a hamburger joint. We can't afford that hotel dining room."

We found a little hole-in-the-wall joint just down the street, where we bought a hamburger with all the trimmings for twenty-five cents for us to share, plus a glass of root beer for each for another five cents apiece. We felt like we had eaten well.

We returned to the hotel, and since it had been a long, tiring day, we each took a luxurious warm shower, brushed our teeth, and then knelt down to say our prayers. Papa pleaded that Dr. Allen would be understanding and open-minded. He reminded God that he felt Lael was a special charge of his and that he wanted His help to work on Dr. Allen so Lael would have all the advantages that the Nampa School and Colony could offer. He thanked God for helping get us to Boise so easily. He also asked Him to bless and protect Mama and the kids and Grandma Fanny. He asked God to also bless our boys in uniform and if at all possible to bring an end to the war. Then he closed by asking Him to protect Joel and Johnny, who would soon be going into the military service. The prayer was touching and sincere. It seemed as though Papa was talking to an older, wiser friend in whom he put much trust.

We slept well. But Papa had set the alarm clock for 6:30 so we could get up, eat, and get on our way to Nampa to meet our ten o'clock appointment. We quickly packed our belongings in Papa's little valise and went downstairs to the lobby, where Papa paid for the lodging. Papa looked at the breakfast menu on the door by the restaurant.

"Let's go find that hamburger joint again," he said.

At the burger place we sat down and looked at the menu. It listed two eggs, bacon, hash browns, toast, and orange juice for seventy cents. I asked Papa what hash browns were. He said they were fried potatoes, which was just what I wanted.

When the waitress came, I spoke right up. "I'll have number two on the menu."

She wrote it down and then asked, "How would you like your eggs and bacon?"

I looked at her kind of puzzled like and then answered with what I thought was a very proper response. "I want them cooked."

She about dropped her pencil. "What I mean is how would you like them cooked?"

I looked at Papa. He politely answered her, "We eat our eggs at home over medium and our bacon crisp." She wrote that down, smiled a sweet smile at him, and gave me a "grow up kid" look.

After Papa had ordered and she left, I asked, "How did you know what she meant by how I wanted them?"

"I learned that while I was in the army in one of the bigger cities. People eat eggs all sorts of ways. Nice places have them basted, over easy, over hard, poached, and some even have what is called eggs Benedict, which is eggs with ham, gravy, and a muffin of some kind, something very elegant but expensive. Also, you can have them with or without pieces of ham cooked in and so on."

He went on to explain what all those different kinds of cooked eggs meant. Someone had said once, and I remembered it, that "travel is broadening." I was beginning to get the idea.

The Idanha Hotel was located on the eastern side of Boise. Nampa was fifteen miles west. With Papa carrying his little valise and dressed in his suit, white shirt, tie, and hat, and with me wearing the same clothes as the day before, we hurried through the maze of streets until we arrived on the western outskirts, where the state highway would take us to Nampa. Breakfast and the long walk through Boise had taken its toll on our time. It was about nine o'clock when we finally set ourselves up at the edge of the highway.

Papa took a look at me and tried to put my blond hair in place. He picked off a few remnants of breakfast around my mouth and chin and then looked me up and down. He placed the extra length of belt in the metal slides provided for it so it would not hang down like a long tongue. Then he turned his attention to his own attire and tried to get the dust off his suit jacket and pants.

Satisfied, he said, "Now let's turn our attention to getting a ride, and when we do, don't let me forget to ask the driver how we get to the State School and Colony when he lets us off."

I said, "OK."

An old farmer came along shortly in a mud-splattered pickup with a big St. Bernard dog in the back and stopped for us. We climbed in with me in the middle again, Papa by the window.

"What's a man and his boy doin' a hitchhikin' in these here parts?"

Papa answered that we were from Ririe, over by Idaho Falls, and needed to go to the Nampa School and Colony because we had a girl there.

"Land o' livin'!" he exclaimed. "You been hitchin' clear across southern Idaho to come here to visit your girl?"

"Yes," Papa quietly responded. The man looked across me at him. Papa's profile against the mud-specked window of the pickup made him look sad and earnest, like he had a lot on his mind.

"Waal, I'll be durned, I ain't never seen the likes o' that before. That girl must be someone special in yur family for you to go to all this trouble to come see her."

"Yes, she is very special to us," was Papa's subdued response.

The old farmer sensed that Papa was becoming anxious about the visit, so he started telling us about Nampa and the vicinity. He said it had a mild climate, much milder than in the higher elevations over by Idaho Falls he figured; in this area they could grow peaches, apples, plums, apricots, and many other types of fruits and pretty much any kind of vegetable. He was a fruit grower himself, had done it all his life, and was right proud of the fruit they produced around here.

"To my way o' thinkin' this here climate is as good as anythin' they can show us in Californy, and we grow just as good a fruit and vegetables as they do."

A street sign said that we were approaching the city limits of Nampa, but I could not see anything of the city. The old farmer said that the city itself was over the hill south, or to our left, but that we were in luck because the school we were looking for was just a couple of hundred yards from the highway to our right on top of a little knoll. He stopped and let us off at the entrance of a roadway that took us up to the school.

Papa asked him what time it was. The old farmer pulled a watch attached to a long silver chain from the front pocket of his bib overalls. He popped the lid open, looked at the watch face, and said it was "a comin' right up on ten."

Papa shook the old farmer's hand. "I'm sorry I was not much company to you on the way over here. I have a lot of things on my mind about this visit. So I apologize and want to thank you very much for your kindness in giving us a lift."

"No apology needed. When a man puts his thinkin' where his rightful priorities lie, that's the sign uv a sound mind and good character. I sense you have some concerns about your daughter, and that's where your thoughts oughta be right now. I wish you well."

I added, as the old gentleman was ready to drive off, "You sure do have a good lookin' dog."

"Yep," he responded. "She's a good un. Name's Daisy. Most a the time, she's a heap smarter than I am."

I waived as they departed. "Bye, Daisy," I said.

Chapter 28

The Nampa State School and Colony

WE WALKED ALONG a two-hundred-yard asphalted driveway leading up a slight grade to a nice turnaround at the front of an elegant looking two-story building with four white pillars in front. I had never seen pillars like those before in eastern Idaho but remembered having seen some on a plantation house in the movie *Gone with the Wind.*

A sign on the building said Administration. As we neared it I saw a man standing in a large second-story corner window. He seemed to take quite an interest in us, as he stood completely immobile looking down. I felt uneasy with him staring down at me, so I turned my eyes back to the ground. Papa had not seen him. For some reason I thought it unwise to mention it to Papa so that he would not look up and alert the man to the fact we were countering his stare.

We entered the building through a fancy double glass door. Papa asked a receptionist on the ground floor where we might find Dr. Allen. She told us to go upstairs, turn left, and walk straight ahead toward the desk where Dr. Allen's secretary would be. At the desk the friendly voice Papa had heard over the telephone greeted us.

"You must be Mr. Moss, and this must be your son."

"Yes, his name is Reed. He's twelve."

"Hello, Reed, welcome to Nampa. Did you have a good trip over? You must have stayed overnight somewhere to be here at this early hour."

"Yes, we stayed at the Idanha Hotel in Boise," I proudly announced. She seemed impressed.

"Well, my name's Diane. I'm Dr. Allen's secretary. Dr. Allen is expecting you, so come right on in."

Papa countered, "Would it be possible for Reed to visit with Lael while I meet with Dr. Allen?"

"Oh yes," she quickly responded. "I just have to call her ward, and they'll bring her right over." She added, "Reed, why don't you sit there in that nice chair while they are bringing Lael, and Mr. Moss, I'll take you in to see Dr. Allen."

I sat down while she took Papa toward Dr. Allen's seemingly spacious office. The man in the light gray suit I had seen observing us from the window appeared at the doorway, shook Papa's hand, and asked, "I noticed you walking up the driveway. Did you have car trouble?"

"No," Papa replied. "We hitchhiked from home to here."

"You what?" exclaimed Dr. Allen. "You mean you hitchhiked clear across the state to get here?"

"Yes, with gas rationing and things being a little tight, that was the only way we could get here."

That was all the conversation Diane and I heard as Dr. Allen took Papa into his office and closed the door.

Diane seemed quite interested in the hitchhiking and asked me several questions about it. I didn't share her interest since I had done so much. I did tell her of our good luck in getting in on the cheese curds.

"Oh, I just love fresh cheese curds myself!" she exclaimed.

I told her about the fantastic ride in the big red Cadillac. She smiled at my excitement. The tables seemed to be turned. She seemed to be used to

Cadillacs, and I was used to hitchhiking. After we had chatted, she picked up the receiver to her phone, dialed a couple of numbers, and waited for someone to answer.

"Will you please bring Lael over to my office now? Thank you."

She hung up and turned to me. "They have her all ready and will bring her right over."

I said, "Thank you," and started to wonder how Lael would look. It had been almost five months since I had hugged her good-bye on that bitter cold morning in January. I thought back about growing up with her, and my thoughts seemed to catch on the snowball incident at school and the time when the teenager from Rigby had called her over to his car in front of our house. I remembered vividly her crestfallen look and deep sadness in both instances.

I heard steps on the stairway leading up to Diane's office and turned to see a lady in a white dress and white shoes helping a person I did not recognize up the stairs. I looked and looked. Could that be Lael? If so, she had shrunk! She was no longer 5'6". She would not measure more than 5'4" at the most. She looked so much older than eighteen. I couldn't believe what I was seeing. She was thin. Her face was drawn.

The nurse brought her to Diane's desk. Lael didn't seem to notice me.

Diane spoke, "Lael, this is your brother Reed," pointing to me. Lael looked at me with a vacant stare. She appeared to be staring at a brick wall, nothing more.

The nurse said, "When you need me to come and get her, give me a call."

Diane nodded and then said to me, "We have a little room where the two of you can visit. We made it especially for visitors to the school."

She led us down a hall to an open door that led into a small room where two nicely upholstered straight-backed chairs stood with a small wooden table separating them. She helped Lael to one chair and pointed for me to take the other.

"If you need me, I'll be at my desk."

I nodded and turned to Lael. She was looking across the table at me but still seemed not to recognize me. Her hands were folded in her lap, and she was rocking slightly forward and back. I pulled my chair around beside her and took one of her hands in mine.

"Lael, do you remember Ririe where you grew up?" There was no response. "Do you remember Grandma Fanny?" Her eyes flickered and she turned toward me. "She said to tell you hello and give you a big hug." Lael smiled, a wan and fleeting, but noticeable, smile nevertheless. I hugged her. "That's from Grandma Fanny." She smiled again.

I took the gum, coloring book, and peanuts from Papa's valise, and one by one I laid them on the table for Lael to see. She took the package of gum but couldn't open it, so I helped her pull out a stick, undid the wrapping, and let her put it into her mouth. She chewed quietly, seemingly absorbed in the sweet taste. A bit of saliva appeared at a corner of her mouth. I grabbed my hankie out of my back pocket and wiped it away as I had seen Mama do.

"Mama said she misses you," I said, looking straight into her crossed eyes.

She repeated, "Mama."

"Do you remember your brother Joel?"

She repeated his name.

"He doesn't know you're here. He's still in Hawaii and thinks you are still in Ririe with Mama and Papa."

She repeated, "Papa."

"I'm Reed, do you remember me? I'm your brother, too." She looked at me. She smiled again. Something was dawning in her mind.

She said, "Helen, Rhea, Ruthie?" in the form of a question. I told her they were okay and wanted me to say hello to her and that they missed her. A light seemed to be turning on in her countenance. She was coming around to some faded memories of home.

"Do you remember Bessie the cow?"

She smiled. "Bessie—had baby calf," recalling that long ago memory.

Bessie had long since been sold to the butcher, and her baby calf had been slaughtered for meat and put into the freezer locker we rented at Brown's

Grocery, but I didn't tell her that.

I asked, "Do you remember the dry farm and Antelope Flats?"

She looked puzzled for a moment, then repeated, "Dry farm," and smiled.

Her hand went back to her lap with the other one. She started to rock forward and back and seemed to go back into her vacant world. She could not hold on to what we were talking about. But she enjoyed the gum, and I enjoyed my little duty of checking the saliva now and then.

We spent almost an hour together going over playing kick the can, run sheepy run, and anti-I-over; feeding the chickens and hogs; and all the other memories of Ririe and the Flats I could think of. Then Diane appeared at the doorway with Papa and ushered him into the room.

"Stay and visit with Lael as long as you would like, Mr. Moss." Diane disappeared back down the hallway.

Papa came around the table. Lael stood up and said, "Papa!" in the sweetest voice I have ever heard. She recognized him. He took her in his arms and buried his head in her shoulder. After a long, tender, and very emotional embrace, he sat her back down in her chair and took the one I had occupied, while I stood and watched. Papa took her hand, held it, and gently rubbed it. He looked into his daughter's face.

"I have good news! Dr. Allen says you are going to be able to stay here at this school." He choked up, pulled a white hankie from his pocket, wiped his eyes, and with a little corner of it wiped a tad of saliva from Lael's mouth.

"He says you have been a good girl, and that makes me very happy. Mama will be so happy to hear that you are okay and that you will be staying here. Grandma Fanny and the kids, too." He choked up again.

Lael looked at him somewhat puzzled. She didn't seem to understand all the emotions he was encountering. But her look was one of fondness and reconciliation. She had a "family" again.

Time became a major player in our visit. We needed to get back to Ririe, hopefully by nightfall. After Papa had recovered his composure and spent as much time with Lael as he felt he could, we picked up the goodies from the table and started for Diane's desk. Papa put an arm around Lael, and together they strolled down the way to Diane with me trailing behind. It was a happy sight, Papa and his daughter walking together.

Before leaving Papa had one last request of Diane. "Would it be possible to say hello to Danny Rosenthal?"

"Why, of course. He'll be excited to see someone from his hometown. He's in a neighboring ward from Lael. Perhaps we could go together, drop Lael off at her ward, and then go see Danny."

Papa took Lael's one hand and I the other as we followed Diane down the stairs and across a large courtyard to another building. There we met the nurse who had brought Lael to Diane's office. Papa thanked her for taking care of Lael. He said that she was looking a little thin and asked how she was eating. The nurse replied that at first she would hardly eat and that was why she was so thin, but she was doing better. Papa thanked her again, handed her the goodies, and asked if she would see that Lael got some of them occasionally. She nodded.

Papa gave Lael a big hug, kissed her tenderly on the cheek, and said, "We have to go back home now, sweetheart, but you be a good girl and do all that they ask you to do so that hopefully they can make you better. We'll come and see you again as soon as we can. I don't know when that will be with the war going on, but hopefully soon. We love you. Mama, Grandma Fanny, Joel, Helen, Rhea, baby Ruth all love you."

"And I love you and miss you," I chimed in.

Lael looked a little crestfallen, as though she had been brought back to a reality she once knew and now was being closed out from it again. But the nurse intervened with a hug around her shoulder and led her back into her ward. As Lael went through the door, she turned her head and looked back. From that distance, coupled with the shadow from the building, Lael seemed to return to her beautiful face and hair. We smiled and waved. She waved and then disappeared into the building.

Diane took us across the way to another building. It was a hub of activity. She led us down a broad hallway and into a barbershop. Both Papa and I immediately recognized Danny. He was older but looked healthy. He was dressed in a barber's white smock and had just finished cutting someone's hair. We walked toward him. He turned and looked our way. He recognized us immediately, smiled, and came toward us. The jiggle of his St. Vitus' dance was gone. With a bit of a slur in his voice and a timid little shake of his head, he put out his hand to Papa.

"Hi, Mr. Moss."

Papa took the hand. "Hi, Danny. You look great, and you're cutting hair. You have worked hard and done well over here. I will tell your mom and dad I saw you and how good you are doing."

You could tell that Danny was retarded by the humility of his look, his timid demeanor, and the slur in his diction. Yet he was able to live with his handicap and had become a productive human being with a definite, if humble, sense of self-esteem.

"Yeah, tell them hi for me and tell them to come see me."

"That's not so easy with the war going on and gas being rationed. We had to hitchhike over here ourselves. But I'll tell them, and I'm sure they'll be here to see you as soon as they can."

Danny smiled at the thought. We visited a few more moments and told Danny all he wanted to know about his family and Ririe. Then we bade him good-bye and went with Diane back to the administration building.

Papa asked, "What did you do with Danny? He couldn't sit still long enough to learn anything, couldn't go to school, just wandered the town."

"Some medication helped calm him down, and that made it so he could concentrate and learn."

"Everybody in Ririe will be so surprised and pleased. We'll be sure to tell them about his great progress." He paused and then asked. "Do you think Lael can make any progress like that?"

Diane responded frankly, but sincerely, "I don't know. I have great confidence in Dr. Allen. If anyone can help her, he will."

Papa thanked her for her kindness and for all they were doing for Lael, and especially for arranging everything for our visit.

She responded, "I'm very impressed that you would hitchhike this whole distance to keep the connection with your daughter. So many people put their children in here and then seem to disappear off the earth. We seldom, if ever, hear from many of them again."

Papa thanked her again, shook her hand, and turned to leave.

I stepped up to Diane. "Thanks, Diane. I guess I should call you by your last name, but I don't know what it is. Please take good care of my sister and tell her whenever you see her that Reed, Joel, Helen, Rhea, Ruth, Grandma Fanny, and Papa and Mama love her and miss her."

Diane laughed. "I better run to my desk and write all those names down before I forget them. But I'll surely do what you ask." She paused, put a hand on each of my shoulders, and looked me in the eye. "You have a good family, Reed. You're lucky. I hope you appreciate it all your life long."

She seemed to be speaking from experiences at the school that were sometimes not so welcome and pleasant, and she spoke with sincerity and emphasis. I extended my hand, mumbled my thanks, and started walking with Papa back down the long driveway to the highway leading back to Boise.

Papa walked with a new spring to his step. As we approached the highway he turned to me.

"Son, I'm anxious to get back to tell Mama, Grandma Fanny, and the kids about my conversation with Dr. Allen. If we get to Boise before the Greyhound bus leaves, we'll take the bus. Besides, if we can catch a bus that leaves in the early afternoon, we can get clear to Idaho Falls and then hitch a ride to Ririe and be home by midnight. That'll save us staying in a hotel, which will pay a large part of the bus fare anyway."

I was tickled with the idea. We hitched a quick ride to Boise and found a bus leaving in thirty minutes for Pocatello. I could tell that Papa's visit with

Dr. Allen had lifted a big burden off him. He seemed to be a new man from the one we had lived with since January 29.

Papa's plan worked. The bus ride was pleasant. We had comfortable seats and sat up so high I could see the ever-changing landscape of southern Idaho. Much of it was desert or arid cattle grazing lands, mountains with some sparse growth of trees, or abundant sagebrush. We passed through Hagerman (where Ernest Hemingway would live some of the time) and saw the water streaming in wide sheets out of the aquifer midway up a sheer wall of lava rock. Papa told me that most of that water flowed underground from way up in the upper Snake River Valley where we lived. In fact, he said that the Big and Little Lost Rivers got lost (went underground) in the desert and probably formed a part of that underground flow.

We passed through the Magic Valley where Twin Falls is the dominant city. We went across the Perrine Bridge on the outskirts of the city and gazed at the deep canyon formed by the Snake River, with lush green acres gracing its banks at the bottom of the canyon. Up above and on both sides of the canyon I saw fertile lands covered with newly planted sugar beets, sweet corn, potatoes, peas, and other crops. These were all being irrigated through a system of canals, which carried precious water from the Snake to the thirsty crops. Papa told me that men had dug those canals with pickaxes and shovels and with horses pulling scrapers back in the "early days." Some canals seemed to stretch for miles and miles, perhaps twenty or longer.

The sun was setting in the western sky as we boarded the connecting bus in Pocatello to go north to Idaho Falls. Soon after we left Pocatello a sign along the highway indicated "Fort Hall Indian Reservation." I saw some teepees along with small adobe-looking buildings dotting the landscape. I also saw vast stretches of flat and tillable land that looked to me like it could be very productive. I asked Papa why it was not being farmed. He said that there was not enough rainfall to make a decent crop, and there had not been any canals dug in this area to bring water to the land.

I told him I thought the storms always came from the southwest, and since this Indian land lay directly to the southwest of the Flats, it should get the rain first and only leave what was left for the Flats. He reminded me that the Flats had those low-lying hills on the southwest—Birdie's Bump being a part of those—and the larger mountains adjoining the Snake River on the north.

"Those two rows of mountains make a perfect catch basin for the clouds. They halt their northeasterly progress long enough to bunch them tighter together and milk them of their moisture over the Flats. A man from the agriculture department told me that the Flats get fourteen to twenty inches of rainfall per year, while the Indian reservation might only get eight to twelve. That makes the difference."

After this trip and my initial inspection of most of southern Idaho, I decided that the upper Snake River Plain and Antelope Flats were some of the best Idaho had to offer. They also had fantastic fishing, boating, hiking, skiing, and other recreation, which much of the rest of southern Idaho lacked. That trip developed in me a deepened appreciation for the area I called home.

The shades of the night were deepening as the bus pulled in to the Greyhound bus station near the middle of Idaho Falls. We set out on foot as fast as we could to get to the northern outskirts of the city onto Highway 26 to catch a ride. We passed a hamburger joint, and my stomach did a flip-flop. We had not eaten since my over-medium eggs and crisp bacon earlier that morning. Papa's gentle prodding kept me going. It was not the first time I had gone without food for a whole day, so I trudged along behind him, trying to turn my thoughts to something besides food.

The third car we saw stopped to give us a ride. He was a stranger heading for Jackson Hole, Wyoming. Papa carried on an animated conversation with him while I lay down in the backseat and tried to let sleep take my mind off my hunger. The ride to Ririe went quickly. I had fallen asleep and was startled when Papa nudged me just as the car was coming to a halt right in front of the door to our house. I was happy to see it. It had been a long, tiring, but eventful and broadening two days.

It was almost midnight. Mama welcomed us at the door. She literally yanked Papa inside by the lapels of his suit coat and wanted to know everything that had happened and how Lael looked. I asked if we could talk about it over something to eat. She quickly seated us at the kitchen table and heated up and then ladled out two bowls of chicken noodle soup. She sat down across from Papa, looked into his face, and saw satisfaction and peace.

"Tell me all about your big trip, but start with Lael and Dr. Allen, and then fill in the other details."

Papa realized that the last two days had been anxious and trying not only for him but for her also. He immediately soothed her mind with, "Lael is thin but is being well cared for and is starting to eat better. She didn't recognize Reed at first. He visited with her while I talked to Dr. Allen. By the time I came in to see her, she seemed to be refreshed enough that she was remembering lots of things about her family and Ririe. She recognized me and said, 'Papa,' the minute she saw me. I have to confess that mentally she has not changed much from when she left home. But the important thing is that Dr. Allen assured me that they will keep Lael there and work with her!"

Mama let out a long, deep breath, and her nose and mouth began to pinch and tighten as she struggled to hold back tears. To her this good news was not a thing to cry about, and she was going to squeeze it off like pinching off a sneeze.

"Tell me what he said. What was his attitude?"

"The first question he asked me was if we had car trouble because he saw us walking up the driveway with no car in sight. I told him we hitchhiked from Ririe. He looked at me at first like I was some kind of a freak. But I really think it made him realize how much we care about Lael. His whole attitude seemed to become one of compassion and understanding. He told me he had retrieved Lael's file and had read the letter we sent soon after Lael came to the school. He wanted to know more and asked me to go into as much detail as my time would allow. I told him everything I could think of and remember: her regal little mannerisms in earlier years, the influenza epidemic, the fire with Merlin and how it affected her, the swing accident, all those things. I told him every detail I could remember about December 7 and how she changed literally overnight. I finished by telling him about the electric shock treatments and how they hurt her and did her no good.

"The farther I went in telling him Lael's background, the more interested he became from a medical standpoint. He asked me lots of questions that I tried to answer as best I could. Those questions seemed to have a medical or psychological connection that he was analyzing as our conversation continued. He said that she definitely has some kind of a psychosis now that puts her on the brink of insanity. Yet to have it come on the way it did, and so suddenly, really intrigued him. After I had finished telling him everything I knew and answered all his questions, he looked at me for the longest time, like he was looking right into my soul.

"Finally he said, 'I would like to work with Lael. We'll keep her here and see if there is any way we can bring her back from this brink.' That was the gist of the conversation. He was so friendly I could hardly believe it, especially after all those letters Dr. Lowe had written and which he must have seen in Lael's file. The visit was nothing like I had anticipated when I was letting all those 'imaginary horribles' go through my mind on the way over there. I think he's going to try to do everything that he can for Lael."

Mama was elated. She looked lovingly at Papa. "Thank you for taking that trip to Nampa. I can see the relief in your face. I think we'll sleep better from now on."

She turned to me. "Speaking of sleep, it's way past your bedtime young man, but first I want to give you a great big hug for helping Papa get hitchhiked clear over to Nampa and back to Boise. I doubt he could have done it without you."

She gave me a hug, then put an arm around my neck, drew close to me, and said, "But first tell me all about your visit with Lael, while Papa was talking to Dr. Allen."

I did, but I abridged it considerably because I was getting sleepy. Satisfied, she kissed me on the cheek, told me to be sure to brush my teeth and say my prayers before going to bed, and then pointed me toward the bathroom.

As I stood brushing my teeth in front of the mirror over the sink, I turned my head, looked out through the open door, and noticed that Mama had come around the table, plunked her 110 pounds on Papa's lap, put her arms around his neck, and was giving him a long kiss. Both of their eyes were closed, so I enjoyed watching them until their lips disconnected and they buried their heads in each other's shoulders. Then I walked past them, smiled a shy smile, got a shy one from both in return, and went downstairs to bed.

Chapter 29

1944

THE WINTER OF 1943-44 was tough on Grandma Fanny. She struggled with colds, sniffles, and a bout of the flu. During that time most of her grandchildren in the area took turns spending the nights with her until the family persuaded her widowed daughter, Eunice, to come from California to live in with her.

The bags under Grandma's eyes were more prominent than ever. She looked tired and old. The cold and flu had affected her lungs. It was difficult for her to cough up enough phlegm to give her much relief. Yet she was still her tough, bright, and independent old self.

My turn to spend the night with her came up in mid-March of '44, shortly before Eunice arrived. Grandma Fanny cooked me a steaming dish of dishrag soup, and later we sat and talked for a spell. While I pulled on my pajamas, she took out her teeth, brushed them and put them in a glass of water on the kitchen table, went into the bedroom and pulled on her wool nightie, and then invited me to come in. We said prayers. She climbed into bed and I into my sleeping bag beside her on the floor.

In that funny way she talked with her teeth out, she mumbled, "Reed,

I'm jist about a goner. You oughta jist take me out in the borrow pit and sprinkle enough dirt over me so I won't stink and leave me be. I ain't worth nothin' to nobody anymore, and as a matter o' fact, I'm jist a great big bother. But I gotta stick around a while cause my grandbaby, Joel, is a comin' home soon, and I gotta be here when he does. He promised me he was goin' ta do a waltz with me when he got home."

She immediately burst into a coughing fit that I thought was going to bring her end right then, and on my watch! But she rallied, and after she got a little strength, she whispered more to herself, but loud enough so I could barely hear, "Gittin' old and wearin' out is plain craziness." I knew from that little outburst she would have strength for the night.

Early in the morning, April 21, 1944, I carried an armload of chopped wood over to Grandma's lean-to. Assembled in her little living room were all of her living children except one who couldn't make it on time. I quietly laid the wood by the stove. Aunt Eunice took my hand and led me to the bedroom door.

"Isn't she beautiful? She awoke about one-thirty, said her arms hurt, her head ached, and she felt sick to her stomach. I tried to help her sit up, but she slumped unconscious in my arms. I called everybody to come. She passed away at ten to five this morning." Then she added, "When she went to bed last night she asked me to read Joel's letters to her. There were seven. She seemed so pleased." Eunice fell silent.

The pillow on which Grandma's head was resting tilted her face toward me. I saw peace. Grandma Fanny's white hair lay like a halo around her wrinkled but serene face. Her eyes and lips were closed. Her hands and arms were crossed upon her chest. She looked as though she was sleeping, but her chest did not rhythmically rise and fall.

Grandma Fanny, born April 12, 1855, in Stubbs Green, England, came to the United States when just a young girl and walked across the plains to the Salt Lake Basin. She suffered the loss of two husbands, a child, and several grandchildren, lived through two world wars and the Great Depression, but never lost her zest for life. She lived eighty-nine years and nine days, long and well enough to become a legend in her time and region. She was laid to rest beside her last husband, Hyrum Ralph Moss, who had preceded her in death thirty-six years earlier on June 17, 1908.

Grandma Fanny didn't make it to dance the waltz with Joel, but she had been there in May 1943, when Johnny came home from his service as a church missionary. She saw him married to his sweetheart, Jessie, that fall. That greatly pleased her. She sat among the dignitaries at the reception for the couple and was greeted warmly by all the guests. Joel and Johnny were her grandsons, contemporary cousins, and a light in her life. They grew up like a pair of twins to her, and she doted over them. It was sad to lose her, but as I've reflected on things later, I'm glad she did not have to endure the trauma of her grandsons' military service or to experience the rest of Lael's travail.

Shortly after his marriage to Jessie, on August 18, 1943, Johnny was drafted into the Army Air Corps. Joel returned home a couple of months after Grandma Fanny died and was also quickly drafted into the Army. The war years were an emotional roller coaster ride for the family. Joel was big brother and half a parent to his younger siblings. Johnny, a first cousin, was intimately tied to our family and was one of Lael's protectors.

Joel went to see Mary Jap as soon as he returned from Hawaii. He was one of Mary's "boys," like Byron. Upon seeing him she rushed to him and gave him a big hug. "You done come home. Yo' Mama be happy now. I have miss you. Yo' Mama and Papa say you eat lots of Japanese cookin' in Hawaii. You bring family and girlfriend and I make you big Japanese dinner."

Joel brought this welcome news home, and arrangements were quickly made for the big feast at Mary's. Mama made us dress up in our best Sunday clothes and inspected us all carefully before we made our enthusiastic march the short distance to Mary's restaurant. Joel brought a girlfriend. I arrived first and was about to open the door to the restaurant when I noticed a sign taped on its window. "Restaurant close tonight 7 p.m. for big party. Please excuse."

Inside, most of the little tables had been assembled together to make a long table with a beautiful white tablecloth spread upon it and chairs neatly arranged around it. Off to the side and near the kitchen were two small serving tables on one of which were sets of chopsticks all neatly laid out, each right beside a setting of knife, fork, and spoon. On the other serving table were several shiny aluminum pots and pans letting off little columns of steam. I opened the door and was overwhelmed by the most delicious of odors.

"Tonight will be Ririe's social highlight of the year," I muttered to myself.

Mary came out of the kitchen and shuffled toward us with that special gait of hers, greeted us warmly, and gave each a big hug as we streamed through the door.

At first Mary declined to eat with us, but Mama insisted, so Mary joined us. First she asked who wanted chopsticks and who wanted knives, forks, and spoons. All opted for chopsticks, but for everyone except Joel and Mary, who knew how to handle them, the eating was too tedious. The chopsticks were soon traded for the other utensils. We ate a lavish feast that Mary had worked feverishly most of the day to put together while still attending to her regular customers. My mind often wanders back to that magnificent event and to its gracious hostess. It grieves me still that Lael could not be there.

Joel went to Fort Walters, Texas, where he trained with the Sixty-First Battalion's artillery unit. When his training was completed he came home on a short furlough. Except for Lael, the family was together again briefly. The mood, however, was restrained, even gloomy. I could see in Mama's face, and especially in her eyes, a haunted look, partially fueled by Byron's death and by the things happening now to her family over which she had no control. She knew Joel's orders required his battalion be sent to Fort George, Maryland,

and from there he would be shipped to Europe to fight the German Army immediately after this brief furlough.

Papa was also deeply troubled. I could see it in his eyes, in the way his lips often became a tight line across his face, in the way he would stop eating and stare off into space. Of the five children he saw at the Grand, and of the three eldest in the picture by the tree stump, one was dead, another had become insane, for want of a better word, and now the oldest son's life would be in jeopardy.

Papa had told me about the big "Battle of the Bulge" that had flared up on the European front. Hitler was trying to stop the Allies before they could cross the Rhine River, force a big breakthrough back to Antwerp, Belgium, and then divide and conquer the Allied armies. He told me that he was sure Joel's battalion would be caught right in the thick of that battle. Its outcome would be a major turning point in the war.

From Fort George, Joel sent Lael a teddy bear. He had already sent her a coloring book from Camp Walters. From Germany he sent her a bracelet and hankie. Lael was his sister. His memories of her were fond ones: her graceful bearing, her infinite compassion, her joy at the sight of animals and flowers and little children. Growing up together with her was something very special to him. I was impressed that he thought enough of Lael to buy her a teddy bear while he had the Battle of the Bulge to face.

That battle was constantly on our minds. We knew what it was like to worry about every knock on the door, fearing it would be a Western Union man coming with that horrible telegram. This haunting fear was awful, something we could not shake off. The anxiety persisted day in and day out. The memory of Byron sharpened its intensity. Only those who have been through it can fully appreciate it..

Chapter 30

Honor and Refinement

DESPITE LEAVING SCHOOL in the seventh grade, Papa was self-educated. He read virtually any book he could get his hands on. Most evenings I saw him reading something. On our almost daily summer trips to and from the Flats, during our overnight stays in the shack, and other occasions, he taught me what he had learned about values, standards, and principles to live by. These were all brought into sharp focus one memorable night and the day thereafter in the same year that Grandma Fanny died and Joel and Johnny went to war, 1944.

It was shortly after Thanksgiving. We had missed Johnny and Joel over the holiday, but the war was going well. Optimism was growing that the war in Europe would soon end. There was a certain euphoria in the air. People were starting to celebrate, however premature that might be.

My teachers had skipped me a grade in grade school. So in 1944 my schoolmates were mostly a year older than I. The peer pressure brought on by this age differential was significant. One Saturday evening four of us were having a get-together at Greg Nelson's house. Greg's parents had taken the bus to see a sick relative who lived out of town. They would not be home till the next evening. We were playing Monopoly. Greg was losing and getting bored.

With a quirky grin on his face, he suddenly looked up from the game and said, "I got a great idea for a fun night." We stopped playing and looked at him. "There's a big western dance up in Alpine, Wyoming, tonight. I've heard they're the wildest dances in Wyoming. I'd really like to see one. All we get to see is those silly school dances since we can't go to the dances at the Ririe Pavilion."

The guy next to me spoke up, "That's fifty miles away. There's no way to get there."

"That's easy," replied Greg.

"What do you mean, easy?"

"We can take my dad's car. It's sittin' right there in the garage."

"That would be stealin' it, and your dad is bound to know you took it just by checkin' the speedometer."

"That's easy, too!" exclaimed Greg. "All you gotta do is unscrew the speedometer cable, and when you get back you screw it back on again." I was getting uneasy.

"What about the gas? Your dad will know it's gone a hundred miles just by checkin' the gas gauge."

Greg countered, "I know where I can get five gallons of gas. When we get back I'll take care of that by myself. So none of you will have to be involved." For some reason nobody touched that with any questions.

Against what little better judgment I had, I went along to see a real live western dance and to please my peers. Greg acted like unscrewing the speedometer cable was a thing he had done a few times before. He handled the car with skill and even negotiated the treacherous Conant Valley Dugway and its hairpin curve near the bottom with ease.

The dance hall was a run-down frame building, built more like a shed than a dance pavilion. There were two bare-knuckle fistfights going on outside as we waded our way through the onlookers. All four combatants were flailing around without doing much damage. A couple of the onlookers were women, probably wives or girlfriends of the fighters. The rest were men who were cheering on their respective heroes.

Nobody asked for any I.D. The ticket price was fifty cents, which was a lot, but we all forked it over and went inside. The dance hall was spacious with a large, dusty dance floor. Shadowy booths lined its sides. Virtually all the booths were occupied because the band had taken a breather. Beer and whiskey bottles adorned most of the tables. At one end of the dance hall was a big banquet table made of a row of wobbly card tables shoved together and covered by a big white tablecloth. On top of that were two galvanized tubs full of chipped ice and beer bottles. Beside those was a big, flat pan that had raw hamburger slapped in little gobs onto thin biscuits. Cowboys and other men were lined up at the table paying five cents for each biscuit and taking them back to their tables. I didn't see any women eating any. I had never eaten raw hamburger and didn't want to start now. Besides, the ticket had taken all my money.

The dance band started up again, but I didn't see much dancing. I saw a lot of foot stomping, and as the evening wore on the couples were mostly trying to just stay on their feet. From all the whooping and hollering going on I got the impression they were having a real good time. We didn't dance. We just sat and watched. I'm sure we looked a little out of place.

Across the room in one dark booth I noticed a man and woman were having a heated argument. I could not hear the words because of the loud music. Just as the music stopped—and it caught her off guard—she shoved the man violently backwards and spoke loudly, "Cal, you ain't worth a bucket of slop!" People started pointing at them and laughing. The woman blushed, and Cal sat looking sort of dumb.

Watching all this unfolding made us forget time. And it flew by! Before we even realized it, it was nearing two o'clock in the morning. I began to fret. My parents didn't know where I was and why I was staying out so late. I hoped they never would!

Greg dropped me off a block from home. It was after three a.m. I ran to the house and around to the back door where I took off my shoes and carried them in my hand. I opened the door without a sound and tiptoed very quietly down the stairs. I quickly undressed and climbed into bed, certain that I had succeeded in not waking the folks. I promptly fell asleep.

Moments later I woke with a start when I heard a slight rustle beside my bed. A chill went up my spine as I saw a shadowy form in the dark sitting on a stool, silently glaring down at me. It spoke with grave authority.

"I will not have a son who has to come into his own house like a thief in the night! Where have you been, and what have you been doing to make you act like that?"

It was my mother. I was no match for her. I told her everything: the speedometer, the trip to Alpine, the gasoline, and the dance.

She muttered four words that kept me from sleep the rest of the night, "We'll see about this!" She turned and walked back up the stairs.

I lay there pondering my fate. After a half an hour, around four a.m., I heard Papa's footsteps crossing the kitchen floor above me. I thought I would be visited. But the footsteps went on through the kitchen into the little washer room and out the back door. I heard the car engine start and the car back out of the garage and drive off down the street. Was he going to get the sheriff? Horrible images crept into my mind in that dark basement gloom. I couldn't take it. I got up, climbed the stairs, and walked into my parents' bedroom. Mama was lying in her bed with her eyes wide open, looking up at the ceiling.

With a quiver in my voice I asked, "Where'd Papa go?"

She looked up at me with a sort of loving disdain. "He drove over to the Willow Creek lookout to watch the sunrise and think about you."

I gulped and tried to make some lame apology. She stopped me with, "There will be some straightening out, so let's just wait and see what happens. You might as well get some sleep till he gets back."

Sleep? All my senses were on edge! I went into the living room and sprawled out on the couch, then nervously jumped up and went to Lael's window to look up and down the street to see if our car was returning. I went in the kitchen and got a drink of water to ease the dryness in my mouth. Then I tried the couch again. The wait was grueling.

Shortly after sunrise, Papa drove back into the driveway, parked the car, and came into the house. He went into the bedroom and in hushed tones talked for a few minutes with Mama. Then he came to the living room. I sat up. I saw a look that said I had let him down. He pulled Lael's window chair over and sat directly in front of me.

"Reed, you know about my experience at the Grand Hotel many years ago. That added a great burden to your mother's and my feelings of responsibility toward you children. We feel we should make sure you learn to be good citizens, that you respect the law and your leaders, live by high moral standards, and get good educations and eventually marry someone trustworthy and respectable."

I knew this. I had grown up with it all my life.

Then he abruptly changed course, saying, "They are starting to have hit parades of some of the modern music. I notice you are taking quite an interest in them. How long do your favorite songs stay popular on the hit parade?"

I was perplexed by the question but answered, "Oh, usually a few weeks, and then they slip back down the scale."

"Has any of those hits remained popular for centuries?"

I didn't know what this had to do with a wild western dance in Alpine, Wyoming, but responded, "I don't know any like that."

"In 1812 Napoleon tried to conquer Russia, just like Hitler has tried to do now. Napoleon's army and the Russians fought horrible battles across Russia. The Russians triumphed, but only after a terrible slaughter. Many years later a Russian by the name of Tchaikovsky composed the 1812 Overture. With music he captured the sounds and emotions of those great battles and the eventual triumph of the Russians. If you listen carefully you will hear the drone of artillery fire, the sounds of the great battles, of men fighting and dying, women and children suffering and dying, too. But when victory comes and the invaders are turned away, church bells ring and a deafening cannonade brings the music swelling up to a thundering conclusion. You can literally feel the surge of joy that floods Russia and its people as they revel in that great triumph. That powerful impact on your emotions is what makes great music endure throughout time.

"We have always had this old upright piano in our home." He reached over and touched its dark surface. "We have it because we feel good music is important. It can capture feelings one cannot describe, and it can elevate our thoughts and emotions. It can spur us on to great achievement. It can help us control our animal instincts. It can refine us!"

Then he asked the question, "Were you refined by what you heard and saw and did last night?"

For want of a better answer, I said, "I don't think so."

Papa nodded. Then he went on.

"Reed, we expect you to be honest. Let me tell you about honesty. I was in Idaho Falls a while ago to a new store opening there. They advertised hamburgers for only ten cents to get people to come. I was standing at the counter when a young woman about thirty-five came into the store with a four-year-old boy. She asked if the manager was there. He was waiting on me, so he asked if he could help her.

"She said, 'Yes, my parents and my family ordered ten hamburgers for a dollar, but when we were driving to our home out of town, we discovered your clerk had given us eleven hamburgers. We decided to eat the extra one, so here is the ten cents we owe you.'

"The manager kind of shuffled his feet and said, 'Oh ma'am, you didn't need to come all the way back here to do that.'

"She responded, 'No, you take that dime. We ate your hamburger!' She grabbed the little boy by the hand and departed. The manager looked at me and said, 'I'd like to hire that little boy when he is about sixteen. He will undoubtedly grow up to be an honest man.'

"To be honest means you do things the way the lady with the little boy did."

Then he asked the question, "Were you and your friends honest by disconnecting the speedometer cable on Greg's dad's car?"

I looked ashamed and cast my eyes down. "No."

"When you took his dad's car without permission?"

My lame answer, "No."

"When you rode on gasoline that you knew would be stolen?"

"No."

Papa wasn't through. "You didn't know Karl Klinger. He lived in Grandma Fanny's lean-to until he went back to Austria to die. Karl often quoted a little poem in his native tongue. 'So jemand boeses ueber dich spricht, das ist ihm erlaubt; Du aber lebe so, dass niemand es glaubt.' In English it means: So someone speaks evil about you, that you have to allow, but you live so that no one will believe it! Occasionally someone will hear, or perhaps even misinterpret, something bad about you. Ofttimes the only way you can fight such things is to be of such high character, to be so honest and trustworthy, that no one will believe those bad things being spoken about you."

Then he asked the question, "Did you live in such a way last night that people would respect and trust you despite what anyone said bad about you?"

I answered with a dejected, "No".

"I expect you to have the type of character that people will trust. Your mother and I expect you to do better than you did last night."

Papa wasn't finished with Karl Klinger. "Karl told me another poem that also goes to the heart of what I want you to know. Translated into English, the poem said, 'I am I know not who. I come I know not from where. I go I know not whereto. I wonder if I'm happy so!' Those few words describe our quest on this earth—to find the answers to that question.

"The answer in a way, I think, is found in an English ballad. It tells about a grizzled old sea captain who had sailed the seven seas throughout his life, had been in many ports, and met many people of differing cultures. He had completed his final voyage and was coming home to retire from the sea. He was so famous some people came to see him leave his ship and ask him questions about his long life on the sea.

"The main question they asked him was, 'What do you have to tell the world after all your travels and getting to know so many different cultures and people?' The old captain answered with only three words, then turned, picked up his duffel bag, and departed." Papa paused.

I impatiently asked, "Well, what were those three words?"

"Seek thy God! That's all the old captain said, but if you earnestly seek God I think you'll find Him and the answers you want. I've found Him. There is a scripture about Him that is very special to me. 'Fear of God is the beginning of wisdom.' Do you want to be wise?"

I answered in the affirmative.

"Then substitute the words 'accountable to' for 'fear of,' and see if it helps you understand the passage. We all like to do respectable things in front of respectable people. That's easy. But what guides our thoughts and actions when we are alone, or when it is dark and no one can see us, or when we are with people that may not be as respectable as they should be? If you sincerely feel that you will be accountable to God no matter where you are and under whatever circumstances, then you will make the decisions you would expect He would expect you to make, and those choices will usually be wise ones. There you have the 'beginning of wisdom.'

"Another man, Immanuel Kant, said: 'Two things fill me with continuing wonder. The heavenly tent over me and the moral law in me." You should appreciate and follow that moral law within you and be accountable to God. Such a course of conduct will pay you big dividends in your life."

Then he asked the question, "Did you feel any accountability to God when you made the choices you did last night?"

"No."

"Were those decisions wise ones?"

"No."

"Did that moral law in you try to tell you something?"

"Yes," I stammered. " I didn't feel good about what we were doing."

"Your mother and I want you to be wise. We want you to be honest and true. In other words, we want you to be a man of honor. Also, we want you to seek for that which is praiseworthy and of good report, like the good music we've talked about, and become a man of refinement. Honor and refinement is what I am getting at. I can only preach and teach, but you have to learn and live.

"Now there is some straightening out to do. You'll have to discontinue running around with those friends. You'll have to find new ones who will meet the standards we've been talking about."

I muttered an objection, "But that'll be hard. I sit in class with them every day. We play on the same ball teams. They'll want to know why. What do I tell them?"

"The truth: that your mother and I have said it must be so because of what happened last night. You don't have to tell them this, but you will have to find better friends to run around with than those."

Papa stood up. I could see firmness and resolve in his eyes. I knew I would be turning a corner, one way or another. He put his hands on each side of my shoulders and looked deeply into my eyes, but said nothing. Then he left the room. I had been firmly chastened. Papa had done a lot of thinking that early morning while watching the sunrise from the Willow Creek lookout.

Turning that corner did, in fact, mean leaving one group of friends to find another, and it was difficult and trying. I felt ostracized by my former friends and was a lonely teenager until I eventually found a couple of classmates whom I liked and who accepted me as a friend. I wasn't afraid of Papa, but I found, whenever I reflected back on that morning conversation, that I could not bear to let the friend, which I knew him to be, down.

Chapter 31

God Does All Things Well

IT WAS APPROACHING MIDNIGHT, February 3, 1945. This was his first mission over Germany. Berlin was the target. Johnny was riding at his turret gunner post along the big underbelly of the B-17 Flying Fortress bomber. Even with the limited visibility permitted by his position he could still see bursts of antiaircraft fire and searchlights flooding the heavens as they approached the city. The plane was rocked by nearby bursts but somehow managed to squeeze through the exploding maze to get to its target. The payload was dropped somewhere upon the vast city. Then the plane made a wide, looping turn to return to its base in England. The turn exposed the full underbelly of the plane to an antiaircraft position based on the outskirts of Berlin.

A massive explosion tore away a large section of the plane. It keeled over and made a fiery, screaming dive into the earth near Neukoeln. No one survived. The plane tore a massive hole in the earth. No one will ever know the thoughts that blazed through the minds of that young crew in those last moments of their time on earth.

Johnny had gone to the Army Air Corps in November 1943, after living with Jessie only three months. But in that time, she conceived. While he was training to be a turret gunner on the B-17, she was carrying his son.

Johnny was granted leave from his base at Lowry Field, Denver, Colorado, to come home to be with his wife when the baby was born on August 23, 1944. The boy was born about four p.m. on the very day Johnny had to leave to go back to Lowry Field. They named him Brent. Johnny got to see him for only a few minutes after his birth; then he was told by the hospital staff that he could not see him again even though he had to leave that night at eight.

Jessie saw Johnny at a base in Lincoln, Nebraska, for four days at the end of December 1944 and the first couple of days of January 1945. She had to leave the baby with her parents. She told Johnny that his son had light blond hair just like his dad. He looked a lot like his dad and was a healthy and growing young boy. Johnny was thrilled to have his dream of becoming a father fulfilled but was distraught that he had seen his son for only those few moments before he would leave to fly air strikes against a desperate enemy.

Johnny, Lael's protector, first cousin, and friend, perished on his first flight over Germany.

Berlin was eight hours ahead of Ririe time, so Johnny was lost in mid-or late afternoon of that same day, Ririe time. The next morning, February 4, 1945, I had awakened early and come upstairs to the living room by Lael's window to study for a school assignment. It was early enough that dark shadows of the night remained abroad in the town even though the sky was beginning to brighten in the east. Fog from the river was rising up in a winding plume along the Snake, past Heise, the Hogsback, and the Flats. I was immediately reminded of that January 29 two years earlier when Lael left our family.

Suddenly I heard some scurrying around in my parents' bedroom. I could hear subdued talking but could not make out what was being said. Something in the scurrying about and the tone of the voices indicated that an urgent matter had come up. Papa came into the living room. He was dressed in his suit and tie. I didn't know of any appointment he had at this early hour, especially dressed like that.

I asked Papa what was going on just as Mama appeared in the doorway, also nicely dressed, with a touch of rouge on her cheeks and a dab of lipstick on her lips.

"We've got to hurry over to Alma and Lizzie's. Something's happened to Johnny."

"What's happened to him?" I asked with a quiver in my voice.

"I don't know."

"Then why do you have to go over to Uncle Alma's and Aunt Lizzie's this morning, and so early?"

Papa looked at me for a moment, hesitating. He seemed on the verge of explaining it to me. Just then Mama stepped to his side and said she was ready to go.

"I'll tell you about it later. Right now we need to hurry over there!"

They disappeared out the back door. I watched from the window as they backed the car out of the driveway, turned north, and accelerated rapidly up the street. The car was trailing a whirling cloud of fumes in the brisk early morning air. Agitated and worried I ran out onto the porch to watch the departing automobile. Any thought of studying had completely vanished. I sat back at the window thinking over what could have happened to Johnny. He had only been in Europe a month or less.

I recalled the snowball incident where Johnny protected Lael. I thought about Jessie. I really liked her. She had a beautiful singing voice, and every time she came to town she would be asked to sing at church or at weddings or at the community center. In fact she sang at the big Christmas party we had just celebrated the past December. Everyone liked Jessie and her blond haired baby boy, and her voice. She shuttled between her home in Riverdale, Utah, and Johnny's parents' home near Ririe.

Amidst all those musings I was startled when I saw our car drive slowly back in front of my window and turn into our driveway. They had been gone less than half an hour, and it took them at least six or seven minutes to get to Johnny's house and another six or seven to get back! Any visit with Alma and Lizzie would have been of very short duration. I rushed into the kitchen and watched impatiently for the back door to open. As my parents entered they were talking to each other with looks of concern on their faces. Papa suggested that we all go in the living room and sit down.

Papa hesitated, looked at Mama, and then back at me. "Listen carefully to what I have to say, Reed. I was in the living room reading last night. Just as I stood up to go into the bedroom, Johnny came to me. He stood over by that chair there." Papa pointed. "He was dressed in his uniform. He looked neat and healthy.

"He said, 'Uncle John, if anything happens to me you get over to see the old folks. Get over there!' That was all. Then he was gone. I sat there dumbfounded and wondering what to do. I went into the bedroom and told your mother, 'something's happened to Johnny.' It was so late we decided we couldn't go see Alma and Lizzie at that hour. So we decided to go over there early this morning. We tossed and turned and hardly slept. That's why we got up so early and rushed over there."

"What did they say? What's happened to Johnny?" I asked, afraid of what the answer might be. I was beside myself with worry. Losing Byron was a horrible tragedy, and now with Johnny this was cutting too close to home, to our family. This was as awful as it could get, unless Joel was killed.

Papa's answer surprised me. "Alma and Lizzie don't know of anything being wrong. Everything was normal in their house. In fact, we got them out of bed. So we wouldn't worry them, I told them that Mother and I happened to be in the vicinity, we were coming back by their house, and thought we would stop in to see how they were doing. We only stayed a couple of minutes after everything seemed to be all right."

He added, "Jessie isn't there. She's in Riverdale."

I was agitated and anxious. Questions blurted out of me. "Johnny is stationed in England. How could you see him? Why did you see him? Why did he tell you to go over there before they even knew something was wrong? Or did you just dream it?"

"No, son, I did not dream it!" Papa's voice was stern. "I was wide awake when it happened!"

"Well, why would Johnny come to you if something has happened to him, but Uncle Alma and Aunt Lizzie and probably Jessie don't know anything about it?" I was almost shouting.

Papa stared at me with a peculiar look on his face. I looked at Mama. She had the same look. "Maybe this is meant as much for us as it is for Alma and Lizzie."

"I don't get it!"

Papa answered with a soft voice. "Suppose Johnny's dead, but nobody here, including his folks and Jessie, knows anything about it? Then suppose the telegram comes in a few days confirming something dreadful has happened to him? What does that mean to me, to us?"

"I don't have any idea!" My worry about Johnny made me speak abruptly.

Papa went on, "Your mother and I were talking about this on the way home. You know that I saw five of you kids before any of you were born or even thought of."

"Yeah," I responded cautiously.

"Well, if that telegram comes saying that Johnny is dead, then I will have come full circle. I will have seen beings—I guess that's the best word—both before they were born and now, with Johnny, after he has died. I will have seen both of the bookends of life." His voice trailed off.

I, on the other hand, was thinking a rather sobering thought: if that telegram doesn't come, and I hope it doesn't, then my dad must be a lunatic who hallucinates. I did not like that option either because I had always trusted my father's word.

On February 26 the telegram came to Alma and Lizzie. They came rushing over to our house to tell the folks that Johnny's plane had been shot down. Papa and Mama sat with Alma and Lizzie in our living room and explained the reason for their early morning visit on February 4 and the visit from Johnny that triggered it. That visit gave Alma and Lizzie evidence upon which they placed great faith that their Johnny, though dead, was okay. Papa told them, "Remember that God does all things well! We may not understand it all, but I think the extraordinary happenings of these past few days help to confirm that fact." Alma and Lizzie found comfort in Papa's comments, despite their grievous loss.

When I heard the news and relived that early February 4 morning hour, I realized then that I had been privy to a prophecy. Intelligence had been communicated to Papa, and from him to me, which foretold the future. Yes, we had lost our Cousin Johnny. But we had also found him. Papa had again been treated to a significant insight into a future event, the coming of that dreadful telegram with word of Johnny's death.

Johnny's remains and dog tags were not found until almost four years after the war in Europe ended. Finally, Cousin Johnny was brought home and given a proper funeral. His casket was draped in the American flag. As "Taps" played at the cemetery, six Veterans of Foreign Wars tenderly folded the flag and presented it to Jessie.

The six veterans straightened themselves up to soldier's attention and gave Lael's cousin, protector, and special friend a hero's final salute. Then they lowered Johnny's casket into a grave located just a few yards north of Merlin's resting place in the Ririe-Shelton cemetery located on the little hill a mile south of Ririe. His tombstone reads:

John C. Moss
Sgt. 350 AAF Bomb. Sq.
WW II PH
Nov. 29, 1921
Feb. 3, 1945

The PH stands for Purple Heart.

Chapter 32

The Search for Understanding (The Palisades)

WE WERE HALFWAY ACROSS the glacier in the Palisades wilderness when, with a sickening scream, Ken Allen lost his footing. He started to slide feet first down the face. As he gathered momentum his body turned sideways and started to roll, his legs and torso horizontal to the glacier, his arms vertical, spread-eagle. He became a human pinwheel, furiously twirling down the steep incline until he glanced off a boulder that slowed his wild descent. His body arched into the air and then flopped lifelessly face down onto a mound of dirt that stopped him. His boots dangled in a little pool of water. It was August 1945, the year the war ended.

My Cousin Cloyd, Uncle Tom's son, twenty years my senior, was the Scoutmaster. He claimed, as our troop began our trek, that he was taking us to paradise in the Palisades area. Cloyd also knew Byron, Merlin, Lael, and Johnny, and he knew I was struggling with what had happened in their lives.

Two days earlier, Ken Allen and the rest of us had jammed our food, sleeping bags, and fishing gear into Cloyd's horse trailer, and with his big station wagon pulling it and hauling us, we left Ririe on Highway 26, cruising through the Flats and on past the two little wide spots in the road, Swan Valley and Irwin. Just after Irwin we turned north on the rutted, dirt road that adjoined Palisades Creek. Three miles brought us to the Palisades Campground. From there only foot and horse traffic could go.

We put on our heavy backpacks and left the campground on a narrow dirt trail that wound gradually and sometimes steeply upward, following Palisades Creek. The creek was named for the numerous descending terraces, like palisades, that formed its downward course to the Snake River. Our trail meandered along the creek most of four miles and crossed it five times, on bridges constructed under the WPA program back in the thirties, until it reached Lower Palisades Lake.

We were breathing heavily after ascending the last hundred yards up the face of a massive rockslide. Tall trees obscured the gouge from which the slide came, but the convoluted debris holding back the creek attested that there had been an earthquake centuries ago that literally tore the adjacent mountain apart. The dam the slide created gave us the first of the three jewels of our Palisades paradise.

Lower Palisades Lake stretched out before us, about a mile long and a quarter-mile wide. The lake's narrow width seemed just a pregnant broadening of the creek. The water's turquoise color around the edges gradually gave way in iridescent hues to a pastel blue in the middle. We stared, transfixed, with our heavy packs and sweating faces. After the tiring climb up, the lake beckoned us like a siren. But there was much more to come.

Our trail skirted the left flank of the lake and then crossed the creek again a mile beyond the lake's upper end. From there we branched off on a trail that headed eastward toward Wyoming. It rose sharply upward another thousand feet, but with the help of artfully planned switchbacks our climb was almost pleasant despite our heavy packs and the fatigue from the distance we had already hiked. Halfway up the steep incline the trail skirted the rim of a deep ravine.

I timidly gazed over the edge and felt a little dizzy looking down a sheer drop-off of three hundred feet. A furious and foamy torrent came gushing out from under a steep earthen wall that abruptly made the ravine into a dead-end canyon. Cloyd told us to stop and take off our packs. We sat with faces glistening from sweat, the backs of our shirts wet in the outline of our packs. Cloyd had something to show us.

"Turn around and look behind you."

To our amazement we saw that a monstrous gash had been carved out of a nearby mountain. The debris had cascaded down to where we were sitting. Through the centuries grass, trees, huckleberry, serviceberry, gooseberry, and other bushes had overgrown the slide area and would have hidden its origin had it not been for the towering mountain above us displaying that awful gash.

"You thought the slide that dammed off the lower lake was awesome." Cloyd said. "That one is pocket change compared to this. One giant rumble of the earth, and this slide sealed off another creek. In a few minutes you'll see the real results."

I looked at the deep ravine, at the sheer wall blocking it but letting water spew out of its base, at the mountain with a massive, treeless gouge across its gigantic face, and felt a tingle go up my spine. The earth rolling in her splendor was breathtaking. It got better yet.

We completed the last switchback and were rounding a slight bend in the trail when the scout in the lead suddenly stopped in his tracks. Lying before us was the second jewel in the triple crown of paradise. Upper Palisades Lake stretched out before us, several miles long and a mile or more wide, a giant emerald shimmering in the afternoon sun. This jewel was the singular creation of the giant rockslide we had just traversed. We were tired, but the lure of the lake moved us onward.

The trail wound along its northern shore but most of the time was several hundred feet above the shoreline. I hungrily licked my lips as I looked down to where large native cutthroat trout were swimming lazily along the shore in the crystal clear water and imagined them sizzling in butter in a frying pan over a crackling fire. My hunger was only slightly appeased by an occasional huckleberry, serviceberry, or chokecherry plucked from plants clustered along the edge of the trail as we continued toward the upper end of the lake.

Once a fat pine hen ran out along the trail in front of us, wiggling its tail and strutting along for all to see, as though it was the grand landlord of all this splendor. We watched across the lake as a mother moose and her calf lumbered unconcerned out of the trees and down to the waterline where they dipped their black muzzles into the cool blue water. On the surface of the lake a short distance from the moose were several ducks drifting aimlessly about. Occasionally one would dip below the surface for a morsel to eat or just to cool off. The silence and serenity were hypnotizing.

We rounded a bend where our trail descended close to the shoreline. From behind a small copse of trees we saw a little furry shape swimming on its back with two little hands feeding a wet, clinging mass of dark green into an angelic face. The mass gradually disappeared behind two large front teeth. Suddenly with a loud splat of its tail, the furry bundle disappeared beneath the surface. Several moments later it reappeared and with a coy grin, settled again onto its back, and started chewing on the grass it had just retrieved.

We arrived at the upper end of the lake where two fierce streams fed into the lake's hungry mouth. Countless small trout were fighting to collect tidbits rushing with the streams' flaring fans into the lake. We walked a short way up one stream and found numerous underground springs feeding it with sparkling clear water, which steadily enlarged its cascading discharge into the lake.

From there I could see the true majesty of the upper lake, especially as the sun began sinking toward the hill on the horizon lying only a few miles to the west. The water glistened in the shimmering sunshine. Trout leaped in golden arcs to nip hovering flies, leaving ever-widening ripples undulating on the otherwise tranquil surface. The slant of the descending sun gradually turned the blue surface to golden as we stood and watched in wonder.

I reached out my cup and filled it with water from one of the springs, then let the clear, cold taste tingle my lips. Coming from its deep underground passage I was sure that the water was potable, so I gulped heartily.

Cloyd said we would spend the night there. But first he challenged us to a swim in the lake. He pointed to a cottonwood tree a little distance back down the trail. It must have been seventy-five to one hundred feet high and was leaning out over the lake, held firm by its onshore roots. A long rope was tied near its tip and hung down almost the full length of the tree. We quickly got the idea. From a small landing place where the rope was tied, we could soar out over the lake and take a twenty-foot leap into the cold water or swing back to the safety of the shore.

We all chose the former. I had not anticipated just how biting cold the water was. Not only did I sink deeply into its depths but also breathlessly. The striking cold was an almost paralyzing contrast against my sweat-bathed skin. It made me gasp and launch myself upward to the beckoning warmth of the sunshine. As I sputtered onto the surface, a serene numbness overcame me, and I swam contentedly for ten minutes or so.

Invigorated by our swim, we raced against the coming darkness to build a fire and cook and eat sizzling hot dogs charred over the flames. We wadded crushed slices of bread around our hot dogs and flushed them down with steaming hot chocolate. Then we climbed into our sleeping bags and slept soundly atop twigs and rocks that should have interrupted our sleep but could not.

Early the next morning we were on the trail again. It climbed steadily upward, winding through small groves of trees where centuries of fallen leaves had created a carpet that gave the trail a spongy softness against our weary, tender feet. Each time we emerged from these little groves, our eyes beheld nature's best, the dense high-mountain flower gardens.

The largest of these brilliant meadows was located in the third and last jewel of our triple crown, Waterfall Canyon. Three-quarters of the way around the backside of the canyon, like a queen's crown observed from back to front, were the sheer walls of the canyon. Some walls were twenty feet high, others five hundred. And around that entire three-quarter perimeter were waterfalls: big, small, short, tall.

But first came the meadow of flowers! They were everywhere and of every color and kind. They waved and bobbed with the drifting breeze and glistened from the mist of the waterfalls. We breathed in their aroma carried to us by the breeze moving gently down the meadow. The greens, the blues, the reds, the violets, the whites and the off-whites had sprung up out of deep and undisturbed soil, aided by the plentiful water. We had been entranced by the upper lake in the setting sun but now, facing into this shimmering panorama with its waterfall backdrop, we were awestruck. None of us, except Cloyd, had ever seen such splendor as that brilliant burst of color framed by the silvery waterfalls.

As we stood at the edge of the meadow, Cloyd explained that on top of the sheer walls was a narrow plateau that spread outward from the rim over which the waterfalls gushed. He told us that the plateau was a hundred or so feet wide in some places and as little as five in others, but in general it was quite level. He pointed toward the farther edge of the canyon and upward to the tip of a mountain where glacial ice still rested in August! From this glacier, Cloyd told us, came a gradual melt that made countless little pools in the lava depressions amidst the plateau. These pools lay directly in the eye of the sun. While the water stood in those little pools, the sun warmed it to a comfortable degree before it was finally pushed out over the rim. In several places this sun-warmed water provided a pleasant shower, especially if the rim over which it fell was only a few feet overhead. (A couple of friends and I tried to shower in a very small waterfall that was three hundred feet or so high and quickly found that a drop of water falling that distance can hit like a bullet!)

Bright little rainbows played among the mists from the waterfalls. A hundred yards ahead of us a fawn with a speckled coat came bounding up out of the flowers, then back down again, playing and prancing about as its mother stood nearby contentedly grazing. It was here, in this majestic setting, that we would spend the remainder of our trip. We unpacked and set up our camp. Then we were free to wander wherever we would like.

Cloyd, three other scouts (including Ken Allen), and I decided to hike on up out of Waterfall Canyon so we could survey it from the top. To our pleasant surprise the trail that brought us to Waterfall Canyon continued on through the meadow and switchbacked up the canyon wall at the center of the queen's crown, then wound its way on over the top. At one turn in the trail we were near the glacier. Drawn to it, we eventually found ourselves at its edge looking down on the unforgettable beauty of Waterfall Canyon.

From that point we chose to traverse a steep portion of the glacier in order to reach some watermelon snow we saw about fifty feet beyond us. Watermelon snow is colored pink from a type of algae, I was told, that flourishes in such snow. Cloyd told us that if we used our imaginations we could even taste sweetness in the snow when we ate it. Cloyd took the lead across the glacier. He kicked out a hole in the icy snow with the first step so that he had solid footing and then went likewise to the next. We followed single file, using the footholds he had made. It was here that Ken Allen fell and lay helplessly, seemingly lifeless, feet dangling in a little pool.

Gripped by anxiety, we quickly but cautiously made our way to where I thought we would find Ken's corpse. Cloyd arrived first and cradled Ken's head in his arms, wiping snow and blood from his blond hair and ashen face. He was alive! More than that, he was awake; and more than that, he only had the wind knocked out of him, no broken bones. There were a few cuts and abrasions, but nothing serious. We were all shaken but intensely happy that, incredibly, Ken had survived. After ten minutes of checking him over and letting him rest, we were able to walk back along the smooth and mostly level shelf of the canyon rim. We waded through some of the warming pools to where the trail brought us back into Waterfall Canyon.

Ken was short and had blond hair. I had always thought of him as a Johnny look-alike. Because of that, his fall awakened hard thoughts of the last moments of Johnny's life when his B-17 made that fiery, screaming dive into the earth. Cloyd must have sensed this because as I climbed into my sleeping bag that night, Cloyd pulled his over beside mine.

"Up there on the glacier today, while we were tending Ken, were you thinking about Johnny?" he asked.

I answered with an embarrassed, "Yes." I didn't like my face being an open book. I was coming into manhood and imagined that such thoughts were not "manly."

"It's only been a little over six months since Johnny was killed," Cloyd said. "It's no wonder we are still thinking about him. We wonder where he is. Did he suffer? What were his last thoughts? Will someone find his body? Believe it or not, I was thinking about Johnny, too, when I saw Ken fall."

"No kidding?"

"Ken's blond hair and his build remind me very much of Johnny. And it's too soon to let Johnny go in our thoughts. It's going to take time to overcome that loss and to heal."

"I know," I said, "but what makes me so frustrated is why did that have to happen to him? He was as nice a guy as I could ever look up to. Even though I was nine years younger than Johnny, he treated me like I was his equal, like I was a man. So why did he have to be killed? Why does God allow wars to happen and leave all this heartache and misery?"

Cloyd thought for some time. "I don't know. I honestly don't know. But I have some ideas that give me some consolation."

"Like what?"

"Remember that big gash torn out of the mountain that slid down and made Upper Palisades Lake?"

"Sure, I just saw it yesterday."

"That slide, and the one that made the lower lake centuries ago, tore up those mountains just plain awful, leaving them with big ugly scars in their faces and a pile of dusty and lifeless rocks and earth at their feet. You could ask, 'Why would God desecrate those mountains so?'"

I turned over, leaned up on my elbow, and looked at him.

"At the time it happened, it would be a fair question. But now look at what those slides have done. They have covered themselves with lush vegetation and formed two beautiful lakes. The creeks they blocked off have continued to flow underneath all that debris and still provide a lush habitat for those trout we love to eat. Looking at all that so-called devastation from our present-day vantage point, I think we could both say, 'Well done, God!' Right?"

"I guess so," was my cautious response.

"And what about this Waterfall Canyon? A geologist told me that it was formed during the ice age, while some big glacier, maybe a mile thick, squatted down like a big mother hen over all these hills and mountains. All that crushing weight carved out this incredible mountain meadow, laced three of its sides with the solid rock frame of a majestic crown, and over a moment or two of millennial time, let beautiful waterfalls pour out over most of its circumference. If you were looking at that glacier in that bygone era, you might have asked, 'What is this cold and barren mess doing here? Why did God put it there? It serves no worthwhile purpose.' From that pre-historic perch, your question would have been valid. But looking at it from our day, our perspective, we would have to say, 'Well done.' Right?"

"Yeah, I can understand that, but what has that got to do with Johnny? And while you're at it, what has that got to do with Lael ending up at the State School in Nampa?"

Cloyd was quiet for some time. I thought he might have fallen asleep. But then he broke the silence. "You never did know your brother Merlin. You were born three years after he died. But I knew him; and I knew, from hearing it from your father, that John had seen his first five kids at a little hotel in Blackfoot. He described Merlin's red pallor and shriveled appearance to my father and also to me quite a while before you were born. Then you kids came along, boy first, girl next, boy next, all just as John had predicted. But Merlin was born completely normal, not reddish and shriveled. That threw the whole family into a tailspin. We wondered if John had told us a fairy tale, Grandma Fanny included, until that awful day when Merlin was burned and died. Then we all realized that something, some intelligence of some sort, had shown your father the future; and that belief was further validated when the next two children, a girl and then a boy, you, came along."

I was engrossed in his story. I hadn't known before this that Cloyd had been privy to Papa's experience.

"I think it's only proper to put a name to that intelligence that showed your father the future, and the best I can come up with is 'God,'" he said.

"Can't you find something special, even sacred, in your father's experience like you can with the mountains, the rock slides, the lakes, and panoramic beauty we see all about us here? I'm sure your dad's experience helped prepare him and your mother for the future. It let them know there would be difficulties but that it was all in God's hands and would be all right. Admittedly, with Lael, things weren't foreshadowed as they were with Merlin, but did they have to be?"

"I think it would have sure helped a lot."

"But why should you and your family be so privileged as to see a prophetic glance at *both* Merlin and Lael, when countless families lose children to death or to insanity or other handicaps without any such favor bestowed upon them? Aren't you being just a little selfish, maybe, when you ask, 'Why couldn't we have been warned about Lael, too?'"

I had no answer. "But what about Johnny?" I said. "Why did he have to be jerked out of his little family and after seeing his son for only a few minutes? What holy purpose can that possibly serve?"

"I don't know," Cloyd swiftly countered. "But as long as God controls the universe, does it really matter? If He showed your dad Merlin's fate and took him back to Himself, wouldn't he have the same capability with Johnny?"

"I suppose," I said as I rolled onto my back and looked up into the stars.

Cloyd continued. "I know your dad saw Johnny for only a moment or so, but it was after he had died, and before Alma and Lizzie knew anything about it. Doesn't that suggest that there is life after life ends here? Perhaps we should measure life on an eternal scale. If we do that, the tragedies we suffer here become infinitely smaller. I would imagine a death or a descent into insanity here in our finite, mortal domain would be nothing more than a little cut or bruise or nosebleed on an infinite, eternal scale. Like the mountains, their gigantic rockslides, and the formation of the lakes over time, we have to be patient and let time take its course and work it all out to God's beneficial end. Given what your family and our family with you have experienced, I see no reason to throw all that away in some fit of bitterness."

I had another question. "When Papa saw us five kids, what was he see-ing? Was I really there? I don't remember anything about it. And what about Johnny? Was that really him dressed in his Army Air Corps uniform when Papa saw him?"

Cloyd thought for a long time. "You've got me there. I don't know the answer, but I've got some ideas. You've seen Gone with the Wind. I think it was the first movie ever made in Technicolor. Clark Gable and Vivien Leigh looked and sounded as real as if you were seeing them in person."

"But," I interjected, "that needed a projector and a screen."

"I know," Cloyd answered, "but the first point is that those images were images of actual people and scenery the movie director wanted us to see. Through modern technology those pictures were stored on film, and when that film went through the projector, those images were brought to life and reflected up on the screen for all of us to experience.

"Think about that, and then think about what we do with the radio, sending voice messages around the world. If we can do those kinds of things, why can't God send messages, or images, or even personages, to wherever He wants? Moses claimed he saw God's burning bush that really didn't burn and that he heard God's voice. The impact of that experience on Moses was so dynamic that he became the leader of the greatest exodus of people out of bondage the world has ever known. The Apostle Paul claimed he saw Jesus Christ and talked with Him long after Jesus had died on the cross. From that moment on Paul dedicated his life to preaching Christianity and died a pris-oner and martyr in Rome.

"If that happened to them, why couldn't God allow you kids and Johnny to appear in some sort of image to your father? You and I know those events have had a powerful effect on him, too! The responsibility he feels toward you kids, his desire for all of you to be educated, to live good lives and be good examples, it seems to almost consume him at times."

"I never thought of it like that. But I know Papa would go into a fit if any of us didn't do our best in school, or even thought of settling for less than a college education, or if we even went a little bit wayward. And I know that

Papa must have seen Johnny after he died, or what appeared to be Johnny, but before Uncle Alma and Aunt Lizzie got the telegram. I was there for that one."

"I think you're getting the idea," Cloyd said. "I wish we knew more about it all. Sometimes I feel like we are on the edge of some vast bounty of knowledge but are just getting a teeny glimpse into wonders beyond our imaginations."

He turned over and went to sleep. I continued looking up into the Milky Way and beyond. I thought about Johnny and Lael. Maybe, just maybe, God does do all things well, in His eternal time frame.

Chapter 33

The Rales

OUR TELEPHONE RANG. Mama answered it, then let out a muffled groan. Joel and Helen were away at college. Our parents, Rhea, Ruth, and I were at home in that early evening of March 14, 1947. We looked at Mama with anxious faces. Dr. Allen was telling her that Lael had died that afternoon and expressing his condolences. Mama was silent, just trying to breathe. After a long pause, Dr. Allen asked what arrangements should be made for her body. Mama, desperately trying to squeeze off the tears, asked him to talk to Papa and handed him the phone. Then she sat down on the couch and buried her head in her hands. Rhea and Ruth rushed to her, put their arms around her, and hugged her as they learned the truth. I stood heartsick and numb as I listened to Papa say he would call an undertaker in Idaho Falls and let him make the arrangements to bring Lael home. Papa's face was a mask of sadness as he tried to keep his composure and respond to Dr. Allen's questions. Lael, my sister, was dead. She was only twenty-two.

During the first two of the four years Lael was in Nampa, gasoline was in very short supply. The government issued gas and diesel ration stamps to farmers for the bare necessities of producing a crop. Automobile travel for business purposes was severely restricted. Leisure travel was virtually impossible. As a consequence, after our hitchhike to Nampa in 1943, there were only five visits to see Lael. During that time, Lael, with someone's help, wrote us one letter of "Lael, Lael, Lael". It was postmarked January 3, 1944.

Mama made three visits by train and usually took a child with her. She and Ruth went once during the summer of 1944. They stayed overnight in a hotel in Nampa. Then little Ruth's short little legs had to endure a very long walk to the school. Money for a taxi was out of the question. Ruth and Mama reported back to an anxiously waiting family.

"At first Lael didn't recognize us. Yet she seemed reasonably happy and smiled a lot. In fact Ruth had a lot of fun with her jumping rope outdoors in the afternoon sunshine. Lael giggled and laughed as she and Ruth jumped side by side. Lael still had the skill to handle her own jump rope."

She continued, "I think maybe the medication is helping because Lael seems a lot happier now. She was not able to do any fancy work, but she was being cooperative and helping with jobs around the laundry and in the kitchen.

"But I am worried about her health. She doesn't gain any weight and has a funny cough that rattles around in her chest. Dr. Allen didn't seem too concerned, but he did say she eats like a bird, so she doesn't gain weight. I gave the nurse a few dollars and asked her to buy her an ice cream cone, popcorn, and other good tasting things, which might get her interested in food again."

Ruth added, "I really had fun jumping rope with Lael. She giggled and it sounded pretty."

Mama said, "I think it helped Lael to see her little sister and play with her."

Mama and Rhea made another trip by train six months later. Even though school was still in session, Mama took Rhea because these little sisters seemed to help Lael feel a sense of family. Lael was still thin and had little appetite. Her cough had worsened.

In late summer 1945, Mama took both Ruth and Helen with her. Two notable things happened on that trip. A nurse, upon observing Helen's compassion and care for Lael, told her she should choose nursing as a profession and help handicapped people like Lael. But after seeing the numerous patients and the seeming hopelessness and helplessness that abounded at the school, Helen told the family she "would not fit the job." Also, she had become an excellent typist and was proud of being the secretary for Mr. Clark, president of Ricks College.

More importantly, Lael's failing health had become more worrisome. She was going downhill, and the pace was accelerating! No one could tell them why it was happening. There was no jumping rope this time. Lael didn't have the energy. When they were alone, Mama raised Lael's dress to look at her legs and backside and was horrified. She was developing sickening bedsores.

The nurse assured Mama that they were tending to the sores but said that with Lael's failing energy, it was difficult to keep her up and walking to maintain her immune system. Mama begged her to help get Lael to eat, to get her up and help her exercise so she could fight off whatever was ailing her.

When Mama returned from that trip she felt something was dreadfully wrong. Lael was even thinner than before, and her mind was not improving now. More dreadful yet was the prospect that the school superintendent might transfer Lael to the insane asylum. She felt completely helpless and hopeless to aid her daughter's welfare.

In the summer of 1946 Papa bought a new Plymouth four-door sedan, replacing the old Chevrolet he had driven during the war. The Plymouth had an incredible suspension system. It rode like the Cadillac we hitched to Boise in back in 1943. Joel had been required to stay with the occupation forces in Europe, primarily France, until June of 1946. As soon as the spring work was done, and now with ample gasoline available, Papa, Mama, and Joel took the first opportunity they could to drive to Nampa in the new Plymouth.

Joel reported that Lael stood in front of them like a doll, glazed eyes, uncomprehending, lifeless! She was very thin and seemed very ill. Her 5'6" frame had shrunk significantly. She looked old. She recognized no one, least of all Joel, whom she had not seen since 1941. He was heartsick. He was looking at someone he knew, but didn't know. They didn't stay long. It seemed to make what little life was left in her uneasy and restless.

The gift list disclosed that they left for Lael "two pairs of anklets, 1 pair of hose, two boxes of fig newtons, 3 candy bars, 1 popcorn ball, and 1 package of popcorn."

The family talked about that trip one evening while seated around the old kitchen table. By coincidence, that day Mama had had a conversation with a lady from the village concerning Lael when she was twelve. The lady's six-year-old daughter had been playing with Lael and some other children near one of the canals that fed the numerous ditches leading to the backyard gardens and corrals. The lady's little daughter fell and scraped her knee badly. She began to cry. Her mother, on seeing the mishap, started out of the house toward the group but suddenly stopped in midstride and watched. Lael, the lady reported, quickly ran to the canal, wet a part of her skirt, came back, and wiped the grime from the knee. Then she bent over the knee and kissed it. The little girl stopped crying. She reached out and touched Lael's cheek. The hurt was gone. Lael was her healer.

Mama lamented, "Lael was always so compassionate. Whenever I had a headache, without saying a word, she would touch my head with her hand. Somehow it seemed to help make it better. It tears at my heart to see her now, so helpless, so vulnerable, so forlorn, so alone in that awful world of hers. It leaves me sad and cold and empty!"

Papa shook his head, reached his arm around Mama, and drew her to him. The rest of us sat silent and grieving.

Through the long harvest season of 1946 and a good part of that winter when the roads were usually impassable, Papa and Mama placed an occasional call to find out how Lael was doing. The news was ominous. She was becoming bedridden, with virtually no energy to stand or walk.

Unable to stand it any longer, and despite the hazard of icy roads in late February, Papa and Mama made one last trip to Nampa. Mama's poignant letter of March 3, 1947, to "Dear Mrs. Bourrett" sums up Lael's unrelenting travail.

I know you are very busy, but wondered if you would please take time to let me know how Lael is. Is she eating any better, gaining any strength?

How are the sores? I hope they are improving. One seemed to have a little infection in it, and caused her considerable pain when lying on that side. She seemed to rest more comfortable when they had a new dressing put on. I know you are doing that quite often so I won't have to worry as much about that part.

I left her some money at the office. Would you or someone please take some and get her an apple or ice cream cone or something to give her more appetite, when you are in town? She seemed so hungry for the ice cream cone I took to her. The juice I left her will get rather tiresome if it isn't changed to something else but I know you will do that as you were very thotful (sic) in bringing her different drinks. Please let me know if I can help her in any way or help you with her by coming down.

We appreciate all you have done and hope we can be with her before she passes on.

Thanks very much. Resp. and best regards to all, also gratitude.

Sincerely, Mrs. Moss (John W.)

Eleven days later came the heartbreaking telephone call from Dr. Allen.

Lael died at 2:22 that afternoon. The certificate does not show any autopsy was performed. Yet it states with certainty that tuberculosis was the cause! Was this the source of the "sounds" Dr. Lowe heard on his first medical examination when he reported, "On auscultation the breathing sounds are increased but no rales are heard… But they have a peculiar sound. The first sound appears to be about the same intensity as the second,"

This raised a haunting question. Did Lael's inability to describe or call attention to the symptoms of this disease because of her mental condition contribute to yet more suffering over her final years?

A concluding paragraph of a letter from Dr. Allen on March 26, 1947, discloses the final irony in Lael's life:

Dear Mr. Moss:

We are glad that we were able to take care of Lael as long as we did, but of course we are very sorry to have lost her. Lael started down hill and there was no chance of replacing her on her feet again. It is to be deplored that we had no X-ray on hand and she was unable to go down town to have an X-ray taken.

No x-ray. No way for anybody to know what was going on inside of Lael's body and no way for her to tell them. It seemed a tortured end to a tortured life.

Mama dressed Lael in a beautiful, plain white dress before she was placed in her modest casket. On the day of her funeral she was carried into the little living room of the family home and placed by the window where she had spent long hours writing her name and peering out into a world we will never know. Here the villagers would come to see Lael one last time before she was taken to the church for the funeral.

The townspeople, especially the mothers and also Mary Jap, who had all taken care of Lael and Danny Rosenthal, came. These loving folk were gratefully welcomed and thanked for their dutiful care for this child of our village. Between his late February visit to Lael and her death, Papa had developed a severe inner ear infection. He could not stand up unassisted and was too sick and weak even to attend her funeral. However, Papa dressed himself as neatly as he could and sat on the couch across from Lael with a bandage around his head to shield the infected ear from any draft. He graciously acknowledged each visitor, as did Mama and the older children.

Two well-dressed strangers appeared at the door, one in a black suit, the other in dark gray. From their attire and courteous conduct it was assumed they were gentlemen of distinction and considerable prestige.

Helen sucked in a long breath and exclaimed, "President Clark and Mr.

Stephenson, you came all this way from Ricks. That is so nice of you to be with us at Lael's funeral."

President Clark was the president and Mr. Stephenson the registrar of Ricks College. President Clark looked at Papa and responded, "We've had the pleasure of having two of the Moss children attend Ricks. We have been very impressed with them. Mr. Stephenson and I felt it our duty and privilege to seize this opportunity to acquaint ourselves with your parents and family and express our condolences for the loss of your sister."

Papa lifted himself up into a bit more dignified sitting position and braced himself against the arm of the couch. He extended his hand to the two men.

"You do us a great honor in coming. I apologize for my condition. I wish I could stand and greet you properly."

"Please remain seated," responded President Clark, who took Papa's hand and then Mama's, adding, "Helen has told us about Lael and the difficulties she and your family have faced over the years. I appreciate Helen very much as my personal secretary and have been delighted with Joel's and her academic achievements at Ricks. It is you who do us the honor in sending them to us. We owe you this visit."

Then he asked, "How old was Lael?"

Papa looked down and swallowed hard. "She was twenty-two last November 10. She went to school here in Ririe, graduated from the eighth grade, and lived with us until she was eighteen. Then she went to the State School and Colony in Nampa, where she lived the last four years."

President Clark turned to Mama and softly asked, "How have you been able to cope as a mother, as a family? To see a lovely daughter gradually deteriorate right before your eyes? I can hardly imagine the heartache."

"It's a greater agony than even the sudden death of a child. I can say that because we have endured both. Yet I would not have traded one moment of Lael's life for any early release from the worry and pain. We learned so much from her and had the opportunity to love her deeply and to be loved by her in return, despite all the heartache of those years."

Mr. Stephenson spoke. "Then it's true that it is better to have loved her and lost her than never to have loved her at all."

"Oh yes, that's so true, Mr. Stephenson. To love a soul like hers is a special privilege. She bore her burden with such dignity and showed such love and compassion. I feel in my heart that she will now be made whole and find peace in some paradise beyond this life." She spoke with conviction.

They both looked admiringly at Mama, shook hers and Papa's hands again, and President Clark said, "I think I understand now what makes your children as they are. Please send us some more."

He and Mr. Stephenson stood beside Lael's casket a long moment, peering down at her wan face and ravished little body, then silently bowed their heads and left.

A half hour before the funeral service began, Papa asked Joel to get the car ready and Helen to help Mama get the other girls ready to go to the church.

He turned to me. "Reed, I want to talk to my daughter. Will you please help me so I can see her and talk to her?"

The room was cleared. Only Papa, Lael, and I were there. I helped Papa up to the casket and put my arm around him to hold him steady. He braced himself against the side of the casket and looked down at Lael.

I looked closely at my sister. Her body had withered away to a mere eighty pounds or less. Her hands stretching out from her long-sleeved white dress were pale and the fingers skinny. Her face looked so withered and old! It was not the face of a beautiful young woman in her prime. It resembled more the face of Grandma Fanny, who had been laid to rest in her ninetieth year. I ached for my sister. Life had been so unfair.

Papa covered Lael's two pale hands with his right and began to speak. "My dear daughter, dear sweetheart, you were so beautiful, so pure, so wholesome when I first saw you. You radiated an affection and sweetness I cannot describe. But I felt it. I had absolutely no idea, no premonition, of what you would have to suffer! But now that the earth has claimed your defenseless and muddled mind, you are set free from its bondage. How pleasant the thought!

You will see the glory of galaxies and suns and planets and universes beyond description. With reason and clarity you will now be able to comprehend some of the great incomprehensibles of the universe, including why God made you thus! You will hear and feel the blessedness of the music of the spheres, music that will be sweeter and more soothing than anything you will have heard here, and you will rejoice in its rhapsody and grandeur. Now that the earth has claimed your tortured body, you will dance, you will run, you will skip, you will leap with joy and gladness, free of its limitations."

His voice caught. He paused and then continued. "You will have Grandma Fanny and Merlin and Johnny and Byron to greet you with hugs and kisses and fill your life with love. That assurance will help us endure and let you go. And your love will live with us and enrich our lives until we can join you and them in a glad reunion.

"My heart is heavy, Lael. I don't know if we did everything for you that we should have done to help you find joy along your difficult pathway in life. Please forgive us if we failed. We need your forgiveness to lift the burden off our hearts."

He paused. His shoulders shook. Tears splashed down his cheeks. He wiped them away with his free hand and then continued in a choking voice, "Please rest in peace, my dear daughter, and come to meet us as we one by one come to you. God bless you and keep you, and may He reward you for being one of His most valiant souls."

Papa then moved his right hand up to her face and stroked her hair, still with that auburn sheen. Then he bent over the edge of the casket and kissed her tenderly on the cheek. I helped him sit back down on the couch and reached him a handkerchief lying nearby.

Mama came into the room accompanied by the funeral director. She busied herself at the casket, straightening out creases in the dress and the long white sleeves. Satisfied, she called the other children to come into the room. Joel was asked to say a final family prayer. As we raised our heads from the "amen," Mama nodded to the director to close the casket. As the lid was slowly lowered over Lael, my eyes caught a sparkle from Lael's crossed hands. I quickly looked closer, and there nestled between her two hands was a little black and white porcelain calf, obviously placed there by Mama. As the casket was sealed, my mind went back to that night with Bessie and the calf, and I thought how nice it was that Mama had provided this special remembrance of Lael, the compassionate. Somehow this little gesture, and the memories it stood for, would help keep us all connected.

Since then the years have drifted by. Many of the bittersweet memories have dimmed. Yet one thing remains constant: Lael comes "ever gentle to my mind." I see a handicapped child, a newborn calf, a butterfly, a snowflake, the fuzz of a dandelion drifting idly with the wind, the foggy plume rising from the Snake, and so many of nature's other wonders that bring her back to me. Will I see her again? I think so. Will she come to meet me when I eventually come to where she is? I think so. It gives me something special to look forward to.

John saw five children. Two have died. Yet five children remain. I do believe God does all things well, in His eternal time frame.

THE END

AUTHOR'S EPILOGUE

Grandma Fanny's "Conditions": Her promise to the Ririe School Board was honored some forty-five years after she died, when Zelma had to go into a nursing home and John had to move in with his children, thus vacating Fanny's original home. The fair value appraisal for the house and lot was $33,000. But the school board only had $25,000 available to pay. John made a gift of the extra $8,000 to the school district and conveyed the property to it.

Johnny's son, Brent: His mother, Jessie, remarried and raised Brent and several additional children to be fine, upstanding citizens. Brent married, became an attorney and later a distinguished District Judge of the Idaho Seventh Judicial District, sitting in Rexburg, Madison County, Idaho. He looks very much like his father.

Mary Jap: Mary lived out her life managing her hotel and café. When she died, a memorial service was held in the Mormon meetinghouse in Ririe. Residents of Ririe and the Flats, and former residents came from far and near filling the large chapel to overflowing. They paid homage to their beloved Mary, and witnessed a touching Buddhist service performed by her long-time Buddhist minister and friend from out of town.

The shack on the "Flats": It still stands, but the front door and all the windows are missing. Soft breezes whistle through it. It has begun to lean now. Strong Idaho winds across the Flats are taking their toll. Some say, "tear it down"; but should you tear down so intimate a memory? And don't such buildings, like photographs, "take us back in time" and keep us well connected with our past?

John and Zelma's surviving children: Joel went on to get a doctor's degree from the University of North Carolina in Sociology and became a university professor. Helen completed her bachelor's degree in Secondary Education from Ricks College. Reed got a Juris Doctor degree from George Washington University Law School and practiced law for 37 years until he retired to a new home on the family farm on Antelope Flats to write this book.

Rhea completed her bachelor's degree at Utah State University in Home Economics and also acquired a teaching certificate. Ruth completed a bachelor's degree in Human Development and Family Relationships at Brigham Young University, and then earned a teaching certificate in elementary education and specialty kindergartens from the University of Utah.

John and Zelma: Zelma died April 16, 1987, at age 91 and 245 days. John died February 7, 1991, at age 98, 132 days shy of his 99th birthday. They are buried beside Lael and Merlin in the little Ririe-Shelton cemetery a mile south of Ririe. They rest just a few yards south of Johnny and his parents.

The Farm Economy: In 1950 John sold his wheat for $3.25 per bushel and bought a new crawler tractor for $5,000, after his longstanding debt had been paid off. Diesel cost at most 20 cents per gallon then. In 2003 our wheat sold for $3.14 per bushel. The same tractor would cost between $80,000 and $100,000. Diesel sells for $1.50 per gallon now.